THE LIFE AND REDEMPTION OF TEDDY MILLER

Book I &II: The Cause of Darkness and The Light from Darkness

John W. Bebout

D1712773

This book is dedicated to the newest stars in my universe, my granddaughters Quinn McGoodwin and Anna Kipling.

BOOK I
THE CAUSE OF DARKNESS

Kate Warne, Image Credit: Chicago History Museum

If the soul is left in darkness, sins will be committed. The guilty one is not he who commits the sin, but the one who causes the darkness.

-MONSEIGNEUR BIENVENU IN LES MISÉRABLES

PROLOGUE

There are few places more beautiful than the Shenandoah Valley in Virginia. Those of us who lived there called it simply 'the Valley,' as if there were no other valleys in the world worthy of more than a passing interest. As children, the Valley helped shape our aesthetic sense and many of us came to recognize the hand of a higher power in its physical perfection. The Valley was more than just the setting for the story of our lives: it was a major character.

Mark Twain wrote that "When ill luck begins, it does not come in sprinkles, but in showers." That was certainly true for the Shenandoah Valley during the Civil War. But the Valley was always fated to suffer great destruction during the War. It was located less than 100 miles from Washington City at its closest point and it trended from southwest to northeast, making it resemble what many called 'a lance pointed directly at the very heart of the Union.' On more than one occasion, Union advances on the Confederate capital of Richmond—which may have greatly shortened the War—were stalled by Confederate actions in the Valley.

As late in the War as July 1864, Confederate General Jubal Early marched north up the Valley and crossed the Potomac River into Maryland. There he defeated a Union force at Monocacy before reaching the very defenses of Washington City itself. Early's raid stunned Northerners. It was 'the old story over again,' editorialized the *New York Times*. 'The backdoor, by way of the Shenandoah Valley, has been left invitingly open.'

President Lincoln had tried to end the Confederate threat in the Valley. From 1862 to 1864, he had ordered Union troops into the Valley on numerous occasions. But as in so many other arenas of the War, he was hobbled by incompetent military leadership and he was unsuccessful in driving the Confederates out. About all he accomplished was to make legends out of Confederate generals such as Stonewall Jackson and Jubal Early for their exploits there. But the tides of war were changing. In 1864, President Lincoln issued orders for what would be the last major military campaign in the Shenandoah Valley. They were succinct and unambiguous: his generals were to close off the northern invasion route used by Early and deny the Valley as a productive agricultural region to the Confederacy. As General U. S. Grant explained it to his soldiers, 'The people should be informed that so long as an army can subsist among them, recurrences of these raids must be expected, and we are determined to stop them at all hazards... Give the enemy no rest... Do all the damage to railroads and crops you can. Carry off stock of all descriptions, and Negroes, so as to prevent further planting. If the war is to last another year, we want the Shenandoah Valley to remain a barren waste.'

Grant's soldiers did their job well. When the War finally ended in the Valley, it ended in a conflagration that present-day residents still refer to as 'the burning.'

CHAPTER 1

The Battle of New Market,
May 15, 1864;

The Shenandoah Valley, Virginia

We take comfort in the sameness of our lives. For the most part, our good days, our bad days, even our very worst days all begin much the same way: we leave our warm beds, do our ablutions and prepare to undertake the ordinary and often mundane tasks required of us. But sometimes fate steps in and events wash over us like a rogue wave, tossing us in directions we could never have imagined. Sometimes, we would give all we own to return to the life we had known no more than 24 hours before.

I was awakened from a fitful sleep filled with dreams red-tinged and violent. I rolled over on my back and listened to the night sounds, searching for what had disturbed me. But I heard only my younger brother Jed's rhythmic breathing as he lay asleep beside me and the sound of chirping peepers that drifted in through my open bedroom window.

I had nearly fallen back asleep again when I noticed it: a slight vibration that moved up from the floor and through the bed frame. Alarmed, I jumped out of bed and ran to the window. There was only the merest sliver of a moon, but it was enough to see as far as the Valley Pike some 200 yards in front of our farmhouse. The road was unpaved and ran from Winchester in the north to Roanoke in the south, perhaps 180 miles. Normally desolate at night, it was alive with a long column of men, horses and wagons. I could see no beginning or end to the line. There was surprisingly little noise beyond an occasional muffled curse at some recalcitrant animal and the snuffling of the horses. The men marched silently. There was no clanking of canteens or mess kits, no talking or singing; there was just the rhythmic drumming of feet and hooves on the packed ground that had the earth vibrating like a guitar string.

Jed startled me as he moved up beside me at the window. I hadn't heard him get out of bed. "Are they our boys?" he asked.

I shook my head. "I cannot tell." The moon-lit scene was all shades of grey. I could make out no color at all. And the men, the animals, the wagons: they were all covered with a layer of dust from the road. More dust swirled around their feet as they walked. From this distance, they gave the illusion of floating just above the surface of the road, an army of ghosts.

Jed began to turn away from the window. "Let us go see who they are," he said, but I grabbed his arm and held him in place. "Wait," I said. I knew that if they were Union troops, they'd think that anyone out this late at night was up to no good. I didn't want to be shot or hanged as a guerrilla. "Best go wake up Daddy," I said. Jed nodded and left the room.

My father and Jed walked into the room a few minutes later. My father 's white nightshirt seemed to glow in the feeble light coming in through the window. His dark hair was slick and wet, and I reckoned he had splashed some water on his face to wake up. The three of us stood staring out the window for a long time as column after column of men and wagons continued to pass. After a while, I repeated Jed's question: "Are they our boys, Daddy?"

My father shook his head. "No, Teddy, they are not our boys." He crouched down and rested his forearms on the windowsill. Then, in a soft, sad voice he recited "'...the sun will be darkened, and the moon will not give its light; the stars will fall from the sky and the heavenly bodies will be shaken.'" My father turned and looked at me. It took me a moment to realize that he was challenging me to cite the chapter and verse of the scripture he had just quoted. I searched my memory. "Matthew 24:29," I finally said. My father nodded, rose to his feet, and turned to leave the room. "Get some sleep, boys," he said as he left. "There's nothing to be done tonight."

When my father was gone, Jed said to me "I do not remember that verse. What does it mean?"

"It tells of the end of the world," I answered. I looked back out the window at the columns of Union troops marching down the road. At that moment, a cloud passed in front of the sliver of moon and all became dark. 'And the moon will not give its light,' I thought. I was suddenly very frightened.

By morning, the columns of troops had passed.

Our breakfast that day was a normal one for our womanless household: my father, brother and I devoured our food as we discussed the chores that lay ahead for the day, each of us talking over the other. None of us mentioned the Union troops we had seen the night before, but I could tell that my father was distracted, and I saw him check his pocket watch several times when he thought no one was looking. After we finished breakfast, he addressed Jed and me: "I'm going up to New Market today, boys. I need some nails to repair the outbuildings and I may as well lay in some other supplies while I am at it."

I felt a stab of apprehension. I knew instinctively that it was unsafe for a civilian to be on the roads while the Union Army was massing in the Valley. I tried to talk my father out of it, to try to get him to postpone his errands until a later time, but he dismissed my pleas with an impatient shake of his head. "I will not have the Yankees dictate when I can run my errands," he said. Then he turned to Jed and said in a softer tone, "And you do what your brother says. Teddy is in charge while I am gone." Jed gave him a sour look but did not backtalk. I had recently turned 16 years old, 2 years older than my brother, and I was the presumptive boss when my father was away.

I cleaned and put away the breakfast dishes while my father and Jed walked out to the barn to hitch our old plow horse to the wagon. When I was finished, I stepped off the front porch and walked through the morning dew towards the barn. The spring sun was warm on my back and the sweet smell of honeysuckle enveloped me. I stopped and looked back at the front porch and I could imagine a better, happier world with my mother sitting there in the rocker, knitting. She would look up, smile at me, and say "You be careful today, Teddy. And watch out for your little brother." A great sense of melancholy settled over me and I ached for the mother I had barely known.

I don't know how long I had stood staring at the front porch, but by the time I got to the barn, my father was already gone.

My brother and I were standing just inside our barn, discussing our chores, when the battle began. We had no warning; there was no sound of marching troops or muskets firing, no distant cannonade. There were just the normal sounds of a spring morning in rural Virginia: birds singing, the sound of bees in the honeysuckle and animals shuffling in their stalls.

A single artillery shell arched overhead and then, its momentum exhausted, fell to earth. It exploded just outside our barn and only the heavy oak door saved us from instant death. The door, riddled with shrapnel, was blown in on us and trapped us against the floor. The concussion had pounded the breath from our chests.

When I came to my senses, I saw dust dancing in the sunlight streaming in through the shattered doorway. I threw the remains of the door aside and found my brother lying beside me, covered in dust and wood splinters. He wasn't moving. I took his arm and shook it. "Jed," I yelled, "Jed!" After a time, he opened his eyes and began to sit up. I saw his lips moving but I heard nothing. "Are you hurt?" I asked. I frantically checked him for blood but found none. He shook his head and his lips formed words I could not hear.

I half pushed, half dragged my brother out of the exposed doorway as the sounds of battle began to grow around us. Soon the ground was shaking beneath us as we huddled in a corner of the barn. There were so many cannons firing near and far that it sounded like one long, continuous roar. Dust, shaken from the rafters by the cannonade, rained down on us like flour through a sifter. Jed put his face next to my right ear and yelled something. When I shook my head, he turned my face with his hands and yelled into my other ear: "Can you hear me, Teddy?" I nodded. He touched my right ear and showed me his fingers, bright with blood. The explosion of the artillery shell had ruptured my right eardrum.

The sounds of battle rose to an unbearable level that assaulted all our senses. It was a mad symphony of bangs and whirs and crashes accompanied by the deep percussion of the cannons. Terrified, Jed and I sat with our knees pulled up to our chests with our arms over our heads until the constant roar of cannons eventually became more sporadic, interspersed with the pop-pop-pop of muskets off in the distance. When I finally dared to look up, it was an astonishing sight: light streamed into the barn through what must have been a thousand holes. Although the barn had not sustained a direct hit, nearby explosions had riddled the walls and roof with shrapnel. That Jed and I were alive and untouched was nothing short of a miracle.

"We need to get out of the barn," I told Jed. Our sense that it provided protection was clearly an illusion. I took his arm and began to lead him out of the barn. "Wait," he said. "What about Gus? We cannot just leave him here."

Gus was our mule, 30-years old and long retired from any real work. But Jed and I would occasionally ride him bareback around the farm to give him a little exercise and he was the closest thing we had to a pet. Reluctantly, I reversed direction and we headed for Gus's stall. Jed ran ahead and I heard him gasp when he got there. Coming up behind him, I saw Gus lying dead on the stall floor.

Blood, made black by dust, was everywhere. Hair and gore covered the stall floor and walls and the stall door had been kicked nearly off its hinges. I reckoned that Gus had been terrified by the cannonade and had tried to kick his way out of his stall until the shrapnel finally found him. I was grateful that I had not been able to hear his struggle to escape above the sounds of battle.

I stared down at Gus until the smell of blood, dung and raw meat overwhelmed me and I felt my legs begin to buckle. I had to grab onto the stall wall to support myself.

Up until that moment, I thought I understood death. Death was a natural part of life on a farm. We slaughtered animals for food, and we killed with mercy those that were sick, injured or no longer able to do their work. There always seemed to be a natural order to things; death, when it came, came for a reason. There were accidents, of course, and tragedies like my mother's death. But death was mostly tempered, doled out in small doses and often a blessing. I raised my eyes to the shattered roof of the barn and listened to the artillery shells exploding off in the distance. I knew that with every explosion I heard, more men and animals were dying. Death seemed to be on a rampage, like a starving animal finally let out of its cage.

Jed began to sob. I pulled him close, wanting to console him, but anxious at the same time to get us away from the barn. Jed turned and buried his face in my shoulder. "What's happening to us, Teddy?" he cried. Then he suddenly became very still and looked up at me with wide eyes. "Where is Daddy?" he asked. "Oh, Teddy, where is Daddy?"

I held him close, aware of the sounds of battle once again beginning to build around us. "He will be back soon, Jed. As soon as the fighting stops, he will come back to find us. Right now, we have to find somewhere safe to hide."

The only safe place I could think of was the cellar under our house. We used it to store potatoes and other root vegetables, as well as preserves and salted meat. It was dark and musty, but fairly large and safely underground.

We peered cautiously out of the shattered barn doorway. We saw no soldiers. Smoke filled every depression in the ground like a layer of noxious fog. It was impossible to see how damaged the house might be through the haze, but I could see it was still standing. Choking on the acrid smoke, we ran around behind the house to the cellar entrance and threw the door open. Once inside, we closed the door, but we couldn't bolt it. There was no lock on the inside. It only took me a few moments to find a candle and some matches we kept near the door. I soon had the candle burning and the light threw long, flickering shadows against the whitewashed walls of the cellar.

Jed and I sat down wearily against the back wall, our hips and shoulders touching. We sat quietly for a long time listening to the ebb and flow of the battle outside our cellar. There was a terrible regularity to it: the sounds of fighting would rise to a crescendo, abate for a time, and then rise again. It was the devil's heartbeat, I thought. Exhausted by fear and comforted by the thick walls around us, Jed and I eventually fell asleep.

CHAPTER 2

The Yankees

Soldiers are often shocked the first time they lay eyes upon their enemies. They expect monsters with red eyes and clawed fingers. Instead, they see men much like themselves: young, scared and homesick. This revelation rarely reduces their willingness to fight, but it often diminishes their ability to hate.

I was awakened by a crash on the floor above our heads. Heavy footsteps followed and I could hear muffled voices. The sounds of battle outside had stopped. I nudged Jed awake and motioned for him to be quiet. There was another crash, and another, and the sounds of laughter.

"What are they doing?" Jed whispered. I shook my head, but I suspected that they were ransacking our house, looking for valuables. I figured they were Yankees because I didn't believe any Confederate soldiers would violate southern property like that. Then it occurred to me that they might find the door to the cellar. I looked around for something with which to brace the door, but it was already too late. The door was suddenly thrown open with a crash.

Accustomed to the dim candlelight in the cellar, we were

blinded by the light suddenly streaming in through the open door. A high, nasal voice in an accent I had never heard before said "Well lookee heah! It appears this cellar has rats."

I shaded my eyes trying to make out the figure standing in front of me, but all I could see was a vague outline in a flare of bright light. A second voice came from behind the first: "Too big for rats, Kevin me boy. I think maybe we caught ourselves a couple of guerrillas."

The first figure moved out of the light and came into focus. I could feel Jed stiffen by my side at the sight of him. He was a Yankee soldier all right, I could see patches of blue peeking out through a uniform caked with dirt. He was rail thin, his hair sticking out like sheaves of greasy wheat from under his slouch hat and his face was blackened with burnt gunpowder. He seemed always to be moving. Even when he stood still, he swayed slightly from side to side. The barrel of his musket was mere inches from my face.

The second man moved out of the light and stood beside the first. He too was caked in grime and burnt gunpowder. His beard was streaked with grey, and he appeared much older than the first soldier. His eyes were wide and white against his blackened face. He crouched down and looked at me curiously. "What is yer name, boy? What are ye doing here?"

"My name is Miller," I said. "This is our house."

"Oh, yer house!" He turned to the other soldier. "Ye hear that Kevin? This is young Miller's house." He stood up and scratched at his beard. "Where is yer Daddy and Momma?"

"Momma's dead. Daddy was out getting supplies when the fighting started. He'll be back for us soon."

"Yer Daddy a soldier?"

"No, Sir. He is a farmer."

The old soldier threw his head back and laughed, startling me, the sound bouncing around in the small cellar. "Of course he is! Everyone in this damned valley is a farmer, to hear them tell it. But I am sure ye all do your part to help the war effort, do ye not?"

I wasn't sure what he meant. "We give a share of our wheat crop to help the Confederacy..."

The old soldier shook his head. "No, no, I mean fight. Even a farmer can pick up a rifle and kill some Yankees, can he not?"

I suddenly realized what he was saying. "My Daddy is no guerrilla!" I said, feeling a panic rising inside me. "He would never hurt anyone, Yankee or not. He is a farmer!"

The old soldier seemed to be appraising me. "Yer a big one, ain't ye?" He stepped backwards to give himself more space to maneuver. "Ye ever kill a Yankee, boy?"

I was too terrified to speak. I just shook my head no.

The old soldier turned slightly towards the other soldier, never taking his eyes off me. "Not so brave in the light of day, is he Kevin? These guerrillas like to scurry around in the dark, ye see, like cockroaches in a tenement."

The old soldier turned back towards me and I watched his eyes sweep the cellar. When he saw the shelves of preserves we kept there, he leaned his musket against the wall next to the young soldier and said, "Keep yer eyes on them, Kevin." Then he walked over and picked up a jar of strawberry jam, ripped the wax plug out and began to eat it with his fingers. I watched him roll his eyes with pleasure. When he was half-finished, he threw the jar against the wall and reached for another. Apparently not finding something to his liking, he threw that one against the wall too, and the next.

I was shocked at the old soldier's wanton destruction. Food was life to us; we had no more than we could raise or harvest.

The old soldier turned and saw me glaring at him. He stood facing me, watching my eyes as he reached behind his back and swept several more jars off the shelves. "Do ye have something you wish to say, young Miller?"

But before I could say anything, Jed spoke up: "I got something to say, you old sum bitch! Why do you not go find a store up in Winchester to attack as all you seem good for is fighting jars of preserves!"

The old Yankees eyes widened and he took a step towards

Jed but I quickly stepped between them. The old Yankee and I stood face-to-face, only inches apart. I could smell the burnt gunpowder that had blackened his face. "Get out of my way," he said.

I said nothing, not trusting what might come out of my mouth, but I did not move. The old Yankee and I stared at each other for several more moments until he turned and walked over to the younger soldier and retrieved his musket.

The two Yankee soldiers stood side-by-side, exchanging glances but seemingly unsure what to do next. Tension filled the room like a black cloud and Jed and I did not dare to move, not even to shift our weight or change the position of our arms.

"We need to get back to our unit, Alfie," the young soldier finally said. The old soldier nodded. "Aye, Kevin, we will as soon as I take care of this guerrilla."

The younger soldier began to sway even more. "I do not know, Alfie, he looks awfully young to be a guerrilla."

The old soldier snorted. "Hell, Kevin, how old do ye have to be to pull a trigger? Do ye not remember the good Union soldier we found murdered up around Winchester? He were hardly older than these two."

"I remember, Alfie, but maybe we should take them to the captain…" But the older soldier was already raising his musket. He was muttering something unintelligible as he leveled it between my eyes and cocked the hammer. I watched as his finger tightened on the trigger, too terrified to move or call out. I knew I was about to die.

CHAPTER 3

6 months earlier...

December 1863—The First Snow

Every season brings its own palette of colors to the Shenandoah Valley: spring is swaths of delicate green set against the dark, freshly turned soil in the fields, a mere hint of the lush emerald greens and soft blue skies of the summer to come. In the fall, the mountains erupt in a multiplicity of colors, which seem to burst into red, orange and yellow flames when touched by the rays of the rising sun. But winter, to me, is the most beautiful season of all. When covered in snow, the Valley takes on an almost spiritual aspect and the sound-dampening snow gives the world a reverential hush. Even playing children seem to lower their voices out of some instinctive respect. I often stand in the snow-covered fields and imagine myself in the center of a grand European cathedral, the walls appearing to me as vast and distant as the Blue Ridge Mountains to the east and the Allegheny Mountains to the west.

I had awakened to a perfect blue sky and the rising sun reflecting off a blanket of fresh snow. It was the first snow of the season and there should have been pure joy in my heart. But I awoke angry and frustrated, blind to the beauty around me because my father and I had argued the night before. It was becoming our new routine.

We had argued about the War, of course. After 4 years of nearly constant conflict in the Valley, the War had insinuated itself into every aspect of our lives. It was all we thought about, all we talked about. It was the unwanted guest who wouldn't leave, the bogeyman under every bed.

The crux of our argument was always the same: I wanted to enlist in the Confederate Army on my upcoming 16th birthday while my father believed I was too young. There appeared to be no room for compromise on either of our parts and I was driven nearly to desperation by my fear that the War would end without my having had a chance to fight.

My father must have thought me foolish to be so unmindful of the tragedy that the War had already brought to the Valley. After all, the cries of grieving wives and mothers had become an aria in a tragic opera being performed the entire length and breadth of the South. But I was young; where there was death and suffering, I imagined only honor and adventure. And when others prayed for an end to the seemingly endless War, I prayed for it to last just long enough for me to snatch some glory for myself.

The evening before, I had followed my father from room to room, giving him no peace and no escape as I argued and cajoled. I finally cornered him in the kitchen where I listed the names of my friends who had enlisted in the Army, some as young as 15, ticking their names off on my fingers like a lawyer making points before a judge. "Nearly everyone I know is in the

Army!" I added, my voice rising.

My father grew quiet as he always did when driven to the end of his patience. I should have recognized this as a warning sign to back off, but I did not. I made the same arguments over and over again, as if sheer repetition would make my father recognize their validity and give me my way.

"Enough, Teddy," my father finally said. "I warn you not to push me too far."

"Then why do you not listen to me? In another year, the war may be over, and I will have missed my chance forever!"

I watched my father struggle to keep his temper in check. "For the last time, you are too young. Besides, you do more good for the Confederacy here on the farm."

God forgive me, but I had a mean streak when I couldn't have what I wanted. "That is the point, is it not?" I demanded. "You want me to hide here on the farm with you while the real men fight this war!"

My father looked as though I had slapped him in the face and I was instantly mortified by my own spitefulness. "Daddy, I did not mean that!" But my father held up his hand to stop me from saying more. "When you are seventeen, I will not stand in your way. Now leave me in peace."

My brother Jed and I pushed our way through thigh-high snowdrifts to get to the barn, the snow creaking and crunching under our feet. I broke the ice in water troughs and buckets while Jed prepared to feed our meager assortment of animals. Our old mule, our plow horse and a half-dozen sheep and pigs waited expectantly. Every eye was turned towards us, every ear cocked in our direction. Hooves clicked against the frozen ground in excited anticipation of the meal to come.

Jed looked over at me. "You are an ass, Teddy."

"Shut up, Jed." I already felt badly enough about what I had said to my father the night before. I didn't need Jed making me feel any worse.

Jed shrugged. "Just telling you what you already know."

I mucked out the horse stall, my breath freezing and hanging in the air like a gauze curtain. I spread fresh straw on the stall floor and watched Jed bustling about filling the feed buckets. Jed was 13 years old, nearly three years younger than I, and the spitting image of our father. He had the same lean build and thick, dark hair. He also had my father's temperament, rarely displaying anger and unfailingly reasonable. He and I were so completely opposite in personality that it sometimes drove me crazy.

Jed looked up from his work and said, "You know, Daddy is never going to agree to anything so long as you keep sassing him."

"I did not sass him!"

"Call it what you want, but you called him a coward."

I spread the last of the clean straw on the stall floor and sagged against the wall. I felt smaller than a horse turd. "You are right, you are right," I admitted. In my heart, I knew that my father would enlist himself if he didn't have Jed and me to care for. He followed the war news obsessively, reading every newspaper he could find. Then when he finished reading them, he would roll out his maps of Virginia, the Carolinas and Georgia and plot the reported positions of the various armies. In the margins of the maps, he made notes about the generals and sizes of the forces that opposed each other. When I asked him about the maps, he said simply 'If I cannot be with our boys then I will follow them with my thoughts and prayers.'

"What can I do?" I asked Jed. "I fear the War will pass me by."

Jed lowered his voice an octave and exaggerated our father's gentle Virginia drawl: "Why, Teddy, you are just too young! What is there about 'too young' that you do not understand?"

I smiled at his impersonation. "Is that your advice? That is not very useful, Jed."

Jed grinned at me. "Then you miss my meaning."

"Which is?"

"Grow up!" With that, Jed turned and ran out of the barn.

I jumped over the stall wall and ran after him. He stopped every few steps to throw snowballs at me, laughing as he ran. He pretended to trip and fall in a snow drift, his arms flailing, until I laughed too and soon my mood lightened despite myself. The animals chewed their food contentedly as they watched us run and play in the snow, totally undisturbed by our yelling and wrestling. After all, it was the first snow of the season and it was beautiful.

That evening, for the first time in what seemed like months, my father and I did not argue. Instead, we all gathered in front of a roaring fire where Jed and I listened as our father read aloud from Charles Dickens' *The Personal History, Adventures, Experience and Observation of David Copperfield the Younger of Blunderstone Rookery (Which He Never Meant to Publish on Any Account)*.

I had read the book and I did not pay much attention to the words as my father was reading them. I was content to let my mind drift, the sound of my father's voice as comforting as a grandmother's hug. I smiled as I watched my father unconsciously caress the spine of the book as it lay open on his lap.

When my father grew weary of reading, he used an old piece of our mother's ribbon to mark his place in the book. He put the book down on the fireplace mantle, positioning it as carefully as if it were a piece of priceless porcelain. "My eyes grow tired, boys, but it is still early. What would you have us do now?"

"Tell us about how you met Momma," Jed said.

My father gave Jed a gentle smile. "Ah, Jed, you have heard that story a thousand times before!" But Jed was adamant. "Please, Daddy," he begged.

My father looked at me. "Teddy?" he asked. I smiled and nodded. I understood Jed's need to be reminded of our mother.

She had died giving birth to him and he had never had a chance to know her. I was barely a toddler myself when we lost her. I closed my eyes and tried to remember what she looked like, but I could not. But I remembered how she smelled and the softness of her touch; and I remembered her voice in the way one remembers fragments of a song heard long ago, recalling the lilt of it if not the specific melody.

My father settled back in his chair. He stared at the corner of the room as if he could see our mother standing there, a smile forming on his lips. "I was barely a man when I came to the Valley looking for work," he began, as he always did when he told this story. "I had 6 sisters and 1 brother, you know, and our little farm near Warrenton could not support us all.

"I will never forget the first time I stood upon the Blue Ridge Mountains with the Shenandoah Valley spread out before me," he said, shaking his head at the memory. "The wonder of it took my breath away. I saw verdant pastures of the richest soil and flowing through the middle of the Valley was the Shenandoah River, glistening in the sun like a sapphire necklace. I felt as though I were looking at the land of milk and honey that God had promised the Israelites!

"One day, as I was walking down the Valley Pike looking for work, I was struck with a terrible thirst. Right out there, as a matter of fact," he said, nodding towards the road in front of our farmhouse. "I looked around for water but saw none, so I came to the front door of this very house to ask permission to drink from the well.

"I knocked and your momma came to the door. My breath caught in my chest and I swear the earth spun beneath my feet. Her beauty pierced my heart, dealing it a wound from which I would never recover; from that instant forward, I would have followed her to the very ends of the earth.

"In my mind, I still see her as she was that day. She wore her hair in braids wrapped around her head like a golden garland and her skin was the color of fresh cream. And her eyes— oh, her eyes! —they were a deep blue that constantly seemed to be changing shades, like the Shenandoah River when the sun plays peek-a-boo behind the clouds." After a moment, he looked over at Jed and me and said "You favor her, Teddy: tall, big-boned and fair. But Jed, I must apologize; the Good Lord apparently decided to bless you with looks from my side of the family. Life is not always fair!" Jed and I laughed.

"I must have looked like a tramp," my father continued, "all sweaty and covered in dust. But she looked at me most kindly and asked what I wanted.

"It embarrasses me to say this, but I could not speak. I shuffled my feet and hemmed and hawed, but no intelligible sound would come out! After a few moments of this, your Momma's Daddy came to the door and stood behind her. 'What is going on here?' he demanded. Your Momma looked at me with twinkling eyes and said to her Daddy, 'This poor soul appears to be a mute, lost perhaps, or seeking food and water.'

"Your Momma's Daddy—your Granddaddy—stepped around her and stood in front of me. My nose came no higher than center of his chest and I had to step backwards to lift my gaze to his face. Now, your Momma's family were all big people, but he was a giant amongst giants! At that very moment, I knew how David must have felt when he saw Goliath step onto the field of battle. I do not exaggerate when I say that your Granddaddy could wash the second-floor windows while standing on the ground floor!" Jed and I laughed at this old joke as if we had not heard it a hundred times before.

"'What do you want, boy?' he demanded, and it took all of my courage not to turn and run away. I willed my voice to return and I stuttered through an explanation. 'Work, Sir. Or water.' I said. 'Work or water.'

"'Well, which is it?' your Granddaddy asked. I glanced over at your mother, but she just smiled and looked away…"

Once again, I let my mind drift. I imagined myself dressed in Confederate grey, marching towards Washington City, my father plotting the position of my regiment on his maps as we marched across Virginia and on to certain victory. How proud he would be! So complete was my fantasy that the pops and crackles of the fire became distant musket fire and the wind in the eaves the rebel yell echoing across glorious battlefields.

By the time my mind returned to the present, my father was reaching the end of his story: "Now your Momma's family, they were Norwegians and direct descendants of the Vikings themselves," he said. "Your Granddaddy, he told me stories about his ancestors invading England that would make your blood run cold! I, a grown man, had nightmares for a week every time I heard them! Anyways, your Momma fell in love with me for reasons I cannot fathom to this day. And when she thought I was taking too long to ask her to marry me, she took me aside and, like a true Viking princess, demanded my heart or my life. 'My heart or my life?' I asked. 'Will I not die anyway without my heart?'" Daddy looked at us expectantly. "And do you know what she answered?" he asked.

Jed and I smiled at each other and recited together, "Marry me and my heart will beat for the both of us.'"

Our father smiled broadly. "Exactly so!"

CHAPTER 4

February 1864—Dangerous Words

The soldiers stand shoulder to shoulder, running down the newspaper page in perfect order. It is their last military assembly. Bowen stands next to Brown and Simms next to Simonson, and so on. Their graves— if you could find them—were similarly arranged. There was no hint of the fear or pain or chaos that had accompanied their deaths. So it was after every major engagement of the War.

One late winter evening a few months later, as we sat in front of the fireplace, I suddenly remembered a message I had for my father. "I almost forgot, Daddy: Reverend Cooper stopped by today while you were in Front Royal." My father looked up from his newspaper, which he must have already read two or three times. "Oh?"

"He said he and his family were leaving the Valley."

My father folded the newspaper and put it aside. "Did he say why?"

"He said his family's lives had been threatened and he no longer felt safe or welcome in the Valley. He wanted to thank you for your support of the church before he left."

My father shook his head sadly but said nothing. "You do not seem surprised," I said.

"I am afraid I am not. Reverend Cooper's remarks have been getting dangerously seditious as of late."

"Reverend Cooper?" I asked incredulously. I thought about the Reverend standing up in his pulpit, his voice so soft that the entire congregation had to strain to catch his words. I could not imagine him even having a treasonable thought.

My father stared at the fire. "We live in dangerous times, Teddy. You must be sure of your audience before you voice, well, opinions that may be misconstrued or used against you."

"But what could Reverend Cooper possibly say that got people so upset that they would threaten him and his family?"

"We had a meeting last week to discuss church business. It was the first time I had seen Reverend Cooper since he had learned of his son's death in the newspaper's list of casualties. The boy's name was Joseph... You had gone to school with him, had you not?"

"Yes. He was two years older than I."

My father nodded. "I believe the boy had been with Lee at the Wilderness... Anyways, I was shocked at the toll the boy's death had taken on the Reverend. He was pale and shrunken, his clothes hanging on his limbs as on a hanger in a wardrobe.

"The meeting went on and on, constantly interrupted by people voicing their opinions about the state of the War. Through it all, the Reverend said little, seemingly lost in his own thoughts. But just when the meeting appeared ready to descend into total chaos, the Reverend pounded on the table to get everyone's attention and said, 'Gentlemen, we would be best served to concentrate our energies on the conduct of the church, not the war.' In reply, Deacon Samuelson said, 'But Reverend, the war does not go well for us. We should use every opportunity to implore God to intercede on our behalf!'

"Reverend Cooper said nothing for several moments and then rose slowly from his chair. Every eye in the room was on him. We expected him to offer a prayer or perhaps a blessing for our boys in the field. Instead, he looked at Deacon Samuelson and said sadly, 'I fear God has forsaken us, Deacon.'

"Deacon Samuelson looked shocked. 'Surely you do not believe that, Reverend!' he said, his voice rising. 'The War has martyred over two-hundred thousand good southern boys!'

Reverend Cooper spoke softly: 'My friend, the War is lost, as it was always predestined to be. God could never, would never, intervene on the side of slavery and injustice. We have strayed from the path He has laid out for us and now we are paying a terrible price.'

"Someone gasped and the room became deathly quiet. Then Deacon Samuelson stood up and leaned over the table, his face growing red and the veins throbbing in his neck. 'It is not your place to judge us, Sir!' he declared.

"Reverend Cooper shook his head slowly. 'It is not my intention to judge you, Sir,' he replied. Then he sat down heavily in his chair. 'I have lost my son,' he said to everyone and to no one, his voice now no more than a whisper. 'He is just one of the thousands of southern martyrs of whom you speak, Deacon. But I take no comfort in knowing that he died to protect our peculiar institution of slavery. I see no glory in his death; I do not believe him to be seated at the feet of Christ in glorious martyrdom. No, God help me, I see his death only as another dreadful, dreadful waste!'

"Reverend Cooper sat with his face in his hands and said no more. There was a terrible sadness about him that filled the room so completely that it was difficult to breathe. One by one, the men at the meeting stood up and quietly left the room. Only Deacon Samuelson seemed about to say more, but he too finally just turned away from the table and left the room without another word."

I sat quietly, thinking about the story my father had just told. The only sound was the wind rustling in the eaves of our house and the crackling of the fire in the fireplace. I glanced over at Jed who was engrossed in drawing on a slate and was paying no attention to my father and me or our conversation.

"That is all he said?" I asked. "We have had guests at our own dinner table who have argued more vehemently against slavery!"

My father moved his feet closer to the fire. "There is a difference between a philosophical debate among friends and public statements by people in positions of influence," he said. "And you must understand, Teddy, that there is currently considerable disharmony in the Valley. Insurrection is a flame easily kindled under the right circumstances."

I was astounded by my father's reply. "You sound like you condone what was done to Reverend Cooper!"

My father looked at me briefly and then back at the fire. "You are young, Teddy. The world is not nearly so black and white as you imagine."

Several days later, we heard that Reverend Cooper and his family had left the Valley.

My father never mentioned the church meeting again, but for me, it was as if I had awakened from a long sleep. I had a hunger to understand what drove men to war and the circumstances that could turn people against a gentle man like Reverend Cooper. I asked questions when and where I thought prudent, but mostly I just listened.

I soon learned that the Valley was a place of widely diverse political loyalties, which I reckoned were the 'disharmonies' to which my father had referred. Although the Valley was predominately pro-South, there were many people who had always resented the large landowners with their wealth and slaves and had never fully embraced the Confederate cause. Others had been reluctant to secede from the Union for any number of other reasons and had remained pro-North throughout the war. This obviously bred a great deal of distrust, even between neighbors and friends.

The South fought for 'state's rights,' I heard repeatedly.

I came to understand that this exalted the powers of the individual states above those of the Federal government. But it was impossible to minimize or ignore the issue of slavery, a seemingly inextricable part of southern life with deep moral and financial significance.

I mentally wrestled with the issue of slavery until my head spun. Part of my problem, I realized, was that I knew personally neither slave owner nor slave and therefore had no point of reference. I had, of course, seen slaves at work in neighboring fields, but that seemed as much a natural a part of the landscape as honeysuckle growing on a fence line.

Maybe my father was right, I thought. Maybe I was just too young to understand the moral ambiguities that surrounded the War. But I did understand the natural resentment people had for those who would force their beliefs and culture on them through invasion and subjugation. I bristled at the thought of interlopers in my beloved Valley and my desire to enlist and fight remained undiminished.

CHAPTER 5

May 14, 1864

Every farmer takes comfort from Psalm 128 when it says, 'You shall eat the fruit of the labor of your hands; you shall be blessed, and it shall be well with you.' But even the strongest among us would sometimes falter when his muscles ached, and it seemed to take an impossible effort to plow just one more row or swing the scythe one more time. At those times, his neighbors sat him in the shade and brought him cool water to drink. They took his burdens upon themselves. They renewed him.

My father loved birthdays and would never let one pass uncelebrated. So it was for my brother's fourteenth birthday on May 14, 1864. My father had been slow-roasting a pig since 5:00 a.m. that morning and he had invited every neighbor that could reasonably reach our house in time for the celebration. Nearly 30 neighbors came, arriving in wagons, on old plow horses and on foot.

Malcolm Davies and his wife and their twin girls lived the furthest away of all our guests, but they were always the first to arrive at our parties. My father said it was because Malcolm could smell a pig roast from three counties away and was drawn like a moth to fire. But Malcolm was a lean, hard man and I had never seen him eat much of anything. I suspected he really came for the jug of whisky that would make its appearance later in the evening. Mrs. Davies, on the other hand, was soft and round and always smiling. She appeared to welcome the opportunity to play mother and hostess to our womanless household. Their twin daughters were 13 years old, one as sweet as their mother, the other mean as an old rooster. Jed called them 'Sweet and Sour.'

As soon as she arrived, Mrs. Davies took over the duties of hostess. She greeted each of our guests as they arrived and made sure that the salads and casseroles they brought with them were properly displayed on a long picnic table my father had set up on the front porch. She complimented every culinary creation. "Why, Mabel," she would say, "please tell me the secret of your poke salad! I do not believe they make better in Richmond!" Mabel would blush and grab Mrs. Davies' hand. Lowering her voice to protect her secret, Mable would confide, "It is important to drain the pokeweed twice when you boil it. And, you must add an egg with the fried onions!"

When everyone had finished eating, the spring sun was already setting. The men wandered down by the barn to sip whiskey and share news about the war. The women gathered on the front porch and talked about—well—whatever it is that women talk about. The children organized a game of hide-n-seek with Jed, the birthday-boy, 'it.'

I was at an awkward age: too old for children's games and too young to socialize with the adults. And my size did not help much. Over the past year, I had grown to nearly six feet tall. Thus, my choices for the evening were limited, at best. So, when Jed turned his back and began counting to one-hundred, I ran around behind the barn and found a hiding place between two large round bales of hay.

The light was fading quickly. I could hardly see what was directly in front of me. Within minutes, I heard someone walk around behind the barn. I hunkered down as low as I could. Once I was sure it was Jed, I would race him for home base. Maybe I would even let him beat me 'home,' seeing as it was his birthday. But it was not Jed.

I heard a body slam against the barn wall. I peeked around the bale but could see only faint silhouettes. A tall man had a smaller one pinned against the wall, their faces only inches apart. The tall man was speaking in a low, hushed voice, but I could feel his anger radiating like heat. "Do you not know what you have done? You have killed us all!" he hissed.

The smaller man's voice was high-pitched and whiney: "I just done my duty! He were a damn Yankee! We sent him off to Hell, where he belongs!"

"You hung an officer, you damned fool! The Yankees will track us down and hang us all. Even our own troops will not protect us for such a crime!" The tall man was quiet for a moment, his hands moving to the smaller man's throat. In a ragged, exasperated whisper, the tall man said, "I should throttle you right now and throw your body in the river!"

"Wait, wait, wait," The smaller man pleaded. "I questioned him good. I have some information..."

The tall man leaned into the smaller one, their noses almost touching. "What information could you have that is worth any of this?"

The words came tumbling out of the small man's mouth: "His name was Thomas Ferguson, a Lieutenant in the 1st New York Cavalry. He said there were 5,000 men in his unit."

The tall man loosened his grip and stepped backwards, apparently surprised by the news that there were so many Union troops in the Valley. The small man continued: "He said they were on their way to join the Yankee Gen'ral Sigel at New Market. He said they were going to 'sweep the Valley clean of Rebs from one end to the other.'"

The tall man was quiet for a moment. "How did he get separated from his men?"

The smaller man shrugged. "He were apparently a

messenger, 'though we did not find any papers on him."

The tall man paced back and forth, clearly pondering everything he had just heard. But I must have made some noise. The tall man suddenly froze and stared in my direction through the darkness. "Is someone there?" he demanded. He moved towards me. I burst out from between the hay bales and ran around the corner of the barn towards safety. I heard the tall man yell after me, "Stop! Come back here!"

I ran into the barnyard where the men and my father were gathered. They were sitting on anything handy, a gallon jug of whiskey passing from hand to hand. I ran to my father, but before I could say anything to him, two men came walking around the corner of the barn, one tall and one short. The short one was Jacob Hayes who lived on the next farm over from us. The tall man was Malcolm Davies.

Malcolm's gaze swept the scene and settled on me and my father. If I had expected him to sneak around in the shadows, I was mistaken. He walked directly to us while Jacob found a seat with the other men. Malcolm stood in front of my father and said, "We need to talk, Eli."

The jug of whiskey came to my father and he offered the jug to Malcolm. Malcolm shook his head. "We need to talk *now*," he said.

My father nodded. He returned the jug to the man next to him and stood up. He and Malcolm turned to walk away from the group of men. I started to follow, but my father held up his hand to stop me. "You go find your friends, Teddy," he said.

I watched my father and Malcolm walk away into the darkness. They walked close together, apparently deep in conversation, but I could not hear anything they said.

When the last remnant of Jed's party had been cleaned and put away, I fell exhausted into bed. But I could not fall asleep. I had told my father what I had seen and heard behind the barn, but he just shrugged it off. "Too much whiskey, Teddy, makes men foolish," he had said. "Jacob was just blowing off steam and talking nonsense."

I took no comfort from my father's explanation. I could still feel the heat of Malcolm's anger as if it had burned my flesh. And the idea of anyone, even a Yankee soldier, being brutally murdered by people who broke bread with us, whom we called 'friend,' was incomprehensible to me. But the most unsettling part of all was my father's seeming indifference to what had happened. I tossed and turned, trying to find a comfortable position in bed until I had finally fallen into a fitful sleep filled with dreams red-tinged and violent.

CHAPTER 6

Kevin and Alfie

At the beginning of the Civil War, both North and South were enthused by an innocence unimaginable even 6 months later. Both sides anticipated a short, glorious conflict. There were dances and parades and pretty girls handed cookies and flowers to the soldiers as they marched. But the War quickly became a living thing, uncontrollable, with a terrible thirst for blood. Suffering and death occurred on a scale never before seen or imagined. By the end of the War, even the stoutest soldiers had despaired of ever seeing home and loved-ones again. To survive, the soldiers said, you had to give up hope; hope could get you killed or maimed.

I had watched the old Yankee's finger tighten on the trigger, knowing that I was going to die. The gunshot, when it came, was deafening in the small cellar and billowing white gun smoke filled the room. I gasped for breath and was startled to still be alive. Then, in a panic, I groped around blindly in the smoke for Jed. When I found him, I pulled his face close to mine. "Are you alright, Jed?" Jed put his mouth next to my good ear. "I am alright, Teddy. I am alright."

I could hear the old soldier raging at the younger man through the blinding smoke. "Damn yer eyes, Kevin, why did ye knock my musket?" As the smoke began to clear, I saw the old soldier standing toe to toe with the younger man, backing him slowly against the wall. "He is a guerrilla!" the old soldier yelled, spittle flying from his mouth. "Do ye not understand what that means?" But then the young soldier suddenly shoved the old soldier backwards. He caught the older man by surprise and the old soldier stumbled and nearly fell.

The young soldier began to raise his musket, saying, "Dammit, Alfie, I ain't survived this damn war this long just to be hung 'cause you shoot some kid, rebel nor otherwise." His musket continued to rise until it centered on the old soldier's chest.

The old soldier slowly put his musket down and raised both his hands. "Now Kevin," he said softly, "ye know I was just thinking about all the boys we lost in this God-forsaken valley. Jest lower your musket and we will talk this out..." But the younger man shook his head. His swaying became worse, and the muzzle of his musket was moving in small, lazy circles. I watched it, mesmerized; it was like watching a snake about to strike.

They are both mad, I thought. They will kill each other or all of us. I tried to move sideways to stand between them and my brother, but the young soldier caught the movement out of the corner of his vision. He swung his musket in my direction. "Stop!" he yelled, and I froze. For several long moments, we all stood where we were, no one daring to talk or move. The air was stagnant and reeked of burnt gunpowder and sweat and I felt as if the cellar walls were closing in on me. I had an almost overwhelming urge to grab Jed's hand and run for the cellar door, but the old soldier seemed to read my mind. "Do not even think about it, boy," he warned. And so, we stood where we were, all eyes on the younger soldier who continued to sway as if buffeted by a wind none of the rest of us could feel.

The old soldier slowly sat down on the cellar floor. "Ah,

Kevin, me feet are killing me! Why do ye not sit down here beside me?" he asked, patting the floor beside him. But the young soldier just shook his head. "Well, suit yerself," said the old soldier as he pulled a clay pipe and tobacco from his pocket. In a moment, he had the pipe lit and was blowing smoke at the ceiling. I found the sweet smell of the tobacco nauseating in the already stale air.

None of us moved or said anything for several more minutes. Finally, the young soldier gave a great sigh like a deflating balloon and sank to the floor next to the old soldier. He laid his musket across his lap and said, "I almost shot you, Alfie."

The old soldier nodded and said, "I reckon you almost did, Kevin." He began tapping the ashes out of his pipe against the cellar floor. The younger soldier's eyes welled up and tears began to run down his blackened face. "I cannot fight no more, Alfie, not you, not the Rebs. I do not want to die, Alfie, not now," he said. "Not after all we been through. Not when it is beginning to look like this damned war might actually be coming to an end."

The old soldier looked up as if he were about to say something, but the young soldier continued on, his voice taking on a desperate edge: "You know I got children, Alfie. Two beautiful little girls I ain't seen in nearly 2 years. And my wife, the sweetest girl you ever met..." His voice began to rise. "I promised her, Alfie, that I would come home! I did not always believe I would, but we are so close now..."

The old soldier put his hand on the young soldier's arm. "Now listen to me, Kevin," he said in a voice so soft I could barely hear him from 5 feet away. "Are ye listening to me?" The young soldier wiped his nose on his sleeve and nodded. "Good," said the old soldier. "God knows, I see no special honor in being the last man to die in a war. But we will finish this thing, ye and me. Someday soon, we will march up Boylston Street in Boston and let all the pretty girls pin flowers on our uniforms. And someday we will tell our grandchildren that we done our duty."

But the younger soldier just shook his head. "I am done, Alfie. I am used up."

The old soldier suddenly raised his voice, startling all of us: "Damn it, Kevin, I will tell ye when yer done!" The young soldier looked at the old soldier with wide eyes. The old soldier lowered his voice again: "Now I want ye to listen to me, Kevin. Will ye do that?"

The young soldier nodded. And so, the old soldier began to speak. He alternately praised and berated the young soldier. He talked about friends, duty, lost comrades and God. His voice rose and fell in a rhythm that seemed to soothe the young soldier.

Jed and I watched all this from across the room. It was as if the two Yankee soldiers had forgotten we were even there, but we dared not speak or move. We watched the young soldier laugh and cry and sometimes lash out in anger against the old soldier. But slowly, ever so slowly, the young soldier calmed. Or perhaps he simply became resigned to whatever fate awaited him. I do not know that I could have told the difference.

Nothing could have prepared me for the scene that awaited us as the two soldiers led Jed and I outside the cellar. My knees buckled and if it were not for the old soldier holding my arm I would have fallen to the ground. Our farm no longer existed. Every tree was blasted to a splintered stump. Every blade of grass was trampled. The air, perfumed with honeysuckle only hours before, now smelled of burnt gunpowder, freshly turned earth—and death. Several horses, the exact number impossible to ascertain, lay bloating in the sun around a large shell crater, still harnessed to their shattered caisson.

I turned to look back at our house. Half of the front porch had collapsed, and every window appeared to be broken, but it was still standing. But when I looked towards where the barn had been, there was nothing. Not even a pile of broken timbers to mark the spot. It had simply disappeared.

I glanced at Jed who was being led by the younger soldier. His eyes were wide and unblinking. I turned to go to him, but the old Yankee tightened his grip on my arm. "Hold on there, boy," he said. "We need to go visit the captain." He leaned close and whispered, "And if he believes ye are guerrillas, ye will not live to see the sun set." Just the idea of hanging us seemed to cheer the old Yankee up and he hummed a tune while he push-pulled me towards three Union officers sitting on horseback near the road.

As we approached, two of the officers saluted the third and wheeled their horses around. In a moment, they were galloping up the road in the direction of Front Royal. The third officer, wearing the epaulettes of a captain, watched us approach. He looked dirty and tired. He slouched in the saddle, his eyes heavy-lidded. His horse was soaked in sweat. "What have we here, Sergeant?" he asked wearily.

I had not noticed the stripes half-hidden beneath the grime on the old Yankee's uniform. He pushed me forward, came to attention and saluted. "We found these two hiding in the cellar, Sir."

"At ease, Sergeant," the captain said, returning the Sergeant's salute with a flick of his fingers. "You boys live here?" he asked.

"Yes, Sir," I answered. "I am Theodore Miller, and this is my brother Jedidiah. This is our farm."

"Where are your parents?"

Before I could answer, the old Yankee spoke up: "They claim their Momma's dead and their Daddy run off just before the fighting started." He lowered his voice, "Seems a bit suspicious to me, Captain, their daddy running off and leaving them like that. Mebbe he has got something to hide. This valley is full of guerrillas, you know. And this one," he said, pointing at me, "he has been acting funny, too. I do not trust the bunch of them."

The captain stared at my brother and me for a moment, and then asked, "When do you expect your father to return?"

"I expect he will come back looking for us now the fighting has stopped," I answered.

The captain suddenly seemed to lose interest. "Alright, Sergeant, you detain and question the boys' father when he shows up." The captain glanced up at the sun, which was getting low in the sky. "It is getting late," he said, almost to himself. "I need to find General Sigel's headquarters before it gets dark. Take a few men, Sergeant, and gather whatever food stuffs you can find. Then burn the farm." He turned his horse to leave.

"No!" I yelled. "You cannot do that! We will starve!" I moved towards the captain, but the old Yankee pulled me back. "Captain, please!" I begged.

The captain spun around in his saddle to face me, his face dark with anger. "This is your war, Reb! You and your kind wanted it and, by God, here it is!" With that, he spurred his horse and galloped off to the north.

The old Yankee let go of my arm and I ran over to Jed. I watched Kevin and Alfie walk back towards the house, leaving Jed and I where we stood.

A great sense of loss settled over me as I stared at the desolation around me, our farm barely recognizable. Everything I had known and loved about my life seemed to have suddenly yellowed like an old piece of parchment, fallen to dust and scattered with the wind. I tried to wear a brave face for Jed, but inside my stomach twisted with fear and dread.

CHAPTER 7

Fire and Smoke

Fire can rob us of all we hold dear, causing us to look upon the ashes with watery eyes and lament all that we have lost. But what sometimes follows is far worse: the loss is so complete that we become like a ship with a severed mooring line, drifting with the tides or driven by the prevailing winds. We become rudderless and ungrounded.

I took Jed by the hand and we walked up to our house where we watched helplessly as the Yankee soldiers continued to tear it apart.

They took everything with any conceivable value, piling it in a horse cart. One soldier danced around the yard wearing one of my mother's old bonnets, much to the amusement of the other Yankees. Another soldier emerged with the few pieces of silverware our family owned, once my mother's prized possessions, stuffed in his pants. Other soldiers made quick work out of emptying our root cellar. They came out with their arms piled high with fruit preserves, sweet potatoes and dried hams. It was all the food we had.

The sun was beginning to set, and the shadows grew long.

When it was clear that there was no more booty to be had, a Yankee soldier jumped into the cart, clucked at the horse, and drove out of the yard and onto the road. He was out of sight in moments.

A light suddenly flared, then another. We watched as two Yankee soldiers held torches high while a third poured kerosene on the front porch of our house.

The old Yankee sergeant walked over to where Jed and I were standing. "It is 'bout time for us to get moving, boys. Sorry I missed yer Daddy."

"You do not have to do this," I said, nodding at the soldiers with the torches.

"Like the Captain said, you Rebs brought this on yerselves. Consider yerselves lucky. If it was up to me, ye would both be hanging from a tree limb by now." He turned towards the soldiers holding the torches. "Do it!" he yelled.

I watched the 2 torches spin end over end through the air. When they hit the kerosene-soaked wood, it burst into flames. In moments, the entire front of the house was on fire.

The old Yankee turned back to me. The light from the fire cast red highlights on his blackened face. "At least you'll sleep warm tonight," he said with a grin.

"You bastard!" I growled at him. Without thinking, I lunged for his throat. But the old Yankee was too fast for me. He sidestepped my charge and brought the stock of his musket down on the back of my head as I went by. The world went dark.

I came to with my head in Jed's lap. "Thank God, Teddy, I thought that old Yankee had killed you."

I managed to sit up. I probed the back of my head with my fingers and my hand came away sticky with blood. I looked around quickly. "Where are they?" I asked.

"They are long gone. You have been out for a while."

My head throbbed with every beat of my heart as Jed helped me to my feet. All that remained of our house was a pile of glowing embers. The air reeked of burning wood, tar paper and kerosene. "No sign of Daddy?" I asked. Jed shook his head. I tried to think about what to do, but my head felt like it was about to explode. The world suddenly spun beneath me and I fell to my knees and vomited. I remained on my knees until the spinning slowed, then stopped. Jed once again helped me to my feet.

"We need to find some place safe to stay," I finally managed to say. "Somewhere Daddy will think to look for us."

"The Hayes' farm is only a mile down the road," Jed said. "But it is not likely they fared much better than we did." He thought about it for a moment, and then said "I think we have a better chance of finding help if we get away from the Valley Pike. There appears to be too many Yankee soldiers moving up and down the Valley. Maybe we should go east, up into the mountains."

I fought against more nausea as I tried to think things through. "Malcolm Davies' farm is up Cedar Valley, well off the main road," I said. I still was not sure how I felt about Malcolm, but my father seemed to trust him. And what choice did we have now anyway? "But how will Daddy know where to find us?" I wondered aloud. "We can't leave a sign with Malcolm's name on it."

"I have an idea," Jed said. I watched him root around in the debris until he found an unburned piece of wood around a foot wide and 2 feet long. He picked up a piece of charcoal and began to write on the wood. When he was finished, he stood the piece of wood against a stump near where the front porch had been. I had to move closer to read it in the dim light from the dying fire. If my head had not been throbbing so badly, I would have laughed when I read it: 'Sweet and Sour,' it said.

CHAPTER 8

Malcolm's Farm

The Valley was beautiful but not geographically equable. The richest land abutted the north and south branches of the Shenandoah River. But as one climbed up into the foothills, the soil thinned, and rocks multiplied in the fields. Farms were smaller and less productive. The people who lived there were tough and pragmatic. They had little regard for the people on the Valley floor whom, for the most part, they considered soft and spoiled. But if they grew to like you, you would never have better or more generous friends.

J ed and I walked all night and most of the next day to reach Malcolm's farm. It had taken us much longer than it normally would have because we had to walk through woods and across fields to avoid the main road where we had seen long columns of Union troops and supply wagons. But the woods held their own dangers.

Not long after we had left our farm, Jed and I were picking our way through the woods in near total darkness when I smelled tobacco smoke. I knew that armies would post pickets around the perimeter of their camps to protect from surprise attacks and I suspected that we had stumbled upon one. I motioned Jed to stop. "Smell that?" I whispered. "I think there's a picket smoking up ahead of us."

We stayed there for several long moments, but we saw and heard nothing. I thought about moving forward but my throbbing head reminded me of what happens when you act without caution. I whispered to Jed that we needed to backtrack and go around the suspected picket. He and I began to slowly retrace our steps when I stumbled over some roots. I caught myself before I fell, but I thrashed at the underbrush as I tried to regain my balance. The noise sounded unnaturally loud in the quiet woods.

"Who goes there?" challenged a voice from no more than 30 yards in front of us. The voice was deep and nasal, the accent clearly Yankee.

"Run!" I yelled to Jed and we both turned and took off running through the woods, the underbrush tearing at our clothes and faces. We must have made a terrible racket. A shot rang out from behind us and I could hear the Minié ball tear through the bushes. We had not gone a hundred yards when another voice, again in front of us, yelled "Halt!" followed almost immediately by a musket shot. Jed and I dropped to the ground and covered our heads with our arms. We had somehow ended up between two Yankee pickets.

I do not know if the two pickets then mistook each other for enemy soldiers, but there soon developed a fire fight that quickly began to grow in intensity. Small pieces of leaves rained down on us, cut from the trees and bushes by musket balls flying both ways over our heads. I could hear men cursing in front and behind us as they reloaded and fired into the darkness. Each picket was no doubt convinced that the entire Confederate army was bearing down on him.

Jed and I took advantage of the confusion by crawling away from the sounds of the fighting. When we were several hundred yards away, we heard a voice yelling "Cease fire! Cease fire, damn it! Cease fire!" The gunfire slowed and finally stopped.

Once we moved out of the Valley and into the foothills of the Blue Ridge Mountains, we did not see any more Union troops. Although Jed and I spoke little, I knew his thoughts were like my own: Where was our father? Why had he not come to find us?

After a steep climb up a rutted dirt road, we came at last to Malcolm's farm. It was hard scrabble in comparison to the rich soil in the Valley. Malcolm had a small log cabin that had to be a tight fit for a family of four. The cabin dated back to the previous century and had been occupied by Malcolm's family for at least 4 generations.

Mrs. Davies opened the door just as I was about to knock. She gasped when she saw us standing there. We must have been a sight: Jed and I were filthy, our clothes stinking of wood smoke, our hair matted with sweat. And I was covered in half-dried blood from my head wound.

"Good Lord, Children!" she exclaimed. "What happened to you?"

I blurted out the whole story, hardly stopping for a breath. Mrs. Davies stood with her hands over her mouth as she listened, her eyes wide with shock. When I had finished, she led us inside and sat us at a long wooden table in the kitchen. She got a clean cloth and a bowl of water and began to clean my head wound. I tried to thank her, but my eyes felt impossibly heavy and I could not find my voice. I was exhausted from our long hike. My head drooped forward, and I nearly fell asleep at the table. Jed had his head on his arms and was already sound asleep.

"Come with me," she said, as she helped me up from the table. She led me into a small bedroom and lay me across the bed. She left the room and came back a moment later with Jed. I fell into a deep sleep.

I awoke to the wonderful smell of bacon frying on the wood stove. I do not know how long I had slept, but I felt rested and ravenously hungry. Even the throbbing in my head had abated some. Jed was no longer lying beside me, and I suspected he was already in the kitchen.

When I walked into the kitchen, Jed and the entire Davies family were seated shoulder-to-shoulder at a table which was barely long enough for them all. Jed was the only one eating. He was stuffing bread into his mouth as quickly as he could lather it with fresh butter. Twin daughters 'Sweet and Sour' gasped when they saw my blood-soaked clothes and wild hair. Malcolm looked at me curiously. "The Missus told me yer story when the girls and me got home last night," Malcolm said. "Jed here, when he were not stuffing his face, filled in some of the details." He motioned for me to sit down in his spot as he got up from the table and walked towards the door. "Have some breakfast, get cleaned up, and we will talk."

I glanced at 'Sweet' Davies, who blushed and looked away. 'Sour' Davies glared at me and it occurred to me that I had kept them both from their bed the night before. Mrs. Davies brought Jed and me plates piled high with bacon and eggs. I do not remember a meal ever tasting better.

When I had washed up, Mrs. Davies gave me one of Malcolm's old flannel shirts to wear. After salvaging the buttons from my torn and blood-stained shirt, she threw it in the fire. I left Jed talking to the twins and walked outside to look for Malcolm.

I found Malcolm out back near his barn. He was sharpening an axe on an old, pedal-powered grinding wheel. A long train of sparks flew every time he touched the blade to the spinning stone. I watched him as he periodically checked the sharpness of the axe against his thumb. When he was satisfied with the edge, he got up and walked over to me. "Here," he said, handing me the axe, "earn your breakfast." He motioned to a nearby pile of partially split firewood.

I walked over to the pile of wood. I put a log on a stump and neatly split it in two with one swing of the axe. I put another log on the stump and repeated the process. After a bit, I took off the flannel shirt and hung it from a nearby tree branch. I did not want to tear it or get it dirty because I strongly suspected I would not get another of Malcolm's shirts.

Malcolm stood with his arms crossed and watched as the pile of unsplit wood dwindled and finally disappeared. When I finished stacking what I had split, he walked over to the shade of a large hickory tree and sat down on some old logs. He motioned for me to follow.

"Afore we start, you oughta know that I tell things as I see them," Malcolm said. "The Missus says I am too blunt and need to temper my remarks some. But I ain't wastin' time beating around every bush I come to. I am telling you this because we need to have a serious talk and I do not have the patience to coddle you. I will tell you what I know and what I suspect. Do you understand what I am saying to you?"

I nodded.

"Good." Malcolm said. "First, you got to be prepared to accept the notion that yer Daddy is prob'ly dead. Best case, otherwise, he is a prisoner of the Yankees."

I just stared at Malcolm. I could think of no words to say.

"He must have ridden straight into the entire Yankee army the other day. If he was able, I am sure he would a come lookin' for you boys by now," Malcolm reasoned.

"But why would the Yankees kill or arrest Daddy?" I asked.

"Why? Because he had no business being out on the road snoopin' around with the whole damned Yankee army marching down the Valley."

"He was going to Front Royal for supplies!"

Malcolm snorted. "He were in the wrong place at the wrong time. Let us leave it at that." I started to argue some more, but Malcolm held up his hand. "Save it, boy. Do you want to hear what I know or not?"

I nodded, fighting hard to keep from being overwhelmed by the despair building in my heart.

"Alright, then," Malcolm said. "I went down into the Valley last night while you was sleeping. Place is crawling with Yankees, but I managed to pick up a little information."

"About Daddy?"

"Mebbe, mebbe not. I ain't sure. I heard that the Yankees arrested 3 civilians suspected of being guerrillas during the fighting yesterday. Two was hung outright and the other is still being held for questioning."

"You think one of them might be Daddy?"

Malcolm shrugged. "Like I said, I ain't sure."

My head was spinning. I did not want to think that my father might already have been hanged. But if my father were the one still alive, I had to find him. I had to convince the Yankees that he was not a guerrilla. "Do you know where the last prisoner is being held?" I asked.

Malcolm stared at me for a moment and then frowned. "I know what yer thinking, boy, but it ain't smart to go marching around the Valley right now looking for yer Daddy. You are old enough they may hang you right beside him."

"Please, Mr. Davies, do you know where the prisoner is being held?"

Malcolm shrugged. "I do not know where he is fer sure," he said, "but if I had to guess, I would reckon he would be at Gen'ral Sigel's headquarters. Sigel's in Mt. Jackson, just north of New Market. Least ways, he was yesterday. They have a small jail there and it would be a good place to hold a prisoner."

"Then I need to go to Mt. Jackson," I said.

I was anxious to be on my way, but it was more than an hour before I was finally able to leave the farm. I had spent most of that time convincing Jed to stay with the Davies while I went looking for our father. He refused at first but finally relented when I convinced him that I could travel faster alone. Time was clearly running out for our father if he were even still alive. And General Sigel might have already left Mt. Jackson or be preparing to do so. I felt sure he would not be taking any prisoners with him.

Mrs. Davies had filled my pockets with bread and ham wrapped in greased paper and Malcolm had found a stoppered bottle for me to carry water in, which I carried in a discarded Yankee haversack. Malcolm grabbed my arm as I turned to leave. "You be careful, boy," he said. I was both surprised and touched. Malcolm had never shown any obvious interest in my well-being before. "Yes, sir," I answered.

A hundred yards down the rutted road, I turned to look back at the little cabin. Malcolm and Mrs. Davies stood watching me leave. Jed sat on the front steps of the cabin with 'Sweet and Sour.' No one waved goodbye.

CHAPTER 9

Abner and Blackie

Kindness is one trait that all human beings have in common. Not that everyone chooses to practice it, of course, although few things bear more fruit for less effort. And when one is the recipient of a kind act, it comes most often as a surprise and usually from someone who can ill afford it, be it a soldier on a battlefield who shares his last sip of water or a busy nurse who takes the time to hold the hand of a dying man.

When I reached the floor of the Valley, I found that the roads were no longer clogged with troops and supply wagons. The battle had clearly moved on. Nonetheless, Yankee messengers occasionally galloped by. They leaned forward in their saddles as if willing their mounts to run ever faster. Their horses were wide-eyed and sweat-soaked. God help you if you did not jump out of their way.

No one paid much attention to me as I made my way up the Valley towards Mt. Jackson. I was only one among many civilians displaced by the fighting. I passed whole families with their meager possessions piled high in small wagons. The men were grim-faced, the women weepy. Children clung to their mothers' skirts.

As a crow flies, it was probably no more than 20 miles from Malcolm's farm to Mt. Jackson but following the winding roads —mostly old cow paths and Indian trails—added at least an additional 15 miles. I reckoned it would take me no less than 10 hours to walk it and I was afraid I did not have that much time. I kept an eye out for an old mule or plow horse I could 'borrow' to speed my trip. But every farm I passed was deserted and I saw no livestock of any kind. The Yankee soldiers were efficient scavengers. And judging by the black smoke I saw rising in thick columns all around me, they had burned what they could not carry. I had about despaired of finding any transportation when I heard a clatter moving up the road behind me. I looked back and saw a wagon rounding a curve in the road. As it drew near, I affected a limp, dragging my left leg behind me as I walked.

The wagon slowed as it pulled next to me. It was painted bright green with red wheels and had a white canvas top. A big sign on the side said 'A. Faulke, Sutler.' The wagon was drawn by a huge black horse, the breed a Percheron I think, with hooves the size of frying pans. The horse's muscles rippled beneath its shiny coat as it effortlessly pulled the heavy wagon forward. Every bump in the road brought a clatter from the back of the wagon from what I assumed were pots and pans available for sale to soldier and housewife alike.

The driver looked down at me curiously. He was around my father's age. He had wild red hair and thick whiskers that covered much of his face. A straw hat was perched on the back of his head and he wore a white shirt and a string tie. "You alright there, Citizen?" he asked.

"Yes, Sir," I answered. "I stepped in a pothole and twisted my ankle some," I lied. I exaggerated my limp a little more, trying to look as pitiful as possible.

"Where you headed?"

"Mt. Jackson. I am supposed to meet my Daddy there. He

went ahead in our wagon to get some supplies." That was mostly the truth.

"Well, I am headed to New Market. I can give you a ride that far if it would help."

"Yes, Sir, I would be grateful."

The man gave me a hand up and I took a seat next to him on the wagon. He clucked at the horse, snapped the reins, and we began to pick up speed as we clattered our way down the road. The man offered me his hand and said, "I am Abner Faulke."

"Teddy Miller," I said.

"Well, Teddy, it is nice to have some company. Blackie here," he motioned towards his big horse, "he does his work well but he ain't much of a talker. And in this job, you spend a lot of time just gettin' from one place to the next." Faulke leaned back in his seat, the reins hanging slack. It appeared that Blackie would just keep moving forward until someone told him to stop. Faulke glanced at black smoke rising like a funeral pyre from a farm we were passing. "War is a wasteful thing, Teddy. My Daddy was a farmer and his Daddy too. Rebels or not, it grieves me to see these people losing everything they worked their whole lives for."

"You come from a farm family?" I asked.

Faulke nodded. "I left the farm when I was 14. My Daddy was a mean old cuss. He would get drunk and beat my Momma. I tried to stop him one time and he chased me off the farm, firing his shotgun at me as fast as he could reload it." Faulke scratched at his beard and laughed out loud at the memory. "It was one of those things our old preacher used to call a 'mixed blessing,'" he said. "If Daddy had not been drunk, he probably would not have been beating Momma. But if he had not been drunk, he probably would not have missed me with the shotgun either."

I did not see anything funny in Faulke's story, but I did not say anything. I reckoned that everyone had their own way of dealing with bad memories.

"Anyways," Faulke continued, "I was not made to stay in one

place for very long. So, I became a sutler. Now I am always on the move and I sell people the things they need to make their lives a little easier." Faulke took a deep breath and recited: "I got pots, pans, buffalo robes, shoes and boots, sugar, and a comb for your hair. I got cigars from the West Indies and fresh fruit when it is in season. Or mebbe your Missus needs a new dress, in which case I have a bolt of fabric straight from Paris herself."

I glanced back at the closed flap to the wagon and imagined the treasures within. "Do you not worry about the soldiers robbing you?" I asked.

"Nah, the soldiers is mostly good boys, even if a little rambunctious at times. Besides, I got me a piece of paper from the War Department authorizing me to follow the army and to come and go as I please." Faulke was quiet for a moment and then added, "But there are more dangerous things than soldiers in this valley, be they Union or Reb."

"Like what?"

"Like the partisans!" he said, spitting out the word.

"'Partisans?'" I repeated, unfamiliar with the word.

"Partisans, guerillas, thieves, murderers, thugs, you take your pick. Anyways," Faulke continued, "they infest this valley like rats in a corn silo. They beat and sometimes kill Union stragglers and anyone who disagrees with their politics." Faulke's voice was thick with contempt: "I have heard that the partisans fancy themselves soldiers without uniforms; I think them cowards and murderers! And I am not alone in this belief: if the Union army catches them, they will hang them without a trial." Faulke reached under his seat and pulled out an old two-barreled shotgun. Both the barrels and the stock had been shortened to make it easy to hide and it was an evil-looking weapon. "But if they try to rob me, I will save the army the trouble of hanging them."

We rode for some time in silence. I felt embarrassed by Faulke's contempt for the guerrillas in our Valley, even though I had no direct involvement with them myself. But just my accidental knowledge of what the guerrillas had done to the

Yankee lieutenant made me feel complicit in their crimes. For the first time, I began to wonder how our own soldiers, the ones who wore Confederate grey and bravely met the enemy face-to-face on the battlefield, felt about the guerrillas.

Faulke's good mood eventually returned and we spent several pleasant hours talking about our families and our plans for after the War. I told him I hoped to be a writer like Charles Dickens. He told me that he wanted to open a real store in a big city like New York or St. Louis where he could find a wife and put down some roots. "Now, do not get me wrong," Faulke said. "Like I told you before, life on the road suits Blackie and me jest fine for now. But I would be a liar if I said that I would not like a woman in bed beside me to keep me warm on a cold winter's night." Faulke looked thoughtful. "I have heard that there are large German communities in the big cities," he said. "Surely there would be some woman there interested in a man like me, yes?" But before I could answer, Blackie lifted his tail and broke wind loudly. "There is my answer!" said Faulke. He and I laughed so hard we nearly fell out of the wagon

When at last we came to New Market, I shook hands with Faulke and prepared to jump down from the wagon. But Faulke asked me to wait as he turned and started to dig through the wagon behind him. After a moment, he turned back and handed me a book. It was a translation of Victor Hugo's *Les Misérables*, published in England less than a year before. The cover was crimson red with gold lettering. It had clearly never been opened. "I cannot accept this!" I said.

"When you publish your first book, send me a few copies and I will sell them for you. Of course," he added with a wink, "I will take a small commission on every sale…"

"No, no," I said, trying to hand the book back to him. "This is too much!" I knew the book was worth at least $3, more than a day's earnings for a farm laborer.

But Faulke would not take the book back. "Truth be told, Teddy, I have a half-dozen more copies in the back of my wagon and I cannot sell a single one of them. Seems I was snookered by a book seller in Baltimore. 'Soldiers love to read,' he said, 'and this book is all the rage right now. They will fly right out of your wagon!' But he had told me only half the truth."

"How so?"

"Well, the book is all the rage, but not with *my* army. The Rebs, now, they have adopted this book as their own, even calling themselves 'Lee's Miserables' after their Gen'ral Lee." Faulke looked downcast. "There is not a good Union soldier that will even touch the book. I have been told it is akin to singing 'Dixie' at a Union square dance."

CHAPTER 10

The Fist Fight

A soldier's perception of a battle is limited by what he can see and hear. He may see his comrades standing next to him or, if the smoke is not too thick, the enemy across the field. He may hear the angry buzz of the Minié balls and the roar of the cannon. But for him, there is no grand, overarching plan where soldiers move like pieces on a chessboard. For him, the fight is intensely personal, often reduced to two men: himself and the enemy soldier trying to kill him.

I began my walk to cover the last 7 miles to Mt. Jackson, my copy of Les Misérables in my haversack. After a while, there was a sameness to the destruction I passed along the way. Where there had been significant fighting, it was if a great tornado had ravaged the land. Everything was shattered, ripped apart and spewed across the countryside. Elsewhere, there was just the endless detritus of war, like driftwood stacked against the shore. Canteens, haversacks, and shelter halves littered the roadside, thrown away by soldiers too exhausted to bear the extra load. Dead horses and mules lay where they had died, bloated and covered with bottle flies. I saw fresh graves that had been dug by the roadside, marked with crude wooden crosses or simply a piece of wood railing or a pile of stones. A great darkness settled over my soul as I wondered if my father lay in one of these shallow graves.

When I at last came to the outskirts of Mt. Jackson, the sun had already set. A crescent moon provided the only light and the warmth of the day had given way to an evening chill. As I rounded the last bend, I saw campfires ahead. I heard banjo and harmonica music, mules braying, pans clattering and loud laughter. The smell of strong coffee and burning tobacco filled the air.

I had not gotten much farther up the road when two Yankee sentries stepped out of the shadows and blocked my way. They looked very young and very nervous. They had bayonets affixed to their muskets, both of which were pointed directly at my heart. Both soldiers had on clean uniforms and looked well-fed. One was square-jawed with bushy eyebrows and sideburns that gave him a wild look; the other was round-faced and beardless.

"Halt!" yelled the round-faced one, considerably louder than seemed necessary. "Who goes there?"

I raised my hands above my head. "My name is Miller," I said. "I am looking for my Daddy." I stood as still as I could, afraid if I moved the young soldiers would shoot me just out of nervousness.

'Round face' stepped closer, the tip of his bayonet hovering just inches from my chest. "Your Daddy ain't here, Reb," he said. "Mebbe it would be best if you just turn around and head back the way you come."

But I had come too far to be turned back now. "Please," I said, taking a small step forward, "I need to talk to someone on Gen'ral Sigel's staff."

My movement startled the two young soldiers. They both stepped backwards and exchanged worried glances. I could not be sure if they were going to shoot me or run away. I raised my hands even higher.

"Dammit, Reb," said the one with bushy eyebrows. "One more step and I will shoot you!"

Before I could respond, another soldier walked up to our group. He was average height but very fat and wore the stripes of a corporal. Every button on his uniform looked as if it were about to pop off from the strain. I was shocked. I had never seen a fat soldier before. Most every soldier I had ever seen, Confederate or Yankee, was as thin as a scarecrow. "What's going on here?" the corporal demanded.

"This Reb says he's looking for his Daddy," answered 'round face.' "He wants to talk to Gen'ral Sigel or some such nonsense. We told him to go back where he come from."

The corporal looked at me with some amusement. "The gen'ral?" he asked. "Not the colonel, or the major, or the captain or even the lieutenant? You must be a mighty important Rebel." He pretended to study my face carefully. "Mebbe your Daddy is Jeff Davis? No... No, I do believe I see some resemblance to Robert E. Lee hisself!" The corporal slapped the round-faced soldier on the back. "Good job, boys! I think you done captured Bobby Lee's son," he said. "This war's as good as over now!" This brought laughter from the two sentries.

Other Yankee soldiers began to wander over to see what was going on. Soon I was surrounded by a dozen or more men. No one told me to put my hands down, so I stood there with my arms raised, feeling foolish. The jokes got louder and coarser as the Yankees debated who my father might be. But I noticed one soldier in particular who played no part in the joking. He glared at me, hatred burning in his eyes. As the other soldiers joked and jostled each other, he moved closer, eventually standing slightly behind me. He was short and a little bow-legged, with ears that stuck out from the side of his head. But he looked very tough. I tried to keep an eye on him out of the corner of my vision.

After another joke that left the Yankee soldiers laughing so hard they were gasping for air, the fat Corporal suddenly decided the fun was over. "Alright, boys, let us break it up and get back to camp afore the Sergeant comes over." He turned to me and said, "Turn around and go back the way you came, young Reb. There is nothing here for you."

Before I could protest, the bow-legged soldier shaved me so hard from behind that I nearly fell. "You heard the Corporal. Move along, Reb," he said, "yer stinking up the place."

I turned to face him. Anger and frustration got the better of me and I said, "Do that again and I will knock you on your ass!"

Everyone stopped moving. A couple of the Yankee soldiers 'oohed' and the crowd began to wander back over to watch this new development. The bow-legged soldier balled his fists and started towards me when the fat Corporal grabbed his arm and held him back. "Take off yer uniform shirt, Reilly," he said. "You get caught fighting in uniform and it will mean a court martial."

Reilly stripped off his shirt and handed it to one of the soldiers watching. I took off Malcolm's old flannel shirt as well and tossed it aside with my haversack. Half-naked, we began to circle each other cautiously, our arms held in front of us like wrestlers. Even at 16 years old, I was a head taller and probably 20 pounds heavier than Reilly. But he was at least 3 years older than me, wiry and compact. He looked like a brawler.

Reilly feinted once and then dove at my middle. I knew better than to let him get in close. My years spent in a one-room schoolhouse with boys older and bigger than me had taught me how to fight. I stepped to the side and brought my fists down on the back of his neck as he charged by. Reilly fell to the ground on his face. The soldiers hooted at Reilly and yelled at him to get up.

I stood and waited cautiously for Reilly to get up from the ground. But when he did not move, I inched closer. For just a split second, I feared he might be seriously hurt. At that moment, he spun over on his back and threw dirt in my face. Temporarily blinded, I staggered backwards as I tried to clear my vision.

The wind was suddenly knocked out of me as Reilly drove

his fist into my side. I flailed around blindly. I got lucky and caught Reilly in the face with the back of my hand, knocking him backwards just long enough for me to catch my breath and for tears to wash the grit from my eyes.

Once again, we circled each other. Reilly's left eye was swollen half-closed from my back-handed slap. My side ached and I suspected I had a broken rib. But I knew this would not end until one of us lay in the dust. Yankee soldiers stood around us in a circle, yelling and cheering. More soldiers appeared to be arriving by the moment. It seemed like the entire war had been reduced to one Yankee and one Rebel boy slugging it out in the dirt.

Reilly charged me. He dove in low and managed to wrap his arms around my legs. In a moment, I was lying on my back in the dust. Reilly jumped on my chest and began to pummel my face with his fists. I tasted blood and a red haze covered my vision. But years of lifting 60-pound hay bales on the farm gave me the strength to easily toss Reilly aside. We both scrambled back to our feet.

I felt no pain. I was only vaguely aware of the jeering soldiers around me. All my fear and anger from the last few days rose inside me. I could taste its bitterness on my tongue. Suddenly, nothing else mattered to me but killing this Yankee soldier who had become a symbol of all the tragedy that had recently entered my life. I dropped my hands and walked towards him, barely even trying to slap away his punches. Reilly landed a few hard punches which staggered me, but I kept moving forward. Even as he was raining blows down on me, I managed to get my hands around his neck. Reilly squirmed and kicked and beat on my arms, but he could not break my grip. I squeezed as I stared into his eyes. I watched him begin to die.

I was only vaguely aware of the Yankee Corporal yelling at me to let Reilly go. Suddenly, there were soldiers pulling us apart. They had to pry my fingers off his neck.

Two soldiers held my hands at my side, but I had no more fight left in me. I sagged against them and slid slowly to the ground. I watched Reilly being helped to his feet by his comrades and then I passed out.

I awoke confused and disoriented on a clean bed with a Yankee officer looking down at me. He had a large, hooked nose and watery blue eyes that looked out through gold-rimmed spectacles. He was wearing a clean white apron over his uniform. "Where am I?" I asked.

"You are in an army hospital," the officer answered. "What is your name, Son?"

"Miller, Teddy Miller."

"I am Captain Williamson, the Chief Surgeon. A couple of soldiers brought you in here a few hours ago. They said you were thrown from a horse."

It felt more like I had been kicked by a mule. I nodded my head vaguely. "I remember now," I lied. "Damn horse always was skittish."

Captain Williamson reached down and lifted my eyelids one at a time. Then he asked me to follow his finger with my eyes as he moved it from side to side. When he was finished, he stepped back from the bed and crossed his arms. "You know, Son, I would not be much of a doctor if I could not tell the difference between a fall and a fist fight."

I glanced away and said nothing. The captain continued: "You have at least one fractured rib, broken knuckles on both hands and your face looks like raw meat. There are bruises all around your abdomen and kidneys, so I would guess you are going to pass blood for a few days. And Lord only knows what else you have going on that I can't see." The captain sat down on a vacant bed next to me. "I have to assume that you put up a pretty good fight, or else the boys would have just left you by the side of the road."

When I still said nothing, the captain just shrugged. "Have it your way," he said. "But you are going to need someone to look after you for a few days. Do you have family here in Mt. Jackson?"

I looked at the captain. "No, Sir. We have—we had—a farm down south of New Market. I came here looking for my Daddy."

"What is he doing here in Mt. Jackson?"

"I do not know for sure that he is. But I heard that a civilian was being held here as a prisoner by Gen'ral Sigel's troops. Daddy was away when the fighting started, and he has not been back since. So, I came here."

"Sigel's gone," said the captain. "General Hunter runs the show now, but he may already be as far south as Harrisonburg." The captain stood up. "Let me ask around and see what I can find out," he said.

I started to sit up, but the captain gently pushed me back down on the bed. "Best if you stay still for a while," he said. "I will be back to check on you later."

As the Captain turned away, I asked "Did they bring in a haversack with me?"

Captain Williamson shook his head. "I do not believe so." I thought about the beautiful book that Abner had given me. Damn Yankees, I thought.

CHAPTER 11

The Pinkerton Detective

In many ways, the War for Southern Independence challenged the image of Victorian domesticity that had defined the lives of women in the antebellum era. In the North and in the South, the war forced women into public life in ways they could scarcely have imagined a generation before. These wartime contributions forever expanded many women's ideas about what their 'proper place' should be.

W hen Captain Williamson returned to the hospital later in the day, he was accompanied by two Yankee officers. They walked directly to my bed. "Teddy," said Captain Williamson, "this is Major Plaunty and Chaplain Strickland. They have some information about your father."

I sat up and swung my feet over the side of the bed. I started to stand up but immediately became dizzy. I sat back down and waited for the room to stop spinning. The two officers waited patiently alongside Captain Williamson. They were strikingly different in dress from one another: The major's blue uniform was all gold braid and shiny buttons while the chaplain wore a plain black coat, unadorned except for a white Christian cross on each of his epaulets. Both appeared to be middle-aged, war-weary and very serious.

I suddenly felt ill, not from my injuries but rather from my suspicions as to why the major had brought a chaplain with him. I managed to stand up as I tried to hold back my churning stomach. "Is my Daddy dead?" I asked.

The major and the chaplain exchanged a quick glance. Chaplain Strickland walked over to me and placed his hand on my shoulder, but I violently shrugged it off. "Just tell me!" I demanded.

The Chaplain held up his hands and backed away. "He is not dead."

Relief flooded my senses. But the Chaplain remained somber, and I realized that there was something more going on. I glanced quickly from the Chaplain to the Major and back to the Chaplain again trying to read their faces. "Then where is he?" I asked. "Can I see him?"

"Your father is in jail, Teddy," said the Chaplain. "He has been charged and convicted of spying against the Union."

For a moment, I had no words. "But that's just wrong!" I finally said. "Daddy is no spy!"

"He was tried and convicted by a military tribunal," said Major Plaunty. "I was there, at least for the end of it. He had a fair hearing."

"How fair could it be when a man is convicted of a crime he didn't commit?" I demanded.

"He had maps and information about Union troop movements on his person when he was arrested," answered the Major.

My head was spinning. I could not imagine my father being a spy. Sure, he followed the war news obsessively, tracking the armies across the South on his maps. And I could not help but wonder if those were the same maps with which he was captured. And if so, why would Daddy bring his maps with him to pick up supplies and newspapers? None of this made any sense to me.

The Major and the Chaplain stood patiently while I tried to compose myself. "What happens now?" I asked. "Does he go to prison?"

The Chaplain looked at me and I saw a great sadness in his eyes. "I'm sorry, Teddy," he said.

I shook my head slowly from side to side as I realized what he meant. "No, no, no, no! You cannot kill my father!" Tears filled my eyes and the three men rippled in my vision like a reflection in a pond.

Chaplain Strickland started to reach out to me but then changed his mind, apparently afraid I would rebuff him again. He dropped his arm back down to his side. "I'm sorry," he said again, his voice breaking. He seemed so sad that for a moment I almost forgot my own pain.

Major Plaunty placed his hand on the Chaplain's shoulder and then turned to me: "Your father is scheduled to be hanged at dawn in two days. He is not allowed to have any visitors. But if you want to write him a letter, I will see that he gets it."

"Please, Major!" I begged. "There must be something you can do."

Major Plaunty shook his head. "I'm afraid there is nothing I can do." He took the Chaplain's elbow and began to lead him towards the hospital door. Looking back over his shoulder he said, "Have Captain Williamson let me know about the letter."

My mind was spinning. I knew that if I let the Major leave, I would never see my father alive again. The Major was just stepping out of the hospital when I shouted, "If my Daddy hangs, you will never know who killed Lieutenant Thomas Ferguson!"

The Major stopped short. With his back still towards me, he asked "What do you know about Lieutenant Ferguson?"

"I know that he was with the 1st New York Cavalry. I know that he had 5,000 men with him. I know that he was hanged by guerrillas here in the Valley."

The Major turned around slowly. Whatever compassion I

had seen in his eyes before was gone. "You have just signed your own death warrant, boy. I will see to it that you hang with your father!"

The Chaplain looked confused. "Who is Lieutenant Ferguson?" he asked. But the Major held up his hand to quiet him.

Anger and desperation built in me. "Hang me if you will, Major!" I said. "Wipe out my entire family if that is what you want to do. I cannot stop you. But I did not kill the Lieutenant."

The Major walked up and stood directly in front of me. "Then who killed him?" he asked softly, his voice barely above a whisper.

I shook my head. "No, Major, I cannot tell you that until I have your word that my Daddy will not be hanged."

For a moment, I thought the Major would strike me. He flushed bright red, and I could see the muscles in his jaw clenching and unclenching. "You are in no position to make demands," he said. "It would serve you well to tell me what you know."

I shook my head. "I am sorry, Major, but I cannot do that."

Major Plaunty stood in front of me for several long moments saying nothing. Then he turned to Captain Williamson: "I want this boy under armed guard at all times, Captain. Send word to me when you think he is fit to leave the hospital. Do you understand?"

Captain Williamson came to attention. "Yes, Sir!" he answered.

The Major spun on his heels and stormed out of the hospital, the Chaplain rushing after him.

Captain Williamson looked at me like it was the first time he had ever seen me. "This is a dangerous game you are playing, Teddy."

Early the next morning, my new guard stopped a woman as

she tried to walk into the hospital. She was tall, slender and very pretty. She was wearing a stylish blue dress and she wore her dark brown hair in a tasteful bun on the back of her head. "I'm sorry, Ma'am, but I cannot allow you in here."

The woman smiled at the guard and handed him a piece of paper. The guard glanced at the paper, handed it back to her and said, "My apologies, Ma'am." He stood aside and let her pass.

The woman walked straight over to where I lay in bed. She frowned as she looked at my bruised face. "Who did this to you?" she asked.

"I fell off a horse," I said.

"Ah, I see." She sat down on the edge of the empty bed next to me. "I am Mrs. Warne," she said, extending a gloved hand.

"I am Teddy Miller." I did not take her hand.

"Yes, I know," she said, retracting her hand. "You are the boy who murdered Lieutenant Ferguson."

My jaw dropped. "I never murdered anyone!"

Mrs. Warne cocked her head slightly and seemed to be appraising me. "That is very sad. Not the part about you not being a murderer, of course! Just the part where Major Plaunty is going to have you hanged for it anyway."

I stared at her. "Who are you?"

"My name is Mrs. Warne, but I already told you that. I would guess what you are really asking is what I have to do with your current troubles." When I did not reply, she continued: "The Union Army has hired the Pinkerton Detective Agency to find the murderer or murderers of Lieutenant Thomas Ferguson. When Major Plaunty reported his conversation with you, I was sent to talk to you. To maybe give you a chance to save your own life."

"But you are a... a..."

"...A woman?" Mrs. Warne finished for me. "That is true. But I am also a detective with the Pinkertons."

I had heard of the Pinkerton detectives. They were famous for saving Lincoln from an assassination attempt in Baltimore in 1861. Now they were involved in spying and intelligence gathering for the Union Army. But I had never heard of a female detective before. I was not sure what to think about it.

"We have been looking for the murderers of Lieutenant Ferguson for a while now," she said. "Bad business, that. We cannot have people going around hanging Union officers." She smoothed her dress over her lap. "I am willing to believe, for the moment, that you were not involved in the Lieutenant's death. But to save your own life, you are going to have to tell me who is responsible."

I shook my head. "If all you want is revenge, you can go ahead and kill me now. But if you want justice, you are going to have to make a deal with me. Then I will tell you what I know about who killed the Lieutenant."

"Justice!" Mrs. Warne exclaimed, laughing. "What a wonderfully romantic notion! Justice, revenge, it does not matter... The Army will never let your father go, Teddy."

"I am not asking for my father to be released. Daddy had to know what he was risking when he rode out into the middle of the battle. I can accept him going to prison if I must. What I am asking is that he not be hanged."

Mrs. Warne stood up. "I do not have the authority to make that deal with you even if I wanted to. But I will discuss it with the Army." She was halfway to the door when she stopped and turned back towards me. "You will know their answer by the next person who comes looking for you. It will either be me or the hangman." With that, she turned and walked out of the hospital. The faint scent of jasmine lingered in the air.

CHAPTER 12

The Deal

Desperate with pain or fear, a soldier will often reach out to God, perhaps for the first or only time in their lives. Exaggerated promises are made in hopes that He will alleviate their pain or allow them to survive just one more day. Theologians generally agree that God does not hold the soldiers to promises made under duress. But the devil is less understanding; promises to him are debts that must always be repaid.

W hile I awaited my fate, and my father's, I began to have serious reservations about how much I really knew about Lieutenant Ferguson's death. I knew the basic facts from what I had overheard between Malcolm and Jacob Hayes during Jed's birthday party, but other than Jacob, I had no idea who else might be involved. I wondered if that would be enough for the Pinkerton detective. I also began to consider the moral implications of what I was trying to do. Was I willing to trade Jacob's life for my father's? Jacob had a family as well. I had gone to school with his children. But Jacob was a murderer, and my father was not, I told myself. At least I prayed to God that he was not. In the end, I figured I would deal with the moral issues later.

It was a day later and the evening before my father's scheduled execution when Mrs. Warne finally returned to the hospital. I was frantic. "My father's execution is set for tomorrow morning!" I nearly screamed. "Where have you been?"

Mrs. Warne looked very tired. She was still in the same blue dress she had worn earlier, which was now wrinkled, and stray strands of hair had escaped from her bun. She waved off my complaints with the comment "I am here, am I not?"

"Did the Army agree to my deal or not?" I persisted.

Mrs. Warne sat down heavily on the edge of an empty bed. "The Army is no longer involved in this matter," she said. "At least, not primarily."

That was not an answer I was expecting. "I do not understand what you are saying."

"Lieutenant Ferguson came from a very important family. His father is—was—Senator Hamilton Ferguson of New York. I just got back from meeting with Senator Ferguson in Washington City."

I sat down on a bed across from the Detective. "What does all this mean to my father?"

"It means that Senator Ferguson has given me the authority to deal with you and your father as I see fit, so long as the Army is satisfied with the end result. It appears that he agrees with your quaint notion of 'justice.' He wants the person or persons who killed his son identified and punished."

I tried to imagine how the Senator must be feeling. So many sons were being wasted by a war that seemed to have no end in sight. I could imagine the glory of facing canon and shot on a battlefield, but to die at the end of a rope? What glory is there in that?

"I hope you know that I am truly sorry for the Lieutenant's

family," I said.

Mrs. Warne nodded. "I believe you, Teddy. But you are going to have to tell me what you know right now if I am going to save your father. The time has come."

"Do you give me your word that my father will not be hanged?"

Mrs. Warne studied me for a moment. "With one condition," she said. "If I ever find out that you are lying to me, or working against me, I will personally see to it that your father hangs. In fact, I will put the hood over his head and pull the lever myself. And I may not be able to save you either. Is that understood?"

"I understand," I said. I stared at her with a mixture of fear and respect. I had no doubt she meant every word she said. In the future, I thought, I need to remember that the detective's beauty is just a facade, a velvet sheath for a steel knife.

We stood in silence while I tried to convince myself that I could I trust the detective. Once I gave up my information, I had no more leverage. But what choice did I really have? I took a deep breath and told her the story of Jed's fourteenth birthday party.

When I had finished, Mrs. Warne stood up and paced the room, apparently deep in thought. After a few minutes, she said "It is not enough."

"But that is all I know!"

"We already know about Jacob Hayes," she said. "I need more."

I was surprised. "You know about Jacob?"

"Jacob Hayes is part of a band of guerrillas that grandly calls themselves 'The Golden Knights.' A few months ago, they raided a Union wagon train and one of the soldiers guarding the train knew Jacob from before the war and recognized him. We did not know he had anything to do with Lieutenant Ferguson's death, of course, or we would have already arrested him."

"Well, now you have him for murder. What else do you want?"

Detective Warne gave me a half smile. "If all we wanted to do was hang Jacob Hayes, we could have done that a long time ago."

"Then what?" I persisted.

"I want them all, Teddy. I want the names of every Golden Knight responsible for the death of Lieutenant Ferguson."

The next morning, Mrs. Warne and I walked to the small jail in Mt. Jackson where my father was being held. Although I was not allowed to speak to him, I could stand in front of his cell door and see with my own eyes that he was still alive. The detective had kept her word.

My father sat on a small bed in the corner of the cell, his head in his hands. His hair was matted and dirty and he looked thin and frail. I could not see his face. After a few seconds, the guard pulled me away. At just that moment, my father looked up, but I could not tell if he saw me or not.

As we walked back to the hospital, Mrs. Warne asked me questions about my father's family. "Tell me more about your uncle. The one that moved out west," she said.

"I never met my Uncle Paul. All I know about him comes from a letter he wrote to Daddy. I do not know if he is even still alive." I told Mrs. Warne about my father reading aloud from a letter Uncle Paul had sent from Colorado years before, his eyes glowing with pride and excitement. "Now this," my father said as he tapped the letter, "is real life adventure, not the fevered imagination of some author sitting in his parlor writing." The letter was filled with stories about chance encounters with famous lawmen and outlaws and near brushes with death at the hands of Indians and grizzly bears. How true these stories were I do not know, but I did hear many years later that Uncle Paul had been killed during a robbery in Virginia City, Nevada. I never learned if he had been the thief or the victim.

"So, no one in the Valley would know him if they saw him?

No one in the Valley keeps in touch with him?"

I shook my head. "I do not think my uncle has ever been in the Valley. Daddy moved here from Warrenton when he started working for my Momma's family."

Mrs. Warne hooked her arm through mine as we walked. Anyone who saw us would think we were great friends out for a morning stroll. I was very conscious of the touch of her arm and the faint scent of jasmine that always seemed to surround her.

CHAPTER 13

Heading Home

A solitary yellow wildflower grows by the road. It is a spot of color against the dark sameness of the destruction that has befallen the Valley. To some, it represents the promise of new life and a new beginning, but to others it is only a reminder of all they have lost. In either case, it elicits tears from nearly every passerby.

W ithin a week, Captain Williamson pronounced me fit to leave the hospital. My father, I was told, had been transferred to the Federal penitentiary in Washington City. It was not clear how long he would be imprisoned, but he was alive, and I felt like a great weight had been lifted from my shoulders.

Mrs. Warne had told me to be ready to leave the hospital that same day. I was talking to Captain Williamson around noon when my guard came to get me and told me that the detective was outside waiting for me.

I stepped outside into brilliant sunshine. I did not at first recognize Mrs. Warne. She was no longer wearing a stylish dress over layered petticoats; instead, she wore the type of plain dress that you might see on any farm woman in the

Valley. Gone, too, was her hair bun. Her hair was now parted in the center, pulled back tightly and covered with a hair net called a 'snood.' Mrs. Warne was sitting in the ricketiest wagon I had ever seen. Every board seemed about to fall off. A skinny old mule was hitched to the front of the wagon, and it looked like any step it took was likely to be its last. "Compliments of the Union Army," she said, indicating the mule and wagon with a sweep of her arm. "What do you think, Teddy?"

"It does not appear to me that this will set the Union war effort back very much," I answered.

Mrs. Warne laughed. I liked the sound of it. "True enough," she said. "Well, climb on up and let us be on our way."

As we were leaving, I said, "I would like to know what you are planning. I would like to know how I am to help you get the names of the Golden Knights responsible for the Lieutenant's death." More importantly, although I did not say so to Mrs. Warne, I wanted to know how many more friends and neighbors I was expected to betray.

"You seem like a bright boy, Teddy. Based on our conversations, have you not discerned what I plan to do?"

I shrugged. "Based on the questions you have been asking me, I would guess that you plan on having someone impersonate my uncle, have him join the Golden Knights and then learn everything you want to know." I turned to face her on the wagon seat. "And I would guess that you need me to vouch for my fake uncle."

Detective Warne gave me a brilliant smile. I felt myself blush from the top of my head to the bottom of my feet. "Well done, Teddy!" she said. "But in this business, simple is usually best."

"What do you mean?"

"I mean that we need not involve a third person. You and I will be able to handle this business all by ourselves." Mrs. Warne squeezed my arm and clucked at the old mule. "I will explain it all during our trip down the Valley."

Surprisingly, the old mule did not drop dead. But the wagon had no springs and every bump in the road jarred us so hard that my teeth began to ache. It was not long before we each took turns walking alongside the wagon while the other drove. It was not difficult to keep up with the pace set by the mule.

Mrs. Warne explained the details of her plan to me while I walked alongside the wagon. It was not exactly simple, but it was straightforward. We were to tell people that my Uncle Paul had died fighting for the Confederate cause in Texas. Mrs. Warne would play the role of my uncle's widow who, having no family or means of support of her own, had come back east to be with her husband's family. And I would join the Golden Knights.

"I think they will believe your story," I said. "But the mere presence of my martyred uncle's widow is not going to get me into the Golden Knights."

Mrs. Warne ignored my sarcasm. "Tell everyone that your father was hanged as a spy. There is no way they can know he is in prison in Washington City. Tell them you want revenge. Tell them that if they do not let you fight with them, you will fight on your own. My guess is they will let you in just to try to keep you from drawing the attention of the Union Army."

"I will need to tell Jed the truth. I cannot let him think Daddy is dead, it would break his heart."

Mrs. Warne brought the wagon to a stop. "Listen carefully, Teddy: you cannot tell your brother. The Golden Knights need to believe that your father is dead. To convince them, you need to convince your brother."

When I did not reply, Mrs. Warne snapped the reins, and the old mule began to pull the wagon forward again. In a softer tone, Mrs. Warne said "They must believe us, Teddy. If they discover the truth, they will kill us both."

We chatted about many things as we slowly made our way

down the Valley, scavenging items from abandoned farms as we went. But I was most curious about how Mrs. Warne had become a detective. "Does the Pinkerton Agency have many women detectives, Mrs. Warne?"

The detective laughed. "No, just me, and I am sure I am more than enough for Mr. Pinkerton to deal with! By the way, you need to start calling me Kate or Aunt Kate, whichever feels more natural to you. It would not do to slip up later on."

I thought about it for a moment. "I think I will call you 'Kate,'" I said, "although I will introduce you as my 'Aunt Kate.'"

Kate glanced at me and smiled. "That will be fine."

"Well, Kate, how did you become a detective?"

"It is not a terribly interesting story."

"I would like to hear it."

Kate shrugged. "I got married in 1856 to a fireman in Chicago. Within 6 months he was dead, killed in a warehouse fire. We had no children and neither of us had any living family. I had no idea what I was going to do with the rest of my life."

"I am sorry."

Kate gave me a sad smile and continued: "I was looking through the local newspaper for jobs one day when I saw an ad for the Pinkerton Detective Agency. I do not know why, but I just knew that was where I was meant to work.

"I marched right down to the Agency and found Mr. Pinkerton seated at an old, beat-up banker's desk. I told him I wanted a job. He asked me what clerical experience I had. I said 'I do not wish a clerical job. It is my intention to be a detective.'

"Mr. Pinkerton looked at me as if I were mad. 'A detective?' he asked.

"'A detective,' I said.

"Mr. Pinkerton seemed taken aback. 'We do not employ female detectives,' he said.

"'Then perhaps you should,' I said. 'Women could be most useful in worming out secrets in many places which would be impossible for a male detective. For example, a woman would be able to befriend the wives and girlfriends of suspected criminals and gain their confidence. And, I am sure I do not have to tell you, men become braggarts when they are around women who encourage them to boast. Lastly, women have an eye for detail and are excellent observers.'"

I laughed out loud at Kate's audacity, what my father would have called 'pluck.' "What did he say?" I asked.

"Mr. Pinkerton stared at me for the longest time. Then he told me to report at 8:00 a.m. the next morning. Within 10 minutes of walking into his office, I had become his first female detective." Kate gave me another of her dazzling smiles and we both laughed.

We passed the hours telling stories about our families and lives. But I could not help but feel my mood darken with every step closer to my farm.

It was Kate's turn to walk as I drove. She walked along with her head down, the hem of her skirt dragging in the dust. As we neared my farm, my mood was fully sour. "I do not think you have entirely thought this through," I said.

Kate looked up at me. "Why is that?"

"Well, for one thing, how and where are we going to live? I told you the Yankees burned my house to the ground. And they stole all of our food."

"You over-think things, Teddy."

I was incredulous. "Over-think things?" I replied. "We have no food, no money and nowhere to live!"

"Can you shoot?"

"What?"

"Can you shoot?"

"Of course, I can shoot."

"Then we will have food," she said. "There is an old shotgun under a blanket in the back of the wagon. And your Uncle Paul —God rest his soul—left me a little money we can use for basic supplies and some building materials." Kate smiled sweetly at me. "Feel better, Teddy?"

I did not. But it was clear that I was not going to win any arguments with her, so I gave up. I snapped the reins at the old mule to try to force a little more speed out of him, but he just ignored me. Totally annoyed with the entire world, I leaned back in my seat and took turns throwing imaginary daggers and Kate and the old mule.

CHAPTER 14

The Little Clearing

"I know I have but few claims upon Divine Providence, but something whispers to me, perhaps it is the wafted prayer of my little Edgar, that I shall return to my loved ones unharmed. If I do not [return], my dear Sarah, never forget how much I love you, nor that, when my last breath escapes me on the battle-field, it will whisper your name."-A letter from Major Sullivan Ballou to his wife, July 14, 1861

By the time we arrived at my farm, we had collected a number of canvas tent halves that had been discarded by Yankee soldiers during the first days of the battle for the Valley (every soldier carried half of a tent; thus, any two soldiers could put their halves together and share a single whole tent). It was Kate's intention to sew several of them together to make a couple of large tents for us to live in during the coming summer while we constructed something more permanent. We also found a few discarded Yankee rain ponchos, canteens, and other useful items. A quick search of the abandoned farmhouses we passed yielded some cooking implements, a few rusty tools and a small potbelly stove we could use for both heat and cooking. But we found no food. We never saw a single farm animal and the cellars we checked were bare.

I almost missed the turnoff to my farm. All the old landmarks had been obliterated during the battle that had raged across our property. But the well was intact and there were even some fence rails that had not been burned by the Yankees to boil their coffee or cook their food. I quickly used the rails to construct a rough corral for the old mule, grabbed the shotgun and walked off to hunt for some food. Kate stayed behind to make camp.

There was a small creek about a mile from our camp where I hoped to find some rabbits. I was not disappointed. Within 30 minutes I had shot three, enough for a good dinner. I carried their carcasses down to the creek where I planned to gut and skin them. But the creek was bordered by thick brush that was covered in new foliage, making it difficult to reach the water. I walked parallel to the creek for several hundred yards as I searched for a place to do my work. I eventually found a small pebble beach with a large flat rock to sit upon. There I cleaned and washed the rabbits. As I turned to return to camp, a flash of sunlight caught my eye.

Curious, I walked in the direction of the flash of light. I fought my way through the underbrush and into a small clearing. There I found the dead body of a Yankee soldier sitting with his back against a tree next to the water, his rusty musket lying across his lap. I assumed the reflection I had seen must have come from the brass buttons on his uniform.

I stood staring at the body for a long while when I sensed something or someone behind me. For a brief moment, I thought that Kate must have followed me to the creek. But when I turned, I saw instead another corpse lying behind me, not 10 yards from the Yankee soldier. This one wore the butternut-colored uniform of a Confederate soldier. He was lying face down, his hands empty, his arms reaching towards the creek. His musket lay alongside him, half buried in the leaves.

It was impossible to tell how long the soldiers had been dead. Both bodies were little more than skeletons clothed in tattered uniforms, the flesh long ago eaten by insects and forest animals. I wondered if they had killed each other. Or had they both simply come to the creek to die from wounds received on the battlefield?

A great depression settled over me. I sat down in the middle of the little clearing and cried for the terrible sadness of it all. Once I started crying, I could not stop. I cried for the two soldiers lying in front of me. I cried for the soldiers in the graves I had seen on my way to Mt. Jackson. I cried for my father in prison. I cried for something inside me that was changing forever; although I did not understand it at the time, I was feeling the softness of my youth petrify even as the tears were still drying upon my cheeks.

When I returned to the camp carrying the three rabbits, Kate clapped her hands with pleasure. "We shall have a feast!" she said excitedly. But when I was close enough for her to see my red eyes, she suddenly grew serious. "Are you alright, Teddy?"

I held up my hands to indicate that I did not want to talk. I sat down on a log that Kate had placed next to a roaring fire and watched her skewer the rabbits on green sticks. When she was finished, she spread the fire out to reveal the coals and placed the skewers over the coals to cook. The air was soon filled with the aroma of roasting rabbit.

We sat quietly while the rabbits cooked, Kate respecting my need for silence. After a while I said "I shall need your help tomorrow. Then we need to go get Jed."

Kate just nodded and said "Of course."

I slept fitfully by the fire while Kate slept in the wagon. By dusk, I was fully awake, so I started a small fire while I waited for Kate to stir. Not long afterward, Kate approached the fire with an old pot we had found and a small bag of coffee. I could not even remember the last time I had had real coffee and I wondered what other treasures she had hidden in the back of the wagon. Neither of us spoke as she proceeded to boil some water. After we finished our coffee, I grabbed a pick and shovel and led Kate to the little creek where I had found the soldiers.

I held back the brambles as best I could for Kate to enter the small clearing where the two soldiers lay. When she saw the dead Yankee, she stopped and looked back at me with wide eyes. I could think of nothing to say. I pointed behind her towards the second corpse and she gave a soft gasp when she saw him. "Dear Lord," she said.

"We need to give them a Christian burial," I said. Kate nodded and walked over to the dead Yankee. She began to look through his pockets and search the lining of his jacket. I was shocked that she would so casually desecrate the soldier's remains. "Kate! What are you doing?"

Kate apparently found nothing on the body and stood up. "Soldiers sometimes sew their names in their uniforms so they can be identified if they are killed," she said. "Unfortunately, this young man did not. Nor does he have a diary or a letter or any other means of identification." She walked over to the Confederate soldier and repeated her search. Again, she found nothing. "I was so hoping we would know their names when we buried them. Perhaps we could have notified their families…" Kate's voice began to waver, and tears welled up in her eyes. "Oh, how I hate this war!" she said.

Together, Kate and I dug two graves in the small clearing. We dug them as deep as we could, hampered by ground thick with roots and rocks. When we were finished, I carried each of the soldiers in my arms as a father might carry his child and laid them gently in their graves. We filled in the graves and piled stones to mark their locations. We vowed to come back at a later time and put up more permanent markers.

Kate and I stood silently over the fresh graves. The only

sound was a breeze moving through the leaves above our heads. I wanted to say something for the two soldiers, to somehow acknowledge their humanity, but I did not know how to begin. Seeing me hesitate, Kate took my hand, and she began to recite a prayer by St. Francis of Assisi. Her voice was soft, barely louder than the rustling of the leaves:

"Lord, make me an instrument of Your peace;
Where there is hatred, let me sow love;
Where there is injury, pardon;
Where there is doubt, faith;
Where there is despair, hope;
Where there is darkness, light;
Where there is sadness, joy.
O Divine Master, grant that I may seek not so much to be consoled, as to console;
To be understood as to understand;
To be loved as to love;
For it is in giving that we receive;
It is in pardoning that we are pardoned;
And it is in dying that we are born to Eternal Life. Amen."

"Amen," I said. Kate and I stood there for a long time holding hands, each lost in our own thoughts.

CHAPTER 15

Back to Malcolm's Farm

We sometimes wear a coat whose seams are held together solely by lies. It remains intact only so long as we continue to adjust and readjust our stories to match a constantly shifting reality. If we lose our place or if we grow confused, we are instantly exposed to the elements from which we have been so desperately hiding; then the truth becomes a bright light in front of which we stand naked and shivering.

K ate and I tied our mule and wagon at the bottom of the rutted road that led up to Malcolm's farm and walked the rest of the way. We were no more than a hundred yards from Malcolm's cabin when Jed walked around the corner of the cabin and saw us. "Teddy!" he yelled. He sprinted across the yard and threw himself into my arms. "I was so worried about you!" he said.

I held Jed for a long time, neither of us speaking. When we finally pulled apart, I saw Malcolm walking towards us. He was staring at Kate. When he reached us, I said "This is our Aunt Kate, Mr. Davies. She was..."

"I heard you was back," Malcolm interrupted, his eyes

moving from Kate to me and back again. "Did you find out what happened to your Daddy?" My heart skipped a beat. I glanced at Jed, who was still trying to process the news of an aunt he never knew he had. But at the mention of our father, his attention immediately turned to me. I looked down at the ground. Here was the moment I had been dreading. "Daddy is dead," I said. I heard Jed gasp, but I could not make myself look at him.

No one spoke. When I finally had the courage to look at Jed, he was standing quietly with his arms at his side, tears running down his cheeks. I raised my arm and he came over to my side. He held me with both arms, and I could feel him sobbing. I looked at Malcolm and said, "The Yankees hung Daddy for a spy." My voice was raspy and full of anger. The story I told was a lie, but my anger was real. At that moment, I hated both Malcolm and Kate; Kate for the deal I was forced to make with her and Malcolm for his association with the Golden Knights. Rightly or wrongly, I believed that Malcolm had lead Daddy into this dirty business, even if just by association.

"He were just in the wrong place at the wrong time," Malcolm said. "He never shoulda been out on the road..."

"Save it, Malcolm," I said. It was the first time I had ever called him by his first name to his face and his eyes widened. "Daddy had maps and details about the Yankee troop movements on him when he was caught. The Yankees had reason to believe he was a spy," I said.

Malcolm shook his head. "I do not know anything about that," he said.

I gently moved Jed away from my side and took a step towards Malcolm. "I heard you and Jacob Hayes behind the barn, remember?"

Malcolm looked shocked. "You do not understand what was happening..."

"Bullshit" I said, inching closer to him.

"Watch your mouth, boy!"

"Or what, Malcolm?" I said, balling my fists.

Malcolm balled his own fists. "Or I will teach you to respect your elders!"

Just when it seemed that we would throw the first blows, Kate forced herself between Malcolm and me. She pushed me backwards and then turned to Malcolm. "I am so sorry, Mr. Davies. Please forgive Teddy. The death of his father has left him angry and distraught."

But I was not finished. I thrust my finger at Malcolm over Kate's shoulder and screamed "Someone is going to pay for this, Malcolm! Someone is going to pay for what they did to my Daddy!" Kate spun around and glared at me. "Stop, Teddy! Stop now!" she yelled. Then more softly, "Think of your brother."

I looked at Jed. He stood staring at me, his eyes wide. I moved towards him, but he stepped backwards away from me. I stood there helplessly, unsure what to say or do. I looked at Kate for help, but she was looking at the front porch of the cabin. When I followed her gaze, I saw Mrs. Davies standing there. She was nervously wringing the apron she was wearing, and the twins peeked out from behind either side of her dress. "What is happening, Malcolm?" she asked.

Malcolm turned and looked at his wife. He looked back at me for a moment and said "Everything is alright, Missus. Teddy has had some bad news is all. Eli was kilt by the Yankees." Malcolm studied my face for a moment. "Even so, it seems Teddy ain't sure who to blame."

"Oh, Teddy, Jed, I am so sorry!" Mrs. Davies said. She scurried over to Jed and pulled his face to her bosom. She raised her other arm to summon me, and I ran to her side. She hugged us both for a long while. She was soft and warm and smelled like fresh-baked bread. I melted into her arms, momentarily at peace.

Mrs. Davies made beef stew and dumplings for dinner. After

several days of eating nothing but wild game roasted on a spit, it tasted so good that I had to force myself not to lick the plate clean. Mrs. Davies beamed as I asked for seconds and then thirds.

After dinner, we all moved outside to the porch. Kate and Mrs. Davies sat on two rickety old rocking chairs while the rest of us found seats on the steps and railings. Kate told the Davies about her marriage to Uncle Paul and how he had died a hero fighting for the Confederate cause in Texas during the battle for Galveston in '63. She said he had made her promise to come back east to his family if anything happened to him as she had no family of her own. Kate was a superb actress. I almost believed her story.

Mrs. Davies clucked and shook her head in sympathy as Kate spoke. Malcolm said little and asked no questions. A while later, Malcolm asked me to take a walk with him. We stepped off the porch and walked a little way down his driveway. It was twilight, stars were beginning to appear in the sky and the air was soft and fragrant.

As usual, Malcolm wasted no time getting to the point. "Whatever you think, boy, I had nothing to do with your Daddy spying on the Yankees, if he even was. Fact is, I tried to warn him about the Golden Knights at Jed's birthday party. They are out of control, in my opinion." He stopped walking and turned to face me. "Whatever you believe, I do not hold with murder," he said. "But the Knights are the only protection I have for my family against the gangs of Union sympathizers and thugs that are roaming the Valley." There was still enough light left that I saw him shake his head sadly. "What choice do I have but to stay with them?"

I had no answer for Malcolm. We turned and started back towards the cabin. "I want to join the Knights, Malcolm," I said. I could sense Malcolm's disapproval. After a moment, he said "I will talk to them, Teddy. But they are likely to think you too young."

I lowered my voice to a harsh whisper as we approached the

cabin: "Tell them I fight with them or by myself. The Yankees killed my Daddy, Malcolm, and I will have blood."

Malcolm glanced sideways at me but said nothing. As we climbed the steps to the cabin, Malcolm said "I am truly sorry about your Daddy, Teddy. He were a good man."

We three men slept under the stars that night while Kate, Mrs. Davies and the girls slept in the small cabin. In the morning, Kate and Mrs. Davies bustled around the kitchen and made us a wonderful breakfast of flapjacks and venison sausage. There was a forced cheerfulness as Daddy's supposed death weighed heavily on everyone's mind. And although Jed seemed to have recovered from my outburst the day before, he had a sadness about him that broke my heart whenever I looked at him. At those times, Kate would not meet my eyes.

As Kate, Jed and I prepared to head back to our farm, Mrs. Davies loaded us up with flour, sugar, and lard. I was sure it was more than the Davies could spare, but she would do no less. Malcolm gave us several pounds of nails and some gunpowder, percussion caps and shot for our shotgun. We thanked them profusely for their generosity. Mrs. Davies hugged Kate, Jed, and I so tightly we nearly turned blue.

CHAPTER 16

We Rise from the Ashes

There is something in all living things which drives them to rebuild in the aftermath of misfortune. Consider the ant reconstructing its mound after every rainstorm or the spider its web. We humans, too, rush to restore some semblance of normalcy to our lives even as the inevitability of future calamities tugs at the back of our minds whispering, 'why bother?'

Kate, Jed and I worked well together, and we made quick progress with our camp. My first task was to construct a privy a respectable distance from our camp and the well. So, I dug a deep hole over which Jed and I constructed a small outhouse with wood and nails we salvaged from the ruins of our farmhouse. When we were finished, Kate smiled at us with gratitude; it had been difficult for her to maintain her dignity in our primitive camp.

Jed and I then spent several days salvaging more materials and building two platforms with tent frames. The platforms were each roughly 10' wide by 12' long. The frames provided for a peaked roof and straight sides and were about 10' high. By the time we were done with their construction, Kate had finished sewing together the Yankee tent halves we had collected on our trip back from Mt. Jackson into several large canvas tarps. Sweating and cursing, we managed to wrestle the two largest tarps over the tent frames and secure them to the platforms. These tarps served as the roof and two sides of each tent. We used four smaller tarps to cover the remaining sides. Exhausted, the three of us sat down heavily on the ground and admired our work. "How splendid!" Kate exclaimed. I had to agree. We now had protection from the elements as well as privacy. We would install our potbelly stove in one tent, where Kate would sleep, and Jed and I would sleep in the other.

With the tents finished, Jed went hunting and I began clearing debris out of the cellar where he and I had hidden on the first day of the battle. With the house gone, the cellar was just a hole in the ground, completely open to the sky above. Nonetheless, I figured that its thick stone walls would make a good foundation for the small cabin I planned to build as well as eventually providing food storage again. I was moving debris out of one corner of the cellar when I heard someone say ''lo, Teddy.' Startled, I looked up and saw Jacob Hayes looking down from above. He stood with his feet apart, a musket cradled in his arms.

I dropped the debris I was carrying and made my way slowly out of the cellar, giving myself time to collect my thoughts. After my conversation with Malcolm, I had wondered whom the Golden Knights would send to talk to me. But I could not entirely hide my disdain for the man I knew to be a murderer. I walked up and stood in front of Jacob, my arms crossed. I did not offer to shake hands. "Mr. Hayes," I said, nodding. He was easily a head shorter than me and nearly completely bald.

"Malcolm said you was back," he stated simply.

When I said nothing more, Jacob shifted the musket to the crook of his other arm and looked around casually, eyeing our mule in its rough little corral and the two large tents. At that moment, Kate came out of one of the tents with a straw broom and began to sweep the tent platform. She was wearing a simple black dress with a white apron tied around her waist. She did not appear to notice us.

Jacob leered at Kate. "I heard about her, too," he said. "But Malcolm did not say how pretty she was." He shifted his musket back to his other arm again. "Must be hard to get any work done," he said, grinning.

I felt myself stiffen. I did not like this little man. I tried to keep my voice even, but what I said came out harsher than I had intended: "What do you want, Mr. Hayes?"

Jacob looked as though I had hurt his feelings. "Damn, Teddy, I just want to give you my condolences, is all. I was mighty sorry to hear about what happened to your Daddy."

"I thank you for that, Mr. Hayes," I said. "I will convey your condolences to Jed as well when he returns from hunting." I waited expectantly but he said nothing more. It began to appear that Jacob was not the emissary I had been expecting. I nodded and turned to return to the cellar when Jacob said, "Hold on, Teddy." He glanced around quickly and lowered his voice: "Malcolm said you was hell-bent to join the Golden Knights."

I turned back to face Jacob, my heart racing. "That is so," I said.

"Then be at the schoolhouse tomorrow night 'round 8 p.m." With that, the little man turned and walked away.

When Jacob was out of sight, Kate suddenly appeared at my side. She stood with her right hand hidden in the folds of her dress. "I am guessing that was Jacob Hayes. What did he want?" she asked.

"Jacob said the Knights are meeting tomorrow night. He told me to be at the schoolhouse at 8:00 p.m."

Kate nodded and removed her hand from the folds of her dress. She was holding a small derringer pistol, fully cocked. She carefully lowered the cocked hammer down on the percussion cap. When she was satisfied that the weapon was safe, she put it in the pocket of her apron and took me by the arm. "Just the look of that man makes me very uncomfortable," she said. Arm-in-arm, we walked back to the tents. Once again, I was amazed at the resources Kate had available to her. I had no idea that she had brought any weapons with her other than the ancient shotgun. I looked around as we walked, half expecting to see a cannon disguised as flowerpot.

Jed had seen no rabbits but had shot 6 squirrels. After they had been cleaned, Kate boiled the meat for 20 minutes or so with potatoes and onions to take some of the wild taste out of it. Then she discarded the water and the cooked vegetables and put the meat in a stock pot with fresh water, fresh potatoes and onions and slow-cooked an excellent stew. The meat was so tender it fell off the bones as we ate.

Kate was in a jubilant mood. I remembered her as I had first seen her, dressed in blue silk with her hair in a stylish bun. I figured she must be getting mighty tired of living the hard life of a farm wife. But with a little luck, all I had to do was attend the meeting with the Knights and provide Kate with a list of the attendees whom she could question about the death of Lieutenant Ferguson. Then her work was done here, and she could return to Washington City, or New York or Chicago, wherever her work took her next.

But I would be left to watch the soldiers come and arrest the men whose names I gave to Kate. I suspected that most of them, if not all, would be imprisoned or hanged. And when the Valley people began to look for the traitor among them, suspicion would surely fall on Jed and me and I was certain we could not safely remain in the Valley. I felt a great sadness descend over me. I watched gloomily as Kate made silly jokes with Jed as they cleaned up after dinner.

CHAPTER 17

The Meeting

Watchful are the Gods of all Hands with slaughter stained. The black Furies wait... - AESCHYLUS, 'Agamemnon'

I spent the next day busying myself with small tasks around our camp. I could not work up the enthusiasm to tackle the larger jobs which I believed were meaningless in our current situation anyway. My dark mood from the night before only worsened and wrapped around my soul like a black shroud. I saw no colors, I heard no birds singing, I felt no joy in the simple act of being alive.

Around mid-afternoon, Kate brought me some water and we sat in the shade of a shattered oak tree which had managed to send up a few meager sprouts. The farm still bore the unmistakable scars of a battlefield.

Kate sat with her knees pulled up tight to her chest, looking like a schoolgirl. But she gave me a hard look. "You are not having second thoughts, are you?" she asked.

I looked at her and shook my head. "No, Detective, I am not having second thoughts. You have wrapped this present up prettily enough."

Kate softened a bit. "It is the right thing to do, Teddy."

"Is it?" I asked. "Malcolm is an example of why most of the men stay with the Knights. They do not condone murder, yet they need the protection the Knights provide." I shook my head sadly. "But they will all hang together, will they not?"

The hard tone returned to Kate's voice: "You cannot be half-in and half-out, Teddy. Other people will be murdered just because Malcolm and the others like him will not speak out. I do not believe that they cannot find another way to band together for protection. And I despise them for their willingness to sacrifice others for their own well-being."

I stood up and stared down at Kate. "And do you despise me for sacrificing my neighbors for my father's life?"

Kate looked startled. "It's not the same thing, Teddy," she said. She tried to say more, but I was already walking away, and I did not hear anything else she said. It did not really matter if she despised me or not. I already hated myself enough for two people.

In the end, all the soul-searching I had done meant nothing. I knew that I would do what I needed to do to save my father's life. After dinner, I walked a short distance away from camp with Kate while Jed cleaned up. When we were far enough away not to be overheard, we discussed how I should handle my upcoming meeting with the Golden Knights. Neither of us referred to our earlier conversation.

"Get in and get out as soon as you can, Teddy." Kate said. "The longer you are there, the more things can go wrong."

I nodded. "Should I arm myself?"

Kate thought for a moment and then said, "I do not think so. You should not appear to have any reason to fear the Golden Knights."

I nodded again and turned to return to camp. Kate grabbed my arm and held me in place. "Teddy, you must be careful.

These are dangerous people."

I turned back to face Kate. Still angry from our earlier conversation, I started to say something cruel to her. But her eyes were wide with fear and concern and I could not. Instead, I placed my hand on hers and told her I would be careful. Then I turned away quickly before she could sense the depth of my own fear.

The night was quiet and dark as I made my way to my old schoolhouse. There was a storm brewing and there was no moon for light, but I knew my way well enough. I had attended school there up until I had turned 15. Jed still attended the school, but only during the winter when work on the farm was minimal.

The little one-room schoolhouse was often used for important civic meetings, at which times it was always brightly lighted with oil lamps. But tonight, as I approached the building, only a mere flicker of light shone through the windows. I looked around for horses and wagons but saw none. I stopped momentarily and a chill worked its way up my spine. Where was everyone?

The porch floor creaked as I approached the front door. I gathered what courage I had left and pushed the door open.

Inside, there was a single oil lamp sputtering on the raised dais where the teacher normally sat. There were two men present, one leaning against the teacher's desk with his arms folded over his chest and a second sitting in a student's desk turned to face the front door. The seated man was Jacob Hayes and there was a Colt 1860 Army revolver on the desk in front of him. The standing man was partially in shadow, and I could not see him clearly.

"Evening, Teddy," said Jacob.

I nodded at Jacob and fought the urge to bolt for the door. "I thought there was a meeting tonight," I said.

Jacob started to speak, but the standing man interrupted him. "I thought it best if we took care of some personal business first," he said.

I looked at the standing man. "Do I know you?" I asked.

The standing man stepped into the light. He was tall and thin, and his shoulders seemed disproportionately wide. I was reminded of a circus strongman I had seen years before. He was clean shaven, and a lock of dark hair fell across his forehead. "You do not recognize me, Teddy?"

"Manson Bowley," I said. Although he was at least 5 years older than me, our time had briefly overlapped at school. I remembered him as a cruel bully who terrorized the younger children, including myself.

"I am flattered!" he said. "I have been away a long time." He turned towards Jacob. "How long has it been, Jacob?" Jacob pondered for a moment. "About 3 years now, Manson."

Manson nodded. "Three years," he said. "You must have been, what, around 12 or 13 years old when I left the Valley, Teddy?"

Jacob chuckled. "You make it sound like you was away on a holiday, Manson," he said. "As I remember it, you left kicking and screaming. And those Yankee soldiers nearly beat your Daddy to death when he tried to help you."

Manson nodded again. "Those were dark days, Jacob."

I could find no words. I simply stared at the man. I had some vague recollection of Manson being arrested early in the war, something to do with stealing Union military equipment. "Do you know where I was during those 3 years, Teddy?" he asked.

I shook my head.

"Those Blue-Belly bastards, they took me to Washington City and put me in the Federal Penitentiary. No trial, no chance to tell my side of the story, no chance to say goodbye to my family. They put me in a cage like an animal and threw away the key."

At the mention of the Federal Penitentiary, I felt my knees begin to buckle and I sat down heavily at an empty desk.

"You know how old I was then, Teddy?"

Again, I could only shake my head. I could not find my voice.

"I was 18, barely a man. They put me in prison with scum, Teddy, men not fit to stand under God's blue sky."

No one said anything for several moments. Then, "Well, that is all in the past, is it not?" Manson asked. "Let us talk about why we invited you here this evening." He sat down at a desk opposite me, scooting his desk forward so he was no more than an arm's length away.

"I liked your Daddy," Manson continued. "He was always kind to me and my family. But to be honest, I cannot see him spying on the Yankees. Your Daddy, he always seemed to me to be more suited to books and female conversation than adventure." He reached over and stroked the back of my head gently, almost affectionately, like an uncle with his favorite nephew. I dared not move. In a soft voice, he said "But look at you, Teddy, a man of action!"

I said nothing as he continued to stroke the back of my head. Then, suddenly, he slammed my face down against the desktop. My vision went red. He held my face against the desk with a crushing strength. I reached up but could not pry his hand off. He leaned down close to my ear and said: "Your Daddy sends his love, Teddy. Prison life seems to agree with him."

I could not move or speak. Finally, Manson let go of my head and sat back in his chair. I sat up and could feel blood running from my nose. The room spun a bit as my eyes once again focused on Manson's face. "We do not have to make this difficult, Teddy," he said.

"What do you want from me?" I asked as I wiped the blood from my nose on my shirt sleeve. I looked down at the blood-stained sleeve and had the ridiculous thought that Malcolm was going to be angry with me for ruining another shirt.

"Well, Teddy, let us start with the truth. Your Daddy and I, we had a lot of time to chat in prison. He told me that he saw you in Mt. Jackson, which surprised him greatly, 'though he was not allowed to speak with you. And not long after, he said the Yankees told him he wasn't going to hang after all." He looked at me curiously, "What do you think changed their minds?"

I momentarily debated how to answer Manson's question. I had told so many lies by this time that I had to sort through them like I was looking for the freshest fruit at a market. Manson folded his arms across his chest. "Take your time, Teddy," he said. "But understand that I ain't a man of unlimited patience."

"I appealed to their humanity, is all," I finally said. "I begged them to let Daddy go, but the best they would do is send him to prison instead of hanging him."

Manson nodded. "Yeah, them Yankees is just suckers for sad stories told by Rebel boys. Ain't that right, Jacob?"

Jacob snickered. "Whatever you say, Manson."

Manson leaned forward in his chair again. "Are you sure you want to do it this way, Teddy?" I started to stand up to get away, but his reflexes were much faster than mine. Once again, he slammed my face against the desktop. I felt my nose break and bright points of light flashed across my vision.

Manson continued to increase the pressure on the back of my head. I felt like my head was in a vise. When I was nearly ready to pass out from the pain, he released me and sat back in his chair again.

"One more time, Teddy: what did you give the Yankees in return for your Daddy's life and why do you want in the Knights so bad?"

I spit out some blood. "Go to hell!"

Manson sat still, arms crossed, appraising me. Then he turned towards Jacob. "What is the name of the other brat?" he asked.

"His brother's name is Jed," answered Jacob, and I felt panic rise in my chest.

Manson nodded. "Go get him and bring him here. Bring the woman too. We will see if Teddy here is so brave with their lives as he is with his own."

"Wait, wait, wait…," I said. "I'll tell you what you want if you just leave them alone."

Manson smiled at me. "I'm not an unreasonable man, Teddy. Tell me what I want to know, and we can end this peacefully."

"The Yankees were going to hang Daddy," I blurted out. "They agreed to spare him if I gave them the names of the members of the Golden Knights responsible for hanging the Yankee Lieutenant."

Jacob became incensed. "You little bastard!" he yelled. "You would kill us all to save your Daddy?"

"Shut up, Jacob!" Manson said. He studied my face for a few moments. "One last question, Teddy: who is the woman and what is her role in all of this?"

I felt my heart race as I looked Manson straight in the eyes, trying not to blink, trying not to let him see the fear in my heart. "Her name is Kate. She is my dead Uncle's widow," I said. "She knows nothing about any of this."

Jacob stood up from his chair, the veins pulsing in his neck. "He is lying!" he shouted. "She has got to be a part of this!"

Manson held up his hand. "It does not matter, Jacob." Manson got up and walked to the oil lamp on the dais. Just before he turned it off, he said "Take him out back and kill him. We will deal with the woman and the other brat later."

CHAPTER 18

The Killing Begins Again

The Colt .44-caliber 'Army' Model was the most widely used revolver during the Civil War. Its design represented the technological pinnacle of gun making at the time. It was also a beautiful weapon that blurred the line between functionality and grace of form. There was not a sharp angle or harsh line anywhere on it; and there was a nearly sensual feel to the powerful, yet almost female curve of its grip with its smooth, rounded wood. It was a great favorite of soldiers that could afford to own one.

J acob followed me out the schoolhouse door with his revolver pressed against my spine. A rain had begun falling, covering everything with a light sheen of moisture. We watched Manson walk away into the darkness, neither Jacob nor I speaking.

"They will find my body here," I said to Jacob, trying to buy myself some time.

"By the time they find your body, everyone in the Valley will know what a traitorous bastard you are. It will be a lesson to others," Jacob said. He nudged me with his revolver. "Now walk."

"They know about you, Jacob."

Jacob stopped. "Who knows what?"

I turned to face Jacob. "The Yankees know that you are a member of the Knights. There was a soldier on one of the wagon trains you attacked who knew you from before the war." I moved closer to Jacob, stopping only when his revolver was pressing against my stomach. "You are already dead, Jacob, you just do not know it yet."

"You are lying."

The rain began building in intensity. "You murdered a Yankee officer, Jacob. No matter how long it takes, they will find you and hang you."

I watched the rain run down Jacob's face and I felt cold rivulets of water trickle under my shirt collar and down the back of my neck. "That may be so," he finally said, "but that will not save you tonight. Now turn around and walk."

I did not move. "You only have one chance, Jacob. Help me and the Yankees may spare your life."

Jacob then did the one thing I did not expect: he laughed. "If I help you, Teddy, the Golden Knights will find me and kill me. But if I do not, the Yankees will surely hang me!" Jacob shook his head. "And who says God does not have a sense of humor?" He wiped the rain from his face with the back of his sleeve and stepped forward, driving the barrel of the revolver deeper into my stomach. "Now walk, Teddy, or I will kill you where you stand." I clearly heard the 'click' as Jacob cocked the hammer on his pistol.

"Then kill me now, Jacob," I said. I was standing face-to-face with him, and I do not think I really believed that he would kill me in cold blood. But I watched his pupils dilate and then a calmness seemed to come over him, as if he had made a great decision and he was now relieved of its burden. "I am sorry it has to be this way, Teddy," he said as he pulled the trigger on the revolver.

There was a 'pop' from the percussion cap, but the gun did

not fire. Jacob quickly cocked and pulled the trigger two more times, but the gun still would not fire. He had been careless, and the rain had soaked the gunpowder. He raised the useless gun to swing at my head, but I grabbed his arm and shoved the little man roughly to the ground. Then I kicked him in the side and took the revolver away from him. I straddled him as he lay in the mud looking up at me, wide-eyed, the rain falling more heavily with every passing moment. I pinned his arms to the ground with my knees and screamed "Damn you, Jacob! You would kill me like a rabid dog?" My fear turned to rage, and I swung the pistol hard against his head. I sat on his chest and called him names and damned his soul to hell until my terror-tinged anger finally subsided. I was left weak and winded.

How long I continued to sit upon Jacob's chest I do not know. When my senses returned, I was still holding the pistol like a club. I looked down at Jacob's face, white and bloodless, washed clean by the rain that continued to fall. I could not tell if he were breathing or not.

I jumped up, horrified, as if I had accidentally touched something disgusting. I started to throw the pistol away, but I thought about Manson Bowley. I knew he would be coming for me and I needed a better weapon than the old shotgun. So, I determined to keep the pistol. Summoning what little courage I had left, I checked Jacob's clothing for extra percussion caps and lead balls but found none.

I stood there for a moment, the rain running down my cheeks like tears. Then I turned headed back to our camp.

I made my way back to our camp as fast as I could. I had no idea how soon Manson would discover that I had escaped and come looking for Jed, Kate and me. But when I burst into Kate's tent, there was a scene of such domestic tranquility that it nearly broke my heart. Jed and Kate had a small fire going in the potbelly stove to take the edge off the evening's chill. Jed lay with his head in Kate's lap as she read from Jules Verne's 'A Journey to the Center of the Earth,' an immensely popular novel at the time. The book must have been another of her hidden treasures.

Kate gasped as I burst into the tent. "Dear Lord, Teddy, what happened to you?" she asked. I could not see my face, but I knew that my nose was swollen, and that blood had drenched the front of my shirt. And I was soaked through to the skin by the rain which was beating against the canvas tent.

"All is lost," I said, fighting to keep panic out of my voice. I related the evening's events to her as quickly as I could. Jed stared at me open-mouthed, trying to make sense out of my references to our father in the Federal Penitentiary in Washington City. He tried to ask questions, but I stopped him with the terse statement that our father was alive, and he needed to give me time to explain.

When I had finished, Kate asked me if Jacob were dead or alive. I told her honestly that I did not know. I remembered the calmness in his eyes and the almost casual way he had pulled the trigger on his pistol and a cold chill moved down my spine. "We must leave now," I said. Kate nodded and immediately began to gather our most important possessions. "I have Jacob's revolver," I said, "but I could not find any balls or percussion caps on him."

Kate glanced quickly at the revolver. "It is a .44 caliber," she said, "the same as my derringer. I have balls and caps."

Jed grabbed my arm. "Daddy is alive?" he asked. For a moment, time slowed and then stopped. It was as if we were living between heart beats and the urgency of our situation faded away. Jed's eyes were wide. "How long have you known?" he demanded.

"Jed, you have to understand...," I answered, but Jed interrupted me: "How long, Teddy?"

We stood no more than two feet apart. I started to answer, but Jed apparently read the answer in my eyes. He turned and walked over to the corner of the tent where he sat down heavily on Kate's bed. "I will never forgive you for this, Teddy," he said.

I stood staring at Jed, not knowing what to do or say. I slowly became aware of Kate speaking to me. "Teddy," she was saying, "Teddy, we need to leave soon. It becomes more dangerous here by the minute."

I looked at Kate and nodded. I glanced back at Jed and then turned to finish helping Kate gather what we would take with us.

We were able to put everything we were going to take with us in one, large waterproof sack. There was not much, mainly extra gunpowder, percussion caps and shot and some dried meat that Kate had prepared a few days earlier. But we had to keep the load light anyway as we would travel by foot to avoid the main roads and populated areas where we might be recognized.

I took a quick look around the dwelling we had made for ourselves. The small fire still popped and crackled in the stove. Even as we had been building our camp, I knew that we would never be able to stay here. But it still pulled at my heart. It had become home.

"Where is Jed?" Kate asked. I spun around and looked at the bed where he had been sitting a moment before. He was not there.

"Oh, damn," I said. "Did you see him leave?" But before Kate could answer, I rushed outside into the night. The rain was still falling hard, and a wind had picked up. I ran to the other tent and then to the privy but there was no sign of Jed. I called his name in the darkness, but the wind snatched my voice away. I doubt that anyone could have heard me call from 10 feet away.

CHAPTER 19

On the Run

When we run, it emboldens those who chase us. It exaggerates their sense of strength and control. But chasing and catching are two different things; it behooves the pursuer to have a contingency for when or if the game stops running.

K ate and I put on the Yankee rain ponchos that we had salvaged during our trip down the Valley. They were made of rubberized canvas and were reasonably waterproof. I threw the gunny sack over my shoulder, and we walked out into the rain and wind. We walked with our heads down, the wind resisting every step we took. As soon as we reached the road, I turned towards Malcolm's farm. I could think of nowhere else that Jed might go. The wind and rain lashed at us and even with the rain ponchos we were quickly soaked to the skin. But I was grateful for the storm; it would make us difficult to track.

We walked for several hours in silence, the wind making conversation almost impossible. Walking had become difficult as well. The road had gone from slick to a sucking mud that threatened to rip the shoes off our feet. The gunny sack began to feel impossibly heavy and constantly tipped me off balance. But we took no time to rest. With the storm raging, and having no shelter, it was easier just to keep plodding ahead.

Sometime later, I felt Kate tug on my poncho. We stopped in the middle of the road and leaned our heads together to be heard above rain beating on our ponchos. "Do you smell that?" Kate asked. I lifted my head and I smelled it too. It was wood smoke. "Could it be a campfire?" Kate wondered.

I shook my head. "I doubt it. I cannot imagine anyone being able to keep a fire going in this rain," I answered. "There must be a house nearby."

I tried to think whose farm we might be near, but I was completely disoriented by the storm and the darkness. We turned and began to walk upwind towards the source of the smoke. We had not gone far off the road when a farmhouse loomed out of the darkness. The front windows glowed faintly, and the odor of wood smoke was strong.

I started to walk to the front door, but Kate held me back. "We need to be careful, Teddy," she said. "There could be deserters in there." She was right, of course. Deserters from both armies roamed the Valley as they tried to make their way home. They were desperate men, fully aware that they could be hanged or shot if they were caught. And desperate men were dangerous men.

Kate and I made our way onto the front porch as quietly as we could. We peered into the window trying to focus through the dirty pane of glass. It took a moment to make out the shape huddled in front of a blazing fire in the fireplace. It was Jed.

I slammed the door open and walked into the farmhouse. Jed spun around, clearly startled. When he realized who it was, he turned back to the fire and said, "Go away, Teddy."

I walked over to Jed, grabbed his shoulder, and spun him around to face me. "What is wrong with you?" I demanded. "There are people out there who want to kill us! We need to stay together..."

Jed stood up and twisted out of my grip. "No, Teddy," he said, "they want to kill *you*." He circled me like a fighter, just out of reach. "What have you done, Teddy? What have you done to make our friends hate us? What have you done that is so bad you had to lie to me about Daddy?" Jed looked over at Kate. "And you," he said. "I have been thinking a lot about you." Jed walked up to Kate. "You are behind all of this, I know it."

Kate tried to reach out to Jed, but he stepped back out of reach. He pointed his finger at her. "Never touch me again!" he warned.

"We need to talk, Jed," I said, "and I can explain all this…"

But Jed was having none of it. "The time to talk has long passed, Teddy. I am not a child," he said, thrusting out his chin as if daring me to contradict him. "I will never understand how you could let me believe that Daddy was dead."

I looked over at Kate, wanting to blame her, wanting to insist that she explain to Jed why we had lied to him. But it was I who had agreed to her plan. It was I who broke Jed's heart that day at Malcolm's farm. I looked down at the floor, ashamed.

Jed walked over and stood in front of me. "Just tell me why, Teddy."

I looked into his eyes. The pain I saw there was like a dagger to my heart. "I did not believe that you could convince people that Daddy was dead if you did not believe it yourself," I said.

Jed stared at me for a long moment. "And who is she?" he asked, nodding at Kate.

"Kate is a Pinkerton detective," I said. "She wants to learn the names of the Golden Knights who killed a Yankee officer. She agreed to spare Daddy's life if I helped her."

Jed looked confused. "Who are the Golden Knights?"

I felt another stab of guilt. There was so much I had not told Jed. Not for the first time, I began to wonder if I had been protecting him or I had simply been ashamed of the deal I had made with Kate. So, I told him what we knew about the Golden Knights, which really was not very much.

Jed stood staring at me as I spoke. When I finished, he said "I cannot believe that Daddy agreed to this."

"Daddy knows nothing about any of this."

Jed shook his head sadly. "Daddy will never forgive you when the Yankees come to hang our neighbors."

I felt myself blush. "Damn it, Jed, at least Daddy is still alive! I do not know what else I could have done!"

"You could have told me what you were involving me in," Jed said. "You could have at least given me a *choice*!"

The old farmhouse was only marginally better than being outside. Rain poured into the house through countless holes in the roof and it ran down the inside of the fireplace, sizzling when it met the hot hearth. The air was damp and heavy, smelling of rotting wood and our wet woolen clothes. We huddled around the fireplace in an uneasy silence while our clothes steamed from the heat of the fire and eventually dried on our backs. I do not know if any of us slept, but for me it seemed like forever before the sky began to lighten.

When dawn came at last, the rain had stopped. Without the storm, we felt open and exposed in the old farmhouse that was located so close to the main road. Kate and I debated the quickest and safest way out of the Valley as I gathered our meager belongings. But whenever I tried to include Jed in our conversation, he ignored me. Finally, he said "I am not going with you, Teddy."

I spun around to face him. "The hell you are not!" I said.

Jed glared at me. "You cannot make me, Teddy. If you force me to go, I will run away from you at the first chance I get."

I started to move towards Jed, frustration and anger building in me. But Kate held my arm and stopped me. "They will kill you, Jed," she said. Jed shook his head. "No, they will not," he replied. "These people are my friends."

I shook my head, remembering the feel of Manson's steel-like grip on my neck. "No, Jed, you are wrong." But Jed just made a dismissive gesture. "I have made up my mind, Teddy," he said. "I will go to live with Malcolm. He has no sons. He needs a man to help with his farm. He will take me in until Daddy can come home again."

Kate started to speak again, but whatever she was going to say was interrupted by a man's voice yelling, "Everybody outside, we have the house surrounded!" My heart skipped a beat. I knew that voice: it was Manson Bowley.

CHAPTER 20

Trapped

"It was not well to drive men into final corners; at those moments, they could all develop teeth and claws."
-Stephen Crane

T he three of us dropped to the floor. I crawled to the back window, hoping not to be seen by anyone outside. A man I did not recognize was sitting astride a large mule, a musket lying across his lap. Moving to the front window, I saw Manson Bowley sitting on horseback with two other men. One of the men I did not know, but the second was a big man, unmistakable with his flaming-red beard. His name was Asa Goodman. He was a friend of my father's and an occasional guest at our dinner table.

"There is at least one man out back," I whispered to Kate. "The one on the spotted horse in front is Manson Bowley, the one I met in the schoolhouse. The large man with the red beard is Asa Goodwin. He is—was—a friend of my father's. I do not know the other man."

I pulled the colt revolver from my belt. Kate had helped me reload it with dry powder and caps the night before. I watched Manson through the corner of the window as he started to dismount from his horse. "I will try for Manson," I whispered to Kate, who had her derringer out and was holding it close to her chest. "You save your shot for anyone who comes through that door." But we had no time to carry out our plan; the front door suddenly slammed open, and I looked over to see Jed standing in the doorway, his hands on his hips. "Who the hell are you?" he demanded of the men in the front yard.

I watched Manson settle back in his saddle, seemingly startled by Jed's sudden and brazen appearance. Jed looked the men over and then recognized Asa Goodwin. "Oh, hello, Mr. Goodwin!" said Jed. "Please excuse my language. When I heard all the ruckus, I thought you were more Yankee bastards here to steal what little I have left." Jed suddenly looked embarrassed. "Again, Sir, I apologize for my language. This goddamn war is inclining me to curse."

Manson looked annoyed. "Come out here, boy, and keep your hands where I can see them," he said. Jed climbed down the steps and stood in the yard facing Will. He folded his arms in front of him. Manson looked over at Goodwin. "You know this boy?"

"That is Eli Miller's boy Jed," answered Goodwin.

Sweat was running down my neck and I held the pistol so tightly that my hand was cramping. If Manson hurt Jed, I would kill him or die trying. My heart was pounding in my chest.

Manson looked pleased. "Ah!" he said. "Then if you would, Jed Miller, please ask your brother and the woman Kate to step out here and join us."

"They ain't here," Jed said.

Manson nodded to the third man who was wearing a floppy felt hat and a bright red plaid shirt. "Go check the house," he said. The man dismounted from his horse and started for the front door.

Jed shrugged. "Do as you like," he said, watching the man approach the farmhouse. "But I ain't fond of being called a liar, especially by some prison rat like you."

Manson's face reddened. He leapt off his horse and grabbed Jed's arm. "What did you call me?" he demanded. I started to stand up, cocking the hammer on my pistol, but Kate held me down. "Wait," she whispered.

Jed tried to pull his arm free from Manson but could not break his grip. "Teddy told me all about you last night before he left. He told me you was a godless heathen who shoulda been drowned in a creek the day you was born."

I was shocked at Jed's language, but no more than Manson. He gave a growl and swung at Jed, his fist catching him on the side of the face. Jed fell to the ground and Manson pulled his leg back to kick him. I pulled free of Kate's hold, ready to run out into the yard shooting, when there was a loud gunshot which startled us all. I instinctively ducked back below the windowsill.

The man in the felt hat, who was just opening the front door, turned and ran back into the yard. A moment later the man on the mule galloped around the corner of the house to see what the gunfire was all about.

Asa Goodwin sat in his saddle, his musket pointed at the sky, a thin wisp of smoke rising from the barrel. "Leave the boy alone, Manson," he said.

Manson turned to face Goodwin. "Do not be tellin' me what to do, Asa," he said.

Goodwin dismounted from his horse and carefully placed his musket on the ground. Then he pulled a large knife from his belt. He walked towards Manson, the knife glinting in the sun with every step. "Strike him again, Manson, and I will surely kill you."

Manson's eyes darted back and forth between Goodwin's face and the knife he held in his hand. "Now, Asa," he said, "you heard what he said to me! I will not be talked to that way by anyone, 'specially not some snot-nosed brat!" Manson slowly moved his hand to the hilt of his own knife.

Goodwin stopped a few paces in front of Manson, and they stood staring at each other. No one in the yard moved or said anything; even the horses seemed to sense the tension and they stood with their ears flat against their heads, their eyes wide.

Just when it seemed like the men would surely attack each other, the man in the felt hat approached Goodwin and Manson, his hands held up in front of him like a minister offering a benediction. "Asa, Manson, now listen to me," he pleaded. "Do not do this!"

"Stay out of this!" growled Manson, who never took his eyes off Goodwin.

Felt hat moved ever closer to Manson, speaking softly in words I could not hear, his hands still raised in front of him. Step by small step, he reduced the distance between them. Manson suddenly appeared to sense that he had let felt hat get too close and he moved to pull his knife from its scabbard. But he was too late; felt hat punched Manson with such force that it lifted him off his feet. Manson was unconscious before he hit the ground.

Goodwin put his knife away and turned to the man on the mule. "Dammit, Ben, you were told to keep an eye on the back of the house. And you," he said to the man with the felt hat, "go and check out the house." But it was already too late for that. Kate and I had escaped from the house by the back window while the men were distracted. Keeping the house between us and the men in the yard, we had made it unseen into the woods. Then we worked our way around to the side of the farmhouse where we hid in some thick bushes. We were just close enough to the house that I could try and offer some protection to Jed if it became necessary and hear at least some of what was being said.

After a quick check of the house, the man in the felt hat walked back into the yard. "There is no one else in the house," he said.

Goodwin turned to Jed. "Where is your brother and the woman?" he asked.

Jed was rubbing his jaw and glaring at Manson lying in the

dirt. "I do not know, Mr. Goodwin. I left our farm last night while they was still packing. All I know is that they were planning on leaving the Valley."

"Why did you not go with them?"

Jed bristled. "I ain't no traitor!" he said.

Goodwin nodded and patted Jed's shoulder. "Do you have a place to stay?"

"Yessir, I reckon Malcolm Davies will take me in. That is where I was headed when the storm hit last night. I believe he could use some help on his farm, what with two daughters and no sons."

Jed and Goodwin spoke for some time more, but I could hear only fragments of their conversation. After a while, they shook hands. Kate and I watched as Jed set off on foot towards Malcolm's farm while Goodwin relieved Manson of his knife and pistol and then threw water in his face from a canteen. Manson staggered to his feet like a drunk on a binge, swinging wildly at anyone near him and cursing Goodwin with every breath. When Manson finally calmed down, they mounted their horses and mules and galloped out of the farmyard towards New Market. But I noticed that they had not yet returned Manson's weapons to him.

When they were out of sight, Kate and I stood up and brushed the dust and brambles from our clothes. I was so angry that my hand shook as I put the pistol back in my belt. "What the hell is the matter with him?" I demanded of Kate.

"Jed?" asked Kate.

"Yes, Jed, who else? He could have gotten himself killed!"

"He probably saved our lives, Teddy."

I glared at Kate. "I had things under control. Jed practically begged Manson to kill him."

"You had things under control, Teddy? Your plan was to fight it out with four heavily armed men with an old horse pistol and a one-shot derringer!"

I gave Kate a sour look but said nothing.

I sat down wearily in the shade while Kate went to find some water. I felt like things were spiraling out of control. Because of my decision to conspire with Kate, I had lost my farm, my friends and now my brother. I felt nauseous and overwhelmed and I wished more than anything that I could sit down with my father for just 5 minutes. I needed him to tell me that I was doing the right thing. I needed him to tell me that everything was going to be alright.

Jed had shown great courage in his showdown with Manson, but he was only 14 years old and I felt a great responsibility for him. If anything happened to him, I could not live with myself. Nor could I ever face my father again. But part of me was angry as well. I felt an overwhelming resentment that Jed would judge me for the decisions I had made. What would he have done in my place? Would he have let our father die? I felt it was too easy for Jed to condemn me now that our father was safe.

I fought the urge to lie back, close my eyes and sleep. I felt a hundred years older than my 16 years. Instead, I forced myself to stand up and I groaned like an old man getting up from a nap. I looked down the road in the direction Jed had gone. I tried to think out my options as logically as I could. But I did not trust my emotions which were clouded by an odd mix of anger and concern.

Kate returned and found me staring down the road. As if she had read my mind, she said "He is safer with Malcolm, at least so long as Manson Bowley is chasing after us."

I turned and looked at her and nodded. "I have come to much the same conclusion," I said. But I could not hide the worry in my voice. Kate placed her hand on my shoulder and said "He is a smart boy, Teddy. And Malcolm will look out for him."

I prayed that Kate was right.

CHAPTER 21

The Farmer's Daughter

War heightens our sense of our own mortality and may cause us to act with less restraint in our emotional lives. Love, especially, demands our immediate and total submission lest we awaken tomorrow with the inconsolable regret that we missed an opportunity, perhaps our last, to seize some happiness in a world gone mad.

K ate and I moved away from the road and found some shade in which to make our plans. Kate made no effort to hide her desire to get away from the Valley as soon as possible. But that was no easy task when you were traveling on foot and half the Valley's population was looking for you. The Blue Ridge Mountains to our east, which had hidden the Confederate Army from Union eyes for so many years, now served as a nearly impassable barrier to Kate and me. We would have to use one of only a half-dozen or so east-west gaps in the mountains to obtain egress from the Valley.

I drew a crude map in the dirt with a stick. I made a long line running roughly north-south, the Valley Pike. At the north end, I drew a circle. "Mt. Jackson," I said. Then I drew another circle further south which I said represented New Market. Further south yet I made a third circle: Harrisonburg. Between New Market and Harrisonburg, I made an 'X.' "This is where we are," I explained. "Because we have not yet reached the village of Sparta on this road, we must still be more than 5 or 6 miles south of New Market." I scratched two lines perpendicular to the Pike. "These are the only two gaps though the mountains anywhere near us: one is east of Harrisonburg, about 7 or 8 miles south of us. The other is east of New Market, roughly 7 miles north of us."

Kate studied the map in the dirt. "Why can we not simply head east and hike over the mountains?" she asked. "It is unlikely that anyone would be able to track us there."

I thought about the Blue Ridge Mountains lying several miles to the east of us. In my mind's eye, I could see them shimmering in the blue haze that gave them their name. They were not very intimidating from a distance. But my father had taken Jed and me deer hunting there several years ago, and I remembered high cliffs of white stone, deep crevasses and steep slopes that left us gasping for breath. Only an occasional game trail provided a path through thick underbrush. "We have no water and little food," I said, "and it would take us days to bushwhack across the mountains. The terrain is difficult and if either of us broke a leg or twisted an ankle..." I just shrugged my shoulders and left the rest unsaid.

Kate stared at the map in the dirt for several moments. "Then which route do you suggest?"

"I am most familiar with the roads and farms around New Market."

Kate nodded. She erased the crude map with her foot and said, "Let us get out of here before we attract more attention."

Kate and I walked parallel to the Valley Pike, keeping it in sight so long as there were places to hide if anyone passed on the road. Where there were only wide fields which offered no cover along the road, we turned away from the Pike and walked parallel to it, returning only when forests once again hugged the road. Our progress was slow.

We walked in silence, not so much for stealth but because we were both trying to calm our racing hearts. By now, every Golden Knight in the Valley was aware of the deal I had made with the Yankees. The situation had become desperate for everyone involved. The Knights knew that if we escaped, we would return with troops and hang or arrest them all, at least the ones we knew about. They could not let us get out of the Valley alive.

"They will try to catch us at the gap," I said. Kate looked at me, alarmed. "How do you know this?" she asked.

"There are so few crossings through the mountains that it does not require many men to watch them all. Or maybe they have just told the local farmers to keep an eye out for us. Either way, it is their best chance to catch us."

As we neared New Market, the amount of forested land greatly diminished and there were few places to hide beside the road. So, we moved a mile or so eastward of the Pike and walked along Smith's Creek which was bordered with trees and shrubs and swampland. We could occasionally catch a glimpse of Massanutten Mountain, part of the Blue Ridge Mountains, lying a mile or so further to our east. It towered above the Valley and its white cliffs seemed to glow in the light of the lowering sun.

Being so close to New Market, we faced the prospect of a miserable night. We could not build a fire out of fear that someone would smell the smoke. That meant we could not boil water to drink. Hunting was also out of the question because of the noise of a gunshot. Dinner would have to be what little dried meat we had left in our gunny sack. Mosquitos thrived in the swampy bottom land, and they swarmed us.

I looked up at the sun, barely a hand's width above the treetops. "I am going to check out some of the farms around here before it gets dark," I said. "I want to see if there is any unusual activity and maybe I can find us some clean water."

Kate slapped at a mosquito on her arm. "I am going with you. I need to get away from these little blood-suckers." But I shook my head. "Best if you wait here Kate," I said. "They will be watching for a man and a woman together. I will be less conspicuous alone."

Kate stared at me, wide-eyed. "You would leave me here alone?" But she knew I was right. She looked over at the land on the east side of the Creek which was rising perceptively up towards the foothills. "Then I will move up into the foothills away from this swamp," she declared.

"Then how will I find you? I am sorry Kate, but you need to remain here on the bank of the Creek. Even in the dark, I can follow the Creek back to you."

"Damn it, Teddy, then you better bring back some water with you. And do not alarm the neighborhood by stealing a pie out of some farmwife's window. That would give us away for sure."

I tied an empty Yankee canteen to my belt and turned to follow the Creek north. As I walked away, I could hear Kate cursing the mosquitos, the Valley and me in equal measure.

Nearly all the farms around New Market had been devastated by the battle that had been fought there, but there were a few located off the main roads that had somehow been missed by both the fighting and the Yankee scavengers. I came across one of these no more than 2 miles from where Kate and I had camped along the Creek.

The farmhouse was undamaged, and the yard was neat and orderly. For a moment, it was as if I had dreamed the War, and everything was back as it had been before. But my left ear was still numb from the explosion of the artillery shell outside our barn, my nose was broken, and I still had a lump on the back of my head from the old Yankee's musket. It was a nice fantasy, but nothing more.

I hid in the long shadows that preceded sunset and watched the house. I saw no movement and I heard no sounds beyond the tree frogs that chirped to welcome the coming night. I could not take my eyes off the well that stood in the yard, no more than 10 steps from the rear door of the house. I licked my dry lips as I thought about the cool, clean water that it held.

After about an hour, dusk had fully settled in. The shadows had merged into a general dark greyness. Having seen or heard nothing the whole time, I moved cautiously into the yard and over to the well. I lowered the bucket into the well, let it fill, and then cranked it back to the top. The only sound was a soft creaking of the handle.

I had just dipped my hand into the bucket to take a drink when a flare of light appeared inside the house. Before I could turn and run away, the back door swung open and a figure carrying a lantern walked out into the yard. I just stood there, water running between my fingers and onto the ground. A female voice said, "I have a gun. Do not move."

I raised my hands slowly. "I am sorry, ma'am, I did not realize anyone was at home. I was just in need of a drink of water." I tried to shade my eyes with my raised hands.

"Who are you? I do not recall seeing you before. Are you a deserter?" she asked.

I shook my head. "No, ma'am. Just a traveler in need of water."

The woman circled me, holding the lantern high. The light was blinding, and I could not make out anything about her. "What is your name?" she asked.

"My name is Jed," I answered. It was the first name that popped into my head.

The woman continued to circle me. "Jed what?"

"Gunnarson." Gunnarson had been my mother's maiden name.

"Do you plan to harm me, Jed Gunnarson?"

"No, ma'am! I mean no harm to anyone! If I may just fill my canteen I will be on my way."

She said nothing for several moments, then "Very well. You do not look very dangerous to me. You may put your hands down." She placed the lantern on the edge of the well and stepped into the light.

I noticed two things at once: first, she was not carrying a weapon and second, she was beautiful. She had long, dark ringlets of hair that lay softly around her face like a frame around a portrait. Her eyes were a piercing blue, and her skin was very fair. I noticed a light dusting of freckles across the bridge of her nose, a small imperfection that, somehow, made her even more perfect in my eyes. She reminded me of pictures I had seen of angels painted by the Italian master Botticelli. I felt my heart race.

"You have nothing to say?" she asked.

"You are not what I was expecting."

"And what were you expecting, exactly?"

"Someone, I do not know, older, I guess. A doddering old farm wife, perhaps, with a broom in one hand and a shotgun in the other. And a big mole right here," I said, pointing to the tip of my nose.

The girl laughed. "As you can see, I have neither broom nor shotgun nor mole!"

"And you have no more resemblance to an old farm wife than day has to night."

"Are you flirting with me, Jed Gunnarson?"

I felt myself blush. I could only hope that it was not obvious in the harsh light from the lantern. But she seemed to sense that I was embarrassed anyway and quickly added: "You may flirt with me if you like! I see so few people my own age. Mostly just old farmers with a pitchfork in one hand and a rake in the other. And it is surprising how many of them have a mole just here," she said, pointing at the end of her nose. We both laughed.

"I am sorry if I startled you," I said. "I would have knocked on the door had I believed anyone was at home."

"My mother is ill, and I have been sitting with her all afternoon while my Daddy is away. I must have fallen asleep. I was just coming out to the well to get fresh water for her when I ran into you."

"Where is your Daddy?"

The girl shrugged. "He went to a meeting in New Market. Something to do with the War, I suspect. It is *always* about the War. All of the men went."

I had a good idea what the meeting was about. I had to resist the urge to run out of the yard and into the darkness. But I was too smitten to move. "You have not told me your name," I said, somewhat surprised at my own boldness.

"Have I not?" She said, smiling. My heart flopped in my chest like a beached fish. "No," I said, "you have not."

She held out her hand. "I am Eugenie Hope Martin." I shook her hand, reluctant to let it go even when she finally pulled it back. I do not believe that I have ever been so much of two minds as I was at that moment: there was nowhere else I wanted to be more, yet I feared that her father might return at any moment. And I doubted that Kate's mood was improving the longer I was gone. But I could not tear myself away from Eugenie. I told her silly stories about my life, exaggerating everything just to hear her laugh. She told me about her family and her dreams of leaving the Valley and living in a big city like Richmond or Baltimore. I learned that we both shared a life-long love of books. I do not know how long we talked.

I was startled by a sudden thrashing in the bushes. It turned out to be only a raccoon, but it brought me back to the danger of my situation. "I really must be going, Miss Martin," I finally said. "Your mother must be concerned that you have been gone so long."

"You are leaving already? Oh, what a shame! If you could only wait until my father returns. I am sure that he will allow you to sleep in the barn tonight."

I smiled at her. "I doubt that your father would be pleased

to find a stranger here, particularly a man, alone with you. It would be best if I move along."

I felt Eugenie's eyes on me as I turned to fill the canteen. "I hope you are not going back into that horrible swamp," she said.

Her words startled me. "The swamp?"

"Your shoes and pant cuffs are covered with mud. We have had little rain recently and I can think of nowhere else with standing water. Surely, it would be easier to follow the Valley Pike." She studied me for a moment. "Where did you say you were headed?"

I tried to recover from my surprise about her reference to the swamp. "Warrenton. Did I not tell you that? I have family there that needs my help with their farm." I looked down at my muddy shoes and pants. "I got lost this morning. I have no desire to return to that swamp."

"Ah. Well, be safe, Jed Gunnarson."

I started to walk away but stopped and turned back to her. "I would like to see you again. When this is all over. The War, I mean."

Eugenie gave me a slight smile. "Perhaps."

I struggled to follow Smith's Creek in the dark, slipping often into the water and tripping over roots and rocks I could not see. But my frame of mind was quite cheerful in comparison to the mood in which I found Kate. "Where have you been?" she demanded. "I thought you dead or captured!"

"I am sorry, Kate. I got caught at a farmer's well and I had to talk my way out of it." I handed her the full canteen, and she drank deeply from it. "You will have to tell me all about your adventure," she said, as she handed the canteen back to me. "But right now, we are getting out of here before these mosquitoes have sucked me dry."

"In the dark? To where?"

Kate motioned across the creek. "Over there, uphill, somewhere—anywhere—away from this miserable swamp and its mosquitoes." So, we forded the shallow creek and followed the land as it rose away from the swamp. We moved purely by feel as there was little ambient light. Brambles tore at our skin, but the mosquitoes dwindled from maddening to just annoying and finally disappeared altogether. We eventually came to a stand of pine trees where the air was heavy with the scent of resin and there was a thick carpet of needles beneath our feet. I was not sure how far we had come from the swamp, but the slope of the land clearly indicated that we were well up into the foothills of Massanutten Mountain.

We sank wearily down to the ground, the needles as soft as a fine cushion. Kate's mood slowly improved. "What did you say to the farmer to keep him from shooting you?"

"Not the farmer," I said, "the farmer's daughter."

I heard Kate sit up a little straighter. I could tell she was smiling even though I could not see her clearly in the darkness: I could hear it in her voice as she said, "Ah, now this is a story I want to hear!"

I started my story from the beginning. I told Kate about watching the house for nearly an hour before I tried to get water and then being surprised by the girl. But when I described Eugenie, Kate asked "Did you say that part about her looking like a Botticelli painting out loud?"

"Of course not!"

"Too bad. How I would have loved to have heard that when I was a girl!" Kate gave out a deep sigh. I could not tell if she was making fun of me or not, so I ignored her comment and continued with my story. But I left out any additional references to Eugenie's beauty or to the musical sound of her laughter or to the sprinkle of freckles across the bridge of her nose. When I got to the part about Eugenie's remarks about the swamp, I could feel Kate stiffen beside me. "That is a dangerous piece of information for her to have," she said.

"It caught me completely by surprise," I admitted. "I made up something about being lost and ending up in the swamp by accident."

"Lord, you men are such fools! Do you not know that we women notice everything?" Kate sat quietly for a few moments. Then, "Do you think she figured out who you really are?"

I shook my head in the dark. "I do not think so."

I could hear Kate lie back in the pine needles. "I guess we will find out tomorrow."

CHAPTER 22

Out of the Swamp

Battles are sometimes won, or lost, by the most unlikely happenstance that no amount of planning can anticipate. Call it luck or fate or even Divine Intervention, but you recognize it when it has happened, perhaps not in the heat of battle, but certainly during a later moment of contemplation.

After a fitful night's sleep, I was awakened at dawn by Kate's hand over my mouth. "Someone is coming," she whispered in my ear. We scrambled as quietly and as quickly as we could to where some pine boughs were drooping nearly to the ground. They provided us with at least a little cover.

Lying on our stomachs, we had a fair view of the land sloping down below us. It was lightly forested with large round boulders scattered here and there. I had no idea how far up we had climbed the night before in our desperate attempt to escape the swamp's mosquitos.

The sound of men on horseback came clearly to us from somewhere below. "Do you think they are looking for us?" I whispered to Kate. She rolled her eyes at me but said nothing.

I rolled onto my back and pulled the revolver from my belt and then rolled back on my stomach. I saw that Kate was clutching her derringer.

I could not hear the men talking, but they seemed to be making little effort to keep their movements quiet. Although we could not see them, we could clearly hear their horses shuffling through fallen leaves. "How many men do you think there are?" I asked Kate. She shook her head at me. "More than a few," she answered, "maybe 6 or 7, maybe more. But I do not like what they are doing. It sounds like they have formed a line between us and the swamp."

I felt my heart sink. "They must be preparing to charge us!" I said. And no sooner had I spoken those words then all the men along the line gave a shout and began to fire their weapons. We heard the horses slipping and sliding as they tried to gain traction in the fallen leaves before charging forward. Their hoof beats were thunderous and echoed through the woods, seeming as loud as, or louder than, the gunshots.

I cocked my revolver and looked over at Kate. She looked back at me and gave me a grim smile. "Make the bastards pay," she said. But the riders did not appear on the slope below us. Instead, we heard the sounds of the horses, shouts and gunshots fading into the distance.

For a moment, Kate and I just looked at each other. "They are charging the swamp!" Kate said incredulously. "They must think we are still in the swamp!"

I understood then: the men had formed a line and then made a coordinated charge into the swamp, firing their weapons and generally making as much noise as they could. "They are trying to drive us out of the swamp," I said. "There will be more men waiting for us on the other side along the Pike." I lowered the hammer carefully on my pistol and took a deep breath. I do not think I had been breathing since we first heard the men and horses.

Kate lowered her head onto her arms, her derringer still clutched in her hand. Neither of us said anything for several minutes.

"I do not want to hear 'I told you so,'" I warned Kate. We both knew that the only way the Knights could have known we were in the swamp was from Eugenie.

"May I just say...?" Kate started. But I shook my head and held up a warning finger.

Kate smiled and I knew she was enjoying this. Too much so, in my opinion. "May we just talk about what we are going to do now?" I asked.

"Certainly, Teddy."

"Good," I said. I gave Kate my most stern look. She just looked away, a smile pulling at her lips.

"Good," I said again. When Kate said nothing more, I said "My thought is to go south this time and try to cross the mountains near Harrisonburg. Most of the Knights are farmers and they cannot afford the time to keep running all over the Valley. And maybe today discouraged them some."

"I would like to try something else first."

"What do you have in mind?"

"I know the Union Army did not leave any occupying troops behind them, but there must be scouts or patrols that come through the Valley from time to time. I would like to see if there are any in New Market before we start another hike. They could provide us safe passage out of the Valley."

As much as I dreaded another hike too, I did not like the idea of going into New Market. "In the entire time we have been hiking up the Valley," I replied, "we have seen no Union troops at all. And Manson was headed in that direction the last time we saw him. Does it make sense to just walk into the spider's web?"

Kate placed her hand on my forearm. "Please, Teddy, let us at least see if there is any help in New Market." She sighed deeply and turned away from me. "I have no more stomach for forced-marches and mosquito-filled swamps," she said.

We took advantage of the last light of the day to cross Smith's Creek. There was no sign of the riders who had come looking for us that morning. But the mosquitos were there to greet us. They swarmed around us, getting in our eyes, noses, and mouths. I swatted at them, but almost reluctantly; after all, they had saved our lives.

It was fully dark by the time we had crossed the swamp and reached the Valley Pike. We turned towards New Market and passed one deserted farm after another. There were thousands of acres of good farmland lying fallow, weeds already grown as high as my shoulders. We never saw another human being.

We stuck to the shadows as we walked into the small town. Oil lights flickered in the windows of the homes we passed, and I envied the families I imagined were seated at their dinner tables, safe and warm and at least temporarily removed from the War. Eventually, the Valley Pike became South Congress Street and South Congress Street intersected Old Cross Road at the center of town.

There was an Inn at the crossroads. If the Yankees were in town, this is where their officers would be. But as we stood in the shadows, we saw no sign of any troops there. The only sound was tinny piano music coming from the bar in the Inn.

Kate looked fully dejected. "It was a longshot," I said. Kate just nodded. I know that she had to be wondering if we would ever get out of the Valley. I started to say more when there was a commotion across the street at the Inn. We stepped back further into the shadows.

The front door of the Inn swung open and light spilled out. Four men staggered into the street. Behind them, a large man with a white apron—probably the Innkeeper—shook his fists at them all. "I will not have you annoying my regular customers!" he said. "Now stay out!"

Kate gripped my arm. "You were right, Teddy," she whispered. "Look who it is!"

My heart sank as I watched Manson Bowley step away from the group of men and approach the innkeeper. He was clearly drunk, swaying slightly and slurring his words: "You would protect a bunch of Yankee sympathizers? They refused to help us with our search! Mebbe you are a traitor too!"

"You are drunk!" said the Innkeeper. "But if you insult me again, I will teach you a fine lesson!" He rolled up his sleeves, exposing beefy forearms. The men in the street, apparently as drunk as Manson, jeered: "A fine lesson, did you hear that? The fat man in the apron would like to teach you a lesson, Manson!"

The men continued to spur Manson on, clearly wishing to see a fight. The Innkeeper was a head taller and 100 pounds heavier than Manson. But I knew just how deadly, and how quick, Manson was. "Go back inside," I muttered under my breath to the Innkeeper. "Do not try to fight this man..."

But the Innkeeper just stood in the doorway with his arms folded. He ignored the jeering men, his eyes following Manson. Manson walked unsteadily towards the Innkeeper, more unsteadily than he had moved just moments before. He is pretending to be more drunk than he is, I thought. I was beginning to understand how Manson's mind worked. He wanted the larger man to underestimate him. He will wait for the man to let his guard down and then he will strike. I wanted to shout a warning, but I knew that would be suicide. Drunk or not, Manson and his men would be on Kate and me in an instant.

I watched Manson stop no more than two steps in front of the Innkeeper. Manson swayed from side to side and muttered something incoherent. He nearly sagged to the ground.

"Ah, you are too drunk for me to dirty my hands on! Take your friends and leave," said the Innkeeper, turning to return inside. But the moment he turned away, Manson was on him from behind. Manson hooked his arm around the Innkeeper's neck and pulled him backwards, bending him almost in half.

The men with Manson cheered.

The Innkeepers face reddened, and he began to claw at Manson's arm. But Manson just squeezed harder. The Innkeeper's arms flailed and then, after a few moments, stopped moving altogether. Manson let him drop to the ground.

"Is he dead?" asked one of Manson's men.

"Not yet," Manson answered. He knelt over the Innkeeper and slapped the man's face, the sound like a gunshot in the quiet night. When the Innkeeper did not awaken, Manson slapped him again, even harder. This time the Innkeeper stirred. Manson put his knee on the Innkeeper's chest as the man began to struggle to get up. Manson casually pulled a knife from his belt and held it against the Innkeeper's throat. The Innkeeper stopped struggling. "Lesson time!" Manson said. "But it is not me who will be going to school tonight."

Manson looked around at his men and motioned them closer. "Gather around, gentlemen, while I tell you something you may not know about the fine aborigines who inhabit our American west," he said. "As best I understand it, they like to take totems or trophies when they win a fight." Manson moved the knife up from the Innkeeper's throat to just under his hairline. "They cut what they call a 'scalp,' a strip of hair and skin, from their victims' heads. It does not appear to matter much if they are dead or alive when they do it. Then they dry the scalp and hang it from their belts."

Manson glanced at his men. "Was this not a fair fight?" he demanded. When they agreed that it had been, he asked "Then am I not entitled to a trophy?" This time he was met with mostly silence. Several of the men looked uncomfortable. Things had clearly taken a turn they had not expected. But it was also plain to see that none of them dared to intervene. Kate whispered in my ear "He is insane, Teddy!"

Manson grabbed a handful of the Innkeeper's hair with his free hand in preparation for scalping him. I could watch no more. "I cannot stand here and do nothing," I whispered as I pulled my revolver from my belt. But Kate did not need any encouragement from me. She already had her derringer in her hand, and it was fully cocked. Without another word, we both stepped out of the shadows and into the street.

We did not say 'hands up' or 'do not move.' We gave them no warning. Kate and I fired our first shots at almost the same instant. After Kate's single shot, I cocked and fired my revolver five more times as fast as I could. I did not aim, I just pointed in the general direction of the four men and hoped not to hit the Innkeeper. I let God decide their individual fates. The gunshots echoed off the buildings, seeming to multiply in number. It sounded like a hundred men firing at once.

Gun smoke hung in the air. Men were running and jumping for cover. I saw the Innkeeper get up and scurry into the Inn. One man lay unmoving in the street. Kate pulled at my arm and yelled that we had to go. We turned and ran back into the shadows before the men even had a chance to return fire. We had caught them entirely by surprise.

We ran down the narrow streets like the devil himself was after us. We turned at random corners and reversed direction several times. Exhausted, we finally sank to the ground behind a stable. We rushed to reload our weapons, our hands shaking, as horses snickered nervously in a nearby corral. We heard men shouting and running down the packed dirt streets.

"That was probably the stupidest thing I have ever done," Kate said. But I could sense her smiling in the darkness. "But, oh, that felt good! My biggest hope is that it is Manson Bowley who is lying in the street back there."

CHAPTER 23

Pursued by the Devil Himself

In a land at war, the devil often hides in plain sight. After all, who notices one more stalk of wheat in a field? Who sees one more tree in a forest? That which is everywhere requires no special concealment.

It was not Manson Bowley lying in the street. Kate and I could hear him begin to take control of the men rushing haphazardly up and down the streets of New Market looking for us. "Rally here, men!" he shouted, "rally here!" Kate and I peeked out of the alley beside the stable and watched as more and more men, apparently townspeople alarmed by the gunfire, begin to cluster at the end of the street. We could not see Manson, but it was a fair guess that he was in the center of the mob. Then we heard Manson exhort the men to action as he began to divide them into small groups. Soon they would be able to search the whole town quickly and efficiently.

Kate and I rushed back behind the stable. "We must leave now!" Kate exclaimed. But before I could even react, she ran over to the horses who were now beginning to whinny and pace excitedly around the corral. They clearly sensed the tension in the night air. "Quick, Teddy, go in the stable and find two bridles! There is no time to saddle them."

When the stable door resisted my attempt to open it, I kicked it in with my foot, heedless of the noise. I knew that the clamor of the frightened horses would attract the men soon enough anyway. I grabbed the first two bridles I could find and rushed back out into the stable yard. Kate and I each cut out a horse from the herd and quickly fastened the bridles over their heads. "Can you ride bareback?" Kate asked. I nodded at her, grabbed my horse's mane and swung up on her back. Truth be told, I had never ridden any way except bareback. We had never owned a saddle. Kate was quickly up on her horse as well.

We spurred the horses down the alley, which was the only way out. Almost immediately, a man appeared at the entrance to the alley. He raised a pistol and fired at our horses bearing down on him and I felt a terrible impact to my left thigh. I cried out in surprise and pain.

My horse, already on the edge of panic, reared back on two legs at the sound of the gunshot. She nearly threw me to the ground. The man at the end of the alley started to raise his pistol again when Kate sped past me. As she came alongside the man, she leaned out with her derringer and fired at the man's chest from no more than 2 feet away. I watched as a spray of crimson bloomed on the man's chest. He looked down at himself, seeming surprised, and then sank slowly to the ground.

Out in the street, Kate pulled back on her reins so hard that her horse skidded to a stop. "Teddy!" she yelled, "We need to get out of here!"

My horse spun around in circles several times before finally allowing herself to be ridden out of the alley. My leg felt as if it were on fire, bringing tears to my eyes. I held on to the reins with my left hand, my pistol in my right.

Once in the street, our only choices were left or right, but men were running towards us from both directions. Kate turned to the left towards a smaller group of men just turning the corner and heading in our direction. We kicked at the flanks of our horses, shifted our weight forward and urged them to run. As we neared the men, we leaned down close to our horses' ears trying to be as small a target as possible.

As we got closer, I could see that there were three men standing side-by-side in the street. Two had their muskets raised. Panicked, I fired at them twice with my revolver, but I was too far out of range. I heard Kate yell over the pounding of the horse hooves "Wait until we are closer!"

I saw the muzzle flashes before I heard the reports, then I heard Kate give out a cry. When I looked over at her, she held her left hand against her face and blood was running through her fingers. But she was still leaning forward over her horse and urging it to run faster.

We closed quickly on the men while they were desperately trying to reload their muskets. The third man stood almost casually as we thundered down on them. He waited until we were almost on them, not moving even when the other two men had jumped aside. Like a trained marksman, he raised his pistol above his head and then lowered it until it pointed at Kate. "No!" I screamed as I fired my pistol at him as quickly as I could cock it and pull the trigger. I missed, but I distracted him just long enough. Kate swerved her horse to the side and caught the man squarely with her horse's shoulder, sending him flying. He landed on the sidewalk looking like a discarded ragdoll. There is no way he could have survived the impact.

We thundered around the corner onto North Congress Street just as more shots rang out behind us. But waiting for us there was a single man standing in the middle of the street with a double-barreled shotgun. We had no element of surprise; the gunshots behind us had marked our progress through the town.

We continued forward, driving our horses like madmen. The horses were terrified and on the brink of madness themselves and I do not think we could have stopped them even if we had wanted to. Neither Kate nor I had any shots left so we veered left and right of the man. I saw his red beard clearly as we thundered past. Asa Goodwin, my father's friend, never raised his weapon. I looked back over my shoulder and saw him watching us as we rode away. He had saved Jed from Manson Bowley and now me. Even through my pain and fear, I wondered if he understood what he had just done. If we lived, Kate would be back for him. He had to know that.

We turned right on Smith Creek Road and galloped on towards the gap between Massanutten Mountain and Kern's Mountain. This route would take us through the little village of Luray and ultimately out of the Valley. But no more than a couple of miles down the road, our horses were on the brink of exhaustion, and we had no choice but to let them walk. We dozed, may be even slept a little, as we slowly made our way east. Even so, we tried to remain alert enough to hear any horsemen who might be chasing us. None came.

When the first light finally arrived, I looked over at Kate and my heart nearly stopped. Her face was covered in dried blood turned black by dust from the road. Her horse, a brown mare, was matted with dried sweat. The mare staggered from exhaustion and her nostrils flared with every breath she took. "Are you alright?" I asked Kate.

Kate looked over at me and smiled. At least I think she smiled. "A beautiful night for a ride, was it not?" she replied.

But I was in no mood for her bravado. "Your face..." I said. Kate raised her hand and gingerly touched her left cheek. "The ball just grazed me, I think. Were you hit?"

I looked down at my left leg. My pant leg was soaked in blood. "I took a ball in my thigh, but it is numb," I answered. "I do not feel anything."

"Are you losing blood?"

I nodded as a sudden wave of nausea washed over me. I nearly fell off my horse. Kate looked around quickly. "There is a stand of trees across the road," she said. "Follow me over there and let me look at your wound."

We rode deep enough into the woods that our horses, should they whinny, could not be heard from the road. Kate helped me dismount, led me under a tree and cut my trousers open around the wound. "The wound goes completely through, and it is fairly shallow," she said. "No bone was hit, thank the Lord." Kate inspected the wound closely. "It appears to be too small to be caused by a Musket... A pistol ball, I would guess."

I nodded. "I remember a pistol shot in the alley."

Kate turned away from me and lifted her skirt. I heard fabric ripping. When she turned back around, she had strips of fabric from her petticoat and one long piece from the hem of her black skirt. "Let me try and stop the bleeding and then we better be on our way."

"We cannot," I said. "The horses are exhausted. We need to find them food and water and let them rest or else we will be on foot by this afternoon."

Kate nodded and began to bandage my leg with the strips from her petticoats. When she was finished, she covered the whole thing with the strip from her dress. I grimaced as she tied it tight. "Are we out of the Valley, do you think?" she asked.

"I am not sure," I answered. I tried to clear my mind. "Did we pass through the village of Luray last night?"

"I remember no villages."

"Then we are still in the Valley," I said, gritting my teeth. The numbness in my leg was wearing off.

Kate sighed. "Well, I refuse to walk again. You try and rest while I go see if there is a stream or pond nearby where I can find some water for the horses."

I leaned back against the tree and closed my eyes. Despite the pain, I was almost instantly asleep.

It was nearly dark when I awakened again. Kate had a small

fire going and she had water boiling. She looked over at me when I stirred. "How is your leg?" she asked.

"It hurts," I answered. Kate came over to me and undid the outer wrapping of my bandage. She replaced the bandage with more strips from her petticoat. She was quick and gentle. "At least we have stopped the bleeding," she said. "But we should get you to a doctor as soon as we can." She replaced the outer wrapping and turned to move away. But I caught her arm and held her in place. When she turned to look back at me, I could see her left cheek clearly. "My God!" I said.

Kate pulled her arm free and moved back to the fire. "I am glad to see that I still have that effect on men," she said.

I was shocked. Kate had cleaned her cheek as best she could, fully revealing her wound. The Minié ball that had grazed her had left an almost 2" score across her cheek which was now scabbed over. But the whole side of her face was swollen, bruised, and discolored. Her left eye was swollen closed. She looked as though she had been hit on the side of her face by an axe handle.

"How are the horses?" I asked, trying not to stare at her.

"I found a small stream not too far from here and there is good grass in the clearings. I let them eat and drink their fill, then I rubbed them down with some moss. They look much better. I checked their hooves as well and found nothing wrong."

I leaned back against the tree again. I knew that tomorrow we would make another run at escaping the Valley. "Why do you think they have not come looking for us?" I asked.

Kate stirred the fire with a stick. "I do not know. Perhaps they think we have already escaped the Valley. Or perhaps we have exacted too high a price. We left at least 3 men dead or wounded last night in New Market."

I closed my eyes. I thought about Asa Goodwin standing in the middle of the road as we galloped past. Why had he not fired his weapon? Not for the first time, I questioned the chain of events I had set in motion. I fell into a fitful sleep filled with dreams of death and regret.

CHAPTER 24

Out of The Valley at Last

They say that a good soldier fights on when all is lost, when there is no hope, when he can do no more than bring more calamity onto himself. But even the best soldier has a point at which he says, 'no more' and gives himself up to his fate. Flesh, even flesh steeled by resolve, is still flesh.

Kate and I had spent another miserable night on the run without either food or shelter. We awoke, unrefreshed, at first light. Kate's face was still swollen and bruised, and her wounded cheek had turned into a rainbow of remarkable colors. As for me, my leg ached and throbbed, my stomach churning from hunger and pain.

Caution would have us wait until dark before we again attempted to escape from the Valley. But we were mentally and physically exhausted, dirty, and hungry and almost at the point of not caring what happened to us. We decided to leave immediately rather than spend another miserable day in the woods. Kate slipped the bridles over our horses' heads and helped me to mount. I nearly passed out from the pain.

We walked our horses out of the woods and turned east on

the road towards Warrenton. In truth, there appeared to be little chance that the Knights were still chasing us. We had not seen nor heard any sign of pursuit in more than 12 hours.

I remember little of our ride. I was sometimes awake, sometimes I dozed on the horse as we walked, but most times I was in a twilight where it was difficult to tell what was real and what was not. I do remember passing through Luray.

Luray was an unremarkable little village with a blacksmith shop, a cluster of brick and wooden houses and what appeared to be a small country store. As we walked our horses through town, we passed a young woman and her child standing in front of the blacksmith shop. The child appeared to be around 3 or 4 years old and had long, golden curls of hair that made its sex indeterminate.

Between Kate's swollen and bruised face and my blood-soaked clothes and wild hair, we must have looked like characters from a nightmare. The child gave out a cry when it saw us and rushed to hide behind its mother's skirt. The mother just stared at us, open-mouthed.

"I am sorry!" I said to the woman as we passed by. I felt terrible about scaring the child. I looked back over my shoulder and kept saying 'I am sorry!' over and over again even when the mother was out of sight.

It was if we were sleepwalking. We let our horses set the pace as we walked slowly towards Warrenton. From Warrenton, we planned to continue to Washington City. We passed through the small villages of Sperryville, Washington and Amissville where we bought some food and filled our canteen with water. But we never stopped for more than a few minutes; I found that if I stayed still for too long, my leg would stiffen up and it was nearly impossible for me to remount my horse.

Some 10 or so miles from Warrenton, we finally found a

Union cavalry troop on patrol. Or rather, they found us.

Kate and I heard the sound of horses only moments before a dozen or so Union cavalrymen, with carbines drawn, suddenly swarmed around us. They circled us like Indians, trotting counter-clockwise, one behind the other. When they stopped, we were fully surrounded with no avenue of escape.

A lean man wearing sergeant's stripes, his jacket piped with cavalry yellow, walked his horse a few steps closer to us. He looked curiously at Kate. "Ma'am," he said, tipping his slouch hat. "Have you been robbed?"

"Sergeant," Kate responded, "my name is Mrs. Kate Warne, and I am a Pinkerton detective. I would like you to take me to your commanding officer immediately."

The sergeant smiled. "A Pinkerton detective?" Several of the cavalrymen snickered. "Is that a fact?" he asked.

Kate gave the sergeant a dark look. "What makes you doubt me, Sergeant? Is it the fact that I have had half my face shot away, the fact that I am sitting astride this horse with my tights and petticoats showing like some common harlot or the mere fact that I am a woman?"

The sergeant blushed bright red. "I am sorry, Ma'am, I meant no disrespect."

"Then I strongly suggest that you take me to your commanding officer immediately."

The Sergeant needed no more encouragement. He led us to an encampment of around 100 'dog tents,' the soldiers' derogatory name for the open-ended tents for which each man carried one-half and with which we had built our camp in the Valley. I had never seen one fully assembled before and I could now see why soldiers were so quick to discard them: open at both ends, they appeared to provide little protection from sun or rain. At the back of the encampment, we could see a single walled tent, which I learned later were always reserved for senior officers, and a handful of A-frame tents for the junior officers.

We found Major Edward Bell, commanding officer of the

Cavalry troop, sitting at a writing desk in the walled tent. He was as handsome as a stage actor, with dark eyes and black, curly hair that hung over the back of his collar. He was resplendent in his cavalry officer's uniform, a fact not lost on Kate. She touched her face and hair self-consciously while the sergeant introduced us to him.

Major Bell, to his credit, did not react to Kate's disfigurement, but I had to imagine that he had seen much worse. He bowed deeply to Kate and then immediately sent for chairs for us to sit in as well as a doctor to look after my leg and examine Kate's face.

I glanced around the Major's tent. It was simply furnished, containing only a small cot and one battered and scarred writing desk. The Major poured two glasses of brandy from a decanter sitting on the desk and handed them to Kate and me. I sipped it curiously; the only alcohol I had ever had before was stolen sips of my father's whiskey. I could feel the brandy slide down my throat and warm my stomach, a not unpleasant sensation.

"Sergeant Tipton told me that you were somewhat insistent to see me, Mrs. Warne," the Major said, smiling. For the first time since I had known her, I actually saw Kate blush. "I am afraid I may have been a little impatient with the Sergeant," Kate said. "And perhaps a bit crude to get my point across."

The Major gave a dismissive gesture. "We soldiers can be a bit thick-headed. Sometimes it helps to give us a poke to get our attention."

Kate took a delicate sip of her brandy. "You are very kind, Major." I could swear Kate batted her eyes at him, or at least her one good eye.

The major placed his feet upon a small crate and leaned back in his chair. "Am I to understand that you are a detective with the Pinkertons?"

Kate nodded. "That is so. And as I explained to the Sergeant, we were hired by the Secretary of War to investigate the death of a Lieutenant Ferguson at the hands of guerrillas in the

Shenandoah Valley."

"And were you successful?"

Kate took another sip of her brandy. "Partially."

The Major looked over at me. "And what role did Mr. Miller play in all this?"

"Now that is a long story, Major."

The major motioned to his aide to refill our brandy glasses. "No time like the present," he said.

It had taken Kate more than 2 hours, and several more glasses of brandy, to tell our story. During that time, a Yankee doctor and an orderly had come into the tent and dressed my wound and examined Kate's face. The doctor had fussed over both of us, tut-tutting as he poked and probed. For some reason, with the Major's brandy warming my stomach, I had found the doctor very amusing. Kate gave me several stern looks but did not interrupt her story.

When Kate had finished, Major Bell looked thoughtful. "That was a remarkable story, Mrs. Warne. But it does not appear that you have identified all the Lieutenant's murderers, these 'Golden Knights' of whom you speak."

"That is true," Kate agreed, "but I am confident that the ones I do know, when they are faced with a hangman's noose, will give up their companions quickly enough to save their own necks."

The next morning, the swelling in Kate's face was greatly reduced while I had developed a high fever overnight. Major Bell provided us with a six-man detail to accompany us to Washington City and they put me in a covered wagon while Kate rode behind. As sick as I was, I did notice that Kate rarely rode alone. It was obvious that the cavalrymen could clearly see the beauty that lay beneath her healing wound, and they vied for her company.

The ride to Washington City was agonizing for me. I was hot, nauseous and every bump sent bolts of pain through my leg. I finally slept—or perhaps passed out—and I remember no more of the trip.

CHAPTER 25

The Hospital

I have been . . . a good deal to Campbell and Armory Square Hospitals, and occasionally to that at the Patent Office . . . Every one of these cots has its history--every case is a tragic poem, an epic, a romance, a pensive and absorbing book, if it were only written. –Walt Whitman

I awoke lying on my back, naked, covered by only a coarse sheet. I struggled to sit up but managed only to raise my head a few inches. I saw that I was on an army cot, one in a line of cots on both sides of a room that stretched beyond my field of view. I fell back into my pillow, exhausted by the effort.

A tall, thin man suddenly appeared standing over me, a ragged Bible held in one hand. I stared up into his hairy nostrils. "Brother," he said, "would you like me to pray for you?" His face was pale, and he had no hair except a fringe of white that circled his head. His demeanor was solemn. But before I could answer, a voice next to me said "He does not want yer prayers, Preacher! Go find another perch, you damn vulture!"

The tall man glanced at the man lying in the cot to my right and said, "May God forgive you, Son." Then he turned and walked away, apparently seeking a more passive place to minister.

I turned my head and looked at the man in the cot next to me. He appeared to be only a few years older than me. He had a wide, plain face and a mop of curly hair. His complexion was sallow, his eyes dark and sunken. He, too, was covered by a sheet but his was pulled down to his waist. He had no left arm, only a short stump covered by bloody bandages. "This place abounds in preachers of every stripe," he said, "from Baptists to Episcopalians, a few Catholics and even a Quaker or two. I have seen no Hindi yet, but I reckon they are here, along with mystics, shaman, and the occasional African Witchdoctor. Problem is, they offer no real comfort to our boys as they are joyless souls."

I simply stared at the man. "Where am I?" I finally asked.

"Where? Why, you currently reside in the Armory Square Hospital in Washington City, Teddy. I like to believe that it is the finest of the 50 or so hospitals in the area..."

Surprised, I interrupted "How do you know my name?"

"Ah, well, the most beautiful woman was with you when you arrived last week! You were delirious with fever and she whispered your name as she wiped your forehead with a cool cloth." A dreamy look came over the man's face. "I suspect it was her ministrations rather than those of the doctors that brought you through your fever. I, myself, advanced in my recovery just by my proximity to her!" He gently sniffed at the air. "Can you smell that? I believe the scent of Jasmine still lingers in the air!"

Most men speak in sentences, I thought, while this one speaks only in paragraphs. "You have the advantage of me, Sir," I said.

"My apologies! I am Albert Camus Covington of the Vermont Covingtons. It is a pleasure to make your acquaintance, even in these unpleasant circumstances."

I attempted to roll over on my side to shake his hand but could not. My muscles would not obey me. Once again, I sank back into my cot, exhausted by the simplest effort.

A male nurse walked up to Albert's cot and said, "Time to change your dressings, Albert." As the nurse began to loosen the bandages that covered his stump, Albert told me how he had lost his arm in some small battle in Virginia that I had never heard of. But it was an exciting story which he told with humor and self-deprecation. "That is a fine story!" I said when he finished. "You should write your memoirs someday."

Albert gave out a deep belly-laugh. "You flatter me, Teddy! But everybody is 'bout sick to death of this war. When it is finally all over—and I pray to God that day is soon—no one will want to hear another word about it. It deserves to disappear into the oblivion of forgotten history, as it is just one more of mankind's more remarkable blunders."

The next day, I received a note from Kate delivered by a Pinkerton Detective. I watched him saunter down the corridor like he was 7 feet tall, though it is likely he barely broke 5 feet. He wore shiny black riding boots and a long, yellow rain slicker. Although his head was bare, he held a soft felt hat crumbled in his hands. "You are Teddy Miller?" he asked when he reached my cot. When I nodded, he reached into his pocket and handed me a piece of folded blue note paper. Without another word, he turned and walked back the way he had come.

The note said simply 'Off to the Valley with cavalry escort. Wait for me where you are. Kate.'

With my fever gone, my health quickly improved. When I could no longer justify taking up a cot on the hospital floor, I moved into the nurses' barracks. I tried to earn my keep by doing what I could to aid and comfort the constant flow of new arrivals.

I had no nursing skills, but I found the soldiers most appreciative of some of the most humble things, from writing letters home to playing simple word games to pass the time. Occasionally, I held a boy's hand while he died. The soldiers always passed with the greatest dignity, teaching all who cared to watch them a lesson in faith and poise. Whatever fear may have haunted them on the battlefield was a stranger here; they died most often with gentle smiles upon their faces.

The Armory Square Hospital was one of the largest in Washington City and I came to know it well. It was built as a model of innovation and had around 1,000 beds. There were 12 pavilions connected by covered walkways with quarters for officers, all types of service facilities and a beautiful little chapel.

Of all the hospitals in and around Washington City, Armory Square was located nearest to the steamboat landing at the foot of Seventh Street and near the tracks of the Washington and Alexandria Railroad, which ran along Maryland Avenue. As a result, it received the most serious casualties from the Virginia battlefields. I never saw it at less than full capacity.

There were Union guards everywhere, but they never seemed to stop anyone from entering the hospital at almost any hour of the night or day. Many people came to volunteer to help the patients, but innumerable others came to simply stroll the grounds and wander through the pavilions where they gawked at the horrible wounds of war. I heard that President Lincoln often came to Armory Square to visit the wounded soldiers, but I never actually saw him do so. I did see the poet Walt Whitman, who was a great favorite of the soldiers. He would bring fruit and sweets to the hospital and kiss every man on the cheek when he was leaving. He was there nearly every day, invariably cheerful and generous with his time.

When I needed time away from the hospital, I would walk over to the Old Capitol Prison on the corner of Pennsylvania avenue and East First street, where I had been told that my father was being held. It was an old, red-brick, three-story building so named from having been the temporary meeting-place of both houses of Congress after the destruction of the Capitol buildings by the English in the war of 1812. I dared not enter the building, but I would stand on the street outside and stare up at the barred windows. I hoped that somehow my father would see me and know that he had not been forgotten.

In these ways, I filled my days while I awaited Kate's return from the Valley.

CHAPTER 26

Kate Returns

We always seem to be waiting for something, particularly when we are young. Perhaps it is a birthday, a holiday, or another step towards adulthood. But as we age, we often face the coming years with more dread than happy anticipation.

It was nearly 6 weeks later when the short Pinkerton detective in the yellow slicker once again appeared at the hospital. He found me reading a newspaper to a young soldier who had been blinded. The detective waited respectfully until I noticed his presence and then handed me another note written on blue paper which said 'Meet me at Willard Hotel tomorrow, 1:00p.m. Do not be late. Kate.' The detective started to walk away but suddenly stopped and turned back to face me. "I have been watching you," he said. "Since you arrived here, I mean. To make sure that you do not leave before you have met your obligations."

I could think of nothing to say. Perhaps I should not have been surprised that the Pinkertons had been keeping an eye on me, but I was.

"Anyways, I just want you to know that you have done a lot

of good here."

I started to respond, but the detective spun on his heels and walked quickly away. I watched the man weave his way through patients, nurses and visitors and then exit the building.

I had no trouble finding the Willard Hotel. It was a huge, rambling structure on Pennsylvania Avenue that had been constructed by joining together several pre-existing buildings. As a result, its height ranged from 3 stories in some places to as many as 6 elsewhere, and the floors did not seem to match up very well from building to building. But there was no way to mistake the hotel's importance in the political life of Washington City. An endless flow of people constantly entered and left the main lobby. I saw military officers of all branches, reporters with their pencils poised over small notepads, well-dressed politicians and not a few ladies who seemed just a bit too dressed up for the middle of the day.

Flanking the main entrance were 2 large men dressed in identical grey suits. They scrutinized the flow of humanity entering the lobby like grizzly bears watching for salmon in a stream. Occasionally, one or the other would reach into the crowd and pull out some individual and push them, not too gently, back into the street. What criteria the two men were using to decide who was worthy of passage and who was not was not clear to me.

I waited until the nearby church bells chimed 1:00 p.m. before I tried to enter the hotel. I was not surprised when a pair of strong arms plucked me from the crowd. "If you have legitimate business here, there is a service entrance in the back," one of the men in the grey suits said. Even as he spoke those words, he was already shoving me back towards the street, his eyes once again scanning the crowd. "I am here to meet Mrs. Warne!" I yelled, trying to be heard over the general clamor.

The big man stopped pushing me and looked at me curiously. "The Pinkerton detective?" he asked. When I nodded, he told me to stay exactly where I was. He walked into the lobby and returned a few minutes later. "Mrs. Warne is in the Blue Parlor," he said. "Walk to the back of the lobby and follow the last corridor on the left. You will see a sign."

It was Kate who answered the parlor door when I knocked. She wrapped her arms around me and gave me a big hug. "Teddy!" she said. "I was so worried about you! The last time I saw you I was not sure that you would live. How are you feeling?"

The scent of jasmine washed over me, and my skin tingled from her touch. "Fine," I managed to stammer, "I feel fine." Kate stepped backwards, her hands still on my shoulders, while she looked me over. At the same time, I studied her face. I could see only a slight welt where the Minié ball had grazed her cheek. It was almost invisible, a fact I attributed to the careful application of some sort of cosmetic.

As if she had read my mind, Kate gave me one of her dazzling smiles. "It is amazing what a little powder can do, is it not?" But before I could answer, a man cleared his throat in the parlor behind us. Kate whirled around and said, "You must forgive me, Senator! Teddy and I have become quite close during our adventures together." For the first time, I noticed the elderly man seated on the sofa. He sat with his legs crossed, a top hat on the cushion next to him. He had a full head of white hair and bushy white whiskers of the type made popular by the Yankee general Burnside.

Kate took me by my hand and walked me over to the Senator. "Senator Ferguson, this is Teddy Miller, the young man I have told you so much about."

The Senator made no effort to rise and he gave me a weak

handshake. "So, this is the young man who promised me justice for my son."

I was taken aback for a moment. "No, Senator, you are mistaken," I said. "I only promised you that hanging my father would not bring you justice. I could promise you no more than that."

Senator Ferguson stared at me for a moment, a frown forming on his lips. Kate started to speak but the Senator held up his hand to stop her. "Do not play country lawyer with me, Mr. Miller. Through Mrs. Warne, you and I have a simple agreement: you are to assist her in learning the names of every man who played a part in my son's murder. For that, I agreed to spare your father's life." The Senator rose stiffly from the sofa and looked into my eyes. "Mrs. Warne has told me about your adventures in the Shenandoah Valley in search of these so-called 'Golden Knights,' and I am not impressed with the little amount of information you provided her about them." The Senator looked over at Kate. "Frankly," he said, "I am not impressed with the job either of you has done."

I glanced at Kate. Her face was flushed, and I could see the muscles working in her jaw. "Senator Ferguson," she said, "we have not yet even discussed the results of my return to the Valley. It seems unfair to..." But the Senator once again held up a hand for silence. He turned his attention back to me. "Should I feel that you have not fulfilled your part of our agreement, Mr. Miller, there will be consequences. Do you understand me?"

I felt Kate squeeze my arm as I fought against the anger building in my chest. "Yes, Senator," I answered.

Kate called for refreshments while the Senator and I struggled to regain our composure. The Senator had retaken his seat, clearly still agitated, and it had taken all of Kate's charm to convince him to remain. When the waiter arrived, Kate started to order tea and biscuits for everyone when the Senator interrupted her: "Get them whatever they want, George, but get me a brandy. Hell, bring me the bottle. You know my brand." The waiter and the Senator were apparently well-known to each other; the waiter bowed slightly and said "Of course, Senator."

After the tea had arrived, I sat awkwardly trying to balance the teacup on my knees while I ate a sweet biscuit. This required nearly all my attention, which was going to make conversation on my part difficult. It occurred to me that this may have been Kate's intention because whenever the Senator was distracted, she would give me wide-eyed looks which could only mean 'behave yourself!' Or maybe, 'for God's sake, keep your mouth shut!'

The Senator drained his brandy the moment the waiter handed it to him. The waiter immediately refilled his glass and placed the bottle of brandy on the table in front of him. The Senator took another sip and settled back in the sofa. "If it is not already obvious to you, Mrs. Warne, I am losing my patience with this whole endeavor. It has been nearly six months since you began your investigation into my son's murder. I was assured by Mr. Pinkerton himself that you were his very best detective. I was also assured that if anyone could identify the perpetrators of this crime, it was you. But what have you shown me? I read your report upon your return from the Valley with Mr. Miller here and I was not impressed." The Senator pulled a bulky document from his coat pocket and quickly flipped through the pages. "The only names of the Golden Knights you provided were Jacob Hayes, believed dead by the hand of Mr. Miller; some man named 'Ben' whose last name you do not even know; Asa Goodwin, a farmer; and Manson Bowley, an ex-convict. And you do not even venture a guess as to who, besides Jacob Hayes, was even present when my son died." The Senator drained his glass of brandy. "Oh, and then there are also the 3 or 4 nameless men you believe you left dead or wounded in New Market. Does that properly summarize where we are?" He tossed the document on the table in front of him.

I glanced at Kate. I wondered why she had not mentioned Malcolm in her report.

Kate took a sip of her tea and placed the cup on the table in front of her. She nodded at the Senator. "That is a fair summary of my original report, Senator. But as you know, I subsequently returned to the Valley with a cavalry escort. I spent over a month searching for the men we had identified. I was convinced that I could pressure them to reveal the details of their organization to me. I believed that they would sacrifice their comrades to save their own necks."

The Senator refilled his brandy glass. "And were you successful?"

Kate raised her chin. I could tell she was still angry about the Senator's earlier criticisms. "Of course."

The Senator looked at Kate curiously. "Then why have you not simply provided me with a second written report, Mrs. Warne?"

Kate lowered her eyes for a moment as if she were considering her words carefully and then looked back up at the Senator. "In the course of my investigation, I have learned the details of your son's death. While they may be painful for you to hear, I think they may also offer you some small degree of solace. I thought it best to share them with you in person."

The Senator put down his brandy glass and looked at Kate with watery eyes. "If you know of any good in my son's death, Mrs. Warne, I will be most grateful to hear it."

CHAPTER 27

Kate's Story

"War is cruelty. There is no use trying to reform it. The crueler it is, the sooner it will be over."   *- General William Tecumseh Sherman*

"On June 7, I dropped Teddy off at the Armory Square Hospital for treatment of his gunshot wound," Kate said. "He had a very high fever and was in and out of consciousness. I was not sure if he would live.

"The next day, Mr. Pinkerton came down to Washington City from New York to meet with me. After I briefed him on what had transpired in the Valley, he agreed that I needed to return and finish this business once and for all. Mr. Pinkerton and a dozen of his men accompanied me back to Warrenton where I once again met with Major Bell and his cavalry troop. Mr. Pinkerton convinced the Major to send 20 of his best troopers with me back into the Valley." Kate smiled at the Senator. "Mr. Pinkerton can be very persuasive," she said. But I remembered how the handsome Major Bell had flirted with Kate. I did not believe that it had taken much persuasion on the part of Mr. Pinkerton.

"The next morning, I was outfitted with a horse and a

repeating Spencer carbine—a magnificent weapon, by the way —and we were on our way back to the Valley. The officer in charge of the troopers was a young lieutenant named Solomon Marcus.

"We arrived on the outskirts of New Market late in the afternoon of the following day. On our ride over from Warrenton, the cavalrymen had ridden in a loose double-column with one scout far out in front of us and another following in our rear. But before we entered New Market, Lieutenant Marcus ordered a parade formation. He and I rode at the front while directly behind us rode two troopers, one carrying a large American flag and the other the company colors. Behind them, the men trotted along in a tight, double-column. The men rode with perfect posture and looked magnificent in their cavalry jackets. The brass on their Spencer carbines, holstered within easy reach on their saddles, glistened in the rays of the lowering sun.

"I looked over at Lieutenant Marcus and asked, 'Is this not a little ostentatious, Lieutenant?'" The Lieutenant smiled at me and said 'We are in enemy territory, Mrs. Warne. While I do not anticipate running into any Confederate troops, a little 'ostentation' may keep the locals from realizing how many are they and how few are we.'

"Thus, we marched into New Market as if we were in a parade down Pennsylvania Avenue in Washington City. Women stood on their porches staring at us and small children peeked from windows and half-opened doors. I saw no men of military age. No one waved or cheered.

"At last, we turned onto Congress Street, and we walked our horses towards the inn at the intersection with Old Crossroad where I intended to question the Innkeeper about Manson Bowley and the men who had accompanied him. But an old man in a bowler hat with a brass star pinned to his chest stepped off the sidewalk and blocked our path. He held up his hand to stop us. 'I am Peter Banks, Constable of New Market,' he said. 'State your business in my city.'

"Lieutenant Marcus and I looked at each other in surprise. 'We are here to arrest a man by the name of Manson Bowley,' answered the Lieutenant, 'as well as any and all acquaintances of his.' The old man with the badge spat tobacco on the road, barely missing the hooves of Lieutenant Marcus's horse. 'You have no authority here, Lieutenant, to arrest anyone.'

"Lieutenant Marcus stared at the Constable in disbelief. 'I can assure you, Constable, that I operate with the full authority of the President of the United States...' But the Constable interrupted him: 'You left the United States some 90 miles east of here, Lieutenant. This here is the Confederacy.'

"I watched the Lieutenant's face flush bright red. But before he could reply, I jumped off my horse and walked over to the Constable. 'I am Mrs. Kate Warne,' I said, offering my hand. 'I am a detective with the Pinkerton Agency. We would appreciate your assistance in locating Manson Bowley and his fellows. In fact, we are prepared to offer a substantial reward for information leading to his arrest.'

"The Constable ignored my outstretched hand while he studied my face. 'Kate, you say? And are you by any chance an associate of a boy named Teddy Miller?'" he asked.

"What do you know about Teddy Miller?" I replied, surprised by the question. I watched a thin smile form on the Constable's lips. 'Well, ain't this a surprise!' he said. And then, faster than I would have expected for a man of his age, he stepped behind me and placed a pistol barrel against my temple. 'Mrs. Warne, I hereby place you under arrest for the murder of Simon Helburg and Martin Malachai and the malicious wounding of Andrew Beaudine. You will be incarcerated here in New Market until such time as a trial can be held.' He began to walk me backwards away from the cavalry. 'If you have any hope for leniency, I would recommend that you produce your accomplice, Teddy Miller, before the trial.'

"Lieutenant Marcus folded his arms across his chest and looked amused. 'May I ask what this is all about, Mrs. Warne?' he asked.

"I tried to ignore the pistol against my temple and the Constable's arm around my waist as he continued to pull me backwards. 'Manson Bowley and his men tried to kill Teddy and me here in New Market,' I answered. 'We objected and 3 of them got hurt. I did not know their names before now. But it appears Manson Bowley told the Constable here who we were.'

"'Ah,' said the Lieutenant. Almost casually, he raised his right arm and made a small circle in the air with his index finger. Immediately, the cavalrymen pulled their carbines from their scabbards and began to move towards the Constable and me. They walked their horses around us, one column going clockwise and the other counter-clockwise until the Constable and I were surrounded. Twenty carbines pointed at us, or to put it more accurately, at the Constable's head.

"Lieutenant Marcus dismounted his horse and walked up to the Constable. He held out his hand and without another word the Constable let go of me and handed him his pistol."

Kate paused her story and poured herself some fresh tea.

"A rather inauspicious start," remarked the Senator sourly. But Kate just smiled at him. "Actually, it was quite fortunate, Senator, because I now had the names of 3 more of the guerrillas than I had had before, including one wounded man whom I could question.

"And did you question the wounded man?" the Senator asked.

"Quite extensively," Kate answered. "His name is Andrew Beaudine and we found him convalescing in a nearby home. He had been shot high in his left shoulder, the ball missing both his heart and his lungs. I reckoned that he had been the man we shot outside the Inn when we interrupted Manson Bowley as he tried to scalp the Innkeeper."

The Senator reached for the brandy bottle. Finding it empty, he grunted and settled back into the sofa again. He glared momentarily at the parlor door as if willing the waiter named George to reappear and then turned his attention back to Kate. "Well, Mrs. Warne, do not make me drag it out of you. What did you learn from Mr. Beaudine?"

"He ultimately named all of the Golden Knights present when your son was killed."

The Senator's eyes widened. "He volunteered this information to you?"

"To be honest, Mr. Beaudine was not initially very cooperative," Kate answered. "But understand that we were within our rights to shoot or hang Mr. Beaudine on the spot. Guerrillas are not afforded the protection of legal due process. So, we hanged him."

We all took a little time to stretch and refresh ourselves as the afternoon light began to fade into evening. By the time we all reassembled in the Blue Parlor, the waiter George had returned with another bottle of brandy for the Senator and had placed a tray of small sandwiches on the table in front of us. There was also fresh tea for Kate and me. The Senator poured himself more brandy, but I did not see him eat anything. I devoured the little sandwiches by the handful.

"Getting back to your story, Mrs. Warne, why would you hang Mr. Beaudine?" asked the Senator. "Was it not our agreement that you bring these people back to Washington City to face justice?"

"Hanging was the only way I could think of to get Mr. Beaudine to talk," Kate answered. The Senator started to protest but Kate held up her hand. "I apologize, Senator, I am not trying to be clever. Please bear with me... As soon as we located Mr. Beaudine, I began to question him. But he was quite uncooperative and rude. Lieutenant Marcus and I came up with a plan to make him see the wisdom of sharing what he knew with me.

"That evening, Lieutenant Marcus told Mr. Beaudine that he would be hanged at sunrise for guerrilla activities and the murder of a Union officer. Mr. Beaudine sneered at the

Lieutenant and said, 'I am not afraid to die.'

"At sunrise the next morning, Lieutenant Marcus and eight of his men bound Mr. Beaudine's hands behind his back and led him outside to a large chestnut tree growing beside Congress Street. They quickly tied a noose around his neck and threw the other end of the rope over a limb. Lieutenant Marcus stood in front of Mr. Beaudine and said 'I believe you to be a murderer and a coward. Therefore, I will not permit you any last words. May God have mercy on your soul.' Then the Lieutenant nodded at his men and several of the cavalrymen began to haul Mr. Beaudine upward by his neck. But they stopped when he was on his very tiptoes and tied off the rope. Mr. Beaudine could still breathe, but every time he moved, the noose would tighten. He was slowly strangling to death.

"When Mr. Beaudine realized what was being done to him, he cried through the tightening noose 'For God's sake, where is your humanity!' But Lieutenant Marcus had already turned his back and was walking away. A tall Sergeant with a pointed black beard walked up and stood in front of Mr. Beaudine and said 'Best save your breath, boy, and you can prob'ly stay on your toes for a fair while. Or you could just lift your feet and end it right now.' Another soldier said 'Aw, Sergeant, do not be telling him that! I have my money on him lasting at least 1 hour.' Another said 'You give the Reb far too much credit! I say no more'n 15 minutes.' And then the rest of the cavalrymen gave their predictions and made bets, laughing, and taunting the slowly strangling man. Beaudine watched all of this with bulging eyes.

"To his credit," Kate said, "Mr. Beaudine lasted for nearly 45 minutes before he expressed a willingness to tell us all he knew. When the sergeant removed the noose, Beaudine could hardly walk as his toes were so cramped and swollen. His attitude, however, was greatly improved."

I watched the Senator grow pale. Perhaps he was shocked by the almost casual way Beaudine had been tortured. Or perhaps he simply had no stomach for the realities of war.

CHAPTER 28

The Death of Lieutenant Thomas Ferguson

There is a mathematical beauty to the flight of a bullet. It leaves the barrel of a gun at speeds approaching or greater than the speed of sound, fighting desperately against gravity and ether to maintain a level path. But inevitably, those two forces dominate the movement of the projectile, forcing it to fall even as it rushes forward. The result is a parabola which is knowable and repeatable and which a sharpshooter can use to deadly effect.

"Lieutenant Marcus and I took Mr. Beaudine into a small parlor at the Inn, his hands tied in front of him," Kate said. "Whatever boldness he had shown the day before was gone. He seemed shrunken, his clothes suddenly appearing too large for him, and he sat with his head bowed. He avoided looking at either the Lieutenant or me.

"Lieutenant Marcus and I sat in silence for several minutes to allow Mr. Beaudine to appreciate the seriousness of his circumstances. He finally looked up at us and asked what we wanted of him.

"I did not know for certain that Mr. Beaudine had been present at the death of your son," Kate said to the Senator. "But I took a chance and said to him 'I want you to tell me about the death of Lieutenant Thomas Ferguson. I know you were there.'

"Mr. Beaudine looked away, but he did not deny my accusation. 'That was a bad day,' he finally said, 'but I want you to know that I argued against killing the Yankee.'

"'That *Yankee*,' I said, my voice rising, 'was an officer in the Union Army. You will refer to him with respect or I will have Lieutenant Marcus finish the job he started this morning...'

"Mr. Beaudine's eyes grew wide, and he nodded quickly. 'Yes, yes, Lieutenant Ferguson,' he said.

"Mr. Beaudine said he was not present when Lieutenant Ferguson was captured, but he agreed to tell me what he had been told about it. But before he started, he insisted that I understand that there had been considerable Union activity in the Valley in the weeks leading up to the fight at New Market. He said that Union cavalry were riding hither and yon, and messengers rode their horses up and down the roads at all hours of the day and night. Everyone in the Valley knew what was coming and they were angry and fearful, and many acted intemperately.

"Mr. Beaudine said there was a farmer named John Bonner who lived up around Hawkinstown who had a pretty hot temper. Apparently, he got sick and tired of watching the Union cavalry riding across his property, burning his fence rails in their campfires, and stealing his livestock. One evening, just before dark, when he heard another Union messenger galloping down the Pike, Bonner figured he would give the Yankee a good scare. He stepped out on the Pike and took a pot shot at the messenger as he charged by..."

"Hawkinstown?" the Senator interrupted. "Where is that?"

"It is on the Valley Pike, no more than 2 or 3 miles north of Mt. Jackson,' I answered for Kate. When the Senator asked nothing more, Kate continued: "Bonner supposedly missed on purpose, but the gunshot and his sudden appearance on the road scared the horse so badly that it reared up and threw Lieutenant Ferguson to the ground.

"Bonner realized that he now had a serious problem. The Lieutenant was lying in the road with the wind knocked out of him but otherwise seemed alright. But Bonner was afraid that if he let him go, the Lieutenant and his troops would come back looking for Bonner. Bonner knew that they would not believe that he was only trying to scare the Lieutenant and had meant him no real harm.

"So, Bonner tied Lieutenant Ferguson up and carted him back to his farm where he locked him in a grain bin. He did not know what to do, so he sent word to the Knights that he had captured a Yankee soldier.

"Manson Bowley, Jacob Hayes and Andrew Beaudine were in New Market when they heard about the captured Yankee. They rode up to Bonner's farm thinking it was a Union deserter or some other soldier that had gotten separated from his fellows. They were not expecting a Union officer.

"Mr. Beaudine told me that when they got to Bonner's farm, Manson Bowley walked up to the Lieutenant and asked what he was doing in the Valley and where his men were. The Lieutenant ignored his question and demanded that he be set free or turned over to the Confederate Army as a prisoner of war. In Mr. Beaudine's words, 'The Lieutenant was acting all high and mighty and that did not set well with Manson.'

"Manson Bowley then slapped Lieutenant Ferguson hard across the face and told him that he was a prisoner of the Golden Knights, and he would be dealt with by the Golden Knights. Outraged, Lieutenant Ferguson threw himself against Manson, staggering him. But the Lieutenant's hands were tied behind his back and there was not much else he could do. Then Manson Bowley struck him again, knocking Lieutenant Ferguson to the ground.

"According to Mr. Beaudine, Lieutenant Ferguson looked up at Manson and told him he will regret the day he was ever born. He told Manson that he had more than 5,000 men with him and to remember the name of the 1st New York Cavalry as they will track him down and hang him as sure as Monday follows Sunday.

"Manson Bowley, he just laughed at Lieutenant Ferguson. 'I wish them luck,' is all he said.

"Mr. Beaudine said he motioned to Manson Bowley, and they walked away out of the Lieutenant's hearing. Mr. Beaudine asked Manson what they were going to do with the Lieutenant. Manson looked surprised by his question. 'Why, we hang him, Andrew,' he answered. 'What would you have us do? Even if we let him go, his fellows is as likely as not to hang us all anyways.'

"Mr. Beaudine told Manson that he thought the Lieutenant might make a deal with them to save his own life. Besides, he said, no good can come from hanging a Yankee officer. But Manson would not listen to reason. Mr. Beaudine said Manson Bowley was 'all hate' since returning from the Yankee prison.

Kate paused her story and took a sip from a glass of water. I looked over at the Senator who appeared to be present in body only. He sat unmoving, his eyes focused on some distant point. I suspected that he was, at least in his mind, standing on the Bonner farm watching the guerrillas debate the fate of his son. He did not appear to notice that Kate had stopped speaking.

After a moment, Kate continued her story: "Mr. Beaudine said that Manson Bowley had immediately called for rope and a horse. He was clearly in a hurry to finish with Lieutenant Ferguson and be on his way. But the execution was a farce, as it was ill-considered and badly performed.

"Lieutenant Ferguson was placed on a horse beneath a large tree on the edge of a fallow field, his hands tied in front of his body. The farmer Bonner stood holding firmly onto the horse's bridle while a rope with a crude hangman's noose was thrown over a convenient limb. Jacob Hayes grabbed the noose and reached up to place it around the Lieutenant's neck. Once the noose was in place, they would slap the horse and leave the Lieutenant dangling in the air.

"But Lieutenant Ferguson had other ideas. Before the noose could be placed around his neck, he viciously kicked the flanks of the horse upon which he had been placed. The horse reared up and then leapt forward, trampling farmer Bonner who had been foolish enough to be standing in front of the horse rather than to the side.

"Lieutenant Ferguson leaned forward, holding onto the pommel with his tied hands. He continued to kick at the horse's flanks as it accelerated across the field, headed for a road on the other side. Mr. Beaudine said Lieutenant Ferguson yelled back over his shoulder, 'I will be back, and we will sweep this valley clean of you Rebs from one end to the other!'

"Mr. Beaudine said that Manson Bowley gave a howl of rage and ran for his musket. He grabbed the weapon, cocked the hammer, and sighted down the long barrel at the rider receding into the distance.

"Mr. Beaudine said that Manson Bowley stood aiming his musket for what seemed an impossibly long time. 'Time seemed to slow,' Mr. Beaudine said, 'the Lieutenant's mount appearing as if running in deep mud, but the distance was ever increasing nonetheless.' At any moment, the Lieutenant would reach the road at the far end of the field and disappear from sight. There would be no time for a second shot.

"Mr. Beaudine said that he watched as Manson Bowley finally pulled the trigger, his body rocking back from the recoil of the gun. He said that he watched the rider continue onward for at least two full seconds before the ball finally caught up with him. But it was the horse that was hit. Mr. Beaudine said that they watched it summersault forward, throwing the Lieutenant to the ground at a full gallop.

"Mr. Beaudine told me that he had never seen such a remarkable shot. But Manson Bowley made no comment, he just leaned the musket against a tree and started walking towards the Lieutenant. Mr. Beaudine and Jacob Hayes, they stood where they were, unsure what to do. Farmer Bonner, who had been trampled, lay nearby writhing on the ground, his cries of pain sounding for all the world like a kitten mewing for its Momma. Spooked, Mr. Beaudine and Mr. Hayes ran to catch up with Manson Bowley.

"Mr. Beaudine said that when they reached the horse, it was lying in the dust, wide-eyed, clearly in pain and unable to get up. He said that Manson Bowley pulled out his pistol and calmly shot the horse between the eyes, ending its agony. The Lieutenant lay several yards away, his body twisted into an impossible position. Mr. Beaudine said that it was clear that the Lieutenant was dead before they ever reached his body. With his hands tied, he could do nothing to break his fall and his neck had been broken."

The Senator suddenly jumped up from his chair and knelt before Kate. He took her hands between his two. "Are you telling me that my Thomas was not hanged?" he asked. "Is that what you are telling me?" When Kate nodded, tears suddenly sprang from the Senator's eyes. "Oh, thank God, thank God that he was spared such an ignoble death!" He got slowly to his feet and bent down to kiss Kate on the cheek. "Thank you, Mrs. Warne, for a greater gift than you know."

The senator turned to return to his seat but then turned again to face Kate. "But Thomas was found hanged alongside the road. How can that be?"

"Mr. Beaudine told me that when they discovered that your son had been killed in the fall, he had some hope that they might still avoid blame for his death," Kate explained. "He argued with Manson Bowley that they should leave the body alongside the road, hands untied, and it would appear as though the Lieutenant had been killed in an accidental fall. But Manson Bowley was angry and declared that Lieutenant Ferguson would not escape the noose so easily. He made Mr. Beaudine and Jacob Hayes carry Lieutenant Ferguson's—your Son's—body back to the road where a hanging was staged. Mr. Beaudine said that when they were finished, Manson Bowley stood in the road with his arms crossed, nodding approval at the gruesome scene. 'Let this be a warning to every Yankee that sets foot in the Valley,' Manson Bowley had declared.

It was nearly midnight when the Senator called for his carriage and bid us goodnight. It was agreed that we would meet at the same time the following afternoon to finish Kate's report.

When the Senator was gone, Kate and I gathered what few belongings we had and walked out of the parlor. As I held the door for Kate, I asked her "Was that true? What you told the Senator about his son's death?" Kate stopped and turned to face me. "Why, Teddy, what a curious question!" Then she turned and continued through the doorway saying nothing more.

CHAPTER 29

Manson Bowley

It is our better nature that creates beauty. But we create evil as well, sometimes by no more than indifference and neglect. In that respect, we must all take some degree of responsibility for the monsters that walk amongst us.

The Senator was a different man when he appeared in the Blue Parlor at a little past one the next afternoon. He was not a big man, but he suddenly filled the room in a way I could not have imagined the day before. The news that his son had died trying to escape, rather than having been hanged like a common coward or traitor, seemed to have revived him. It was no longer difficult to picture him prowling the halls of Congress with clerks and lobbyists attaching themselves to him like Remora to a shark. He had an unmistakable aura of power about him.

We took our seats, and the Senator wasted no time: "Well, Mrs. Warne, whom did you bring back for me to hang?"

Kate seemed unfazed by the Senator's bluntness. "We have Andrew Beaudine, Senator. Four of Lieutenant Marcus' troopers brought him back to Washington City when we had finished interrogating him." The Senator cocked his head.

"And?" he asked.

"It is a short list, I am afraid." Kate answered. "Of the men who were directly responsible for the death of your son, that is. I do have a few peripheral players in custody, known members of the Golden Knights such as Asa Goodman, Ben Steiner and..."

"I have no interest in conducting a pogrom," the Senator interrupted. "I am sure each of the guerrillas you captured will ultimately be punished commensurate with the severity of his crimes. But I continue to be primarily interested in the men responsible for the death of my Thomas. You have yet to account for all of them."

Kate nodded. "Of course," she said. "As you know, 4 men were responsible for your son's death: Andrew Beaudine, Jacob Hayes, the farmer Jack Bonner and Manson Bowley. Andrew Beaudine is in our custody; Jacob Hayes was killed by Teddy and Jack Bonner died of the injuries he sustained while trying to hang your son."

"And Manson Bowley?"

"Manson Bowley is dead," she answered.

Kate said that tracking down Manson Bowley had been fairly easy. "The Valley has been devastated by the Union Campaign," she explained, "and there is little work to be had. Mr. Beaudine told us that Manson Bowley was scraping out a living by trading his labor for food at a couple of still-functioning farms around Mt. Jackson and New Market. He gave us the names of several farmers who might have seen him recently. Lieutenant Marcus and I, and our 16 remaining troopers, left New Market immediately to begin our search for Manson Bowley.

"The first two farms we stopped at were unfriendly and uncooperative. Their disdain for Lieutenant Marcus and his troopers, and me, was intense. The men stared at the ground and would not meet our eyes; but the women were more open about their feelings. They glared at us with such pure hatred that I half expected them to spit in our faces. At both farms, we conducted a thorough search, but we found no sign of Manson Bowley. But our luck changed when we reached the third farm on our list, which was owned by a man named Franz Blosser. The farm was located about a quarter mile east of the Valley Pike and had a long driveway bordered on two sides by fallow fields. There was no way to approach the house without being seen.

"Halfway up the driveway, we saw a woman run out of the farmhouse. She ran down the driveway towards us, waving her arms and screaming 'He has my little girl!'

"She was a middle-aged woman, her hair covered by a flowered scarf and her skin brown and wrinkled from years of working in the sun. She was sobbing and gasping for breath, all the while begging us to save her daughter. I jumped down from my horse and tried to console her or at least calm her enough to understand her story. I asked her who had taken her daughter. 'Manson Bowley,' she answered. 'He saw you coming down the driveway, grabbed my Mary and ran into the barn.'

"I asked her how old her daughter was. 'Ten,' she answered.

"Lieutenant Marcus immediately had his men surround the barn with orders that they not shoot unless directly threatened. 'Is he armed?' I asked the woman. She nodded and said, 'He always carries a pistol tucked in his belt.'

"Lieutenant Marcus and I stood back from the barn out of pistol range. We could clearly hear the young girl in the barn calling for her Momma. We could also hear Manson Bowley yelling at her to stop crying. 'Manson Bowley!' I shouted. 'I am here to arrest you for the murder of Lieutenant Thomas Ferguson.'

"From inside the barn, Manson Bowley said 'Is that the Lady Pinkerton Detective I hear? Well, Miss Kate, it appears we are never long apart! Have you and your Blue-Belly friends come to hang every Golden Knight in the Valley?'

"'No,' I said, 'just you.' Manson Bowley laughed and said, 'You have a small problem there and her name is Mary.'

"Fear crept up my spine for I knew the evil of which Manson Bowley was capable. I yelled at him that if he had even a shred of honor, he would let the girl go.

"This provoked a response from him of surprising intensity: 'You dare to speak to me of honor?' he replied angrily, his voice rising. 'Where was the honor when you Yankees threw me, as a mere boy, into a jail full of killers and sodomites? Where was the honor when my Daddy was beaten so badly trying to protect me that he could never work again?' Manson Bowley was quiet for a few moments, then said in a calmer voice 'You take your friends back down to the end of the driveway and agree to give me a 30-minute head start, and I will let the girl go.'

"'I cannot do that,' I answered.

"'Then you will be responsible for the death of this little girl,' he said. 'In any case, I will not go back with you to face the gallows.'

"And so it went, back and forth, for the next 20 minutes or so," Kate said. "Lieutenant Marcus and I had just about decided to agree to his terms—while leaving a single sharpshooter behind—when there was an escalation of crying and yelling coming from the barn. The little girl had fully panicked and was crying and screaming for her Momma at the top of her lungs. We could hear Manson Bowley yelling at her to be quiet, but the more he yelled the louder the girl cried. Suddenly, there was a single pistol shot and all became quiet.

"For one long moment, no one moved. Then the little girl's mother screamed and fell to the ground, sobbing. I yelled to Manson Bowley, 'If you have hurt that girl, I will take two days to kill you!'

"'No more threats, Miss Kate, not today!' he yelled back. And with that he threw open the barn door and ran straight at the nearest trooper, firing his pistol as fast as he could cock it and pull the trigger. It seemed that every trooper fired as one and Manson Bowley fell dead to the ground."

The Senator sighed and said, "That was too good a death for him. And the girl? Had he killed her?"

"No," Kate said. "He had fired his pistol near her head, startling her into silence. Then he had told her that if he heard one more whimper, he would kill her and her whole family. We found her cowering in the corner of the barn. She did not speak even when her mother came to get her."

CHAPTER 30

Goodbye

I do wonder what my life would have been like if I had never met you. I know there are roads I would not have traveled and paths of others I would not have crossed. But even now, when I see you in my dreams you are still at the center of everything.

Kate handed the Senator a thick sheaf of papers. "This is a copy of my summary report to the Provost Marshal, Senator," she said. "It covers the time from my assignment to the murder of your son to my second return from the Valley. It lists the names of all the guerrillas we captured and brought back to Washington City, including Andrew Beaudine. It also describes the crimes of which each have been accused. In those instances where the guerrillas are deceased, the report describes the circumstances surrounding their deaths.

"In regard to the death of your son, Lieutenant Thomas Ferguson, he is described as having been killed while trying to escape. His bravery and resolve are indisputable.

"I make no recommendations in the report regarding punishment for any of the guerrillas as I believe that to be the prerogative of the Provost Martial.

"If you have any questions after you have had a chance to review my report, Senator, please contact me at any time through the Pinkerton Detective Agency." And with that, Kate officially ended her investigation into the death of Lieutenant Ferguson.

The Senator bowed slightly to Kate and said, "I am much pleased with the work you have done, Mrs. Warne, and I will make my satisfaction known to Mr. Pinkerton."

The Senator placed his hat upon his head and turned to face me. "As much as it troubles me," he said, "I will honor our arrangement, Mr. Miller, and I hereby declare our agreement satisfactorily concluded. But I fear I was blinded by my desire to see my son's murderers brought to justice and I have allowed your father to escape his fair punishment. God only knows how many good Union soldiers died because of the information he passed on to the Confederate Army." The Senator turned and left the room.

After the Senator was gone, Kate said "Let us take a walk. I am tired of these four walls." So, we left the Willard Hotel and walked slowly up Pennsylvania Avenue in the direction of the President's House. The sun had just set but the day's heat still lingered, and the only breeze came from our own movement. Kate slid her arm through mine. "There are some things you should know," she said, "and it is best if we discuss them where we cannot be overheard."

"About my father?" I asked, my heart racing.

"Yes. And your brother as well."

I stopped and turned to face Kate, but she said "Please, Teddy, let us keep walking. The air is stifling when we are not moving." We continued our stroll up the Avenue. "Do not tell me anything has happened to them, Kate," I said. "I could not stand it if anything has happened to them, not after all of this."

Kate squeezed my arm. "They are well, Teddy. I do not mean to frighten you. But to your father first: he is being moved to a different prison."

"Moved? But why?"

"The Provost Marshal has sentenced your father to 30 years at hard labor for his espionage against the United States. In a few weeks, he will be on a boat headed for Key West and then on to Fort Jefferson in the Dry Tortugas to begin serving his sentence."

My breath caught in my chest. "But 30 years is a life sentence for him! He will never leave prison alive!"

"Remember that the usual punishment for espionage is death by hanging. The Senator honored his agreement with you by sparing your father's life. But not even Senator Ferguson—if he even wanted to—could get the Provost Marshal to agree to a lesser punishment for such a grave crime."

A great darkness settled over me. "And my brother?" I asked.

"He is well. I made an excuse to Lieutenant Marcus to visit Malcolm's farm as we were rounding up the known Golden Knights."

I thought about the Yankee cavalry riding up to Malcolm's small cabin. It must have terrified Mrs. Davies and the twins. And I tried to imagine how Malcom and Jed might have reacted if they thought the cavalry had come for them and what foolish bravado they might have employed. As if reading my thoughts, Kate said "Malcolm walked right up to us, told us who he was and demanded to know why we were on his property. Jed stood on the porch, his arms folded across his chest. Behind him, I could see one of the twins peeking out through the partially opened cabin door.

"Malcolm stared at me but did not acknowledge that he knew me. I said 'I am Mrs. Kate Warne, Pinkerton Detective, and this is Lieutenant Marcus of the Army of the United States. We are in search of a guerrilla by the name of Asa Goodwin. I have been told that he was recently seen here at your farm.'

"Malcolm tilted his head and regarded me as if I were a mad woman. But he played along. 'You was told wrong,' he said. 'There ain't no Asa Goodwin here.'

"I was about to say something more when Jed took a step towards the cabin door. Every trooper grabbed his carbine from its scabbard and pointed it at Jed. 'Do not move!' I yelled at Jed. Jed stopped and slowly raised his hands.

"Before things could escalate further, I said to Lieutenant Marcus 'I want to talk to that boy.' I jumped off my horse and walked up to Jed, grabbed his arm, and began to lead him away from the troopers where we could talk without being overheard. Jed tried to pull away and said, 'I told you never to touch me again!' But I whispered harshly to him to shut up if he wished to save Malcolm's life. He glared at me but said nothing more.

"Away from the troopers, I told him that I was not there to arrest Malcolm, that I had news for him about his father and you. I told him about your father's prison sentence and that you had been wounded in New Market. At that time, I did not know if you would live or die so I could not offer him much comfort.

"He told me that he was well, and that Malcolm was grateful for his help with the farm. Beyond that, he said little."

Kate and I had reached the President's Park across from the White House where we found a bench and sat down. It was fully dark now and lights glowed behind the windows of the Executive Mansion.

"That is all he said?" I asked. "Jed asked nothing more about me?"

Kate placed her hand on my forearm. "He has been deeply hurt, Teddy. You must give him time."

We sat quietly for a few minutes. When I sensed that Kate was getting ready to leave, I asked "Why did you not arrest Malcolm, Kate?"

Kate seemed to consider how to answer me, then: "Had I believed Malcolm to be guilty of any crimes, I would not have hesitated to arrest him. But the most he seemed guilty of was associating with the Golden Knights; and if bad judgement were a hanging offense, there would be few of us spared the noose."

We had just begun our walk back to the Willard hotel when Kate reached into her purse and took out a folded piece of blue paper. Glancing around quickly, she said "Listen carefully to me, Teddy. You must be in Key West on August 28. That is the date your father will arrive there for transport to Fort Jefferson. I have arranged for a man named Captain William Caster to let you have one hour with your father before he leaves Key West. This may be your last and only chance to talk with your father as there are no visitors allowed in Fort Jefferson."

Kate lowered her voice. "Captain Castor owns a fleet of sloops, one of which they use to ferry prisoners from Key West to Fort Jefferson. You must never mention his name to anyone, and you must not agree to pay him any additional money. He is already well-paid. You will find him any evening in a bar called the Crow's Nest on Greene Street. When you find him, hand him this note. It says simply 'Kate says hello.' Do you understand what I am telling you?"

I felt my eyes well up with tears. "I do not know how to thank you."

We stopped walking and Kate turned to me. "You have been a great help to me, Teddy, and I am very grateful." She reached out and pulled me close, overwhelming me with her nearness and the ever-present scent of Jasmine. "Goodbye, Teddy" she whispered in my ear.

CHAPTER 31

Heading South

Any soldier who has experienced combat will tell you that the best battle is the one that was never fought. This concept may be antithetical to the politicians and generals, but they are rarely the ones left dead or maimed on the battlefield. It has nothing to do with courage or patriotism; no one loves peace more than a soldier.

I had only a vague idea where Florida was, let alone Key West and the Dry Tortugas, so I stopped at a bookstore on 'K' Street in Washington City to do some research. The owner of the store, a kindly looking man with a round face and thinning dark hair, led me to an Atlas of the United States. "May I ask what you are looking for?"

"Key West, Florida," I answered.

"Ah," he said, carefully opening the atlas to a map of the east coast of the United States. Pointing, he said "Here is the state of Florida. Do you see the archipelago extending from the southern end? Those are the Florida Keys. Key West is at the very end of the island chain. "

"And the Dry Tortugas?"

The store owner pointed a small distance west of Key West. "More islands. About here, some 70 miles from Key West, I believe."

I glanced at the separation between Washington City and Key West and sighed. "It must be a thousand miles away."

The owner glanced quickly at a table in the back of the atlas and said "Twelve-hundred and nine miles, to be exact." That did not make me feel any better.

The owner extended his hand and said "I am Edward Sessions. I was about to have some tea when you came in. Would you care to join me?"

I introduced myself and said I would like that very much. I followed Edward through a maze of aisles bordered by towering piles of books and periodicals. The smell of leather bindings and aging parchment enveloped me. I took a deep breath and filled my lungs with it. Edward looked back at me and smiled.

We came at last to a small room at the back of the store. There were more piles of books squeezed into every corner, but there was a small clearing with a table, 2 chairs and a small stove. A tea kettle was steaming on the stove top.

As he prepared our tea, Edward said "Key West, the Dry Tortugas. How wonderfully exotic! Do you plan on visiting them?"

"I must meet my Daddy in Key West before the end of next month. But I am at a loss as to how to get there."

Edward stared thoughtfully into his teacup. "Although Florida has seceded from the Union, Key West remains in Union hands and must be resupplied by sea. I believe there are supply ships that sail from Baltimore to Key West. Perhaps you could book passage on one of them."

I shook my head. "I have little money."

"Then work for your passage on one of the ships."

"Do you think I could?"

"There is a merchant Captain who comes in here often. He is a learned man who purchases books to read during his voyages. He has told me that the Navy and the Merchant Marine have claimed nearly every able-bodied sailor from Maine to Maryland. He is forever complaining about how hard it is for him to find dependable crewmen. The same must be true for all the commercial ships. I do not believe that you will have any difficulty finding a ship."

A week later and I was seasick and heaving my breakfast over the side of the *Nordic Angel*, a three-masted barque sailing from Baltimore to Key West by way of Cape May, New Jersey, and New York City. She had been hired by the Union Army to monthly resupply the garrison at Fort Taylor in Key West. Because of loading and unloading at each port, I was told that it would take around 3 weeks—with a favorable wind—to make it to Key West.

I was not born to be a sailor. On the ship, I found it disconcerting that things were always moving, always creaking, and moaning and sliding from side-to-side. And although I was used to hard work as a farmer, I found a sailor's life exhausting. The salt air was nearly as corrosive as acid, requiring constant maintenance of the ship: chip, paint and repeat was the crew's motto. Rotating work shifts, or watches as the sailors call them, caused the days to blur into the nights and I learned to sleep whenever and wherever I could.

The *Angel's* crew was of questionable character, experience and usefulness and I associated with them as little as possible. But the Bosun—a petty officer who is responsible for the maintenance of the ship and its equipment—took a liking to me and I to him. He was probably 10 years older than me, and his name was Sam Tuttlesworth. Sam had been born in Bangor, Maine and he was just the latest of the generations of sailors in his family. Sam taught me how to do my job on the ship. He also taught me little tricks to make life at sea more tolerable, such as filling my pockets full of crackers on which I could nibble all day. A full stomach, it turns out, will generally keep you from becoming seasick.

One evening, as we were on our final leg to Key West, Sam and I were standing at the railing watching the sunset. The ocean had turned from a greasy grey color to an astonishing blue during the day. Sam said that meant we were now in the Gulf Stream, a warm river of water in an ocean of cold water. He glanced up at the three masts where the sails strained against the rigging. "Good wind," he said. "We should be in Key West day after tomorrow if it keeps up."

"You know I mean to leave the ship in Key West, Sam," I said. Sam looked around quickly and lowered his voice. "Somehow, I never figured you for a sailor, Teddy, so I ain't much surprised. But be careful who you say that to. If they catch you jumping ship, they will beat you and drag you back to the ship in chains. Can you not just complete this cruise and use your pay to book another passage?"

I shook my head. "I cannot explain, Sam, but I must be in Key West on the 28th of this month."

"Then stay away from the wharves and bars until you see the *Angel* leaving harbor. When the officers realize you are missing, they will send a party ashore to look for you, but they cannot delay our sailing for too long."

I said I would do as he suggested. Sam leaned his elbows on the railing. "Be careful in Key West," he said. "It is as far south in North America as you can get without being in South America and it attracts men and women of questionable principles. They will slit your throat for a penny and a drought of beer."

"How is it that Key West has remained in Union hands for the entire War?" I asked.

Sam gave a laugh. "While the Key Westers may be mean, underhanded, and unscrupulous, they ain't the brightest or most highly motivated group of human beings on this planet. I thank God for that, or they might be truly dangerous.

"As I understand it, for 3 days after Florida seceded from

the Union, Fort Taylor was manned only by a handful of Union engineers there to make repairs. Now understand that whoever controls Fort Taylor controls Key West and local Confederate sympathizers could have walked straight into the fort and captured it with a toy gun. But, for whatever reason, they did not. I reckon that the capture of the Fort just never reached the level of importance of their evening bacchanal along Duval Street.

"But to be fair, mebbe Union and Reb are equally affected by life under the tropical sun. I say this because, in hindsight, our Union boys was not terribly foresightful neither. It took them the better part of 3 days just to realize that a handful of engineers probably could not hold the fort against a determined assault. So, a Union Captain named Brannan or Brennen or some-such—without orders, I was told—finally moved 44 men into the fort. When the Rebels awoke the following morning, the 'Battle for Key West' was over without a shot being fired and Key West has remained in Union hands ever since."

CHAPTER 32

Key West

The tropical sun slows a man's reason even as it heightens his desire for excess. It flows through his bloodstream like cheap rum, both exhilarating and enervating in equal measure. In the end, his regrets are often similarly split between things done and undone.

Fort Taylor loomed over our starboard side as we entered the harbor at Key West. It had sheer, red brick walls that rose 50 feet above the water. It was 3 stories high with the top 2 floors containing innumerable gun rooms. I overheard one of the sailors saying that the Fort even had its own desalination plant to make fresh water.

We tied up to the city pier around 9:00 a.m. and commenced unloading supplies for the Fort. I worked alongside my fellow sailors and stevedores hired from the city to unload the ship. The heat was suffocating even as our officers pushed us to move ever faster. Sweat poured off our bodies and made our hands slick and our grips uncertain. More than one sailor dropped his load, sometimes injuring himself or some other sailor or stevedore unlucky enough to be nearby.

By mid-afternoon, our holds were empty. Head down, I

walked off the ship with the departing stevedores. No one from the ship seemed to notice and, in a few minutes, I had disappeared into Key West, wandering aimlessly through the streets just to put distance between me and the wharfs.

I eventually made my way to Front Street where I would have a view of any ships leaving the harbor. I sat down under a shady tree, not hiding exactly, but safely away from the crowded wharf area. A local church bell chimed 6 p.m. just as I saw the *Nordic Angel* make her way into the main channel and sail out of Key West. The ship was barely out of sight when I went looking for the Crow's Nest Bar and a ship's Captain named William Caster.

As I wandered through Key West, I passed block after block of pleasant-looking homes with well-kept gardens bursting with exotic plants and flowers. After the contemptuous remarks Sam had made about the 'Key Westers,' as he had called them, I was expecting mostly slums such as I had seen around the harbor in Baltimore. But, as I would learn later, Key West was one of the richest cities in the United States. Many fortunes had been made from fishing and salt production, not to mention pillaging the many shipwrecks on nearby shoals. The latter was of questionable legality, however, as some people claimed the ships had been lured to their doom by purposefully misleading navigation lights.

Even the Crow's Nest Bar was a surprise. Rather than the waterside dive full of sailors and prostitutes I had been expecting, it was attached to a hotel with a fine outdoor dining area set up under palm-frond umbrellas and colored paper lanterns. I heard female laughter and the clink of fine crystal.

I stood across the street, uncertain what to do. I was filthy and sweat-stained from unloading the ship. I doubted that anyone would let me within 100 feet of the Crow's Nest. Dejected, I turned around and headed back to the waterfront.

On my way back to the wharf area, I talked to a couple of young sailors, easy to recognize in their canvas trousers and frocks, about where to find a bath. They told me there was a bathhouse with a Chinese laundry attached to it on Caroline Street and I was soon soaking in a large copper tub while an elderly Chinese woman took my clothes next door to be washed. The water was cold and refreshing in the tropical heat. After scrubbing off the day's dirt, I fell asleep in the tub. I do not know how long I slept, but sometime later I was awakened by the same Chinese woman holding my freshly laundered clothes and a mostly clean towel.

I was twenty-cents poorer, but I felt like a new man. It was now around 9:00 p.m. and the sun was just setting as I made my way back to the Crow's Nest.

As I walked into the bar, which was really no more than an alcove off of the restaurant, I was stopped by a well-dressed man who appeared to work there. He was not unfriendly, but he made it clear that the sailors' bars were back by the wharfs. "I am looking for Captain Caster," I said. "I have a message for him."

The man held out his hand. "Then give it to me and I will see that he gets it."

"I cannot do that. I was told to hand it to him personally." The man studied me for a moment and then said, "Wait here."

A moment later, the man returned with a short man wearing a bright green velvet jacket, white shirt and pants and a purple cravat. He looked as little like a sea captain as any man I had ever seen. "I am Captain Caster," he said.

"My name is Teddy Miller," I said as I pulled the folded sheet of blue paper from my pocket and handed it to him. He scanned it quickly, then refolded it and put it in his pocket. He looked at the well-dressed man who had stopped me and said "Thank you, Thomas. Please tell my guests I will be back in a moment." Thomas bowed slightly and walked away towards the restaurant.

Captain Caster took my elbow and led me towards a fine mahogany bar. Behind the bar were shelves filled with bottles of every shape and color. "Would you care for a drink, Mr. Miller?"

"No thank you, captain," I said, which made the captain laugh. "A sailor that will not accept a free drink," he said. "I have never heard of such a thing!"

"And a ship's captain in a green velvet jacket," I said, "I have never seen such a thing!" And that made the captain laugh even louder. He slapped me on the back. "It is my wife's idea. Now that we are rich—I salvaged an old Spanish galleon full of gold two years ago—she does not believe I should be seen dressed in canvas jackets and trousers anymore." He shrugged. "But if dressing like this keeps her happy, then that seems little enough to ask." He motioned to the bartender who was standing a discreet distance away. "Bring me rum, Willie, and cold water for my friend here."

When we had our drinks, Captain Caster said "I have done work for Kate in the past. When she asked me to find a way to get you one hour alone with your father, I agreed. Not that I need the money anymore, but Kate is difficult to say no to. Did she tell you that your father is to be transported from Key West to Fort Jefferson on the 28th of this month?" When I nodded, he said "He will be taken to the Fort on a Sloop I own and is captained by a friend of mine.

"I have arranged that your father will be the only prisoner on board that day. You will be allowed to speak to him for exactly 1 hour, not a moment more. If you get caught, we will all find ourselves guests of Fort Jefferson.

"The name of the Sloop is the *Bahama Belle*. You will find her tied up at Pier 4. Be there at 9:00 a.m."

I thanked Captain Caster and walked slowly back towards

the wharfs. It was already August 26 and I had just one more day to think about what I would say to my father.

CHAPTER 33

Aboard the Sloop Bahama Belle

If the soul is left in darkness, sins will be committed. The guilty one is not he who commits the sin, but the one who causes the darkness. -Monseigneur Bienvenu in Les Misérables

I did not sleep at all the night before I was to meet with my father. I ached to see him again and to hear his voice and my mind raced with all the things I wanted to say to him. I tried to prioritize them in my mind so as not to run out of time for the important ones.

I got to the pier early on the 28th and paced nervously while I waited for the church bells to announce 9 a.m. At the scheduled time, I stepped aboard the *Bahama Belle*. I viewed her with my newly acquired 'sailor's eye,' noting that she had a single mast and what was called a fore-and-aft rig with one head sail. She looked fast and I reckoned she could make the 70-mile trip from Key West to Fort Jefferson in around 12-14 hours with a good breeze.

A sailor met me at the gangway. He did not introduce himself nor did he ask my name. He pointed to a hatch with a ladder leading below and said, "one hour." Then he turned and walked off the ship.

I climbed down the narrow ladder. The heat inside the ship was stifling and I was nearly overcome by the smell of unwashed bodies and human waste which seemed to have permeated the very wood of the ship. When my eyes adjusted to the dimness, I saw that the entire space below decks had been divided into two compartments by a wall of iron bars with a large, padlocked door. On the other side of the bars, a man sat on a crude wooden bench. His wrists and ankles were manacled. A third chain connected the wrist and ankle manacles and was padlocked to a large eye-bolt attached to the deck. Nearby was an overflowing pail provided for the prisoner to relieve himself, although how he could manage that chained as he was, I could not imagine.

The man did not look up as I approached the bars. "Daddy," I said.

My father looked up. I was so shocked by his appearance that tears sprang immediately to my eyes. His hair was long and unwashed, his skin sallow and his eyes sunken and surrounded by dark circles. His beard had turned a dirty grey and he was thinner than I could imagine a man could be and still be alive. "Daddy, what have they done to you?"

My father said nothing, staring at me as if he were no longer sure of his own reality. "Who are you?" he asked.

"It is me, Daddy," I said, tears running down my cheeks and falling to the filthy deck. "It is Teddy."

"Teddy?" A light of recognition came into my father's eyes. "Oh, Teddy, I have been so worried about you!" he said. "Step into the light so I can see you." I stepped sideways into a pool of light coming through the open hatch above and I heard my father gasp. "You are so thin," he said. I watched my father raise his hand and reach towards me, and although he was 10 feet away, I could feel his fingers trace the outline of my face.

I closed my eyes and let his touch drive away all my fears and anxieties. It was a moment of perfect joy, and I was at peace for the first time since the battle or the Valley had begun.

How long we stayed that way I do not know, but eventually the heavy manacles on my father's wrists pulled his arm down. When I opened my eyes, he was smiling at me with tears brimming in his eyes. "I had despaired of ever seeing you again," he said.

"I never gave up hope, Daddy. We will all be together again, I promise. I will find a way."

My father smiled at me. Then he asked me about Jed. "Is he well? Is he at the farm?"

"Jed is with Malcolm, Daddy. He is well, 'though he misses you terribly."

"Then who is taking care of the farm?"

I dropped my eyes. "There is no farm, Daddy. The battle rolled over it and whatever was still standing, the Yankees burnt to the ground."

"Then there is nothing left?" he asked, seeming to find the idea incredulous. "What about our neighbors?"

"There is hardly a working farm anywhere in the Valley. All the stock and Negroes have been carried off and the fields lay fallow."

"And the War, then? How goes the War?"

"Not well. The Yankee Gen'ral Grant has Richmond under siege. It is feared that if Richmond falls, the Confederacy will quickly follow."

My father let out a deep sigh. "Then all is lost," he said.

"We still own our land," I said quickly. "We can rebuild the farm even better than it was."

My father lowered his head into his hands and muttered "Better that I should have been hanged than live to see my Country defeated."

"Do not say that, Daddy!"

My father sat unmoving for several moments, the only sounds coming from the creaking of the ship as it rocked gently in its berth. Then he lifted his head to look at me, a quizzical expression forming on his face. "When I was in jail in Mt. Jackson, I thought I saw you standing outside my cell," he said. "Was that you?"

"Yes, I had come looking for you. But they would not let me speak to you."

"But how did you find me?"

"Jed and I took shelter at Malcolm's farm after the Yankees burnt us out. Malcolm heard that 3 civilians had been captured during the first day's fighting. Two had been hanged outright as guerrillas and the third was being held for trial as a spy. He reckoned the last prisoner was being held in the jail in Mt. Jackson, so I went there to see if it was you."

"I had been sentenced to hang, too," my father said. "But the day I was scheduled to die, I see you outside my cell and then I am told I was to be spared." Daddy cocked his head at me like he was studying a curious insect on a windowsill. "Now I am on my way to Fort Jefferson and here you are again. Were you also in Washington City while I was in prison there?"

My pulse quickened. "I had been shot, Daddy, and the Yankees sent me to a hospital there."

My father's eyes widened. "Shot! Do the Yankees make war on children now?" His voice took on an edge of concern: "Are you well now? Are you telling me the truth about Jed? Is he alright?"

"Jed is well, Daddy, and has not been injured. He is at Malcolm's farm as I told you. I was shot in the leg and am now fully recovered."

"Thank God, thank God for that! I am sorry, Teddy, I am sorry I was not there to protect you from those Yankee bastards!"

At that moment, I knew I had reached a cross-road in my life and what I said next would, for better or worse, affect my relationship with my father for the rest of our lives. I took a deep breath, wiped my nose on my shirt sleeve and said, "The Yankees did not shoot me, Daddy."

My father looked at first confused, but then his eyes widened, and he said "Oh, Teddy, what have you done?"

I told my father everything, rushing through the story so as not to run out of time. When I had finished, my father at first said nothing, sitting there stunned on the wooden bench. Then, he let out a cry so wretched that it nearly broke my heart: "No, Teddy! Why would you do those things?"

Feelings of resentment and anger rose out of all the other emotions churning inside me. "Why?" I answered. "I did it to save you! Everything I have done has been to save you! What would you have had me do?"

"To save *me*?" my father asked, his voice rising. "Look at me Teddy!" But I dropped my eyes and could not look at him. "Look at me!" he demanded again, and I raised my eyes. "I am sitting here in my own filth, and I am on my way to a prison from which I will probably never return. Why did you not just let them kill me? That would have been the merciful thing to do."

"I could not," I said softly. "Jed and I need you too much." But if my father heard my words, he did not respond to them. "How could you betray our neighbors and our country, Teddy? How could you murder Jacob Hayes? My God, Teddy, Jacob was our friend! You had gone to school with his children!"

My father tried to stand up, but the weight of the manacles pulled him back down on the bench. He shook the chains in frustration and said "Was ours not a Christian home? Did I teach you nothing about goodness and loyalty and patriotism?"

"You taught me love," I answered, trying to hold back sobs.

My father shook his head. "Love of God, love of neighbor and love of Country. Not love of self! What you did, Teddy, you did for yourself, not for me."

Every word my father said to me was like a punch to my body. I felt my father pulling away from me and desperation built in my heart. "You are right, Daddy, everything you say is right! Tell me what to do to make it better! I am so sorry. Please, tell me and I will do it!"

But my father just shook his head and then recited from 2nd Kings, his voice breaking: "*And when she looked, behold, the king stood by a pillar, as the manner was, and the princes and the trumpeters by the king, and all the people of the land rejoiced, and blew with trumpets: and Athaliah rent her clothes, and cried, Treason, Treason.*"

My father's choice of verse chilled my blood and I shivered even in the tropical heat. Although my father sat no more than 10 feet away, he shrank in my vision and seemed to become more distant with every passing moment. I reached through the bars to try to grab him, to try to hold him in place. "Daddy, please!" I yelled.

My father slumped forward against his chains as if the last of his strength had deserted him. His voice barely above a whisper, he said "Leave here, Teddy. I do not ever want to see you again."

I stood there, shocked at his words, and feeling like my heart had just been ripped from my chest. "You cannot mean that!" I yelled. "I am your son!" I wanted to run to my father, to lay my head against his chest, to beg his forgiveness. I believed if I could just reach him, he would have to forgive me and tell me he loved me. "Daddy, please!" I begged as I grabbed the cell door and tried to tear it apart with my bare hands to reach him, to touch him. I shook it and pulled at it like a madman until I finally slid to the deck, exhausted, my fingers cut and bleeding. But my father would not even look at me and he said nothing more. I sat on the deck sobbing until the sailor came to tell me my time was up.

The sailor looked down at my face, wet with tears and covered in snot, with contempt. "Time to leave," he said.

I reached out and grabbed his ankle. "Please," I begged, "just a few more minutes…" But the sailor violently pulled his leg away. He reached to a sheath on his belt and pulled out a knife.

"I was told 1 hour and not a minute more. Now, you can climb that ladder, or I will carry your body up it."

I stared at the knife in the sailor's hand. It was of the type carried by many seamen with a short, slightly curved blade useful for cutting lines and ropes. I knew it would be razor sharp and I should have been intimidated if not terrified. But instead, I had to fight against the urge to grab the sailor's arm and pull the blade across my own throat.

I rose unsteadily from the deck and looked over at my father. He was still slumped forward against his chains, his face still turned away. The only sounds came from our shoes against the ladder and the incessant creaking of the ship as the sailor followed me above decks.

CHAPTER 34

Aftermath

His voice haunts me still, coming to me as it does in the deepest parts of the night. His face is always shrouded and lost in shadow but his words—oh, his words—how they reverberate through my mind and tear my very soul from its attachments.

I wandered aimlessly around Key West For over a week. I did not eat or bathe and I slept in the parks where I was harassed by constables as well as thieves looking for easy prey. My self-pity was so complete that I wished only to die. What lucid moments I had were spent trying to understand how I had lost everything: my family, my home and even my country. I played my father's final words to me over and over again in my mind until my soul was numbed.

Eventually, I chose life over death. I wish I could say that I received some enlightenment, like a sign from God, perhaps. But in truth, my will to live simply exceeded my desire to die. Filthy, my stomach distended from hunger, I sought work in the bars and brothels of Key West.

To most of the 'Key Westers,' I was invisible. They simply did not see me, and they stepped around me on the sidewalks as if I were dog droppings. But the bartenders, prostitutes and laborers were invariably kind and generous towards me. Perhaps they saw themselves as only a fragile step above the position in which I found myself.

Henry Olsen was the bartender at *The Happy Cork*, a bar on Duval Street where I found work cleaning and restocking. Henry was a large man with a larger laugh and a true joy of living. He had been a sailor until a fall from the rigging had left him crippled and dependent on a crutch to walk. But Henry had a way of making the best of most everything and, in his hands, the crutch became an amazing tool. He used it to reach high shelves where he would knock over a bottle and nonchalantly catch it in midair with his free hand, often without seeming to watch the bottle fall. At other times, he would use it to push a full shot glass to a patron at the opposite end of the bar with amazing delicacy and never spill a drop. And on more than one occasion, I had seen him knock a rowdy sailor unconscious with it.

When business was slow, Henry would tell me stories about his travels around the world. His descriptions of foreign ports were colorful and often profane, and he claimed to have fathered 32 children in the Orient, although each time he told the story the number of children grew. Henry had bright red hair and a large belly that hung over his belt, and he would say "Teddy, if ever you see a red-headed Chinaman with a pot belly, ask their name. If they answer 'Henry,' you will know my story is true."

Henry and I grew close and he played a role in my life somewhere between big brother and father. More like a big brother, as I think about it, as Henry was fully a part of the hedonistic lifestyle that defined Key West. But he helped me find cheap lodging, listened to my complaints, and gave freely of his advice.

I never told Henry why I was in Key West or even mentioned

the Valley. Even so, I was certain that everyone I met could see that I was a traitor, as if it had been emblazoned on my forehead. I rarely looked anyone in the eyes.

I slept all day and worked all night. The physical world and my soul had seemingly merged, and I lived life fully in the darkness.

I wrote letter after letter to my father. I begged for his forgiveness, and I begged for his understanding. I begged to be given just one more chance. Day and night, I fantasized about rescuing him from Fort Jefferson. Surely, I thought, he would have to forgive me then. But with every week that went by without a reply from him, my hopelessness grew.

To what depths I might have sunken I do not know, but I saw no restraints on the slope to perdition. As I observed it, the downward slide was quick and certain. Every night, I watched men try to fill the emptiness in their lives with alcohol and debauchery and none were successful. But just when I had about despaired of finding any purpose to my life, I met Elwood Haney.

Elwood had been a regular at the *Governor's Pub*, one of the dozen or so of port-side bars in Key West. But for whatever reason, he had worn out his welcome there and was now a member of the clientele of the Happy Cork. He was there nearly every night until we closed.

There are mean drunks and there are funny drunks and there are drunks who sit quietly at a bar waiting for their time on this earth to run out. Elwood seemed to be of the latter type. For weeks, I had never heard him speak a word except to order his next drink. But one night as I was sweeping up in preparation for closing, he motioned me over with a wave of his hand. "What is your name, boy?" he asked. When I told him, he pulled a few coins out of his pocket and handed them to me. "Be a good fellow, Teddy, and get me a bottle of rum to take home with me. Oblivion at the Happy Cork appears to be an unobtainable goal tonight."

I took the coins and fetched him a cheap bottle of rum. When I went to hand it to him, it seemed that Elwood saw 2 bottles rather than 1 as he reached twice for thin air. When he finally connected with the actual bottle, I asked him if he needed help getting home.

Elwood reached for his last drink on the bar. "Kind of you, Sir," he said. "It appears 'the gentleman hath drunk himself out of his five senses.'"

"Shakespeare," I said.

Elwood paused as he was lifting the shot glass to his lips. "Shakespeare?" he asked.

"You quoted Shakespeare. The Merry Wives of Windsor."

Elwood placed the shot glass back down on the bar and cocked his head at me. "Stand me up and knock me down," he said. "I had about despaired of ever meeting another cultured man in this tropical wasteland. What did you say your name was?"

"Teddy. Teddy Miller."

Elwood smiled broadly at me. "Well, hello, Teddy!"

Elwood and I became friends, not good friends, perhaps, as he was often brooding and noncommunicative. But when the mood struck him, we would talk for hours after the bar had closed. I learned that he had been born to wealthy parents in Atlanta but had to flee Georgia for his life after getting the mayor's youngest daughter in a family way. "Now I could have saved myself a great deal of trouble by simply marrying the girl," Elwood explained. "But God forgive me for saying so, the poor thing was one of the homeliest creatures I have ever seen. That I had managed to impregnate her at all speaks to the wondrous power of alcohol to bend our perceptions."

After leaving Atlanta, Elwood had wandered up and down

the east coast taking any job he could find. But when the War started, he found himself stranded in Key West for the duration. To support his drinking habit, as he put it, he had worked at any number of jobs from laborer to fireman to bookkeeper.

Elwood never discussed his jobs in chronological order, but rather as they applied to whatever conversational point he was making. And the one job he never seemed to talk about at all was his current one. One night I asked him, "What is it that you do now, Elwood? You have never told me."

Elwood looked around quickly and then lowered his voice: "You must understand, Teddy, that I have not been the most motivated employee. I rather dislike getting up in the morning, keeping regular hours and taking orders. So, it wasn't long before I ran out of employment options here in Key West."

I tried to imagine what kind of work Elwood could be doing that clearly made him so uncomfortable. After once again checking that no one was paying any attention to our conversation, he said softly "I haul coal out to Ft. Jefferson."

At the mention of Ft. Jefferson, my breath caught in my chest. Elwood must have thought I was reacting in disapproval to what he had just told me. "Now, Teddy, I know what you are thinking… you think I am a traitor for supporting those Yankee bastards and that I have forsaken our beloved Confederacy. But I have no choice if I am to keep body and drink together. There is no one left in Key West who will give me work."

I suddenly felt as if the sun had just broken through the clouds after weeks of rainy days. I felt something stir in my soul that I had thought gone forever: hope. I placed my hand on Elwood's forearm and said, "Let me tell you a story, Elwood, for I believe God has brought you and I together for a reason."

Less than a month later, I was a crew member aboard the sloop *Lucille* making my first coal run to Fort Jefferson. I had told Elwood only parts of my story, concentrating on my father's trial and imprisonment. As much of a drunkard and rascal as Elwood was, he was still a southern patriot and I doubted he would react well to some of the decisions I had made in the Valley.

Elwood had put in a good word for me with the master of the *Lucille*. Coming from Elwood, this may have done more harm than good, but experienced sailors were still hard to find, and I was hired on the spot.

The *Lucille* carried 70 tons of coal destined to support the ships of the Union navy and she rode low in the water. We did no better than 4 or 5 knots even with the stiffest breeze and I had a lot of free time. I would often sit in the shade of the mainsail and think about my father and the future. I would listen to the flapping of the sails and the gentle hiss of the bow wake and imagine my father's surprise and gratitude when I came to rescue him. But I had darker daydreams, too, where my father refused my help and averted his eyes from my own, his love for me dead, drowned in a sea of hurt and disappointment.

I did not know what my future held. But whatever it was, I approached it inexorably at 5 knots under fair skies and calm seas.

BOOK II
THE LIGHT FROM DARKNESS

CHAPTER 1

Fort Jefferson, Dry Tortugas

October 1864

Fort Jefferson Prison

Dear Father,
   Through your silence, you have made it clear that I no longer hold a place in your heart, but I beg you to at least acknowledge my letters so that I may know you are well.
Your loving son,
Teddy

Key West, Florida

T he sloop Lucille labored through a slight chop, barely making 5 knots even under the stiffest breeze. She was loaded with more than 70 tons of coal destined for the Union navy at Fort Jefferson in the Dry Tortugas and she rode low in the water. Emerald swells broke against the side of the ship, and the bow wake was a soft hiss barely audible above the flapping sails.

I was new to the crew. I had found my way on board with the help of my friend Elwood Haney. Elwood was a member of the sloop's crew as well as a regular at the bar where I worked. He had convinced the *Lucille's* captain to take me on.

Elwood and I were on a mission. My father was a political prisoner at the fort and Elwood had agreed to help me rescue him. We had no real plan on how to do so, but I was 17 years old and everything seemed possible, no matter how improbable. The first goal, we reckoned, was to gather as much information as possible about the prison at Fort Jefferson.

The *Lucille* approached Fort Jefferson from the south and tied up at the south coaling docks. To the north, the fort loomed like a red-brick behemoth, bristling with gun ports; but it somehow seemed derelict at the same time as the tropical climate was already attacking the mortar that held the bricks together. The fort was surrounded by a foul-smelling moat that received the waste from its privies. The heat was indescribable, and it sucked the last drops of moisture from our bodies as we struggled to unload our cargo of coal.

One solitary Union soldier stood guard on the wharf as we went about our duties. He sat on a folding chair in the shade of a small building, his musket leaning casually against the wall. His uniform shirt was unbuttoned nearly to his belly button and his slouch hat was pulled low over his eyes. It was not clear if he were even awake.

I observed as much as I could while I shoveled coal. Clearly, this was not your usual prison. I saw some civilians, whom I assumed were political prisoners, wandering alone along the white sand beaches. They were not accompanied by guards. Elsewhere, what appeared to be Union prisoners (mostly deserters and thieves, I later learned) came and went from the fort almost at will. The guards gestured and joked with their prisoners and each other.

The sun was low in the sky by the time we had off-loaded the last of the coal. As Elwood had predicted, our captain informed us that we would be staying the night at the fort and returning to Key West in the morning when the tides were more favorable. Elwood and I went to sit in the shade near the Union guard. Elwood pulled out a silver flask of whiskey and took a long swallow. I could sense the guard watching us out of the corner of his vision.

Elwood offered me the flask, but I declined. Elwood shrugged his shoulders and gestured to the Yankee soldier. "How about you, Soldier? Wet your whistle?"

The guard glanced around quickly and then got up from his chair. He walked over to us and took a swig from the proffered flask. He handed it back to Elwood and said, "Why thank you, Elwood!" which surprised me greatly. But then I remembered that Elwood had made this trip many times before.

The guard sat down next to us. Up close, he was much older than I had first realized, but I reckoned the Yankees used their younger men for the fighting, not guarding prisoners. He looked at me curiously as he extended his hand. "William Carr."

"Teddy Miller," I said, shaking his hand.

The guard accepted the flask again and took a long swallow before handing it back to Elwood. "Mother's milk," he said with a sigh.

Elwood glanced around and asked, "Where is the pub and bawdy house you promised me during my last visit? I see nothing but the same sand and scrawny palmetto bushes."

The guard laughed. "If you look carefully, you will see the same bad food and bad water too. I sometimes wonder if they built this place to punish the prisoners or the guards." The guard stood up, groaning at the effort, and said, "I best get back to my post. Thank you kindly for the drink, Elwood."

Elwood tipped his hat at the guard and said, "Always good to see you, William." Then, almost as an afterthought, Elwood said, "If you are of a mind, William, meet us at the north dock after your watch ends and we will have a wee dram to help us sleep."

"Why thank you, Elwood, I believe I will! My watch ends at 8 o'clock, if that is agreeable."

"8 o'clock it is."

The heat did not seem to abate even as the sun continued to sink on the horizon. Elwood and I sought shade in the shadow of the *Lucille* and wiped our brows with our bandanas, filthy with coal dust. "And I used to complain about Atlanta summers," Elwood said, shaking his head. "Now, at least, I have lost all my fear of hell, as this place must surely be worse." I ignored Elwood's complaining and said, "I want to thank you again, Elwood, for helping me. If we are caught, we may find ourselves on the inside of this fort looking out. Or worse."

Elwood shrugged his shoulders. "Truth be told, I am grateful to you, Teddy. You have added a little excitement to my life." I understood how Elwood felt. Key West, although a part of Florida and the Confederacy, was fully under Union control and separated from the rest of the state by a naval blockade. Time moved slowly as we waited for some conclusion to the War.

"Do you think we can get any information from him? William, I mean?"

Elwood shrugged. "They keep the fort as dry as a vicar's garden party, and William does love his whiskey." Elwood patted the pocket where his flask was kept. "He has an incentive to keep the conversation going."

Around 8 p.m., Elwood and I made our way past the fort and over to the north coal dock. There was little activity there and we found a place to sit on the wharf, our feet dangling over the edge of the black, creosote-treated wood. There were no prisoners about, and I reckoned they were locked up for the night. The light was nearly gone when William Carr ambled up to us and sat down. "Another day in Paradise," he said.

Elwood took out his flask and passed it to me, then William. William took a greedy swallow, then a second, and passed it back. "Thank you again, Elwood."

I took a second to study the guard. I sensed immediately that he was no bumpkin. Best to stick as close to the truth as possible, I thought.

After another round, I said to the guard, "William, I would like to ask you a question about one of your prisoners."

The guard tensed and was instantly alert and I knew I had been right in my assessment of him. He got to his feet and started to walk away. "I am disappointed, Elwood, that you and your young friend think I can be bribed by a few sips of whiskey."

"Please, William, wait! It is not what you think," I said.

The guard stopped and turned back towards me. "Then tell me what I should think. But know that one wrong word and I will march you both up to the fort and into a cell."

"It is my Daddy," I said. "He was sent here to serve 30 years at hard labor. I have sent letter after letter to him, but I have heard nothing back in return."

The guard seemed to be evaluating me. "You are telling me the truth?"

"I only want to know if he is alright."

The guard sat back down and reached for the flask. "What is his name?"

"Eli Miller."

The guard thought for a moment and then shook his head. "I never heard of him."

"But you must have!" I persisted.

The guard said, "I wish I could help you, Teddy, but there are nearly 900 prisoners here, both military and political. I do not even know all of the guards."

I felt my heart sink. "Well, William, I thank you for your frankness," I said. I felt deflated.

I could feel the guard watching me. He must have felt some pity for me because he said, "I will tell you what I can do. My friend works for the Commandant, and he may be able to check the files for you. I will ask him in the morning."

"We leave on the tide tomorrow, William, will you be at the wharf?"

"I will be there before you sail. Now, Elwood, pass that flask of yours."

The guard was as good as his word. No more than a few minutes before we were to leave, I saw William walking down the wharf towards us. I jumped over the gunnel and ran to meet him. But before I could say anything, William stopped and looked me in the eyes. "I am sorry, Teddy."

I felt a cold chill run down my spine and my legs nearly buckled. "What did you learn, William?"

"Your Daddy is dead, Teddy. He died within 2 weeks of reaching here. Dysentery, they say."

CHAPTER 2

Into the Future

Dearest Jed,

It is with a heavy heart that I write to tell you that Daddy died in Fort Jefferson prison. They tell me it was dysentery and that he passed away within 2 weeks of his arrival.

I met with Daddy briefly when he was on his way from Key West to Fort Jefferson. I want you to know that he asked about you and expressed his love and devotion.

You are always in my prayers and it is my fervent hope that we may someday reconcile.

God be with you.

Your loving brother,

Teddy

Key West, Florida

I remember little of the trip back to Key West. Elwood tried to comfort me, but I was inconsolable. "I have lost him forever!" I said.

Elwood gently touched my arm. "He knew you loved him, Teddy. I am sure that was of great comfort to him. It should be of comfort to you now."

"Oh, Elwood, I am afraid he did not. There are things you do not know about me, things that I did, things that he never forgave me for." I took a deep breath as a witch's brew of emotions flooded over me: I was desolate at the thought of never speaking to my father again, heartbroken that I would never have his forgiveness and angry at everyone and everything. Guilt gnawed at my innards.

Elwood squeezed my arm and said softly, "You are still but a boy, Teddy. What is it you could have done to warrant such guilt?"

"People died because of me. Even my own brother Jed has disowned me."

Elwood and I sat silently for a long time. Finally, he said, "Let me tell you what I have learned about guilt, Teddy. It is the one thing about which I may properly be called an expert." Elwood pulled out his flask and took a long drink. "Guilt!" he said. "I have fought it, wallowed in it and even bragged about it. But if I am honest, I have also let it become a shield against self-knowledge and change. It is a wonderful excuse to do nothing." Elwood passed me the flask. "The past is best left in the past. Do not squander your future by letting it consume you."

After I learned about my father's death, I had no choice but to let go of my obsession to rescue him and somehow recover his affection. I gradually began to think about the future again. I had looked backward for so long, dwelling on things done and undone, that the world had become a colorless place where joy and happiness were strangers to me. I needed to live again. I needed to feel the simple joy of being alive.

I thought about the Shenandoah Valley. I thought about my brother and my friends. And I dreamt about a girl named Eugenie. I put pen to paper and began to write:

Dear Miss Martin,

I beg of you that when you check the signature at the bottom of this letter you do not immediately discard it, but rather you give me even the briefest moment of your attention. I know that I have done nothing to be deserving of such a gift, but perhaps you will take pity on a man whose heart now rests in your tender hands.

I cannot presume that you remember me from our brief meeting in June of last year. But it is seared into my heart, and I can see it as clearly as if it were yesterday: I had come to your farm seeking water one evening when you surprised me at the well. Your face was hidden behind the glare of a lantern, but the sound of your voice stirred my heart, full as it was of promise for moments yet to come. And then, when I saw your face, I was lost. Even the greatest painters could not have envisaged a greater beauty than yours, from the soft curls that framed your face to your dazzling blue eyes. Not a day goes by that I do not see your face the moment before I fall asleep and the moment after I awaken; and I hear your voice in every breeze that rustles the treetops.

Please let me know by return post if I may continue to write to you. I do not know if I shall be able to breathe again until I receive your answer.
Your servant,
Teddy Miller
Key West, Florida

But I did not possess the courage to post the letter to Eugenie. I simply could not bear one more rejection in my life. I crumbled up the letter and threw it in the trash.

I dedicated myself to my regular employment at the *Happy Cork*. I worked nearly around the clock, only snatching an hour or two's sleep here and there. It was exhausting and invigorating at the same time; at long last, I felt like I was at least taking some action in preparation for the next stage of my life. Every night I would take the pennies I had made that day and add them to a jar I kept hidden under my bedroom floor.

While I labored in Key West, battles great and small were won and lost by both the North and the South. There seemed no clear certainty which side would ultimately prevail. The Union had endless supplies of soldiers and matériel, but their will to continue the fight was being tested; the Confederates, on the other hand, had the will to fight but only dwindling resources. In any case, the casualties kept accumulating, filling the newspaper pages day after day.

CHAPTER 3

Meet Quinn MacBrùn

I need a hero, I'm holding out for a hero 'till the end of the night. He's gotta be strong and he's gotta be fast. And he's gotta be fresh from the fight. I need a hero, I'm holding out for a hero 'till the morning light. He's gotta be sure and it's gotta be soon. And he's gotta be larger than life, larger than life. — Bonnie Tyler

One day in late October, it was a quiet evening at the Happy Cork. There was little conversation between our regulars as most sought oblivion in sour silence at the bar and rickety tables. But sometime around midnight, the front door was flung open with hurricane-like force. Every head turned to watch a tall, redheaded man in a burgundy jacket burst through the doorway. "Good evening, Gents!" he said in a booming voice with a thick brogue. "Drinks are on me!"

A startled silence came over the bar. Then, all at once, a great cheer went up. The men raised their mugs and shot glasses in a toast to the generous stranger.

"My name,' he said, "is Captain Quinn MacBrùn."

"Greetings, Cap'n!" came the reply as mugs and glasses were

again lifted in tribute.

Captain MacBrùn slapped two $20 double-eagle gold pieces on the bar. Henry stared at them transfixed. I suspected you could buy the whole bar for far less. "What is your name, bartender? Henry, you say? Well, Henry, keep the drinks flowing until you run out of spirits or cash."

Henry grabbed the gold coins and stuffed them in his apron pocket. "Aye, Cap'n," he said. Then to me, "Best get some more rum from the back, Teddy." Henry, rushed from bar to table to bar again, refilling the now free drinks as fast as they emptied. Given the clientele of the *Happy Cork*, that was at a remarkable rate.

Captain MacBrùn wandered around the bar, scanning the patrons like a housewife searching out the best fruit at a market. He made one circuit, then another and announced, "I am master of the good ship *Quicksilver*, the fastest side-wheeler this side of Glasgow, and I am..."

"Never heard of her," interrupted a voice from the back of the bar. A hush went over the patrons. To keep the free drinks coming, they would not have questioned the captain if he declared himself to be the Pharaoh of Egypt. They squinted in the dim oil light to see who was attempting to kill the golden goose. "Who said that?" demanded the captain.

A sailor I knew only as 'Ben' stood up and crossed his arms. "I did," he said.

Captain MacBrùn walked up to him, looked him in the eye, and nodded. "I like a man who speaks his mind. Are you an Ordinary or Able seaman?"

"Able, Cap'n, as I have crewed both merchant and military vessels in my time."

"How well do you know the Florida straits? The coastal waters?"

"Like I know every bawdy house between Baltimore and Key West," he answered.

The captain laughed. "Then hear me out, sailor. I may have something of interest to you." The captain walked back to the bar. "As I was saying, I am master of the *Quicksilver*, and I am looking for Able and Ordinary sailors to sign on for a short cruise. I will pay 2 double eagles to every Ordinary Seamen upon completion of the round trip, and 4 double eagles to every Able.

The bar became so quiet you could hear the beer foaming in the mugs. "That cannot be," someone whispered. "Surely you are joking with us, Cap'n," said another. "No one pays a sailor that much money," said a third. Ben chimed in: "He is a blockade runner, you idiots! That is not so much money if you are rotting in a Yankee prison."

The men looked at the captain. "Is that true?" one asked.

The captain shrugged. "Call me what you will. I am simply a Southern patriot who trades southern cotton or salt for weapons and other matériel in Nassau. The fact that I, and my crew, are well-compensated for this work is understandable as there is some risk." The captain downed a mug of ale in a single, long swallow. "Although to be fair," he continued, "the risk is mostly mitigated by two factors: one, the *Quicksilver* can run at nearly 15 knots, far faster than most of the Yankee blockaders; and two, it is I who skippers the *Quicksilver*."

The captain put down his mug, leaned against the bar, and folded his arms across his chest. "Well," he asked, "who wants to join me?" There was a long moment of silence, then Ben stood up again. "Ah, what the hell. Count me in, Cap'n." Captain MacBrùn reached into his jacket pocket and pulled out a notebook and a pencil. "Full name?" he asked. Then, "Common or Able?" And so it went until he had 3 new crew members signed up. He gave each of them a single gold eagle worth $10. "For expenses," he said. He told them to meet him at a bar called "*Marye's*' in Boot Key on November 23 when an overhaul on the *Quicksilver* was scheduled to be completed.

As the Captain reached for his coat and prepared to leave, I asked him if he had room for one more. He looked me up and down, then shook his head. "I have no room nor time for a Landman," he said.

"I have some experience as a sailor, Cap'n. I crewed a supply ship from Baltimore to Key West and manned a sloop delivering supplies to Fort Jefferson in the Dry Tortugas. You will find me very dependable." I looked at Henry, "Is that not true, Henry?" Henry nodded his head. "That is true, Cap'n. I would hate to see him go."

The captain cocked his head at me and then reached again for his notebook. Before he could ask me, I said, "Theodore Miller, Common."

CHAPTER 4

One Last Goodbye

I've never forgotten him. Dare I say I miss him? I do. I miss him. I still see him in my dreams. They are nightmares mostly, but nightmares tinged with love. Such is the strangeness of the human heart. I still cannot understand how he could abandon me so unceremoniously, without any sort of goodbye, without looking back even once. The pain is like an axe that chops my heart. — Yann Martel

I spent the next few days getting my affairs in order. Because my life was uncomplicated, that did not require a great amount of time or effort. But before I departed Key West for Boot Key, I had some other unfinished business to attend to. As I had no idea when or if I would return to Key West again, I was determined to visit my father's grave before I left.

I asked around Key West where the prisoners who died at Fort Jefferson were buried. I was told by a former guard that if a dead prisoner's body was not claimed by a relative, it would be buried in a common, unmarked grave on Bird Key. I knew that Bird Key was located a few miles east of Fort Jefferson but still nearly 70 miles from Key West.

Getting to Bird Key was not the issue it might have been under normal circumstances. I used some of my 'expense' money to hire a salt-trader named Ernesto Álvarez to take me there a day later his sloop. Captain Álvarez was a handsome man, perhaps ten-years older than me, with dark curly hair and a bright smile. His eyes nearly jumped out of his head when he saw the hard cash I was carrying. "Nine to twelve hours out, depending on the breeze," he said, "and nine to twelve back. And we will need to spend the night at that God-forsaken place. I will not test the shoals in the dark." He looked at me and smiled: "$5 should cover it."

I smiled back at him. "I am not looking to buy your boat, Cap'n. Three dollars and you provide the food and water." When he hesitated, I said, "Three gold coins, no Confederate script." He smiled again: "Done!"

The next day, I arrived early at the slip where Captain Álvarez's sloop *Marisol* was moored. She had a single mast with one headsail in front of the mast and one mainsail aft. This was called a 'fore-and-aft rig' and could be configured for speed or ease of handling. Captain Álvarez had clearly gone for ease of handling as the *Marisol* had triangular sails fore and aft (called a 'Bermuda rig'), making the vessel so easy to sail that one person could do it alone if necessary. She was clearly a workhorse, not very pretty, but she looked seaworthy.

I got to know Captain Álvarez and his crew of one as we made our way slowly to Bird Key. Ernesto, as he preferred to be called, explained that they were both Cuban immigrants who had left their country because there was great unrest, and a revolution was simmering. He had only the slightest trace of an accent. "When the revolution comes, many landowners will lose their property and their fortunes. Rodrigo and I," he said, indicating the crewman manning the helm, "borrowed money from our families and bought this sloop to seek our fortune here. When we are established, we will bring our families here to be with us."

When I complimented his flawless English, Ernesto attributed it to his mother, who had been born in the United States. "My mother passed away 10 years ago, God rest her soul. She always insisted that both Spanish and English be spoken in our home. And she always had the latest books shipped in from England, which she would read to me in the evening when I was young: books by Hawthorne and Melville and poets like Whitman, Byron and Browning."

"We have a lot in common," I said. "My Daddy loved to read. He believed that everything you need to know about life you can learn from the Bible and Shakespeare." A memory of the evenings my brother and I spent sitting around the fireplace listening to Daddy read suddenly popped into my mind, and a great sadness threatened to overcome me. But I shook it off and said, "I met Walt Whitman once."

Ernesto looked at me with an expression of pure awe. I thought he might ask to touch the hand that had shaken Whitman's. "Really? When?"

"Not even a year ago. He would come to a hospital in Washington City to visit the soldiers. He would bring sweets, tell stories, and kiss every soldier good-bye when he left. The soldiers loved him."

"You were a soldier?"

"No, but I had been injured and I was imposed upon the Yankee doctors."

Ernesto waited expectantly for more of the story, but when I said nothing, he seemed to sense that I did not wish to say more. He asked, "But you are well, Teddy?"

"I am well."

"Then that is all that matters." He smiled brightly at me, "Let us discuss Dickens!"

And so, we passed the time pleasantly, discussing literature as the *Marisol* made her way to Bird Key. But as the hours passed, my emotions continued to build, both apprehension and anticipation growing in equal measure.

The sky was a perfect blue and the breeze moved us along at a good clip; 'plain sailing,' as a sailor would say.

We were nearly upon her before we saw Bird Key rise up out of the sea. No part of the island appeared to have an elevation of more than 3 or 4 feet. In size, it could not have been more than 2 acres as I could easily see the length and breadth of it. I saw no outbuildings. The only manmade structure I could discern was a rickety looking pier on the south side of the island.

Ernesto tacked the *Marisol* alongside the pier and Rodrigo jumped off to secure the lines. The sun was lowering and that made the heat somewhat bearable as there was no shade anywhere. I saw nothing on the island except small cacti and a few scraggly bushes.

"Rodrigo and I will catch some dinner while you visit the island," Ernesto said. "Meet us back at the boat when you are finished."

"Do you not want to set up camp on the island?" I asked.

Ernesto crossed himself saying, "*Este es un lugar malvado, un lugar de almas perdidas!* This is an evil place, a place of lost souls! We will not set foot upon it. We will eat and sleep on the *Marisol*." I was surprised that Ernesto, for all his sophistication, was so superstitious. But he was a sailor, after all.

I picked my way carefully down the wobbly pier towards the sand beach, which was blindingly white in the tropical sun. I walked towards the center of the island, making my way between the cacti and bushes. The nearly constant wind had left the sand looking almost manicured, as if someone had raked the entire island that morning. I found no signs of a grave. The only objects I saw that could conceivably mark a mass grave were three stones. They did not look natural to the island, and I suspected they were ballast stones. They seemed to mark three corners of a plot around 100' by 50'. I do not know if there had ever been a fourth stone. I looked for writing on the stones but found none. If there ever had been any inscriptions, they had long ago been sandblasted off by the wind.

But I had found my father. I could feel him. I knelt on the sand. "Oh, Daddy," I cried aloud. Tears sprang from my eyes and sobs wracked my body. I looked around at the barren waste and thought about our beautiful Shenandoah Valley in Virginia. I remembered how much my father had loved it: 'When I first lay eyes upon it,' he would say, 'I thought this must be the land of milk and honey that God had promised the Israelites.' From that to this, I thought. From that to this desolate place.

I knelt there for a long time, thinking about my father. I thought about the home he had made for my brother and me. I thought about the evenings we had spent sitting in front of the fire while he read to us. And I thought about his gentle smile and seemingly endless patience. But I also thought about the tragedies that had befallen my brother and I since the Union Army had burnt our farm during the Battle of New Market. Anger and resentment began to build in me, pushing aside the grief that constricted my soul.

I stood up and took several deep breaths to try and calm myself, but I could taste the bile on my tongue. "I never had a chance to ask you, Daddy, about the day the battle began. Why did you leave us alone that day? Did you not know what was happening? I was only a boy, Daddy, and I did not know what to do!" I received no answer beyond the sounds of the distant, gentle lapping of the sea against the shore and the crying of the seabirds that whirled across the sky. "Were you a Confederate spy like the Yankees claimed? Is that the answer?"

My legs grew week and I knelt once again on the sand. "Was the cause you chose greater than your own sons?" I cried. I covered my face with my hands and sobbed.

When the sun had fully set, I stood and wiped the tears from my eyes. "I am leaving the Keys, Daddy. I do not know that I will ever be back again. I hope you know how much I loved you." I had walked only a short way back towards the *Marisol* when I stopped and turned around. "I cannot say I am sorry anymore, Daddy. If I had it to do all over again, I would still do all I did to save you from the hangman. There could never be a cost too great."

CHAPTER 5

Leaving Key West

And the danger is that in this move toward new horizons and far directions, that I may lose what I have now, and not find anything except loneliness. — Sylvia Plath

T he Happy Cork had closed for the night and Henry sat watching me place chairs on the tables and sweep the floor. "I am sorry to see you go, Teddy."

I stopped my work and smiled at him. "I hope you know how grateful I am to you, Henry. You gave me work and a place to stay when no one else would. I owe you more than I could ever repay."

Henry shrugged off my gratitude. "You are a good man. I have never been disappointed with your work." He hesitated for a moment and then added, "This job will always be here for you if you ever need it."

"Thank you, Henry. But the time has come for me to make my way home."

Henry hobbled over to me on his crutch and gave me a huge bearhug. By the time he let me go, I had nearly passed out from lack of air. As he stepped back, I swear I saw a tear in the corner of his eye. I had only seen Henry cry once, and that was when he dropped a bottle of premium rum. I was deeply touched and almost cried myself.

Henry turned quickly away and made his way back to the bar. "God go with you, Teddy," he said over his shoulder.

The next morning, I packed my meager belongings in an old seabag. When I had finished, I reached under the floorboards where I had hidden my money and pulled out an oily package tied with a rawhide strip. As I untied and opened it, the smell of gun oil filled the air. I carefully lifted out a Colt .44-caliber 'Army' Model revolver. I inspected it for rust and found none. Satisfied, I rewrapped the pistol and shoved it to the bottom of my seabag.

I looked around for anything I might have forgotten and then walked out of the *Happy Cork* forever.

As a crow flies, Boot Key is about 50 miles from Key West. I could have sailed directly there, but I still had the better part of two weeks left before I was to meet Captain MacBrùn at *Marye's Bar*. I therefore determined to lallygag my way along, hopping from island to island by whatever means available.

With my seabag slung across my shoulder, I walked past some brightly painted little cottages on the outskirts of Key West. The road was unpaved and in ill repair, and it became deeply rutted as I made my way further out of town. Soon it disappeared into a narrow trail used only by fishermen and cows.

When I reached the coast, I walked along the shore until I found a small marina with several fishing boats. There, I negotiated for a ride to Boca Chica Key. I also gave a boy 2 pennies for the straw hat he was wearing. The sun, even in late fall, was brutal.

It was less than 10 miles from Key West to Boca Chica, and the fisherman who dropped me off could not understand why I even wanted to stop there. "Nothin' but salt marshes and mangrove trees," he said. "And mosquitos as well as biting midges, biting flies, thrips, no-see'ums and every other creature that God created for no other purpose than to annoy mankind."

We landed on a coral-strewn beach ringed by skeleton-like, dead mangrove trees. I followed a trail inland which eventually led to a small clearing with a ramshackle looking cabin. The cabin appeared to be constructed of flotsam and jetsam found on the island's beaches. There were boards of all shapes and sizes attached somewhat haphazardly to make the walls. There was even a weathered sign for a bar in Key West that served as a shutter for one of the windows. The roof was scrap tin.

When I walked into the yard, I called 'Ahoy!' to announce my presence. After a moment, a voice responded from within the cabin, "Who goes there?"

"My name is Teddy Miller. I am making my way up the Keys."

A tall man walked out the door. He was wiping his hands on a bright, flowered apron while he eyed me curiously. "Why did you not simply sail to the mainland?"

"I have a job waiting for me on Boot Key. But I have some time on my hands, so I reckoned I would explore."

The tall man laughed. "Like Kit Carson and John Wesley Powell, that kind of explorer? Well, you are a little late, Son, as I have been 'exploring' this little corner of paradise since 1843."

I laughed back. "Nothing that grand, I can assure you. Just a chance to see something new as I do not know if I will ever return to the Keys."

"Well, come inside boy, afore the sun melts your brain."

Inside, the cabin was surprisingly cool. It was neat and orderly with comfortable-looking furniture. The tall man had obviously been sweeping the floor as a straw broom leaned against a large table in the kitchen. When he saw me glance at the broom, he said, "Women's' work, I know, but my missus is out catching our dinner. A little sweeping is a fair trade, I think, for some time out of the sun." He reached over and shook my hand. "Henry Geiger," he said.

"Nice to meet you, Henry." Henry offered me some cool water and we sat down at the wooden table. "What do you think of the Keys so far, young explorer?" he asked.

"Beautiful," I said. "I am most impressed by the variety of wildlife, from the alligators and snakes to the little white-tailed deer. And some of the larger islands are so lush, they appear almost Eden-like."

That made Henry laugh again. "Eden-like? Well, this is the land of plenty... plenty of mosquitos!" It was an old joke that I had heard told many times before in Key West, but it made Henry slap his knees with merriment at his telling.

I sipped at my water and studied Henry. He had bright blue eyes that stood in sharp contrast to his deeply tanned skin. His hair was neatly trimmed and completely white, although he did not appear to be more than 50 years old. He was a far cry from the 'wild men' I had been led to expect in the Keys by the Key Westers. He seemed in no hurry to return to his sweeping, so I asked, "What brought you to settle here?"

Henry shrugged. "My missus and me, we used to live in Key West, where I made a living working with the wreckers who salvaged the shipwrecks on the reefs. We had two sons. When they growed-up and moved away, the missus and me determined to have no more to do with Key West. We had tired of the debauchery and the drunks relieving themselves in our little garden. When we heard about land being available here, we moved over. Never regretted it a'tall."

At that moment, a woman dressed in a man's shirt and trousers walked in through the front door of the cabin. She was carrying a large fish with yellow fins that she plopped on the table. "Henry Geiger," she said, "what excuse have you found this time to keep from cleaning the house?"

Henry jumped up from the table and gave his wife a kiss on the cheek. "This here is Teddy Miller, Lovey. He is exploring his way through the keys and landed on our doorstep no more'n 30 minutes ago. Teddy, this is my wife Lovey."

I rose to my feet and shook her hand. Her grip was dry and strong. Unlike her husband, Lovey's hair was a dark auburn which she wore tied loosely in a bun at the back of her head. She too was deeply tanned. "I caught a lovely fish today and it is more than enough for just Henry and me. Will you join us for dinner tonight, Mr. Miller?"

"Please call me Teddy," I said. "And I would very much like to join you for dinner."

I learned that the fish was called a 'yellow-fin tuna.' Henry took it outside and cleaned it, then cut it into several thick steaks rather than filets. Lovey seared the steaks in a cast iron skillet in butter, salt, and lemon juice from a tree that grew in the yard. She served them slightly rare, and they were unlike any fish I had ever had before. Surely, the best restaurants in Key West could not have prepared it better. Lovey beamed at me when I complimented her cooking.

Lovey sent Henry and me out onto the front porch while she cleaned up the kitchen. "Ah, Teddy," he said, "you know your way to a woman's heart! Lovey will remember your compliments for months to come." Henry pulled out a clay pipe, filled it with tobacco, and took a deep draw. The sweet smell of tobacco complimented the evening air already fragrant with tropical scents. I leaned back in an old rocker and felt a great contentment. I began to understand why Henry and Lovey loved it here, even as I smacked a mosquito off my cheek.

"How many people do you reckon live in the keys, Henry?" I asked.

Henry scratched at his cheek. "Other than Key West? Well, let us see: Most every major island in the lower keys is occupied. No more'n 1 or 2 families sometimes, but occupied, nonetheless. Besides Lovey and me, one other family of 4 lives on this key. Mebbe 19 more on Cudjoe, one or two on Sugarloaf, twenty-some on Vaca. Also, twelve or thirteen hardy souls on Indian Key last time I was there. Half is farmers, half is seamen."

Lovey came out on the front porch and sat on Henry's knee. "What are you boys talkin' about?" she asked. Henry patted her leg. "Just tellin' Teddy here about the number of people living here in the lower keys. I ain't familiar enough with the middle and upper keys to make a guess, though I hear more and more Bahamians is comin' to settle them. Good sailors, them, and they know how to farm this type of soil as well."

We chatted throughout the evening. Henry and Lovey seemed to enjoy my company and I certainly enjoyed theirs. Finally, when none of us could keep our eyes fully open, we said goodnight. Henry and Lovey offered me their little barn for the night which I gladly accepted. With a full belly and fragrant hay for a pillow, I slept like a baby.

The next morning, Henry offered to take me to Sugar Loaf Key, the next stop on my trip. I tried to pay him, but he refused any money. Lovey gave me a sandwich wrapped in waxed paper and made sure I had fresh water in my canteen.

We made our way on choppy seas with a clear sky of the brightest blue I have ever seen. Henry's little sailboat heeled over under a stiff breeze, and we made the 5-mile trip in less than an hour.

CHAPTER 6

Life and Death in the Keys

Death is beautiful when seen to be a law, and not an accident. It is as common as life. --Henry David Thoreau

I had planned the remainder of my trek across the keys based on the information Henry Geiger had given me. I reckoned that by sticking to the populated islands, I was more likely to find sustenance as well as a ride to the next key.

I caught rides between the islands, or sometimes clusters of islands, on about anything that floated. For a few pennies, or sometimes for free, local fishermen and traders would take me from one settlement to another a few islands northeastward. I rode in everything from flat-bottomed rowboats to small sloops and fishing boats. In this way, I traveled from Sugarloaf to Cudjoe and finally to Big Pine Key.

I must have passed hundreds of islands, most small, desert-like, and uninhabited except by the ubiquitous seabirds; others were large and lush. As I had told Henry Geiger, I was deeply affected by the beauty of it all. When our boat would startle some birds on an island, they would rise almost as one and fill the sky with color and motion.

When at last I came to Big Pine Key, I was within a week of my appointment with Captain MacBrùn on Boot Key. The fisherman with whom I had caught a ride, dropped me off on a white, sandy beach with the high-tide level marked by a long line of dried seaweed. Huge coconut palms shaded the edge of the beach.

As was my habit, I walked along the shoreline looking for a path headed inland. When I rounded a bend, I saw two dark-skinned men and a boy in wooden canoes. One man had white hair and there was a small boy with him, perhaps 5 or 6, certainly no older. The second man appeared much younger. They were on opposite sides of what looked like a large bed of seagrass, separated from each other by several hundred yards. The seawater was so clear that the boats appeared to be floating in air.

I found a shady spot under a tall palm tree and sat watching the men and boy. They were fishing with round nets, weighted on the perimeter, which I knew to be 'cast nets.' Fishermen would use these nets to catch baitfish such as sardines, pigfish, and glass minnows. The baitfish would then be used to catch larger fish.

I marveled at the men's efficiency. I watched the old man cast the net and immediately pull it in, all in one fluid motion. Then he emptied the net on the canoe floor, and the boy threw out what was not useful to them and placed the rest in a container of some kind. Then they repeated the process.

I was taking a sip of water when I saw the old man, who was in the canoe closest to me, slip as he cast the net. His head hit the gunnel of the canoe so hard that I could hear it from 200 yards away. I watched as the canoe capsized and the old man tumbled into the sea, taking the child with him.

I stood up and yelled for the younger fisherman. When he

turned to look at me, I pointed in the direction of the older man's canoe and took off running down the beach in the direction of the capsized boat. When I was adjacent to the canoe on the beach, I was still at least 50 yards from it. I threw myself into the sea and swam towards the canoe. The water was blood warm.

I am not a strong nor experienced swimmer, but I still made it to the overturned canoe before the other fisherman arrived. I looked over my shoulder and saw him paddling madly towards us, but he was still 100 yards away. I saw no one on the surface of the water. Exhausted already, I took a deep breath and dove beneath the surface. I saw the old man sinking to the bottom while the young boy was struggling to reach the surface. I grabbed the boy's shoulder and started to pull him up to the surface. But his skin was slick from the seawater, and I lost my grip. He immediately began to sink. My lungs were burning from lack of air as I struggled to get to him. Just when I thought we would both drown, I finally reached him and somehow pulled him to the surface. We both gasped for air and the boy went into full panic. He wrapped his arms around my neck, choking me, and I could barely keep us both above the surface of the water. I swallowed water with every breath I took. Suddenly, a pair of strong arms grabbed the boy from around my neck. The second fisherman had arrived, and I gratefully grabbed on to the gunnel of his canoe for support. "¿Mi tío? My Uncle?" he asked. I had no breath with which to speak so I pointed beneath the overturned canoe.

The fisherman slipped over the side of his canoe and into the water carefully so as not to capsize it, then dove beneath the surface. He was under so long that I feared he may have drowned too. But he finally broke the surface with his arm around the chest of his uncle, who was clearly dead.

The younger man let out a howl of pain and loss. Then, together, we managed to get the old man's body into the canoe. The younger man paddled us to the beach while I held onto the gunnel. I sprawled on the beach gasping for breath as the younger man carried the old man to a spot above high tide and lay him in the shade.

When I recovered my breath, I walked up to the younger man. He was sitting next the body while holding the boy tightly to his chest. They were both trembling and tears were running down the man's face. He pulled the boy closer and then touched my arm: "Thank you," he said, sobbing, "for saving my boy." I did not know how to answer, so I simply nodded and sat down next the man and his son. We sat in silence for a long time.

When the man seemed to have regained his composure, I asked, "Would you like me to help you take your uncle home?"

The man shook his head. "We may not touch him again, " he answered. "That is our custom."

We sat silently in the shade again for a little while until the fisherman asked me if I had a gun with me. When I said I had an old pistol in my seabag, he asked if he could borrow it. I pulled it out, loaded it and carefully handed it to him. He took the pistol, stepped away from us, and fired it into the sky as fast as he could cock and pull the trigger. When it was empty, he handed it back to me and sat back down. "They will be here soon," he said. "We all heard the screech owl, the *'stikini,'* last night. We knew someone was going to die. They will be expecting shots to announce a death." Then, almost to himself, "I never expected it to be my *tío*."

As we waited for whomever was coming, the fisherman and I introduced ourselves. His name was Amos Morgan Semissee and his son was Billy. He was, he said, a 'Black Seminole,' an escaped slave, who had taken refuge with the Seminole Indians in Florida after he escaped from a Georgia plantation. "Although I allied myself to the Seminole, and even took a Seminole wife, I was still a slave in their eyes. They called me a 'maroon,' a word meaning 'fugitive'. I was free to fish or farm as I saw fit, but the Seminoles would take part of it every year as payment for their protection." He shrugged his shoulders. "A master is still a master, and a slave is still a slave," he said. "So, I packed my family up and moved here."

Amos glanced over at the body of his uncle and sighed deeply. "My *tío* was widowed and lived alone. But he was beloved by our village for his piety and generosity and will be greatly missed. He was a special favorite of my son, who he would bounce on his knee and tell ridiculous stories to. Billy would laugh until tears ran down his cheeks." He smiled slightly at the memory. "Today, he was teaching Billy to fish as he had taught me." Tears suddenly sprang from his eyes again and he crossed himself. "I came so close to losing my son today!"

CHAPTER 7

Death and the Black Seminoles

We who are left behind watch you on your way. The long prison of the years unlocks its iron doors; go free now, into the beautiful land. Forgive us who suffer in this clouded world. Guide us and wait for us, as we wait for you. We will meet again. We will meet again. — William Nicholson

P eople began arriving by canoes, rowboats, and fishing boats. Soon there were some 10-12 people milling around, and I noticed that none approached or touched the body. The old man lay as Amos had left him on the edge of the beach. Finally, an old woman arrived in a flat-bottomed boat rowed by a young man. She was as black as ebon, her skin sunburned to a leather-like appearance. She wore a long denim skirt with a brightly flowered blouse. Her hair was streaked with grey and white, and I could not even guess at her age. She carried a patterned blanket with her. She was obviously of some importance as the crowd parted for her as she made her way to the body.

When she reached the old man, she crossed herself and knelt beside his body. She placed her hand on his forehead, lowered her head, and prayed softly for several minutes. When she had finished, the young man helped her to her feet, and she covered the old man with the blanket. Why she had the right to touch the corpse when others did not, I did not know. She turned towards the crowd of people that had surrounded her and said, "Construct a litter to move his body to my canoe. I will select 4 bearers to carry it." She scanned the crowd and pointed to three men. Then, she turned and pointed at me. "Y tú," she said. "And you."

I was surprised. I turned to Amos, who was standing beside me, unsure of what to do. "It is an honor," he whispered to me, "in recognition of the bravery you showed when saving my son."

After the old man's body was placed on a litter, the three men and I carried him to the old woman's rowboat. When the body was placed in the boat, the woman shooed us away and the same young man as before took the oars.

I rode with Amos and Billy in their canoe to No Name Key, which was no more than 1 mile east-northeast of Big Pine. The little boy clung to his father's leg the entire trip. He never said a word.

The settlement on No Name Key was the largest I had yet seen in the lower keys. There appeared to be more than 20 homes, even though not all seemed to be occupied. We carried the old man's body to his home, a small wooden cabin near the center of the village and carried it inside. There, a fire was roaring in the fireplace although the outside temperature had to be nearly 90 degrees. Amos said that the fire would be allowed to burn out naturally before the old woman I had seen at the beach would prepare the body for burial.

I followed Amos to his house which was located not far from his uncle's. Amos said that the fire would burn all night and nothing more would be done until the morning. He invited me to eat with his family and then sleep in a hammock on the front porch. I readily accepted. We went inside for some shade and cool water.

Inside, Amos's wife named Amesta was crying hysterically, kissing the boy over and over again. When she saw me, she fell to her knees, wrapped her arms around my legs, and thanked me effusively for saving her son's life. She was speaking in a mixture of English, Spanish and a third language I did not recognize. But the meaning was clear.

After a few moments, Amos helped her to her feet, and she fell into his arms. "God was with us today, Amesta," he said. "He sent Teddy here to save our boy." Amesta smiled and seemed to calm somewhat as she wiped tears from her cheeks. She looked up into her husband's eyes: "I am so sorry about *Tío* Che-da-ka." Amos nodded but said nothing more.

Amesta was short and stocky with a round face and large, sparkling brown eyes. I thought her very pretty. She wore her hair wrapped with a bright scarf, which seemed to be a custom on the island as I had seen other women dressed the same. She prepared us a wonderful dinner which I enjoyed immensely. The mood was heavy, though, so there was little conversation.

After dinner, Amos and I took a walk around the small settlement. "There are 4 Maroon families here. There had been 2 more, but they left to find work in the other keys. There are a few white families and quite a few Bahamians." Amos gave me the names of different people whose homes we passed, showed me the village cistern, and pointed out other places of local interest. When the sun fell below the treetops, we made our way back to Amos' house again.

When Amos and his family went to sleep, I settled into the hammock. But I did not sleep well as I had terrible dreams. More than once, I woke up holding my breath and then gasping for air as I broke the surface of an imaginary sea.

After breakfast, Amos invited me to attend his uncle's funeral. He suggested that I change into whatever clean clothes I had with me, as that was their custom. Around 9

a.m., Amos and his family emerged from their house in what appeared to be their best clothes. We walked together the short distance to his uncle's house, where several people had already gathered. They, too, were dressed in what we back home would call their 'Sunday best.' More people began to arrive, and the yard began to fill up, but like the day before, no one went near the body in the cabin.

Amos whispered to me, "We wait for Señora Suc-car-see. She is the woman who took the body of my *tío* from the beach yesterday. Only she can touch a dead body." Curious, I asked, "Why does only she have this right? Is she a medicine woman?"

Amos shrugged. "She holds no special rank in the village. But she was chosen by God to deal with the dead. I do not know why. Perhaps she herself does not know why either. She just knows." It was a calling, I supposed, not unlike someone who joins the priesthood or becomes a doctor or nurse. They just know that was what they were meant to do.

Maybe a half-hour later, Señora Suc-car-see walked into the yard. She was accompanied by the same young man who had rowed her boat the day before. He was, I later learned, her nephew. The crowd parted and the Señora walked alone into the house without saying a word. Amos told me that she was preparing the body for burial. The corpse would be washed, and prayers said. If there were any live embers left in the fireplace, she would sprinkle them with water.

When the Señora was finished, she summoned some men to carry the body on a litter to a small family graveyard at the edge of the village. We all followed behind the litter, no one speaking. When we arrived at the little graveyard, a grave had already been prepared and the body was carefully placed in it. Four men carrying muskets stepped to the four corners of the grave. The man on the north side fired in the air first, then the man on the west fired, then the man on the south and, finally, the man on the east.

A woman walked over to the grave carrying a pile of freshly laundered clothes and some food and placed them carefully in the grave. A second woman carried a steaming hot cup of coffee which was also placed in the grave. Two men covered the body and offerings with what looked like Elm bark. Only then was the grave filled with dirt.

When the last shovel full of dirt went into the grave, everyone began clapping loudly, which startled me. They smiled brightly at each other. But I noticed that everyone stepped carefully around the edge of the grave. Amos told me not to step in any of the new dirt from the grave. "If you do," he said, "sickness will follow you right back to my house."

Several men quickly built a lean-to over the fresh grave and covered it with more Elm bark. It was, Amos said, to keep the rain from soaking into the newly turned earth. Then we returned to the uncle's cabin. This time, only the uncle's immediate family was allowed in. I saw smoke begin to rise from the chimney and knew they had relit the fire. What else they did, I did not see. But only a few minutes later, they invited everyone into the cabin where the kitchen table had been piled high with food and drink.

It was a true feast, which had been prepared by Amos's wife Amesta and a few neighbors. There was fresh game, including racoon and pig, fry bread, and a soup called *sofkee* which was made from a fermented lime- and lye-soaked corn gruel. It was all new and wonderful to me.

CHAPTER 8

Boot Key

We do not get to choose how we start out in life. We do not get to choose the day we are born or the family we are born into, what we are named at birth, what country we are born in, and we do not get to choose our ancestry. All these things are predetermined by a higher power. By the time you are old enough to start making decisions for yourself, a lot of things in your life are already in place. It's important, therefore, that you focus on the future, the only thing that you can change.
— Idowu Koyenikan

T he night of the funeral, I was again invited to eat with the Semissees. I had told Amos that I would leave right after the funeral, but he insisted that I stay with them one more night as they wanted to thank me again for saving Billy. I learned later that making dinner was a special concession to me; the Seminoles had no set meal schedule, no breakfast, lunch, or dinner. They would keep a pot of sofkee or a spit of wild game on the fire all day. People would eat when hungry.

The mood at the table was greatly improved from the night

before. Uncle Che-da-ka had been buried according to tradition and was fully provisioned—and presumably happy—and little Billy filled the house with laughter and life. We talked about many things, but I was especially curious about how Amos and Amesta had met and fallen in love. After all, they came from such different worlds. Amesta glanced at her husband and laughed. "He was the most arrogant man!" she said. "He would prance around the village as if there were no other men in the tribe. Everything about him seemed to say, 'Look at me!' The girls would all laugh at his bravado, but secretly they all hoped to catch his eye."

Amos put his arm around his wife and pulled her close. "You know I never had eyes for anyone but you." Amesta laughed, "Liar!" she said. "You followed Jennetta Mokoyike around like a lost puppy. It was only after she married someone else that you turned your attention to me."

Amos looked at me and pretended to be shocked. "Such a story! Do not believe her, Teddy. I lost my heart the first time I looked into her beautiful eyes, and she knows it."

Amesta smiled at her husband, and then said, "What about you, Teddy? Is there *una chica especial*, a special girl, in your life?

"There is," I said. I suddenly felt myself blush. It had just jumped out of me. I had never said it out loud before, never admitted it to anyone else. I had only a moment to wonder why that was so. Was it because I was afraid it was just a boy's foolish dream? But before I could think about it more, Amesta cocked her head at me and said, "Well, what is her name? Is she pretty? Where did you meet her?" Amos laughed and took his wife's hand in his own. "Give the boy a chance to answer, Amesta!"

"Her name is Eugenie," I answered. "And, yes, she is very pretty." I thought about how she had looked that night I had first seen her. "Yes," I said again, "she is very pretty," which made Amesta smile.

Once I started talking, I could not seem to stop. "When

I have earned enough money, I will return to Virginia and try and make amends with my family and neighbors. This is a promise I made to myself at my father's grave." Tears unexpectedly filled my eyes and I turned away from Amos and Amesta. I felt Amesta touch my hand.

"And if Eugenie will have me," I continued, "I have determined to marry her and make a new life for us both."

Amesta squeezed my hand. "That is a wonderful thing, Teddy! ¡*Debes estar muy emocionada*! You must be so excited!" she said. "Does she know you are going to ask her to marry you?"

I shook my head. "Not yet." I did not add that I was not even sure if she would remember me, let alone agree to see me again.

Over the course of the evening, I talked about my hopes and dreams and future plans. Amos and Amesta listened patiently to me and offered gentle suggestions here and there. There had been something so comfortable about sitting around a table with those wonderful people that it made me feel like I could trust them with my deepest hopes and fears. I eventually realized that what I was feeling was the love and acceptance of a family. So, even while I still mourned the loss of the family I had once known, I determined then and there to build a new one.

The next morning, I said goodbye to Amesta and Billy. There were many tears shed, not the least of which were mine. Billy held my hand and called me *Tío Teddy*, which affected me greatly. Amesta made me promise to stay safe, kissed me on the cheek, and hugged me.

Amos and I walked across the village and down to the shore where his wooden canoe was beached. We pushed it into the water and jumped aboard. Then Amos paddled us to Boot Key, almost 10 miles away. The trip took us a little over 3 hours.

I was shocked at my first view of Boot Key. There appeared to be little 'island' to it. All I could see was acres and acres of mangrove trees and only small hammocks of solid land. Amos assured me that there was a small marina on the north shore as we made our way around the island.

Amos called the mangrove trees 'walking trees.' I could see why: the trees had a tangle of roots above water that gave the impression they could walk away if they so desired. The water was saltwater, unlike the freshwater swamps I was used to, and shallow. It was also crystal clear, and I saw many fish, an occasional crocodile and quite a few sea turtles. Birds by the thousands took to the sky as we passed by. I recognized the pelicans, spoon bills and bald eagles, but there were many others whose names I did not know. The abundance and variety of life was staggering.

At last, we came to a rickety wooden pier with a small cluster of wooden buildings on stilts around it. One of the buildings had a lopsided sign on it that read 'Marye's Bar.' I saw only one ship tied to the pier, a 'scow schooner,' a shallow-draft ship with a square bow and 2 masts. She looked top-heavy and unstable.

I sat in the canoe staring at the ship for several moments. It was greatly in need of painting and seemed to be years past its prime. It was not the ship I had imagined Captain MacBrùn skippering.

When it could be put off no longer, Amos and I hugged and prepared to say our goodbyes. Part of me wanted to tell him to turn the canoe around and I would spend the rest of my life at peace in these beautiful islands; but the other part of me knew that my life, and my fate, lay waiting for me in Virginia. I told him how grateful I was for his generosity and friendship, but I had no words to express my gratitude for the sense of family he and Amesta had bestowed on me.

We made no empty promises to meet again, at least in this life. "You will always be in our prayers, Teddy. *Buena suerte y que Dios los proteja.* Good luck and God protect you."

I climbed out of the canoe and up onto the pier. I stood there, my heart heavy, watching Amos paddle away until he disappeared around the island. Then, I turned and walked into *Marye's Bar*. I had made it on the appointed day.

CHAPTER 9

Thirty Pieces of Silver

Very little would have been needed for the tears of Judas to be allied in the memory of mankind with those of Peter. He might have become a saint... — François Mauriac

Even given the low standards set by the sailors' bars in Key West, Marye's Bar was primitive. The bar itself was 3 boards lain across 2 sawhorses with an oil lamp sputtering at one end. Behind the bar, there were kegs of beer and ale and bottles of what appeared to be whisky and rum. There were no barstools, but I saw perhaps a half-dozen tables spread about the interior, several of which were occupied. There were two windows, but they had been covered by brown paper and they let in little daylight. In the dim light, I could make out no detail about the men sitting at the tables.

I stood at the opposite end of the bar from the bartender. He was a sour-looking man wearing a filthy apron. I called for the bartender, but he seemed to ignore me. Then, a familiar voice said from one of the tables behind me, "His name is Fritz, and he is deaf as a stone, Teddy. Wave your hands until he notices you."

So, I waved my hands when Fritz seemed to be looking anywhere in my general direction. Eventually, he wandered over to me. "Yeah?"

"Beer," I said. He nodded and turned to a tapped keg without any further difficulty communicating. I reckoned he must read lips. He placed a foamy mug in front of me and I finished it in one, long swallow. It was warm but deliciously refreshing. "One more," I said, as I placed some coins on the bar. When I had the beer, I walked towards the table in back from where the voice had come.

As I got closer, I could make out a sailor I knew as Ben and a man dressed in dark clothes sitting next to him. "Ben!" I said, "I thought that was you!" Ben and I had signed on to Captain MacBrùn's crew on the same night at the *Happy Cork*. I started to extend my hand when I saw that the man seated next to Ben was wearing a Union Navy uniform. An officer's hat lay on the table beside him. I froze in place.

"Teddy!" Ben said. "Where are my manners? This here is Lieutenant Valentine of the Key West blockade squadron." I turned to run to the door, but 4 men rose out of chairs in the shadows at the back of the bar. They, too, wore Union Navy uniforms and they carried muskets with bayonets set. "Halt!" one of them yelled, and I stopped where I was. I turned back towards Ben. "You bastard," I said.

"Relax, Teddy," Ben said. "Have a seat. Have another beer. MacBrùn should be here soon and then we can all get on with our lives. Well, at least I can. You and the rest of your wannabe buccaneers will be spending the rest of the war in prison."

I took a seat at a table with 3 other men. I did not know any of them. Ben signaled to the bartender and a fresh beer was placed in front of each of us. "Generous," I muttered sarcastically.

"He can afford it," said the man to my left. "He gets a bounty for every blockade runner he turns in: $100 for each Able and Common sailor," he explained, "and $200 per officer. And I think there is an extra bonus on the head of Captain MacBrùn, but how much I did not hear."

I sipped sullenly at my beer which had suddenly lost its flavor to me. "How many of us have they caught so far?" I asked. The man shrugged. "There are just the 4 of us that arrived today, but I do not know how many men arrived early and may be imprisoned elsewhere."

I looked over at Ben and the Union lieutenant. They were not speaking. I got the feeling that Ben was something the lieutenant tolerated, a necessary evil, but that he was not particularly fond of his company.

We sat there in relative silence for some time. Around mid-afternoon, voices could be heard outside the bar. One of the Union sailors rushed to the door and peeked outside. "MacBrùn just arrived in a flatboat," he said. "The two men rowing are leaving, and he is coming in alone." The Lieutenant signaled to another of his men to take a position on the other side of the door.

When we heard footsteps approach, I was tempted to cry out to warn Captain MacBrùn; but when I felt the prick of a bayonet in my back, I kept my silence. The door was thrown open with a crash, and I began to wonder if the good Captain ever just walked in normally through a doorway. When he stepped out of the glaring light pouring in through the open door, there was an audible gasp from the bar. Captain MacBrùn was wearing the full-dress uniform of a Confederate naval captain. He was resplendent in light blue trousers and a matching woolen coat that fell beneath his knees. On his sleeves, he wore gold braid designating his rank and perched on a wild mass of red hair was a kepi-style officers' hat. He looked as if he were attending a ball in Richmond.

Captain MacBrùn quickly scanned the room, much better lighted with the door open, and saw the Union officer and his sailors. If he were surprised, he gave no sign of it. He walked straight up to the Union lieutenant and said, "Have you come to join us, Lieutenant? Always room for another good sailor."

"I have come to arrest you, MacBrùn, for blockade running.

I would suggest..." But the Lieutenant never got to finish whatever he was going to say. Captain MacBrùn's face turned beet red, and he took a step towards the lieutenant: "You are addressing a senior officer, Lieutenant! You will come to your feet, salute, and address me by my rank!"

The Union lieutenant jumped to his feet so fast that he tipped his chair over backwards. He saluted and said, "I am Lieutenant Valentine, Cap'n MacBrùn, and I have come to arrest you for blockade running."

Captain MacBrùn returned his salute and said, "That is better." He pulled up a chair and sat down with the lieutenant and Ben. Ben had the good sense to get up and move to another table. MacBrùn signaled the bartender to bring him an ale. Lieutenant Valentine started to object, but MacBrùn held up a finger. "A little celebration, Lieutenant, before you carry out your duties. After all, today you captured one of the most famous blockade runners in the south: me. Who else has made more than 20 successful runs through the Union blockade? Aye, it is a good day for you."

Lieutenant Valentine tried to regain control. "I must remind you, Sir, that whatever you say to me will be reported to the court."

Captain MacBrùn finished his ale and slammed the mug down on the table. "Then," he said dramatically, his voice carrying clearly throughout the bar, "*If it were done when 'tis done, then 'twere well it were done quickly.*"

Lieutenant Valentine's mouth fell open. Nothing seemed to be going the way he expected. I almost felt sympathy for him. After all, how do you prepare for a Shakespeare-quoting, fire-breathing, redheaded narcissist like Captain MacBrùn?

Lieutenant Valentine's sailors lined us up and prepared to lead us out of *Marye's Bar*. My heart sank as I realized that my journey home was over even before it began. And I cannot pretend that I did not see the irony of likely sharing the same fate as my father.

CHAPTER 10

Theater in the Round

*The best way of successfully acting a part is to be it. —
Arthur Conan Doyle*

W e walked out into the blazing sunshine with Lieutenant Valentine and his four armed sailors behind us. We had all no sooner cleared the doorway then Captain MacBrùn said loudly, his brogue rolling around every word, "I can call spirits from the vasty deep," which I remembered from Shakespeare's Henry IV. Everyone turned to stare at him. When nothing happened, he bellowed again, "I can call spirits from the vasty deep, dammit!" A head popped up over the eaves of the bar roof above our heads: "Sorry, Cap'n." It was a man I had not seen before, and he was pointing a musket at Lieutenant Valentine. Captain MacBrùn looked around expectantly, but apparently did not see what he was looking for. "If I have to say that damn line one more time, I will keelhaul every one of you!" Three, then 4 more men appeared from behind the buildings. They too, were armed. I suspected the other roofs held armed men as well. The 4 Union sailors looked questioningly at Lieutenant Valentine. But before he could say anything, Captain MacBrùn said, "No one needs to die today, Lieutenant. Have your men stack their arms."

Lieutenant Valentine glanced around quickly, noting the location and number of Captain MacBrùn's men. Apparently finding the odds against them unacceptable, he said, "Stack your arms, men." He pulled his pistol from its holster and handed it, handle first, to Captain MacBrùn. "Very well, Captain. But I consider us to be prisoners of war and demand to be treated as such."

Captain MacBrùn laughed and refused the lieutenant's pistol. "You are my prisoners, Lieutenant, which I promise is several steps up from the level of civility you will find in a Confederate prison. Now, let us get out of this sun."

As Captain MacBrùn was ushering the lieutenant back into the door to *Marye's Bar*, the lieutenant glanced quickly down the waterway, then looked away. Captain MacBrùn must have noticed because he asked, "Looking for your longboat, Lieutenant? My men captured it this morning. But do not fret, your men are all well and will join us here soon."

Theatre, I thought. With Captain Quinn MacBrùn it is all theatre. His life is a play, written, directed, and starring the good captain himself.

Inside the bar, Ben sat sipping a beer at a table in the back. If he were concerned over the day's developments, he did not show it. Captain MacBrùn walked up and stood in front of him, reciting, "*So Judas did to Christ; but he, in twelve, found truth in all but one...*" But the Shakespeare was lost on Ben who just stared sullenly into his mug. Captain MacBrùn said, "Before I decide what to do with you, tell me one thing: what is the bounty the Yankees have placed on my head?"

Ben looked up from his beer. "Five-hundred dollars," he answered.

"Yankee or Confederate script?"

"Would not take neither, myself. Only Gold."

"Fair price," said Captain MacBrùn nodding his head. "Smart you are to stick to gold." He whirled around and signaled to Fritz, twirling his hand in small circles to indicate 'drinks all around.' But just that fast, Ben stood up and pulled out a knife he carried on his belt. He placed it against Captain MacBrùn's neck, pressing the blade so hard that a small rivulet of blood ran down under the captain's uniform collar. The knife was a type most sailors carried, the blade perhaps 3 inches long with a slight curve. It was used to cut ropes and lines and sailors kept them razor sharp.

"Now, Laddie," said the captain, "If you would just put that toy knife away, we can settle this..." But Ben just pressed harder and hissed, "For God's sake, will you shut your mouth? One more word and I swear I will kill you right now." Then, to the Union sailors, "Gather all the muskets and throw them out the window. Now!"

The sailors looked at Lieutenant Valentine, who nodded his head. "Do it," he said.

The sailors tore down the brown paper and began tossing muskets out the window. When the men had been relieved of their weapons, Ben backed the captain slowly towards the bar door. None of us had any doubt that he would use the knife if we tried to interfere. When they had exited the bar, I could hear Captain MacBrùn say, "Where are you going, sailor? There is no way out."

"Shut up, Cap'n, I cannot think!" We watched all this from inside the bar through the open door. Ben pulled the knife away from the captain's throat as he wiped his brow. He desperately surveyed the pier, no doubt looking for a way of escape. But there was no boat other than the scow schooner and no land to swim to. He gave a deep sigh and a calmness, perhaps acceptance, suddenly seemed to come over him. "Well," he said, "it looks like we both die today, Captain." Ben again started to place his knife against the captains throat when there was a gunshot from within the bar. Ben, surprised, looked down at blood pouring from a wound on his side. He turned toward the bar and a second shot caught him in the heart. He was dead by the time he crumbled to the pier.

Lieutenant Valentine stepped forward, smoke still rising from the barrel of his pistol. He looked briefly at Ben's body, then holstered his pistol and returned to the bar.

When everyone had settled into the bar again, Captain MacBrùn raised a mug of ale. "To Lieutenant Valentine," he said, "a gentleman and a marksman! An enviable combination!"

Lieutenant Valentine gave the captain a sour look. "With all due respect to your rank, Sir, you are a scoundrel and a reprobate. But in *my* Navy, justice is doled out by a court, not by some rogue sailor."

Captain MacBrùn laughed and slapped the Lieutenant's back, spilling some of the lieutenant's beer. "Perhaps someday I will taste Union justice. But not today, Lieutenant!" He yelled for Fritz to serve another round and then cursed when the bartender did not hear him. Eventually, a fresh round of drinks was placed before the officers and sailors.

In the midst of Captain MacBrùn's celebration, 2 more Union sailors were led into the bar by some of MacBrùn's men. They had apparently been left on a longboat waiting for a signal from Lieutenant Valentine to come pick up him and his prisoners. The sailors sat down with their peers, looking surprised by the general mood of cheerfulness. Fritz immediately brought them mugs of beer.

Finally, Captain MacBrùn stood up and said, "I hate to break up this party, gentlemen, but it is time for my crew and I to be on our way. The Lieutenant's longboat tells me that there is a Union gunboat anchored somewhere over the horizon, and I would prefer not to be here when they come looking for him." Lt. Valentine glared at Captain MacBrùn but said nothing. "By the way, Lieutenant Valentine, I am afraid I must relieve you of your longboat. It seems a fair bounty for the local men who helped me."

Captain MacBrùn pulled a coin purse out of his pocket and placed several gold coins on the bar. "Fritz," he said to the bartender, "keep the Lieutenant and his men well-nourished and well-hydrated until their friends come to pick them up." With that, he whirled around and stormed out the door. Exit stage left, I thought.

Out on the pier, Ben's body had been lying in the sun for several hours. One of the Captain's men asked, "What about him?" Captain MacBrùn looked at the body for a moment and then said, "Throw him off the pier. The 'gators will take care of him."

Two men reached for the body, and I yelled, "No, Cap'n, please! This man deserves a Christian burial, whatever his transgressions!" The captain held up his hand to stop the men from throwing the body off the pier and squinted at me. "I know you," he said. "You are the landman from Key West."

I bristled at the insult. "I am a Common Sailor, cap'n, not a landman. I ask only that you grant this man a Christian burial." When the captain did not answer immediately, I said to the men around us, "Should you fall in battle, is this the fate that awaits you as well? Do you want your body disposed of with no blessing, no simple prayer to speed your soul along?" Several of the men shuffled their feet and muttered their disapproval.

Captain MacBrùn glanced impatiently at the sun, which was already dipping towards the horizon. "What is your name again?" he asked.

"Miller," I answered.

"Very well, Common Seaman Miller, find some volunteers and dispose of this man's earthly remains as you see fit. But it must be done quickly, as it is dangerous to linger here too long."

Only the Lead Deckhand, a kindly man named Oliver Sykes, volunteered to help me. But it was enough. We placed Ben's body on an old piece of canvas, surrounded by pieces of whatever scrap metal we could find. Then, Oliver expertly sewed the body into the canvas. When he had finished, we bound the canvas-wrapped body from head to foot with rope.

Oliver and I placed the body on a board at the very end of the pier where we assumed the water was the deepest. After a prayer was said, we would lift one end of the board and Ben's body would slide into the water and sink, weighted down by the scrap metal. The bindings would provide some protection from scavengers.

The captain had been sitting in the shade watching us while his crew readied the scow schooner for departure. When we had finished preparing the body, I asked Captain MacBrùn if he would like to say something over the departed, but he dismissed me with an impatient wave of his hand. But several other crew members left their duties to stand with us at the end of the pier. Even one of the Union prisoners asked to participate.

Oliver carried an old bible with him, dog-eared from years of use. He took a deep breath and began to recite a catholic prayer often employed for burials at sea:

Lord God, by the power of your Word you stilled the chaos of the primeval seas, you made the raging waters of the Flood subside, and you calmed the storm on the Sea of Galilee. As we commit the earthly remains of our brother, Ben... Oliver hesitated. "Does anyone know Ben's last name?" he whispered. The men looked at each other and shook their heads.

Oliver continued:

As we commit the earthly remains of our brother, Ben, to the deep, grant him peace and tranquility until that day when Ben and all who believe in you will be raised to the glory of new life promised in the waters of baptism. We ask this through Christ our Lord.

Amen.

When he had finished, we lifted the end of the board and Ben's body slid into the water. No one moved or spoke for several moments, and then we all turned to return to our duties.

CHAPTER 11

Across Alligator Reef

No difficulty can discourage, no obstacle dismay, no trouble disheartens the man who has acquired the art of being alive. Difficulties are but dares of fate, obstacles but hurdles to try his skill, troubles but bitter tonics to give him strength; and he rises higher and looms greater after each encounter with adversity. — Ella Wheeler Wilcox

The scow schooner moored next to Maryc's Bar was named Kay and she was around 60 feet long with a beam of about 23 feet. She had two masts and a bowsprit more than 20 feet long to accommodate a triangular foresail. Although a square bow increased her cargo capacity, it greatly decreased her speed. As her draft was only 4 feet, she was ideal for inland and coastal waters. But I could not imagine her as a blockade runner.

We made the *Kay* ready to sail under the less-than-tender ministrations of the Chief Mate. His name was Andrew Fast, and he wore the sour expression of a man constantly put-upon by life. Everything that was said or done seemed to have no other purpose than to antagonize him and he constantly snapped at the men to work harder and faster. But I did develop some empathy for the man when Oliver described to me the Mate's duties. "He is," explained Oliver, "first lieutenant, boatswain, sailing-master, and quartermaster. The captain tells him what he wants done and leaves it to him to see that it is done and done well. He also keeps the ship's log and is responsible for the safe delivery of the cargo." Oliver shook his head, "It is a big job for one person, but I have found him to be a fair man, if sometimes overwrought."

We sailed west-northwest until we cleared the tip of Vaca Key. Then *Kay* turned east-northeast destined for who-knew-where. We, the crew, were apparently told no more than we needed to know.

Kay stayed within the shallow and hazardous waters of the Florida Bay. Oliver said our charts were primitive, but we had several sailors aboard that had fished these waters their whole lives. Captain MacBrùn depended on them to point out the hazards that abounded in the shallow water.

Encountering the Union blockade in these waters was unlikely, but the captain was cautious. He set up lookouts to watch for smoke or any other sign of another ship. He himself stood at the bow with a spyglass at the ready. He looked for all the world like the Emanuel Leutze's painting of Washington crossing the Delaware.

I reckoned we were making around 5 knots. After about 6 hours, Captain MacBrùn changed our course to southeastward and ordered us to anchor between 2 keys. Ahead of us, we could see the vast Atlantic Ocean glistening under the tropical sun as long swells rolled in under us. The island to starboard, I was told, was Duck Key, while to port lay Long Key.

When the sun had begun to settle beneath the horizon, Captain MacBrùn ordered us to make ready to sail. The sails were unfurled, and I watched as a sailor climbed the rigging to attach a lighted red lantern to the top of the aft mast. We were moving the moment the anchor broke the surface. In the failing light, we made our way from between the 2 islands and out to sea.

◆ ◆ ◆

The scow *Kay* rolled and tossed in the Atlantic swells. It was an overcast night and there was not even enough ambient light to tell where the ocean ended, and the sky began. It was eerily quiet, and it sometimes felt to me as if we were floating on air, the scow rising and falling on random air currents.

After about an hour, we began to hear the sound of waves breaking and the captain ordered us to heave to. All motion ceased except for a slight drift with a breeze from the south.

Suddenly, a lookout yelled, "There, cap'n, off the port bow! A signal light!"

We all turned to look and saw a dim, white light flashing: two long flashes, one short and another long. The pattern was repeated over and over. Oliver leaned over and whispered in my ear, "It is the letter 'Q' in Morse Code. It is the *Quicksilver*. She is in the deep water on the other side of the reef." I felt my heart jump.

Captain MacBrùn yelled to the Mate, "Acknowledge her signal, Mr. Fast." The mate flapped the cover of an oil lantern with the same pattern of flashes several times. There was one last flash from the *Quicksilver,* and all went dark. The captain sent a sailor up the mast to extinguish the red lantern.

We unfurled the sails and sailed a short distance parallel to the reef. There were no navigation markers of any kind and no stars to follow. Why the Captain turned to cross the reef at the point he did, I do not know. Perhaps it was instinct or perhaps he had some piece of information that I did not. But at the appointed place, he yelled "Hard left rudder, helmsman!" and we entered a maelstrom of breaking waves and cross-currents. The *Kay* heeled hard over, and men grabbed the gunnel to save themselves from falling overboard. "Steady as she goes, Helmsman! Steady as she goes!"

No more than a few hundred yards and we would be across

the reef. But just before we reached the deep water beyond, the *Kay* grounded herself. Men were thrown off their feet and unsecured equipment went flying. There was a terrible sound of grinding and scraping, and the scow spun part-way around as if on a fulcrum. The sails flapped uselessly as they spilled their wind.

The captain gave rapid orders to the helm in hopes of turning the *Kay* back towards open water, but the scow did not respond. Just before I was sure the ship would be breached, a large wave rolled beneath us and lifted us temporarily off the reef. The scow suddenly responded to the rudder and the sails filled with wind again and we slowly—agonizingly slowly —made our way off the reef and into the deep water of the Atlantic Ocean.

Somehow, the *Kay* had held together, although she was taking on water from various split seams. Captain MacBrùn seemed unperturbed. "Signal the *Quicksilver*, Mr. Fast," he said. "Tell them that we are across."

We patched the *Kay* as best we could before longboats from the *Quicksilver* picked us up and attached a tow rope to her.

I slept that night in my own bunk, located in the aft section of the *Quicksilver* with the rest of the deck crew. I was assigned no watch that night and I went to bed with a full stomach from a hot meal served in the crew mess. Men stirred and tossed and snored around me, but I slept soundly.

Oliver woke me at 7:30 a.m. and we went to the mess for breakfast together. Afterwards, as Lead Deckhand, he was obliged to explain my primary duties. They did not differ much from the work I had done on other ships: chip, paint, repeat. We worked side by side through much of the morning and Oliver told me about the *Quicksilver* and Captain MacBrùn. "The *Quicksilver* is a magnificent ship," he said. "She was built in Glasgow around 1855, and when the War broke out, Cap'n

MacBrùn brought her over to assist the Confederacy against the blockade." Oliver lowered his voice: "Truth be told, I do not know how much the captain actually believes in the Southern cause. But he helps to procure much needed supplies and, in the process, has made himself and the ship's owner, very wealthy. A good cruise can yield a profit of more than $60,000."

I was dumbfounded. I could not even imagine so much money. Oliver continued, "The *Quicksilver* is the largest ship I have ever served on. She is well over 200' long with a beam of 34'. Her full complement is 40 officers and men, while we have perhaps 30. But we will make do.

"She has two forms of propulsion, steam and sail. Huge coal-burning boilers drive the two side wheels and give her a top speed of around 10 knots; her square-rigged masts, along with small fore-and-aft sails, can add as much as 5 knots more to her speed. She can outrun most Yankee blockaders."

"Most?"

Oliver smiled. "Most."

CHAPTER 12

Life on the Quicksilver

No man will be a sailor who has contrivance enough to get himself into a jail; for being in a ship is being in a jail, with the chance of being drowned... a man in a jail has more room, better food, and commonly better company. — Samuel Johnson

There is often a misconception among landmen that sailors are mostly idle at sea. On a well-ordered vessel like the Quicksilver, nothing could be further from the truth. Except for at night and on Sundays, no sailor was allowed to stand idle on the deck. Every officer seemed to see it as his solemn duty to keep the men busy at all times, even when there was nothing to do. Many a piece of brass was polished multiple times in a single day.

Days were rigidly scheduled. Mornings began at daybreak when the decks were washed, scrubbed, and swabbed. Then the 'scuttled butt,' a wooden cask used to contain fresh water for a day's use, was filled with fresh water and the rigging was coiled. This usually took until 7:30 a.m. when breakfast was served.

The workday officially began at 8:00 a.m. and lasted to

sundown except for an hour for dinner. But it did not end there. Every seaman stood 2 watches a day, which rotated through a 4-day schedule. The net result was that a sailor got 8 hours of uninterrupted sleep only every 4 days. We quickly learned to sleep anywhere at any time we were not on duty.

The watches, to me, were the best part of being a sailor. If the ship were anchored, watches were spent making sure that the anchor did not drag, updating charts and mending sails and equipment. While the ship was at sea, there were numerous watch activities for a deck hand, from lookout to manning the helm and the 'lee helm,' which transmitted speed information to the engine room.

I found that I had a natural talent for steering the ship. There was an art to keeping the ship on course, especially when the seas were rough, or the winds were high. Deviating from the proscribed course, even by a degree, could take the ship miles away from the Mate's carefully plotted destination.

The ship's officers quickly recognized my talent on the helm and asked for me on nearly every watch, especially in bad weather. I enjoyed it immensely, the challenge of it as well as watching the changing colors of the sea from the wheelhouse. I was also privy to conversations between the captain and his officers.

I was surprised to learn that the *Quicksilver* had already been to Nassau to deliver a cargo of cotton and salt. She had been skippered there by another Confederate naval officer while Captain MacBrùn completed his recruitment trip to the Keys. Due to sickness and attrition, the *Quicksilver's* crew had been reduced in number so much that the men left had to stand double watches.

The *Quicksilver* had obtained 300 cases of Austrian rifles and a quantity of saltpeter in Nassau in exchange for the cotton and salt. It was all worth a staggering $180,000. It was now Captain MacBrùn's job to get them safely through the Union blockade and into the hands of the Confederacy in Wilmington, North Carolina.

There was a new moon forecast for 5 days hence. All else being equal, the lack of moonlight would make for near perfect conditions to run the blockade. Captain MacBrùn and his Mate picked a point near Masonboro Inlet, to the north of Wilmington, where they would wait for darkness in one of the many smaller inlets before making a dash for the port on the appointed day.

Captain MacBrùn and the Mate made good use of the 5 days available to them to reach Masonboro Inlet. They were concerned that the crew was mostly green and had not yet been forged into a team. Training became their priority, and every day—sometimes several times a day—the ship's bell would be rung 5 times at 5-second repeats. It was the signal for us to take our 'action stations.'

A crew member's action station may or may not be the same as his duty station. I was assigned to the helm while others prepared the ship for action, above and below deck. The deck crew scrambled up and down the rigging, furling or unfurling the sails, while the stokers madly shoveled coal into the boilers, their skin black from coal dust and glistening with sweat. Junior officers shouted orders which sometimes countermanded each other. It appeared to be a chaos from which order was only gradually extracted.

If the Captain was displeased with speed or efficacy of the men's' work, he dressed the Mate down in language embarrassing even to the saltiest sailor. But he never addressed the men directly himself. It was the Mate who dispensed the captain's displeasure and, on occasion, discipline.

By the time we reached the coast of North Carolina, we reacted to a call to action stations like an experienced crew. Even the Captain could no longer find a reason to berate the Mate and we were proud of the crew we had become.

CHAPTER 13

Happy New Year, January 1865

All the diamonds in this world That mean anything to me Are conjured up by wind and sunlight sparkling on the sea I ran aground in a harbor town Lost the taste for being free Thank God he sent some gull chased ship To carry me to sea...— Bruce Cockburn

The year 1864 became 1865 as we made our way up the coast towards Wilmington. There was no break in our routine and many of the sailors were not even aware of the occasion. But truth be known, most of us were in no mood for a celebration anyway. The war news had become ever more dire. Two weeks earlier, Sherman had captured Savannah, ending his march across Georgia. And, more recently, the Confederate Army under General John Bell Hood was thoroughly defeated in Tennessee.

When I was not sleeping, I spent nearly all my time on the helm. Captain MacBrùn kept the ship in a constant state of readiness. Although he said little about it even to the Mate, I could see that he was concerned about being intercepted by the Union blockaders. His worry was understandable as we had recently learned that Wilmington was the last southern seaport on the east coast still open to blockade runners and commercial shipping. That meant that the entire Union Navy could concentrate their attention on a relatively small area.

It was nearly 8:00 a.m. on January 3 and I was at the end of my 4:00 a.m. to 8:00 a.m. watch on the helm. It had been a stressful night, and I was tired and hungry. We were close enough to the port of Wilmington that we had to be constantly on the lookout for Union blockaders. It was dangerous work. We showed no running lights at night and collisions were a real threat. It did not help that a heavy fog had settled over us at dawn and we could barely see the bow in front of us. Again, we could provide no warning to other ships, no foghorn or bell.

The captain called for all ahead slow as we entered the fog bank. But he told engineering to keep up a full-head of steam in case it was needed. The fog damped all sound, and we could barely hear the slap-slap-slap of the sidewheels. But the silence was suddenly broken by a lookout yelling, "Ship dead-ahead, Cap'n!" The Mate sounded the collision alarm on the ship's bell at the same instant that the captain yelled, "Hard right rudder!" I spun the helm hard over to starboard.

Through the thick fog, a Union sloop-of-war suddenly appeared in front of us. She was so large, and we were so close, that she filled my entire field of view. It seemed to take the *Quicksilver* forever before she began to respond to the rudder. Captain MacBrùn ordered the starboard paddle wheel into reverse and the whole ship shuddered as it changed direction. But the *Quicksilver* began to pivot, and we passed the sloop port-to-port. The Captain ordered the starboard sidewheel into forward again and told me to hold the course we were on. "Steady as she goes, helmsman!"

It seemed to me that I could have reached out the wheelhouse windows and touched the side of the sloop as she passed by. A voice came from the sloop, amplified by a megaphone: "Heave to or we will fire on you!" Captain MacBrùn's response was to order the lee helm to flank speed. Dense black smoke billowed from our funnel. A moment later, the Union sloop fired a round of canister shot at us, a cluster of lead balls, that raked the aft deck. A stray ball crashed through the wheelhouse, nicked the helm, and barely missed the captain. He did not seem to notice, but my fingers stung from the ball's impact on the helm. The sloop fired another time, but the shot fell short. It appeared we were slowly pulling away from her.

"Luck only," said the Captain to the Mate. "She did not have a full head of steam because she was not expecting any company tonight. But you can bet her stokers are hard at work. She will keep coming." The Mate nodded. "I will see to our sails," he said.

Our adventure might have been over, at least for the moment, if the fog had not lifted. But the pervasive grayness was soon replaced by a brilliant blue sky and almost unlimited visibility. We had nowhere to hide, and the Union sloop-of-war could be seen no more than 2 miles behind us.

We crew remained at our action stations, although the Mate allowed me a half-hour to eat some breakfast. When I returned to the wheelhouse, all seemed as before, except when I glanced back at the Union sloop: she was clearly gaining on us. We had all the sail up that the *Quicksilver* could carry, and the engineers were squeezing out every possible rpm from the sidewheels. But we were losing the race. We would never make it to dark when we had some chance of escape.

"It is that damn Welch coal we carry," the Mate said to the captain. "It does not burn hot enough to keep up a good head of steam. Now, if we had some good American anthracite…"

The captain smiled at the mate and said, "We Scots have a saying, *'If wishes were horses, beggars would ride.'*" When the Mate made a sour face, the Captain put his hand on his shoulder and said, "We have another saying, too, that *'There is nothing either good or bad but thinking makes it so.'"*

The Mate grinned at the captain. "I thought it was Shakespeare, not the Scots, said that." The captain shrugged. "Where do you think Shakespeare got it?"

It was a nightmare in slow motion. The Union sloop continued to gain on us until she was about a mile behind us. At that point, she started firing at us with a 12-pounder cannon she carried on her bow. She fired solid shot, which was wildly inaccurate at that range; nonetheless, it was a fair reminder of what was yet to come. But by the time the sloop closed to a half-mile, her 12-pounder was more accurate, and solid shot fell with regularity around us. Hitting a moving target from a moving ship was more luck than skill, but we could see the shot flying through the air and there was a disconcerting optical illusion which made every shot appear to be coming straight at us.

Through it all, Captain MacBrùn sat quietly in the captain's chair, only speaking to order small course changes to make the wind most favorable for sailing. If he were concerned about the approaching sloop-of-war, he did not show it. The sun was getting lower in the sky, but I did not believe that we could outrun the Union sloop until darkness fell. I winced at every shot that fell near us.

Captain MacBrùn finally called for his chief engineer. A grizzled old man, covered in grease and coal dust, stepped onto the bridge. I was surprised when the captain addressed him by his name rather than his rank or rating: "Well, Charlie, how many times have we found ourselves in this position before?" The engineer gave the captain a toothless grin. "Once or twice't," he answered.

The captain grinned back at him. "Then I suppose you know what to do?"

"Aye, Cap'n. It is all prepared."

The captain gave no further orders for several minutes other than to close the dampers, which would hold in the smoke from the boilers. And then, suddenly, there was a noticeable increase in our speed. The *Quicksilver* seemed to jump forward. The sloop-of-war soon fell back and the constant barrage from the 12-pounder ended.

As the sun was setting, the captain ordered the chief engineer to open the dampers and make black smoke. The captain watched the sloop through his telescope until it was lost in the darkness. At that moment, he ordered the damper closed again and a hard-right turn to starboard.

The Union sloop was sure to head to the spot where they had last seen our smoke. But when they got there, we would be long gone and off on an unknown course.

The captain cancelled the call to action stations and the men not on watch made their way wearily to their bunks. In our berthing area, I asked Oliver how the engineers had suddenly gotten so much speed out of the *Quicksilver*. "An old blockade runner's trick," he answered. "A couple'a 500-pound bales of cotton are soaked with turpentine and burned in the boilers. Burns a lot hotter than the Welch coal we carry."

CHAPTER 14

To Bermuda and Back

We rebelled, even if only temporarily. For a few hours every day, we dropped the rock, left the mount, and turned our backs to the toil and responsibility given and demanded of us by our gods and the authorities appointed to maintain them, and turned instead toward the reprieve we could only seem to find as we closed our eyes and slept together in those craters. We had committed the unforgivable sin of our age, against our age, and we found rest. —Jack Foster

Whenever I entered the wheelhouse to stand my watch the next morning, Captain MacBrùn and the Mate were having a heated discussion. They glanced at me briefly, then looked away as if I were invisible. So it was to be a Common sailor.

"We have lost all surprise, Cap'n. They will be waiting for us at the harbor entrance. We need to find another port..." The captain shook his head. "There is no other port."

"Then let us return to Nassau where we can recoup at least some of the cargo's value."

Captain MacBrùn placed his hand affectionately on the

Mate's arm. "The War is nearly over, Andrew. Are you so anxious to return to ferrying ladies bonnets and French bon-bons around the Mediterranean? Let us make this final delivery, for I do not believe there is a Yankee sailor born that can stop us." The Mate only nodded, whether in resignation or agreement I could not tell.

The captain stared out the windows for a moment and then said to the Mate: "Plot us a course to Bermuda. We will reprovision and let the Yankees stew for a while."

The Mate left the wheelhouse for the chart house and returned a few minutes later carrying a chart. The captain glanced at it and then said loudly: "Helmsman, come right to 1-2-0 degrees!"

"Right to 1-2-0, aye, Sir," I answered. Then, when the ship had aligned with the new course, "Steady on 1-2-0, Sir."

"Very well," said the captain.

Less than 48 hours later, we were pulling into St. George's Harbor on the northeast end of Bermuda. After the lushness of the Keys, it seemed somewhat forlorn to me. All I saw was windblown sand dunes, limestone, and coral rocks, with a few scrubby bushes added for a spot of color.

We were not permitted to leave the ship, but from what I could see, St. George's seemed to be a prosperous seaport. Oliver told me that Bermuda was a place that was frequently used as a stopping point for the blockade runners on their runs to and from the Southern states and England. We took on coal, fresh water and food and left almost immediately. The Union Navy occasionally blockaded the harbor and the captain thought it best if we did not linger.

We picked our way carefully through the coral reefs that surrounded the island and out to sea. Soon we were headed to Wilmington and whatever fate awaited us.

Captain MacBrùn had determined that January 15 would be the date we would try to reach Wilmington harbor. He chose the day because of a combination of the time of maximum high tide (calculated for 1:30 a.m.) and a waning moon. I understood that a high tide gave the shallow-draft *Quicksilver* the ability to move even closer inshore than the large blockaders. And, as it was still 10 days away, I fervently prayed that the extra time might also cause the Union Navy to let their guard down a bit.

With 10 days to spare, Captain MacBrùn took us south to the warmer weather off Florida. There we drilled and honed our skills, but always with a wary eye on the horizon. At night we ran with no lights and the paddle wheels were feathered to minimize the noise. Any sound we made louder than a sneeze was answered with a quick rebuke from the officers.

On January 12, the Mate plotted a course that would have us at the Cape Fear River entrance around midnight on the 14th; on the day of the 15th, we would find a small inlet in which to hide until the appointed time that night.

As we steamed north, the weather became colder and colder. The sea, once a cobalt blue, became a greasy grey and dark clouds tumbled above our heads.

CHAPTER 15

Fort Fisher

And in that time. When men decide and feel safe. To call the war insane, Take one moment to embrace. Those gentle heroes. You left behind. —*Krzysztof Kieslowski*

W e arrived, undetected, at the latitude of the New Inlet late on the night of January 14. Although we saw no Union blockaders, we knew they were all around us. We stayed far out to sea until we were well north of New Inlet. Then, we moved closer to shore and continued north until we came to a small inlet which the Mate knew to be deep enough for us to hide in. We spent the rest of the night and the entirety of the following day in the inlet, hoping not to be discovered by some random Union naval patrol.

At 1:30 a.m., the captain ordered all ahead slow, and we emerged from the inlet and into the Atlantic Ocean. Because I had overheard the Mate and the Captain discuss it many times, I knew that the blockaders could be expected to station their ships in a line across the entrance to the New Inlet channel. Because of their deep draft, there was always a space between the last ship in line and the shore. With luck, we could squeeze unnoticed through that opening. Once we had passed the blockade line, friends on shore would shine dim lanterns to guide us under the protection of Fort Fisher. The blockaders would not dare to pursue us under the guns of the fort.

We started our run with all our lights extinguished, the damper closed to prevent smoke, and the paddle wheels feathered to further reduce their splashing. Whatever noise remained was masked by the waves breaking against the shore.

My heart was pounding against my chest and sweat kept running into my eyes as we passed through the line of blockaders. The shore was on our starboard side, and we could make out the faint outline of a sloop-of-war to our port. I expected at any moment to hear some Union lookout raise the alarm. But then we were past, and my heart slowed. The captain smiled at the Mate and slapped his back. But any celebrations were short-lived. It was our own lookout who shouted, "Ship off the port bow!"

The captain rushed to the window with his telescope. "Small Yankee cutter," he said. Before he could say more, the Union cutter fired off several rockets to alert the blockaders to our presence. Almost simultaneously, the cutter fired a round of canister at us that tore through the wheelhouse, killing the lee helmsman where he stood. Aft of us, the last blockader in the line moved up behind us and fired several solid shots that only barely missed us. "Hard to starboard!" the captain yelled, and I spun the helm over as fast as I could. Ahead I could see waves breaking on the shore, and it was only at the last moment that the captain ordered the helm hard to port.

The sloop behind us fired again, this time finding their mark. Several solid shots tore through the hull. I heard men scream from somewhere in the bowels of the ship.

Again, the cutter in front of us fired canister at us, this time carrying away the forward mast.

Because the lee helm had been destroyed, Captain MacBrùn used the voice tube to order the engine room to make flank speed. In a moment, the *Quicksilver* lurched and quickly began to pick up speed. The captain ordered me to steady the helm, and to my horror, I saw we were centered on the small Union cutter. The Mate said, "There will be no turning back from this, Cap'n." But the Captain did not answer, and he did not order a course change.

The Mate sounded the collision alarm on the ship's bell while the Union cutter desperately fired round after round of canister at us. But they were fired in haste, poorly aimed, and did little additional damage. The cutter had begun a hard turn to starboard when we rammed her.

The collision tore off the cutter's bowsprit and left a gaping hole in her hull. We were all thrown forward by the impact. But the Captain was quickly back on his feet, and he ordered the paddle wheels reversed. The ship shuddered and there were a few moments of hesitation before the *Quicksilver* began to back away from the Union cutter, which was taking on great volumes of water and was clearly mortally damaged. But the cutter Captain must have anticipated our intention to ram him as he had formed a group of 6 boarders on his bow. Two were thrown into the water by the impact, but the 4 others tried to scramble over the bow of the *Quicksilver*. Strapped across their backs, they carried muskets with bayonets fixed. But the gulf between our ship and the cutter became too great too quickly. The men jumped back to their own ship. One snapped a quick shot at our wheelhouse, and I heard the angry buzz of a Minié ball go past my ear and a thud as it embedded itself in the wall behind me.

I was relieved that the boarders had not made it across. Four armed men could easily have captured our vessel as we carried no defensive weapons of any kind. This had always seemed odd to me, but the captain explained to me during one late watch that blockade running was a 'gentlemen's game,' played by gentlemen's rules. "It is a combat of skill and pluck against force and vigilance," he said. There was usually little physical danger as the rules required that the blockade runner must put up no resistance. The blockader, then, would employ no more violence than necessary to stop the blockade runners. But if the blockade runner resisted with force, the goal of the blockaders changed immediately from 'capture' to 'destroy.' When we rammed the Union cutter, it was seen as a declaration of all-out combat. God help us, I thought.

By now, the sky was filled with signal rockets from all the blockaders, and it was nearly as bright as daylight. Explosions and crashes assaulted our ears, and it seemed the whole world had gone mad. I had expected more fire from the Union sloop-of-war behind us, but I guess they were afraid of hitting their own ship. But once we were clear of the sinking cutter, solid shot again began to fall around us. The captain kept us close to the shore, heedless of any obstacles that might be there. We raced at flank speed along the coastline.

The captain turned to the Mate and said, "Make signal to the shore." The Mate lighted an oil lantern and flashed it at the shore. In moments, three dimly lit lanterns could be seen on a distant hillside. These 'range lights' had been placed several yards above each other on the slope. When the 3 aligned, we would be in the channel to the Cape Fear River. And a few minutes after that, under the protection of the guns in Fort Fisher.

We held our course and speed until the lanterns finally aligned themselves, one above the other. The captain gave me helm directions to follow the channel.

A great silence had descended on us. The sloop-of-war behind us had dropped back and was no longer firing at us. I gave a great sigh of relief as the captain gave orders to slow-ahead. It appeared that the Union blockaders had no stomach to face the big guns in Fort Fisher. The captain ordered our running lights put on and our ensign raised so that we would be recognized by the gunners in the Fort.

I had just started to get my breathing under control again when there was a series of flashes at the fort, then a sound like distant thunder. Moments later, the water erupted alongside the ship. Several columns of water rose 50 feet higher than the wheelhouse, drenching the ship.

"Why are they firing at us?" asked the Mate, a desperate tone in his voice. But before the Captain could answer, there was another series of flashes at the fort. "God protect us, they have our range now!" said the Mate, crossing himself. This time, the explosions straddled the ship and sea water washed over the deck.

"Hard left rudder, Helmsman!" yelled the captain. "Order flank speed, Mate."

But the Quicksilver could not react quickly enough. I watched with horror as the cannons at the fort fired again, first the flashes, then the booms and then... only darkness.

The *Quicksilver* must have sunk in moments. When my senses returned, I found myself floating in the freezing water holding on to a piece of flotsam. I could not recall if I had jumped off the ship or had been knocked off by the explosions. The water around me was covered in flaming debris and bodies.

CHAPTER 16

Plucked from the Sea

The problem with surviving was that you ended up with the ghosts of everyone you'd ever left behind riding on your shoulders. — Paolo Bacigalupi

T he flaming pieces of wreckage sputtered out one-by-one, and all became dark. The moon was only a smudge of light, and the stars could not be seen through a haze of smoke that had settled over the water. The tide had turned, and I could feel myself being pulled out to sea. I tried to call out for help, but I could make no sound at all.

I was holding on to a piece of wood that gave me some buoyancy, but I could not pull myself up on it. My fingers had no sense of feeling and would not seem to do what I asked of them. I tried kicking my feet towards shore but that only threatened to pull me off the board.

The freezing water had burned like a thousand hot needles when I first went overboard. Then, I became numb and now, a surprisingly warm sensation had come over me. It was as inviting as a feather mattress, calling for me to let go of the board and slip beneath the cold, inky water. I just wanted to go to sleep, to shed the fear that besieged me. I no longer felt the cold.

Just as I let go of the wooden board, just as I sank below the surface of the water, a pair of strong arms pulled me over the gunnel of a flatboat and onto the bottom. I was immediately wrapped in a heavy wool blanket.

I could only see the man's back as he worked the oars. Something about the man looked familiar to me. Between violent shivers, I asked, "Jed?"

My brother looked back over his shoulder at me and smiled. "Teddy! You are alive! I was not sure there for a while."

"What are you doing here?" I managed to croak. Jed put the oars down and turned to face me. "Saving your ass, looks like."

I would have stood up and embraced him if I could have, but I did not even have the strength to undo the blanket around me. "What happened?" I asked.

"Well, it appears you ain't one of the smartest blockade runners. The Yankees captured Fort Fisher the day before yesterday, and you sailed right into their trap. Now, they are attacking Wilmington itself."

I contemplated that for a moment as I watched my brother brush a lock of his dark hair out of his eyes. I had seen my father do the same thing many times and my eyes welled-up with tears. "Daddy is dead, Jed. Did you get my letter?"

Jed did not answer. His face began to ripple in my vision, and everything went black.

Just as I let go of the wooden board, just as I sank below the surface of the water, a pair of strong arms pulled me over the gunnel of a flatboat and onto the bottom. I was immediately wrapped in a heavy wool blanket.

A man I did not know looked down on me with concern in his eyes. "You will be alright now, Son. We will get you to shelter right soon enough."

"Where is my brother?" I asked.

The man seemed to misunderstand what I was asking. "I am

sorry," he said, "I found no other survivors."

When we reached the shore, a young boy, maybe 15 years-old, sat waiting in a flat-bed wagon hitched to an old mule. "Help me get him in the wagon," said the man. Together, the man and the boy lifted me out of the flatboat and into the wagon. My shivering had not abated, and the bed of the wagon shook along with me. "I found no others alive," the man said to the boy. "Now we need to get this one to warmth and shelter as soon as possible." The boy nodded and climbed onto the wagon, clucked at the mule, and snapped the reins. The wagon gave a lurch, and we began to move.

I awoke naked and tightly wrapped in blankets lying on a sofa next to a roaring fire. I had mostly stopped shivering, although every once and a while a lone shudder would begin between my shoulder blades and then move down the length of my body. Sitting near me, I recognized the man and boy who had saved me from the water. There was also a frail-looking woman with them.

The man must have seen my eyes flutter open, because he walked over and looked down at me. "You are awake?" he asked. I nodded my head. "How are you feeling? You have been sleeping for hours." I tried to answer, but all I could manage was a meaningless croak. "We took your clothes to dry. Meantime, I can lend you some of my clothes when you feel the need." He turned and motioned to the woman, whom I assumed was his wife. She walked over to me carrying a steaming bowl of something. She dipped a spoon in the bowl and held it to my lips, but I just shook my head and pulled away. I felt nauseous and wanted nothing to eat.

"You need to eat something hot," the man insisted. "Your innards are still frosty. You ain't out of the woods yet." Reluctantly, I accepted a spoonful of what turned out to be chicken broth. As I swallowed it, I could feel the warmth spread throughout my body. It tasted and felt wonderful. I smiled my thanks to the woman as she patiently spoon-fed me the entire bowl.

I must have fallen back asleep, because when I awoke again it was dawn, and I was alone in the parlor with the man. He was sitting across from me in an old horsehair-stuffed chair, his chin on his chest, snoring softly. The boy and woman were nowhere to be seen.

I wrestled with the blankets and managed to free my arms. I scratched gratefully at my scalp where my saltwater-soaked hair, now dried by the fire, lay matted against my head. The man must have heard my movements. When he saw I was awake, he said, "You have much of your color back again. I ain't no doctor, but I reckon you will live."

"Thanks to you," I croaked. I asked for water, which he brought me in a large tin cup. When I drank it all, he brought me another and settled back in his chair. "What is your name, Son?" he asked.

"Teddy Miller. I am—was—the helmsman on the CSS Quicksilver."

The man reached over and shook my hand. "My name is Walter Cheeley, and you met my son Charlie and the missus. We all took turns watching you last night. I reckon the missus will be down any time now to fix some breakfast. You hungry?"

"Starving," I answered honestly.

Walter leaned towards me and lowered his voice: "Afore the missus comes down, there is something you should know. Our two oldest boys were both in the Army and both were killed the same day. It has been nearly 6 months, and my missus has not spoken a word since we learned of their deaths." Walter hesitated. "Jest do not want you to mistake her grief for anything else as she is a fine woman."

After a wonderful breakfast, Walter and I again sat in

front of the fireplace. I placed one of the blankets across my shoulders as I still could not seem to get warm. "How did you come to find me last night?" I asked.

Walter shrugged. "As you will see when you are on your feet again, we live on a small inlet jest north of the Fort. I am a blacksmith, and I did a lot of work there, repairs and such. But I knew the Yankees had captured the fort a day or two ago, and when the big guns went off last night, Charlie and I rushed to see who was on the receiving end." Walter shook his head for a moment and continued: "I ain't never seen anything like it. There was a big side-wheeler flying a Confederate ensign, of all things, surrounded by what seemed to be the entire Union fleet. Rockets were flying like the 4th of July and cannons were booming.

"I saw the side-wheeler ram a smaller Union ship, and I thought 'that'll damn well do it.' The Yankees will be out for blood now.

"Charlie and I grabbed some blankets and ran down to where we keep our flatboat on the inlet. I rowed out looking for survivors, while Charlie brought our wagon to the beach."

CHAPTER 17

Mourning

Camp of 1st Battalion, near Petersburg
Aug 23, 1864
Mr. & Mrs. Walter Cheeley

It is a painful task for me to Communicate the sad fate of your sons Frank & Walter jr. (my own Comrades) who were struck on the 21st inst by ball and canister shot & never recovered after. I was in Command of the Skremeshers about one mile to the front & every inch of ground was well contested until I reached our Regt. The Yanks made the attack in 3 lines of Battle. As soon as I reached our line I met Frank and he ran & met me with a canteen of watter. I was near palayed. He said I was foolish I dident let them come at once that the ol Co C was waiting for them. I threw off my Coat & in 2 minutes we were at it hand to hand. They charged us twice & we repulsed them. They then tried the Regt on our Right & drove them which caused us to Swing back our right, then charged them on their left flank & in the charge Frank fell from a ball through the heart. It was likely mercifully quick. Walter turned back to aide his brother and was swept away by canister shot may the Lord have mercy on his Soul. They never flinched from their posts & were loved by all who knew them. They were given a Christian internment alongside of Sergt Markum Ingraham, Sergt Jeremiah Gallagher of our Co & 5 others of our Co that you are not acquainted with. Our Co lost in killed wounded & missing Twenty as follows killed 8 wounded 10 & missing 2 although we fought the Yankeed 10 to one on the 2nd & killed or captured a whol Corps. There was never a battle fought with more determination. Mr. &

Mrs. Cheeley please excuse this letter as I am confused & I hope you will take your trouble with patience you know that God is mercifull & good to his own. I lost two loyal comrades in them. No more at present from your Sorrowing friend.
Wm. C. Ertmann, Lieut Co C, Regt P.V.

By the next day, I had recovered enough to wash myself in a basin of hot water provided by Mrs. Cheeley. After dressing in my freshly laundered clothes, Walter and I took a walk around his property. We walked down a path leading to the beach where I could see Fort Fisher looming to the south. I had expected a brick edifice bristling with gun ports like I had seen in Key West, but instead saw just mounds of earth. Walter explained that the dirt mounds had been used to elevate the cannons by more than 12 feet, extending their accurate range over a mile. I assumed that dirt made a good choice for a fort as it would absorb the shock from any projectiles aimed at it. In any event, the destructive power of the new rifled cannons had about made brick forts obsolete.

Walter gave a loud sigh when he saw the large Union flag flying over the fort. "The end comes," he said, "but so slowly! Had the War ended even just 6 months ago, my boys would still be alive."

We continued our walk over to the little inlet where his flatboat was tied to a small wooden dock. The dock was made so perfectly that every seam was nearly invisible, and it had been creosoted to protect it from the elements. I reckoned the quality was about what you might expect from a man of his profession. We found a fallen tree and sat side by side. He pulled a piece of paper from his pocket and handed it to me. It had been opened and refolded so many times that it was tearing at the folds. "About my boys," Walter said. "It was written by their officer, a fine boy who grew up just up the road."

I read the letter and handed it back to Walter. "That is a fine letter. Your boys were very brave, and they were clearly loved by their comrades. You must take some comfort in that." But Walter surprised me with the vehemence of his answer: "I take no comfort from that letter, 'though I musta read it a hundred times. They are all the same, you see, all the letters sent to grieving families. 'Your boys were brave,' they say, 'your boys were beloved by their friends,' they say, 'they did not suffer,' they say,' your boys received a Christian burial,' they say!" Walter stood up and turned back towards his house. "When I dream of my boys, I see only anxiety and suffering; I fear to know the real truth of it."

CHAPTER 18

Kindness and Courage

In the end, though, maybe we must all give up trying to pay back the people in this world who sustain our lives. In the end, maybe it's wiser to surrender before the miraculous scope of human generosity and to just keep saying thank you, forever and sincerely, for as long as we have voices.— *Elizabeth Gilbert*

When it became obvious to Walter that I was well-enough to travel, we sat down at the kitchen table in front of an old map of the Carolina coast from Murrell's Inlet in South Carolina to Cape Hatteras. "This is us," Walter said, pointing to a place on the map where the Cape Fear River entered the Atlantic Ocean. "As you can see, we are at the bottom of a large peninsula with Wilmington at the top." He scratched at his beard. "Problem is, the Yankees have surrounded the city and there ain't no way around it from the south. Walk north up the peninsula about 15 miles and the whole Union Army will be there to greet you.

"Now, we got a whole different set of problems if you try to get across the Cape Fear River to the west shore where you can walk inland and be on your way. First, you gotta try and run past the blockade again, then the fort. And even if you make it, the Yankees have every damn type of boat known to mankind patrolling the river day and night."

I felt my heart sink. It was like being back in Key West again, trapped on all sides by the Union blockaders. But before I could despair for too long, Walter said, "There may be one way. My brother owns a small fishing boat. If he was willing, he could take you up the coast to somewhere north of Wilmington, mebbe Hampstead, about 40-45 miles up the coast. From there, you could make your way inland."

Do you think he would do it?" I asked.

Walter shrugged. "Only one way to find out. He only lives a couple of miles up the coast from here; I'll send Charlie over tomorrow to fetch him."

Around noon the next day, Charlie walked into the kitchen with a man I assumed was Walter's brother. But you would never know it from his appearance: he was as physically different from Walter as two brothers could be. Where Walter was short and wiry, his brother was tall and stocky; and where Walter was pale from working indoors, his brother was burnt dark brown from the sun. And I could see his hands, a fisherman's hands, scarred from years of hooks and lines.

Mrs. Cheeley ran over to him, and he threw his arms around her. She disappeared into his embrace. "Louisa," he said, "you have been in my thoughts." They said nothing more for several minutes. Finally, they separated, and Walter brought his brother over to meet me. "Andrew, this here is Teddy Miller, the sailor we fished out of the water the other night." Andrew looked me up and down and extended his hand. I shook it, self-conscious of the softness of my hands compared to his.

We sat down at the kitchen table and Walter produced a jug of whiskey. He poured us each a shot. The whiskey was rough, and I had to stifle a cough. Walter explained my situation to his brother, and when he was finished, he asked: "What do you think?"

Andrew motioned for another shot and looked at me curiously. "Had you not heard about the capture of Fort Fisher?" he asked. I explained that we had had no contact with anyone after we left Bermuda. "Well," said Andrew, "I admire your Captain's gumption, as ill-advised as it was. Had you simply heaved-to, you would have received no more than a short prison sentence. But to ram a Yankee cutter, what a beautiful suicide!"

I saw nothing beautiful about it. All the sacrifices, all the pain and suffering, all seemed more and more to me as no more than empty gestures as the War continued to grind on.

Andrew stood up to leave and said, "I will take you up to Hampstead, we will be jest a couple of fishermen heading home. I hope we can fool them Yankee boys, if they come pokin' around, as I can ill-afford to lose my boat. We will leave on the tide tomorrow, roundabouts 10 a.m., I reckon." He looked at me critically. "And try to look like a sailor," he said. "You look more like a landman than Walter."

The next day, I had my last breakfast with the Cheeleys. I thanked them profusely for all they had done for me. "You saved my life," I said. "You nursed me back to health, fed me and dressed me. I wish I had some way to repay you."

Walter smiled at me. "It was God that led me to you that dreadful night. To save even one life during this terrible time is a blessing to everyone. And a gift." Mrs. Cheeley reached over and covered my hand with her own. Though she said nothing, I felt her kindness and compassion clearly enough. I wished with all my heart that I could take away the pain and loss that haunted them both. "I will keep you in my prayers," I said.

Around 9:30 a.m., Charlie walked with me to the home of his uncle. Like Walter, he lived on a small, deep-water inlet which provided shelter for his boat. It was a short walk from the Cheeley's as we were there in less than 30 minutes. Andrew Cheeley came out to meet us when we arrived. He rubbed Charlie's head and shook my hand. "Morning, Teddy." He looked me up and down and a slight smile came to his face, but he did not say anything. I had artfully dabbed some dirt streaks on my freshly laundered sailor's jumper, and I had not shaved. It was my best effort at looking more like a sailor.

Andrew handed me a heavy wool overcoat of the type worn by sailors everywhere. I took it gratefully as the day was overcast, cold and windy, promising to return the coat when we reached Hempstead. Andrew put his arm around Charlie and said, "You take good care of your Momma, she needs all the help and love you can give her. Tell her and your Daddy I will stop by when I return from Hampstead."

Andrew and I walked down to a small inlet at the north edge of his property. There I saw a fishing boat of the type called a 'sailing smack' tied up to a long pier jutting out into the inlet. Her name was the *Darby,* and she was much larger than I had expected from Walter's comments. I guessed her length at about 40 feet and her beam at 10 feet, but her size was exaggerated by a bowsprit that must have added another twenty-odd feet. "How much sail does she carry?" I asked Andrew.

"When we are working, anywhere from 1,000 to 1,250 sq. ft., although I have heard of smacks this size rigged to carry as much as 2,000 sq. ft." She must be fast for a fishing boat, I thought.

I could see that the tide had peaked, and the inlet was beginning to empty. Andrew made the boat ready for sea and we tacked down the inlet and into the open Atlantic. As if to welcome us, the sun suddenly came out and the ocean changed from grey to deep blue. Andrew added more sail, and I took a deep breath of the fresh, salt air as the boat began to gently heel over.

A smack the size of the *Darby* normally required a crew of 3 to 4 people, but Andrew and I worked well together. Because the wind was from out of the north, the same general direction we were travelling, we were required to tack often. Changing direction over and over again required a great deal of quick action with the sails and tiller and it was exhausting work for just two men. Even in the freezing temperatures, I was soon soaked in sweat.

By mid-afternoon, the wind had shifted more from the west and the sailing became much easier. Andrew pulled the sails in tight and, aside from making slight adjustments to the sails, we could at last sit back and rest for some periods of time.

It was difficult to judge our speed or position as there were few landmarks on the shore. But there were enough for Andrew to declare that we had passed Wilmington. "I believe we have passed the most dangerous part of our trip," he said. "It would appear that the Yankee attack on Wilmington has progressed enough that they no longer need to station ships off the coast." But not 10 minutes later, we spied smoke on the horizon from several vessels and they seemed to be heading in our direction.

CHAPTER 19

We Parler with the Yankees

Appear weak when you are strong, and strong when you are weak. — Sun Tzu"

B ad luck if they see us," said Andrew. "They had no way to know we were here. Just bad luck is all."

We watched as two Union ships passed by no more than 2 or 3 miles away. At first, it seemed as though they might not have seen us, but then their lookouts must have spotted us. Great columns of black smoke suddenly belched from their funnels as they made steam and turned to intercept us.

Andrew cursed under his breath and said, "Heave-to, Teddy. It could go bad for us if we do not react quickly enough for some bored Yankee sailor." I immediately set about slacking the sails, thereby stalling our forward progress.

When the two Union ships got close enough, we could see that they were 'steam frigates,' frigate-style ships equipped with a full set of sails as well as steam engines and a propellor. They were huge, a third-again longer than the *Quicksilver* had been. And they carried more than a dozen cannons and more than 450 men.

With amazing delicacy, one of the ships coasted and then

stopped next to us, making not even a ripple to rock us. The ship loomed above us like a great cliff over a canyon.

We saw a head pop over the frigates railing some 30 feet above and stare down at us. It wore an officer's hat and carried a megaphone. "Identify yourselves!" it boomed.

Andrew cupped his hands and yelled back, "We are the smack *Darby* out of Wilmington. I am Andrew Cheeley, and this is my nephew Teddy."

A second head joined the first. The two heads communicated for a moment and then, "You appear to be a fishing smack, but I see no fish. Nor do I see any nets nor traps. What is your purpose for being out here today?"

"I am returning my nephew to his family in Hampstead."

A third head joined the two already peering over the railing of the frigate. Another brief conversation was held and then, "To whom do you owe your allegiance?"

"Why, the Confederate States of America, of course!" yelled Andrew, and I felt my heart jump. I did not like the direction this was taking. "My nephew and I are out this day to capture Yankee war ships. You have fallen into my trap, Sir, and I demand your immediate surrender. You may lower your sword on a line to me if that is more convenient for you."

There was a moment of shocked silence and then gales of laughter from above. "Ah, be on your way, Reb! The eagle has no time to waste on a minnow." The three heads disappeared.

There was a rumble from deep in the frigate's hull and the ship began to pull away. I took a breath for what seemed like the first time since the frigates had appeared on the horizon.

The *Darby* had a deep draft, and we were little disturbed by the long swells that rolled underneath us. Andrew sat in the stern with his arm over the tiller, making small adjustments to our course when he deemed necessary. He had a look of contentment on his face of the type that only sailors know when they are at sea. Occasionally, he would gesture to me to adjust a sail or coil a line, but we mostly just sat in companionable silence.

Hampstead was a small village located on the North Carolina coast and protected by a large barrier island. The entrance from the Atlantic looked tricky to me, but Andrew knew the location of the navigation aids and we were soon pulling safely into a small marina.

I saw a few fishing boats and piles of crab traps on the pier. If I needed another clue as to what the main occupation of the village was, the hanging fishnets left little doubt. "Nice place, Hampstead," said Andrew. "Mostly fishermen, of course, but a few farmers also. Acres and acres of blueberries and tobacco growing not too far from here."

After we secured the *Darby* to the pier, Andrew led me to a small building not far from the marina. When I saw it was a general store, I turned to Andrew and said, "There is nothing here for me, Andrew, as what little money I had lies at the bottom of the Cape Fear River."

Andrew smiled and patted my arm. "Let us help you out, Teddy." When I started to object, Andrew held up his hand to stop me. "I figured you to be a stubborn man, Teddy, stubborn and proud. But you must let me honor a promise I made to Louisa before we left. She and Walter gave me some Yankee cash to help you on your way and I told Louisa that I would see to it that you were provisioned before you continued your journey."

I shook my head. "I think they can ill-afford it and I cannot accept it."

Andrew gave me a hard look. "As you wish, Teddy, but then you must repay your debt to me. This trip was not without its dangers."

My mouth fell open. "But, Andrew, if only I could! I have no money…"

"There is only one way, then: accept my brother's generosity and allow me to fulfill my promise to Louisa." He cocked his head at me. "Well?"

I had to smile. I knew I had just been snookered by a fisherman turned country lawyer. "Very well, Andrew. But you must tell them how grateful I am and that I will return the money as soon as I am able." Andrew smiled back. "Will do," he said.

When we left the store, I was carrying a new backpack and assorted things necessary for survival on my trip north: I had a canteen, a cooking kit, a knife, and assorted foodstuffs. I also had some extra socks and underwear and a toothbrush. I felt rich and truly blessed. And when Andrew turned to leave for home, he pressed the remaining change into my palm. "Stay safe, Teddy."

I left the village and stepped smartly through knee-high grass, leaving a wake in the damp sward. Although I made minor detours around natural obstacles, my path was unvaryingly north. I was, you see, headed home.

CHAPTER 20

Sweet William Sweet

January 26, 1865

The most beautiful people we have known are those who have known defeat, known suffering, known struggle, known loss, and have found their way out of the depths. These persons have an appreciation, a sensitivity, and an understanding of life that fills them with compassion, gentleness, and a deep loving concern. Beautiful people do not just happen. — Elisabeth Kubler-Ross

I n a little less than a week, I had made it within a few miles of Goldsboro, North Carolina. There I made camp in some woods adjacent to the road. I had just begun to cook some beans when a Yankee stepped out of the darkness and approached me. He was a huge man, easily a head taller than me, and dressed in the uniform of a Union infantryman. I noticed he was not carrying a musket. "Can you spare some food?" he asked, "I have not eaten in several days."

I motioned to the man to sit next to the fire with me. "You are welcome to share what I have." I held out my hand. "I am

Teddy Miller."

The Yankee enveloped my hand in his. "I am William Sweet," he said, "but everybody calls me Sweet William." He shrugged his shoulders. "Could be 'cause the Army always calls your name backwards, you know? Like 'Samuels, Ben and Sweet, William.'"

I smiled and nodded. "Where is your unit?"

Sweet William scratched at his beard. "Well, they was in Savannah when I left. By now they are probably somewhere in South Carolina."

"Are you a deserter?"

Sweet William shook his head. "No, Sir, I was just sick of the war and decided it was time to leave. Not that my friends had not tried to talk me out of it. 'Now, Sweet William,' they said, 'it ain't the best idea to just skedaddle. If they catch you, they will shoot you.' But I just threw the last of my belongings into an old haversack, reckoned the direction of north, and walked out of camp."

I did some quick calculations and figured that Sweet William had already walked more than 300 miles, in a Yankee uniform, through enemy territory. It had to be some kind of miracle that he had not already been shot, hanged or arrested. "Where are you headed, Sweet William?" I asked.

"Home. I work on a little farm in upstate New York. When I get there, I will never leave again. And I will open my heart to God and pray that I can forget the things I saw when I stood on the very precipice of Hell."

Sweet William helped me to gather dead tree branches which we piled upon the fire. When the fire was roaring, we moved closer, leaving only our backs exposed to the bitter cold night. I immediately sensed his intrinsic kindness and thought about the road still ahead of me, a road I knew to be filled with dangerous predators, human and otherwise. A man of Sweet William's stature would be an obvious deterrent to most. "Sweet William," I said, "tomorrow I continue my journey north. It is my intention to cross into Virginia around Roanoke Rapids. After that, I will head more westward towards Lynchburg. I would enjoy your company if you are so inclined."

Sweet William smiled broadly. "Why thank you, Teddy, your company will surely speed the trip!" Then, "But at what point will you turn west? I feel it is my best and shortest course to continue North through Richmond."

Richmond? I thought. Sweet William means to walk through the capital of the Confederacy wearing a Union infantryman's uniform. But I said nothing, figuring I would try to argue him out of it later. I pulled out a worn and oft-folded piece of paper on which I had written some directions I had copied from a map while still back in Hampstead. I said, "Around Belfield I plan to turn towards Appomattox and Lynchburg. Stay with me that far and you will be no more than 80 or so miles due south of Richmond."

Sweet William turned out to be a wonderful traveling companion. He was invariably cheerful, and he told entertaining stories about his friends and family; but he would not discuss anything to do with the War. If I would bring up the subject, he would look away and refuse to respond. The miles seemed to melt away and we were soon north of Rocky Mount and headed for the Virginia line.

It was the dead of winter and there was little food to be found in the fields and orchards we passed. Occasionally, we would find a few root vegetables that had been missed during the harvest, and here and there, a few apples still hung from the higher branches. And we were further restricted in our food sources because we had no weapons and could not hunt.

Sweet William had brought no food with him and carried no canteen for water. Neither did he have any money. He was, I realized, like a migrating bird, trusting that God would provide for his sustenance along the way. And, somehow, God did.

Most of the people we met were kind and generous with what little they themselves had.

Almost no one paid any attention to Sweet William's uniform. Nearly everyone we passed seemed worn out, physically and emotionally, by the War. They walked slowly, hunched over and hollow-eyed. If they even looked at Sweet William, it was no more than a momentary glance because of his remarkable size. But there were exceptions. We did meet some people who seemed fueled by hatred. You had the feeling that if their hatred were ever extinguished, they would deflate and fall to the ground, an empty vessel.

We had just such an encounter in a small town called Weldon near the Virginia border. Sweet William and I were walking down the street past some houses. On the front porch of one, a woman was sweeping off some snow when she saw Sweet William. For a moment, she did not move or say anything. Then she let out such a cry of pain and anguish that Sweet William and I froze in our tracks. Her cry echoed down the empty street.

The woman ran down the steps towards us, screaming, "Murderer! You killed my son!" She ran at us, carrying the broom like a club. "Murderer!"

I instinctively took a step backwards as she ran straight towards Sweet William. I saw her raise the broom handle to strike him and then suddenly stop, a quizzical expression on her face. I glanced over at Sweet William where he stood with his arms at his side. He had a gentle, almost childlike expression on his face and a single tear was running down his cheek.

"Why have you come here?" she demanded. "To remind me of my loss? To tear open again the wound in my heart?"

Sweet William shook his head. "No, Ma'am, I mean you no pain."

The woman stared at Sweet William for the longest time, then dropped the broom. She seemed to shrink in my vision, and I thought for a moment that she might fall. She sighed deeply and said, almost to herself, "You are just a child. They are all just children."

I reached over to steady the woman, but she shrugged off my help. Her full attention was on Sweet William. "Are you a deserter?" she asked him.

"No, Ma'am." Sweet William wiped his cheek with his shirtsleeve. "I done my duty to man and Caesar well enough, now I am going home to try to make my peace with God."

Tears began to roll down the woman's cheeks. "Do you have a mother waiting for you?" This elicited another tear from Sweet William, and I felt my own eyes begin to well up. "Yes, Ma'am, I do. 'Though I do not know if she thinks me alive or dead."

"Oh, you must write her! Do not let her be consumed by fear. Tell her you are coming home so that she may fill her mind with happy thoughts of reunion."

Sweet William looked down at his feet and said, "I do not know how to write, Ma'am. I have depended on my friends for what letters I posted in the past."

The woman glanced at me for a moment, seeming to say, 'What kind of friend are you to let this man's mother worry for nothing?' Then she turned again to Sweet William, "It is freezing out here. Bring your friend and come inside."

On the way into her house, we saw a neighbor standing outside by his own porch holding a shotgun. I reckoned he had come out in response to the woman's screams. She looked at him and said, "It is alright, Ed. Go back to your family." The man nodded and turned to go back inside.

She led us into a cozy parlor where we sat in front of the fire. On the mantle above it was a daguerreotype in a gold gilt frame with a black ribbon across one corner. It showed a curly haired young man in a Confederate officer's uniform. His cheeks had been tinted pink, making him look for all the world like a child playing soldier. I could clearly see the resemblance to his mother.

The woman must have noticed me looking at the picture. "That is my son Marshall," she said. "He was killed at

Spotsylvania Court House in May of last year." I tried to say how sorry I was for her loss, but she did not seem to hear me. "I have been trying to prepare myself for the day when I would see Yankees walking down our streets: what would I say, what would I do? But I never imagined it would be today."

We sat in silence for a few moments before she said, "Where are my manners? I am Mrs. Cole."

"I am Teddy Miller," I said, "and this is Sweet William."

Mrs. Cole repeated, "Sweet William?" Then after a moment, "Yes, I can see that." She turned again to me. "Are you a soldier as well, Mr. Miller?"

"No, Ma'am," I said. "Like Sweet William, I am just trying to make my way home."

Mrs. Cole served us hot tea and biscuits and then left the room. She returned a moment later with some writing paper and an envelope. "Now, Sweet William," she said, "we shall alleviate your mother's suffering. You will dictate and I will write. Do you understand?"

Sweet William nodded. "Yes, Ma'am."

CHAPTER 21

Rest and Replenishment

It's only after we've lost everything that we're free to do anything. — *Chuck Palahniuk*

Within two days, Sweet William and I had reached Belfield, Virginia. It was there that we said our good-byes. I shook his hand and gave him half of what little money I had left, as well as my canteen and other camping gear. It was my intention to find work in Belfield and replenish myself, mentally, physically, and financially, before resuming my trip.

Sweet William protested my gifts until I had assured him that I would have no need of any of it for some time. He thanked me profusely, picked me up in a rib-cracking bear hug and promised to keep me in his prayers.

When he had placed me back on the ground, I said, "Sweet William, will you not consider by-passing Richmond and taking a more indirect route? I fear for your safety."

Sweet William shook his head. "God protected me in battle when every man around me fell. I will trust Him to help me find my way home."

Belfield was part of a two-town settlement on the Meherrin River. A sister village called Hicksford lay across from it on the opposite side of the river. The village appeared prosperous with well-kept little wood cottages and a brick-front main street. Dominating it all was a large mansion called 'Village View.' I would soon learn that the front parlor of the mansion had served as the site of a council of war for Generals W.H.F. Lee (Robert E. Lee's son), Wade Hampton and Matthew Butler not two months earlier when they defended, unsuccessfully, nearby railroad lines.

After some looking, I found lodging in a rooming house run by a widow named Clara McHinney. Mrs. McHinney had lost her husband, two sons and a nephew in the War. To support herself, she rented out two bedrooms in her house. It took all the money I had left, but I had room and lodging for one week while I searched for work.

The bedroom was small and somewhat shabby but exceptionally clean and the food prepared by Mrs. McHinney was plentiful and good. After just one night out of the cold, and with a full belly, I was much refreshed. The next morning, I put on my wool coat and set out to find employment.

The village was not large, but it was on a main route to Richmond and there were always many travelers passing through. Consequently, the village had an inn much larger than would normally be expected for its size. The inn was called 'The Crossroads," a wooden structure three stories tall, with a dining room and bar on the ground floor.

When I approached the manager of the inn and told him of my bartending experience, he hired me on the spot. Without him saying so directly, I understood that there were not many young men available for work in the village. Like everywhere in the South, most men of working age were in the Army. Fields lay fallow and laborer jobs went unfilled. "Bartending plus clean-up and stocking," he added. We shook hands and I walked away the newest employee of The Crossroads.

I worked at the inn 6 days a week from 7:00 a.m. to closing with Mondays off. The pay was good, and I managed to put away a couple of dollars most weeks after paying Mrs. McHinney for room and board. I felt my strength returning, but I determined that I would remain in Belfield until the War moved on from Richmond and Petersburg and I could safely return to the Shenandoah Valley. The days turned into weeks and then months.

I followed the War through the newspapers. It had become a slow-motion tragedy for the Confederacy, a cruel dénouement to years of loss and suffering. A month after I arrived in Belfield, Sherman left Savannah and captured Columbia, South Carolina. Not long after, Confederate defenders were forced to evacuate Charleston and the City of Wilmington finally fell.

Each day seemed to bring news of another Confederate defeat: the attack on Fort Stedman, called by some 'Lee's Last offensive,' failed. Then, after losing The Battle of Five Forks, Lee was forced to abandon the Petersburg-Richmond siege lines.

The customers at The Crossroads became increasingly more morose as the weeks dragged on. Conversation was generally limited to ordering another drink or commenting on innocuous things like the weather. The War was hardly mentioned, although it raged no more than 50 miles north of us; but sunken, red eyes hinted at sleepless nights and the personal loss of friends and family members to the seemingly endless bloodletting.

Although few dared to say it, many just wished for the War to end, regardless of the victor. We all sensed that whatever the South had been, it was already no more, ruined by the very War meant to preserve it.

On April 12, 1865, I awoke to a newspaper headline which screamed, LEE SURRENDERS! While there were still Confederate armies in the field, the War was effectively over. I folded the newspaper, placed it on my dresser, and began to make my way over to The Crossroads to start my shift.

It was a beautiful spring day, and the morning sun warmed my shoulders as I walked. But there was no gaiety in my heart, no spring to my step, only a sense of profound loss. It seemed to take great effort just to place one foot in front of another. I suddenly realized how much of an inseparable part of my life the War had become. It was a part of every loss I had suffered and part of every plan I had made. In my mind, I heard the cannons firing, men screaming and then—silence.

I stopped in the middle of the street and lifted my face to the sun. *I closed my eyes, and the sun's warmth became my mother's hands cradling my cheeks. 'You made it, Teddy,' she whispered in my ear. 'You survived!'*

I opened my eyes but saw only indistinct shapes that had been imprinted on my retina by the sun and floated just outside my vision. They numbered not in the tens, or even the thousands, but in the hundreds of thousands. I knew what and who they were: I recognized my father, still wrapped in chains from head to foot; and there was Jacob Hayes, the man I had killed, standing with his feet apart, a musket cradled in his arms. Behind them, multitudes of men in blue and grey uniforms shuffled and murmured.

When I reached *The Crossroads*, I gave my notice.

CHAPTER 22

The Valley

Nevertheless, I long—I pine, all my days— to travel home and see the dawn of my return. And if a god will wreck me yet again on the wine-dark sea, I can bear that too, with a spirit tempered to endure. Much have I suffered, labored long and hard by now in the waves and wars. Add this to the total— bring the trial on! —Homer

I reckoned that the most direct route back to the Shenandoah Valley from Belfield was through Lawrenceville, then to Farmville, Lynchburg and finally Buena Vista. As a crow flies, it was probably no more than 160 miles, but the roads meandered on their way north and the distance to be travelled was close to twice that.

In Lawrenceville, I purchased an old mule to speed my trip. Without pushing myself too hard, I could walk around 18-20 miles a day; but with the mule, I could cover 30 miles without killing him or myself.

The roads were clogged with Confederate soldiers heading home after Lee's surrender. Very few of them carried weapons of any kind, whether by choice or mandate I did not know. They were all skeletal thin and there was a depressing sameness to their appearance as their uniforms had been reduced to rags and most had no shoes. They would meet no one's eyes as they passed by; the famous Confederate pride, cause of so many unlikely victories, seemed to have been replaced by shame and hopelessness.

There was desolation everywhere. Fields lay fallow that should already have been showing the first growth of the season and civilians, displaced by the War, mingled with the soldiers on the roads. Many had carts piled high with their belongings. The men and women walked alongside the carts, their cuffs and hems dragging in the dust. The children sat perched on top of the precarious piles.

I had gotten no farther than Blackstone, Virginia, when I heard the news of Lincoln's assassination. Blackstone was a small village where two roads crossed, and it possessed a small tavern. Posted on the front door was a 3-day old copy of the front page of the National News out of Washington City. The headline was stark: LINCOLN SHOT. It was clear that he was not expected to live.

I felt sick to my stomach at the shock of it. Suddenly feeling a need for human company, I went into the tavern and found a spot at the bar. There were a lot of customers for being so early in the day, and the mood was somber. Men spoke in soft voices, but the topic was always the same: Lincoln and what his assassination meant for the South.

"Hurrah for Wilkes Booth," said a man at the end of the bar. "Good riddance to that flim-flam, goober-digger Lincoln!"

"Ah, Sam, you are a right fool," said another. "Lincoln was no friend of the South, but he were at least inclined to temper his response to those who took part in the rebellion."

"True enough, " said a third man. "No tellin' how the new President will treat us. Tomorrow, we may be readin' about Bobby Lee hisself being hung from a lamp post. Then who is next?"

And so it went. I finished my beer and returned to my mule, little comforted by anything I had heard in the tavern. As I rode out of Blackstone, I wondered if anything in human history had ever been made better by murder.

A few days later, I stopped at a turn in the road just outside of Buena Vista where the Shenandoah Valley lay spread out before me. I tied the mule to a tree and found a seat on a slab of white rock. The sky was cloudless and there was little haze. I could see nearly the entire width of the Valley.

From a distance, little seemed changed in the Valley below. But I knew too well the destruction that had been wrought on it by Grant's orders to his soldiers to leave the Shenandoah Valley a 'barren waste.' My family farm had been burned in the resulting conflagration.

There was little sound beyond that of my mule munching on a small patch of grass. I filled my lungs with the familiar air and gave a sigh of contentment. While I did not know what even the very next day would bring, I was home. For the moment, that was enough.

Over the next few days, I made my way up the Valley, passing through familiar towns and villages. First, Lexington where I picked up the Valley Pike and then through Staunton and finally Harrisonburg. I remembered the last time I had made this trip, especially the funereal columns of black smoke rising from the burning farms. There were no fires now, but the fields lay fallow and overgrown with weeds. The farmhouses still standing were clearly abandoned, every windowpane broken, and the porch roofs sagging.

At last, I came to the turnoff to Cedar Valley, where Malcolm Davies' farm—and my brother Jed—were located. I dismounted from the mule and led him up the deeply rutted driveway.

When I reached Malcolm's farm, I was surprised by what I saw. While the little cabin looked the same, the fences had all been repaired and there was a new barn. There was a prosperous air to it all that had not been there before. Clearly, Jed was being of considerable help to Malcolm.

I saw Jed walk out of the barn carrying a hammer and some boards. He stood staring at me for several moments, and then threw the hammer and boards to the ground. He ran at me and, for just a second, I thought he was going to throw himself into my arms. Instead, he began to pummel me with his fists. I had to cover my face with my arms. "You bastard!" he screamed. "You let me think you dead!"

I tasted blood and my vision turned red. I could not make myself strike back at him even in defense and I started to slump to the ground. Malcolm suddenly appeared and pulled Jed off me. While he held Jed back with one arm, he said, "What are you doing here? We thought you had died in Washington City."

"I wrote," I said, wiping my bloody mouth on my shirt sleeve. "Did you not get my letters?"

"We got no letters."

I sat down heavily on the ground. I looked over at my brother but had to look away. I could not bear the hurt I saw on his face.

"Go get your brother some water, Jed," Malcolm said.

Jed looked at Malcolm with disbelief. "Water?" he asked. "I would rather cut my own throat than serve him!"

"I said get him some water."

Jed folded his arms across his chest and glared first at Malcolm, then at me. "You ain't my Daddy, Malcolm, do not be tellin' me what to do."

I expected an angry response from Malcolm, but he surprised me when he responded with a soft voice: "He is your brother, Jed. Whatever anger you feel towards Teddy, do not let it cloud your humanity."

Jed's mouth dropped open, and he just stood there for a moment or two. Then he said, "Alright, I will get the damn water." He spun on his heels and headed for the cabin. Malcolm yelled after him, "Do not let the Missus hear you cuss, boy! I mean it!" But Jed, if he even heard Malcolm, did not respond.

While Jed was gone, Malcolm helped me walk to some shade under a large oak tree where I sat down on a log. "Jeb was near ruined when he thought you dead. First, he loses his father, then you."

"But I thought he hated me."

Malcolm shook his head, "He were just a boy when you left him here. Hell, he still is. One day, he will understand why you did what you did to save your Daddy's life. I try to tell him that life ain't as black and white as he thinks it is."

I had to smile. "My Daddy used to tell me that."

"Eli is a smart man."

At the mention of my father's name, Malcolm must have seen some reaction from me. "Did something happen to your Daddy?" he asked.

I started to answer when I saw Jed was returning with a cup of water. He nearly threw the cup at me, and half of the water ended up on me and the ground. "Do not choke," he said.

"Jed, I know you are angry, but I really need you to listen to me. I have some important news about Daddy."

Jed froze. "Is Daddy dead?" He apparently read the answer in my eyes before I could reply, and his eyes grew wide.

"I am sorry, Jed, but I know of no other way to tell you this: Daddy died in prison, not two weeks after he arrived at Fort Jefferson."

Malcolm reached over and took Jed's hand. "How did he die?" Malcolm asked.

"They say it was dysentery." I wanted to reach for my brother, to hold him close, but I dared not; I was too afraid of what kind of reaction that might elicit from him.

CHAPTER 23

It is Always about Kate

Land is the only thing in the world that amounts to anything, for 'Tis the only thing in this world that lasts, 'Tis the only thing worth working for, worth fighting for - worth dying for. — Margaret Mitchell

Jed, Malcolm, and I sat at the long table in the kitchen of Malcolm's cabin. Mrs. Davies and her twin girls bustled around behind us preparing for the evening meal. "That Pinkerton woman stopped by here some months ago," said Malcolm. "She said you had been shot and were in a Yankee hospital in Washington City. She said she did not know if you would live or die. So, when we heard no more, we had to figure you were dead."

I nodded my understanding. "She stopped by only to check on you and Jed, to see if you were well. She did it for me."

Malcolm gave out a laugh. "Hah! Well, she nearly scared the bejesus out of us in the process." Mrs. Davies walked up behind Malcolm and whispered, "Watch your language, Malcolm!"

"Sorry, Missus. Anyways, she comes riding up the driveway surrounded by 20 cavalrymen, all with those new repeating rifles. I figured she was here to arrest the whole bunch of us."

Jed spoke up for the first time, his voice bitter: "She grabbed my arm and pulled me aside. She told me not to antagonize the cavalrymen for my own and Malcolm's sake. Then, after turning my world upside down, she left, just like she always does."

"Kate cares about you and Malcolm," I said. "It was risky for her to come here."

"Kate cares about us?" Jed asked incredulously. "It was Kate talked you into betraying your country! It was Kate made you lie to me about Daddy being dead! It was Kate who left you dying in a hospital while she ran off playing hero soldier!"

I felt myself blush as I tried to hold down my rising anger and frustration. "How many times do I have to tell you, Jed, that I made a deal with Kate to save Daddy from the hangman?" Malcolm started to interrupt when I said, "Wait, Malcolm. Let us settle this here and now." I turned again to Jed. "Tell me," I demanded, "what would you have done to save Daddy? Or would you have just let him die? You say I betrayed my country by turning in some murderous thugs here in the Valley as a trade for Daddy's life. Is that where your loyalties lie? Tell me, Jed!"

Jed looked as though he were about to burst into tears. "Tell me, Jed!" I shouted at him. Malcolm and Mrs. Davies looked away in embarrassment. Jed turned and ran out the cabin door.

I started to follow him when Malcolm grabbed my arm. "Let him be, Teddy."

Mrs. Davies had prepared a wonderful dinner, though none of us had any appetite. Jed had reluctantly returned to the table, although he would not look at or speak to me. After dinner, the twins cleared the dishes and Malcolm fetched a bottle of whiskey and three glasses. I was surprised when he poured one for Jed, as young as he was; the other two were for he and I. Malcolm raised his glass: "To your Daddy, boys, Eli was a good man and a generous friend."

"To Daddy," I said. Jed just stared sullenly at his drink.

We finished our drinks and I told them about my meeting with my father on his way to prison. "He asked about you, Jed, and sent his love." I saw Jed's eyes begin to water, but he looked away and said nothing.

Malcolm shifted uncomfortably in his seat and said, "I got some news for you, too, Teddy, and I guess I cannot be putting it off no longer. The Yankees paid us a visit a month ago looking for Jed. They said, 'cause your Daddy was convicted of espionage against the Union, all of his property had been confiscated. Said it was the law and all. They made Jed sign a bunch of papers, said he did not have a choice. Either sign away the farm or go to prison."

I felt my mouth fall open. "We have lost our farm?"

Malcolm placed his hand on my arm. "This has happened to others here in the Valley," he said. "I am told that you can petition the Union government and sometimes receive money towards the value of the land. But you will need a lawyer."

I suddenly felt anchorless, as if I were adrift in a void with no up, no down, no right or left. The land—my land—defined me. It made me a part of the Valley and the Valley a part of me. Who was I now, I wondered? Who would I ever be? Even with all the tragedy of the last few years, I never felt more lost than at that moment.

I spent the night on Malcolm's porch sleeping in an old rocking chair. The twins had given me a pillow for my head and a blanket to keep me warm. The next morning after breakfast, I said good-bye to Malcolm and Mrs. Davies and thanked them for their generosity. I was surprised when Jed offered to walk me down the driveway.

"Malcolm says I judge you too harshly, Teddy. I do not yet know if that is true. But I know I was lost when I thought you dead. And if I had known about Daddy..."

I reached for Jed, but he held up a hand to stop me. "This is not settled yet," he said. "Those were strong words you threw at me last night."

I nodded, willing to accept anything for some chance at reconciliation. "I love you, Jed."

Jed just looked at me for the longest time and then turned to walk back up the driveway towards the cabin. I watched him walk away, hoping he would look back at me. He did not.

CHAPTER 24

The Farmer's Daughter

Only once in your life, I truly believe, you find someone who can completely turn your world around. You tell them things that you've never shared with another soul and they absorb everything you say and actually want to hear more. You share hopes for the future, dreams that will never come true, goals that were never achieved and the many disappointments life has thrown at you. When something wonderful happens, you can't wait to tell them about it, knowing they will share in your excitement. They are not embarrassed to cry with you when you are hurting or laugh with you when you make a fool of yourself. Never do they hurt your feelings or make you feel like you are not good enough, but rather they build you up and show you the things about yourself that make you special and even beautiful. — Bob Marley

When I reached the Valley floor, I mounted the mule and turned us north towards New Market. About 5 miles out of town, I began to dead reckon my way to a farm I had visited just once before. After a few wrong turns, I finally found it around a mile off the Valley Pike and almost dead east of New Market.

It was already beginning to get dark, so I decided to camp for the night and visit the farm in the morning. I found a meadow with good grass for the mule and built a campfire. I soon had a pot of coffee boiling. I had no appetite and contented myself with the coffee while I stared into the fire.

I remembered being so confident when I told my plans to Amos and Amesta on No Name Key. How long ago was that? I wondered. I seemed to have lost all sense of time. A few months, certainly no more, and yet in that time the War had been lost, Lincoln had been assassinated and I had lost my land. I threw the remainder of my coffee on the fire and made ready to sleep. Tomorrow, I would call on Eugenie.

The farm was as I had remembered it from my first, and only, visit nearly a year earlier. It was just far enough off the Valley Pike that it had escaped the attention of Union troops and scavengers. It had to be one of the few still-working farms in the Valley.

I stood at the front door of the farmhouse, and it took every drop of courage I had to knock on the door. I sensed that the next few minutes would determine the course of the rest of my life.

The door opened and my heart skipped a beat. Eugenie stood before me, even more beautiful than I had remembered. At first, she looked puzzled, then her eyes widened, and she said, "You! What are you doing here?"

I do not know what reaction I had expected from Eugenie, but this was not it. "You said when the War was over, I could come to see you..." But I got no farther before Eugenie interrupted, her voice dropping almost to a whisper, "You are such a fool! Do you not know that the Sheriff is looking for you?"

I tried to make sense of what Eugenie was saying, but everything was going in a direction I had not expected. "The Sheriff? But why?"

Eugenie shushed me and glanced back over her shoulder, then stepped out onto the porch as she quietly closed the door behind her. She grabbed my elbow and led me off the porch and around a corner of the house. "If my Daddy sees you, he will shoot you like as not. You need to leave right now."

"But why is the Sheriff looking for me?" I asked again, desperately trying to understand.

"Murder. For the Murder of someone named Jacob, is all I recall."

Jacob Hayes, I thought. The man who had tried to kill me behind the schoolhouse. "That is not as it seems," I said.

Eugenie shook her head. "It does not matter," she said, her voice taking on a desperate edge. "You must leave."

Eugenie turned and started to walk away when I said, "Please, I need to see you again."

She stopped and turned again to face me. She lifted her eyes to mine and said sadly, "You come into my life as a fugitive and then vanish. Now, here you are again, still a wanted man. What am I to make of it all?"

I could feel that I was losing her. I said desperately, "Please, Eugenie, just let me talk with you. There is much you need to understand. I promise you that I am not the man you perceive me to be."

When she did not answer, I stepped closer and looked into her eyes. Every fiber of my being wanted to reach out and touch her face, but I dared not. "I just walked a thousand miles to see your face. And I would walk another thousand, and then another to spend just a moment with you. Please do not push me away."

A tear rolled down Eugenie's cheek and she dropped her eyes from my own. "I risk everything if I agree to see you again. My father would never understand." she said softly.

I was devastated that I caused her even a single tear. I

suppose I should have left at that very moment, to spare her from any more pain that I might cause. But I could not. "An hour, no more," I said.

Eugenie gave me a weak smile and nodded her head. "Tomorrow my father spends the afternoon in New Market. Come over after noon and we can talk." She glanced at the house, "Now you must leave before we are discovered."

Back at my camp, I found a soft, mossy place to lie down. I needed to think everything through. The joy I felt that Eugenie had agreed to see me again, if only for an hour, was tempered by this new knowledge that I was wanted for Jacob's murder. It seemed like everything I needed in my life was snatched away just at the very moment they were almost within my grasp. Feeling desperately sorry for myself, I cried out loud, "Daddy! Please, tell me what to do. I am lost, Daddy." The mule raised his head and looked at me with wide eyes; but whatever wisdom he may have had, he did not share it with me.

CHAPTER 25

Understanding

*My thoughts reel for something to save me from falling
into the invisible pit of misery. — Dave Cenker*

I started the day with a bath in a nearby creek. It was still
early May, and the water was very cold, but I felt clean and
refreshed as I changed into my other set of clothes. A little
after noon, I began the walk over to Eugenie's farm. Despite my
trepidation over recent developments, I could not deny the joy
that was building in my heart with every step I took.

Eugenie was sitting on a swing on the front porch when I
arrived. I could tell by the look on her face that she was of two
minds about our meeting. She gave me a brief smile and said,
"One hour, Teddy, that is all."

I first sat beside her on the swing, but she pointed to another
chair. "There, please." After I had moved, she said, "You have
something you wish to discuss with me?"

I was surprised by her brusque tone. I had lain awake half
the night before thinking of things I wanted to say to her.
But now that the time had come, I forgot everything I had
rehearsed. I looked down and my feet and stammered, "Oh,
Eugenie, I do not know. I just wanted to see you again and

explain some of the terrible things you have heard about me."
I looked back up at her. "But mostly, I just wanted to see you
again."

Eugenie said nothing for a few moments, then shook her
head sadly. "But why, Teddy, you know that nothing can ever
come from this."

An icy fear gripped my heart. "Please do not say that!"

Tears began to roll down Eugenie's face. She took out a
handkerchief and dabbed at her eyes. "You are wanted for
murder. You need to leave the Valley right away. You know they
will hang you if they catch you."

I shook my head. "No, I will not run away. I am no murderer,
whatever they say." I looked deep in her eyes and said, "My fate
is here in the Valley, and I believe you to be a part of it."

"But, Teddy, you do not even know me!"

Afraid I was going to lose her, I blurted out, "I love you,
Eugenie. I have loved you since the first moment I saw you out
by the well."

Eugenie looked at me with wide eyes and started to speak.
But before she could say anything, I said, "I ask nothing in
return but a chance to earn your affection. Please do not turn
me away."

One hour turned into two and then three. Eugenie and I had
left the porch and were walking along a small stream at the
back of her property. It was a beautiful spring day, and the air
was perfumed by the wildflowers growing everywhere.

We talked about many things, my family, her family, and
the recent death of her mother after a long illness. I do not
remember ever feeling happier or more content than I did at
those moments. But there were still some serious topics that
needed to be addressed.

"I need to speak about Jacob," I said, "as it weighs heavily
on my heart." We stopped walking and Eugenie turned to look

at me. "Although I killed Jacob in self-defense, I cannot fully justify his killing in my own mind."

"I do not understand. Is not self-defense always justified?"

"Some might think not. I killed Jacob while acting against the perceived interests of the Confederacy. Had I been acting in support of my country instead, perhaps I might be judged less harshly, even by myself."

Eugenie still looked confused, so I asked her to sit down on a log while I told her the story of my father's capture and my subsequent deal with the Union army. By the time I was finished, the shadows were getting deep, and Eugenie was anxious to get home before her father. She reached over and briefly touched the back of my hand. I felt my heart race and just for a moment, time stood still. I would have been happy living in that moment for the rest of my life.

I walked Eugenie most of the way home where we said our good-byes. We agreed to meet again the next day at the little stream. We both knew we were playing a dangerous game.

CHAPTER 26

Caught

Character is doing the right thing when nobody's looking. There are too many people who think that the only thing that's right is to get by, and the only thing that's wrong is to get caught. —*J. C. Watts*

E ugenie told me that her father had inherited a general store in New Market years before. He paid someone else to manage it, but once Eugenie's mother had died, her father had leased all his land to other farmers and spent more and more time in town. Eugenie thought it was because he found the farm too lonely after his wife's death. Whatever the reason, he was seldom at the farm.

Eugenie and I spent every opportunity over the next few days walking around the perimeter of the farm and the small, secluded stream became our favorite spot to sit and talk. Eugenie made us picnic lunches and we spent hours talking about happy things mostly, and what we wanted for the future. One day I reached over and took her hand and she smiled at me with a smile as bright and warm as the sun. But the more intertwined our affections became, the more we had to find a way to deal with my status as a fugitive.

We talked about my options, of which there were not many. Several times, Eugenie tried to talk me into leaving the Valley, but I refused to even consider it. Then, one afternoon while we sat beside the stream, Eugenie unexpectedly said to me, "If you will not leave the Valley without me, Teddy, then I will go with you. I cannot bear the thought of you being hanged or imprisoned."

I did not know how to respond. It was the first time she had expressed to me the depth of her feelings. I took her hand and said, "I love you too dearly to give you the life of a fugitive. I need to fight this here and now. I am no murderer, and I will not let our life together be tainted by a lie. All I ask is that you pray for me and wait for me until there is some resolution."

Eugenie gave out a deep sigh and I could see she was fighting back tears. "I hope we do not live to regret your decision, Teddy."

I squeezed her hand and said, "I will turn myself in to the Sheriff. If they think me a murderer, let them prove it."

I left Eugenie at her farmhouse and made my way back to camp. The mule was still tied to a tree and was contentedly munching on a patch of grass. But I noticed that some of my belongings had been moved and I immediately sensed that I was not alone. I was turning to run away, my heart pounding in my chest, when a voice called out, "Do not move, boy!"

I instinctively dropped to my knees behind a large tree just as a shot rang out. The ball hit the tree not six inches above my head and I was showered with splinters and bark. I let out a curse and ran through the trees, away from the shooter. I had not gotten ten yards before another man stood before me, his musket at his side. I charged him and caught him with my shoulder before he could raise his musket. He tumbled to the ground and shouted, "He is getting past me!"

I kept running as fast as I could, the bushes and brambles

tearing at my face and clothes. I could hear the men behind me crashing through the woods, cursing, and yelling, and I expected another shot at any moment. I almost thought I had gotten away when I reached the Valley pike; but there waited a man on horseback with a large dog on a chain leash sitting beside him. He said, "Do not make me release the dog, boy."

I stopped and tried to catch my breath. The man casually walked his horse over to me, stopped, and sat staring down at me. He said nothing as two men came running out of the woods. They lay their muskets on the ground when they reached us and stood gasping for breath, bent over with their hands on their knees. They were both young, probably not much older than I, and dressed like farm laborers.

The man on horseback was not much older, but he looked more affluent, perhaps he was a farm manager or owner. Without warning, he reached down and struck me across the face with his riding crop. I grabbed my cheek and cried out in surprise and pain. I could feel blood running between my fingers. I started to protest when he drew back the crop and swung again at my face. This time, I blocked most of it with my forearm. "You best kill me," I said. "I will allow no man to beat me like a dog."

The man on horseback laughed. "This boy throws empty threats around like seed in a hen house." He jumped down off his horse and stood facing me. "You made a big mistake coming here and tomcatting around Miz Eugenie."

I tensed, ready to throw myself at this man regardless of the consequences. Hate and anger burned inside me. Coming from his mouth, even Eugenie's name sounded obscene. But before I could move, the two farm hands pulled my arms behind my back and tied my hands.

But the man on horseback was not finished yet. He removed the collar from around the dog's neck and placed it on mine. Then he attached the chain leash and tied the loose end to the pommel of his saddle. "You bastard!" I said. "You will pay for this."

The man on horseback ignored my threats. He clucked at his horse and began to walk, but I dragged my feet and refused to be led. The man stopped his horse and turned to face me. "Makes me no never mind," he said, "whether you walk, or I drag you. Either way, we are going to see Mr. Martin."

CHAPTER 27

Farmer Martin

I must be cruel only to be kind; Thus bad begins, and worse remains behind. — *William Shakespeare*

Along the way to the Martin farm, the man on horseback would occasionally trot the horse, making me run to keep from being dragged. By the time we reached the farmhouse, I was exhausted and fell to my knees. The two farm hands trotted into the yard just behind us. The man on horseback yelled, "We are here, Mr. Martin. We have caught him."

After a few moments, the front door opened, and a tall, thin man walked out onto the porch. He leaned heavily on a cane as he walked. He had snow white hair and a white beard that stood out in sharp contrast to his weathered skin. "Good job, Simon," he said. He walked over and sat down heavily on a rocking chair and turned it to face me. "Did you really think I would not find out about you and Eugenie? You were not nearly so discreet as you thought. Several people saw you two walking in the fields and woods."

"What do you want with me?" I asked, as I struggled back to my feet.

"Want? Why I mean to hang you, Mr. Miller."

Before I could respond, Eugenie came walking around the corner of the house carrying a basket of eggs. When she saw me, chained and covered in blood, she dropped the basket and let out a scream. "Daddy, what have you done!" She started to run to me when Simon jumped off his horse and blocked her path. She stopped and turned again to her father. "I never knew you capable of such cruelty, Daddy."

Mr. Martin's face turned beet red, and he yelled, "Get in the house, Eugenie, and stay there!" When she did not move, he ordered Simon to take her inside.

Simon reached out to grab her arm when I said, "Touch her and there will be an accounting." Simon spun around and said, "Keep your mouth shut!" He took a step towards me and drew back his arm as if to strike me. But Eugenie yelled, "Stop, Simon, for God's sake!" Simon reluctantly dropped his arm and Eugenie turned and ran into the house, sobbing. The door slammed behind her, as loud as a gunshot.

Simon's dog, a huge beast with large yellow eyes, walked over and lay at his feet. Simon reached down and scratched the dog's head as he waited for Mr. Martin to tell him what to do next. The two farmhands stood shuffling their feet and staring at the ground.

Mr. Martin said nothing for several long minutes. Whether he was feeling any of Eugenie's condemnation, I do not know, but there was no mercy or compassion in his voice when he spoke to me: "You would take my daughter away from me? You are not worthy of one hair on her head!" His tone was so contemptuous of me that I thought he might spit. "Yet she pines for you, a murderer and a traitor. Well, I will not stand for it." He turned to the farmhands and said, "Billy, you go get the wagon. Edward, get a coil of rope from the barn. This day we will see justice done."

Billy and Edward were just leaving the yard when Eugenie reappeared on the front porch. Everyone turned to look at her. She was carrying a double-barreled shotgun almost as long as she was tall. But she looked comfortable holding it and I had no doubt she knew how to use it. "There will be no hanging today, Daddy."

A look of shock, then anger, passed across Mr. Martin's face. "Put that gun away, Eugenie!" But Eugenie just smiled, even as tears were streaming down her face. "You taught me how to shoot, Daddy. Why do you not tell the boys here what a good shot I am?"

Mr. Martin's face was red, and the veins bulged in his neck. "Put the gun away, Eugenie. Do as I tell you."

Eugenie ignored her father and said, "Untie him, Simon." But Simon just stood there. "Sorry, Miz Eugenie, I cannot do that."

"Untie him, Simon."

Simon took a small step towards Eugenie, his arms wide in supplication. "Now, Miz Eugenie, why do you not put down that shotgun before someone gets hurt."

"Come no closer, Simon," she warned. But Simon took another step towards her and she fired. The sound of the gunshot startled everyone. She had aimed at the ground in front of Simon, but some of the pellets must have ricocheted off the hard earth and struck Simon in the shin. He gave a cry of surprise and pain but did not stop moving towards Eugenie. "I know you, Miz Eugenie, and I do not believe you capable of killing me."

It was so quiet that we could all clearly hear the sound of Eugenie cocking the hammer on the second barrel of the shotgun. Even Simon hesitated.

"And I know you, Simon, all these years you have worked for Daddy. And I know that you love nothing on this earth so much as yourself. Except maybe him." Eugenie turned the shotgun until it was pointed at Simon's dog.

Simon's eyes grew wide. "You would not!" he said.

"For the last time, Simon, untie him."

Simon looked towards Mr. Martin as if asking what should be done. But Mr. Martin just looked down at his lap, seeming to acknowledge that he had lost control of the situation. "Let him go, Simon," he said.

Simon hesitated, seeming to debate whether to obey Mr. Martin's orders. After a long moment when no one moved or said anything, he walked over to me and removed the dog collar and chain. Then he untied the ropes that bound my hands. He whispered in my ear, "This is not over yet. No girl in petticoats will save you from the hangman."

I rubbed the circulation back into my hands and my eyes locked with Simon's. "Pray they hang me, Simon."

CHAPTER 28

I Surrender

I have been driven many times upon my knees by the overwhelming conviction that I had nowhere else to go. My own wisdom and that of all about me seemed insufficient for that day. — *Abraham Lincoln*

I sat on the edge of the well in the backyard while Eugenie wiped the dried blood off my face, exposing a long welt across my left cheek. Her shotgun stood leaning against the well next to us. "You were very brave," I said to hcr. She stopped her ministrations and put her finger to my lip. "We are in this together, Teddy."

"We are now," I said. "They will not soon forget you shooting Simon in the ankle."

Eugenie smiled. "You know that was an accident! But I will enjoy every day I see him limping around the property." She grew serious: "But what do we do now, Teddy?"

"I will surrender to the Sheriff at once. Others will come looking for me and I will not put you in danger." I took her hands and smiled at her. "After all, there may be more than two of them and your shotgun only has two barrels."

"Oh, Teddy, do not joke! I cannot bear the thought of losing you. What if..."

But I did not let her finish. "I will clear my name and then no one can stand between us." I held her tightly in my arms and closed my eyes. I saw two futures, one filled with joy and contentment, the other with loss and regret. Which will it be? I wondered.

After my wound had been cleaned, Eugenie and I determined to leave for the Sheriff's office as soon as possible. We did not know where Simon was, and we were afraid he might return with more men. We heard no more from Eugenie's father, which was also unsettling. "I need to get my mule and belongings before I leave," I said.

Eugenie gave me a look that women usually reserve for their husbands and idiots. "Are you out of your mind, Teddy? You would go back in those woods alone?"

"But my mule..."

"I will send Billy and Edward to retrieve your things later." When I looked surprised, she said, "They are good boys. They are just afraid not to do as Simon tells them."

I touched the welt on the side of my face and winced from the pain. "Who is Simon anyway?" I asked.

Eugenie picked up the bloody rags she had used to clean my wound and placed them in an old burlap bag. "Simon Pitchford. He is my Daddy's farm manager, and his Daddy was the farm manager before him. I have known him since we were both children." When I said nothing, Eugenie continued, "He has always been a bully. I think he may have hoped for something to develop between he and I, but I imagine it is the farmland that he really wants." She looked into my eyes, "I suspect that you were an unwelcome surprise."

Eugenie and I rode into New Market in her father's horse and wagon. No amount of arguing would convince Eugenie of the danger, but she rode with her shotgun leaning against the seat between us.

It was a short ride from the farm, but somehow news about my impending surrender had already circulated among the townspeople. Where we turned north onto the Valley Pike, small groups of people had gathered and stood alongside the road. Several of the men hissed "Murderer!" and "Traitor!" at me as we passed by. The women stood with frowns on their faces, clearly displeased with Eugenie. But Eugenie sat tall in her seat and defiantly held on to my hand.

The jail in New Market was a less than imposing structure. It was a single-story, concrete building with no windows and a single door on the front. It sat not 50 yards from the Sheriff's office/home, which was constructed of the same material.

Standing in front of the jail, hands on his hips, was the sheriff, Douglas Martin. I would soon learn that he was Eugenie's cousin. "'Genie!" he said. "I see you have brought me the fugitive."

Eugenie walked up to him and kissed him on the cheek. "I have, Dougie, and I hold you personally responsible for his well-being."

"No harm will come to him while he is in my care," he assured her. Then he turned to me: "You are Theodore Miller?"

"I am."

He smiled and shook his head. "I do not know if I can remember another time when a fugitive voluntarily came to me." Then he turned my face with his hands and asked, "Who did this to you?"

When I said nothing, Eugenie spoke up, "Simon."

The Sheriff shook his head. "He is a bad apple. I do not know why your Daddy keeps him on."

I followed behind as the Sheriff took Eugenie's arm and led us into the jail. He turned to me on the way in and said, "Well, Mr. Miller, here is your home for the next few months."

CHAPTER 29

Meet Sheriff Martin

I am convinced that imprisonment is a way of pretending to solve the problem of crime. It does nothing for the victims of crime, but perpetuates the idea of retribution, thus maintaining the endless cycle of violence in our culture. — Howard Zinn

The little jail was clean. Beyond that, I could find little good to say about it. The building had been divided into two rooms by an iron cell wall. In the cell itself, there were two cots with horsehair mattresses and a bucket for relieving oneself. The front half of the building contained a beat-up desk, a potbelly stove, and a few chairs. The only decorations were some wanted posters, yellowed, and crumbling with age.

Eugenie sat at the desk while the Sheriff and I took a seat on the rickety chairs. I expected to crash to the floor at any moment. Eugenie looked at the Sheriff and said, "Teddy acted in self-defense, Dougie. He is no murderer."

The Sheriff looked at me with a skeptical expression on his face, then turned his attention to Eugenie. "That may be, 'Genie, but legal steps have been taken and now this matter can only be settled in court."

"I understand none of this," I said. "I never heard of charges being filed against me."

"Then you must not have been in the Valley for the better part of the last year. People have spoken of little else since the Coroner's Inquest," said the Sheriff. Eugenie looked at me and nodded. "That is true, Teddy." The Sheriff continued: "Mrs. Hayes came to me a day after Jacob Hayes' body was discovered to report his murder. She told me that she had been told it was you that had killed him.

"We took his body to Doc Heinemann, who is also the County Coroner. Two days later, Doc opened a formal inquest into Jacob Hayes' death.

"Doc called something like seven or eight witnesses, some who claimed direct knowledge, others who had heard rumors."

I interrupted the Sheriff, "But who claimed direct knowledge?"

"There were no witnesses to the actual killing. But a farm laborer named Manson Bowley claimed that he had met with you and Jacob Hayes the night he was killed, and that Jacob was alive when he left."

I sat there trying to understand everything I was hearing. When I asked nothing more, the Sheriff continued: "Manson Bowley was well known to be of questionable character, but no other witnesses came forth to dispute his story."

"I do not suppose that Manson mentioned that he had left with orders for Jacob to kill me," I said bitterly. Eugenie reached across the desk and touched my hand. Then she turned to the Sheriff and said, "That seems a weak case, Dougie."

The Sheriff shrugged his shoulders. "Doc seems to agree. He handed down a rather unhelpful verdict that neither condemned nor exonerated the killing." The Sheriff seemed to search his memory for a moment and then said, "As I remember it, the verdict was something like 'Jacob Hayes, farmer, came to his death in the County of Shenandoah, State of Virginia, on June 2, 1864, of a head wound purported to have been inflicted by Theodore Miller.'"

"Then that should be the end of it!" exclaimed Eugenie.

"It might have been," the Sheriff agreed. "It would normally be my decision whether to file charges against Teddy. And given the weak verdict from Doc Heinemann, I probably would not have. But the day after Doc announced his verdict, Manson Bowley filed first-degree murder charges against Teddy with Augustus Forsberg, the Justice of the Peace."

"He can do that?" I asked.

"He can," The Sheriff answered. "Virginia is one of the only states that allows private citizens to file criminal charges. And 'though I have never seen it done, the State even allows private prosecutions."

Eugenie gave out a deep sigh. "Then what is next, Dougie?"

"Well, I reckon since Mr. Miller is now in custody, the Justice of the Peace will schedule a preliminary hearing to learn if there is sufficient cause to believe Teddy guilty. If not, Teddy will be released. But if he thinks there is, it will go to trial."

The Sheriff allowed Eugenie and I to have a few minutes alone before he put me in the cell. I wiped tears from her cheek as I tried to reassure her that everything would be alright. She promised to visit me the next day and bring me some books to read.

Eugenie returned to the jail the next morning, loaded down with novels and books of poetry. The Sheriff helped her unload everything and bring it into my cell. Then he left us alone after telling me I could stay outside the cell, but I was not to leave the building.

I held Eugenie close. "How are things at home?" I asked.

"Daddy has not said a word to me since yesterday. He will not even look me in the eyes."

"I am sorry."

"Daddy will come around," she said.

"And Simon?"

"Simon? Well, he wears a large white bandage on his ankle and limps around the farm, cursing every time he puts weight on his injured leg." I smiled at the picture that formed in my mind.

Eugenie squeezed my hand. "There is something we need to discuss, and I want you to keep an open mind. Will you do that for me?"

When I nodded my assent, Eugenie said, "You need a lawyer. A good one."

A lawyer? The idea had not even crossed my mind. "But I have no money, Eugenie."

"Well, I do," she said. When I started to protest, she held up her hand to stop me. "You need a lawyer, Teddy. I will not risk our future on the whim of some small-town Justice of the Peace."

But I shook my head no. "I will not have it, Eugenie! I will not allow you to use your money to hire a lawyer!"

Eugenie dropped my hand. "You will not allow it? Is that how you think our marriage will work? You think that you will rule by proclamation, like a Russian Tzar?" The temperature in the jail suddenly seemed to have dropped. My mouth worked but no words came out. Finally, "But it is not right, Eugenie."

Eugenie batted her eyes at me. "Will you break my heart because of male pride?"

I knew when I was beaten, and I reached again for her hand. "Well, where do we find a lawyer?" I asked.

CHAPTER 30

J. John Johnson, Esq.

It is a pleasant world we live in, sir, a very pleasant world. There are bad people in it, Mr. Richard, but if there were no bad people, there would be no good lawyers. — Charles Dickens

J. John Johnson sat at the desk in the jail with Eugenie and me arranged in front of him like students in a Civics class. He was a large man with a friendly face, watery eyes that peered out through gold-rimmed spectacles and a big personality. He was also Eugenie's great Uncle on her mother's side who had recently retired to the Valley after a distinguished career as a lawyer in Richmond. He preferred to be called 'JJ.'

JJ had just finished lecturing us on Virginia law and he confirmed what the Sheriff (JJ's grand-nephew) had told us about the oddity in the law that allowed civilians to file charges and even prosecute alleged wrongdoers. "They must have some standing with the court, of course," he added. "There are several ways that this may occur, and in this case the petitioner alleges that he fears Mr. Miller may intend to harm him as well."

JJ rifled through a pile of papers on the desk in front of him. "Ah, here it is," he said. "This is the Statement of Charges made by Manson Bowley on June 9, 1864, one day after the coroner issued his verdict. The Statement formed the basis for the murder charges Mr. Bowley later filed with the court. It contains Mr. Bowley's description of the accused and the details of the crime, 'though I suspect most of the wording came from the coroner's report." JJ studied the document for a moment. "The motive proposed by Mr. Bowley is that Jacob Hayes was killed to keep him from revealing Teddy's collaboration with the Union."

"What do you think about our case, Uncle?" Eugenie asked.

JJ sat back in his chair. "Without a witness to the actual killing, this will come down to who is more believable, Teddy or Mr. Bowley." JJ, apparently believing we were finished, began to pick up the papers on the desk and put them in an old briefcase. "I rather look forward to cross-examining Mr. Bowley," he said. "Dougie tells me he is quite a rascal."

Eugenie and I exchanged glances and JJ asked, "What is it?"

"Did the Sheriff not tell you that Malcolm Bowley is dead?" I asked. "He was killed by the Union cavalry."

JJ stopped what he was doing. "Oh," he said.

"Does that make a difference, Uncle?"

"Well, it is difficult to cross-examine a dead man." JJ sat back down. He studied us over the rims of his glasses. "Is there anything else I should know?"

Over the next few days, JJ asked me question after question about everything to do with Jacob Hayes, the guerrilla group called 'The Golden Knights' and my deal with the Pinkertons. He asked many of the same questions over and over, only changing the order and emphasis of the questions. When I lost patience, Eugenie would squeeze my hand and say, "Do what Uncle JJ asks. He is the only one who can help us."

While JJ was still planning my defense strategy, General Simon Bolivar Buckner surrendered the Confederate Army of the Trans-Mississippi. Nine days later, on the second of June 1865, the Civil War officially ended. It was an anticlimactic event; there had already been Grand Parades in Washington City for both the Army of the Potomac and General Sherman's army. Only the assassination of Lincoln tempered the Union's celebrations. We also got word that the Justice of the Peace had announced a date for the preliminary hearing: June 24, 1865. It was barely a month away.

One night near the end of the month, I was shaken awake. The Sheriff stood over me holding an oil lantern. "Wake up, Teddy!"

I held up my arm to shield my eyes from the light. "What is wrong?" I asked.

"We need to get you out of here. Grab your shoes and follow me. I will explain on the way."

The Sheriff led me to his house next door. There were no lights on and there was no hiding the urgency in his voice: "I was just told that there is a mob coming for you. Apparently, they do not care to wait on Lady Justice." He peered out the window, then turned back towards me. "If they are determined, there is no way I will be able to stop them. I want you to stay here and watch from this window. If they breech the jail and do not find you there, they will come here looking for you. If you see me overwhelmed, I want you to leave through the back door and hide in the woods. Do you understand?"

I nodded and had just started to say something when a flicker of light shone through the window. "Damnation," said the Sheriff as he grabbed a shotgun standing next to the door. Then he rushed outside.

The Sheriff stood next to the front door of the jail, his

shotgun cradled in his arms. A mob of perhaps twenty men approached. Several were carrying torches and one carried a coil of rope. They all wore bandanas over their faces. I could see that a few of the men were armed as well.

The sheriff addressed the man carrying the rope: "You are up late, Daniel."

Daniel tore off his bandana and threw it on the ground. He turned to the men behind him and said, "I told you these bandanas were a stupid idea!" He turned back to the sheriff. "You know why we are here, Doug. Jest turn the boy over to us and be done with it."

"Now, Daniel..." the Sheriff started to say when another man in the mob shouted, "Turn the boy over now." Then another and another.

The Sheriff scanned the mob and held up his hand. Remarkably, the mob quieted. "Now, Boys, you know I ain't gonna shoot you." He leaned the shotgun against the wall. "I know all of your Mommas, and what would they think of me? Heck, most of us, we all go to church together."

Now unarmed, the Sheriff took a step closer to the mob. He could have reached out and touched many of them. The Sheriff looked from man to man. "But let me tell you what I will do: harm a hair on that boy's head and I will hunt each of you down. I will tie your hands and drag you out of your homes in front of your wives and children. I will lock you in this very jail. And then I will file murder charges against every last one of you."

The mob began to look uncertainly at each other and several even took a few steps to leave when a voice in the back said, "Bravado is all it is! Stand fast, Boys, and let us finish what we started."

The Sheriff walked back to the jail door and retrieved his shotgun. Then he turned again to the mob. When he stepped towards them, they parted, opening a clear path leading to a man at the back. He, too, wore a bandana, but I could recognize him from fifty yards away: Simon Pitchford.

The men formed a circle with the Sheriff and Simon in the center. Simon took off his bandana and sneered at the Sheriff: "I ain't afraid of you, Dougie."

The Sheriff said calmly, "No need to be afraid of anything, Simon. Jest go home."

"Or what, Dougie? You gonna arrest me? I kinda like the idea of being thrown into a cell with that scalawag." Simon held out his hands as if asking to be handcuffed.

"Or I will beat you into the dust," the Sheriff said.

Simon smiled. He lowered his hands and said, "Then put down that gun and we will see who lies in the dust." But it appeared the Sheriff had no intention of fighting Simon; before Simon could even react, the Sheriff spun and smashed him in the face with the butt of his shotgun. Simon fell to the ground, unconscious.

The Sheriff turned again to the mob. "Fun is over, Boys, time to go home."

No one else argued and I watched the mob walk away in groups of two and three. They left Simon where he lay.

CHAPTER 31

The Prosecution

My job as a prosecutor is to do justice. And justice is served when a guilty man is convicted, and an innocent man is not. —Sonia Sotomayor

J J tried to get me released on bail while we waited for the Hearing to begin. But the Prosecutor, a man named Alexander Botelier, who had been appointed by the Governor, argued that I was a flight risk and could not be trusted. Besides, he said, with me facing such serious charges, who could be sure that I would not try to eliminate more of the witnesses against me? The Justice apparently agreed with Botelier, and I was remanded to the little jail.

On the walk back to the jail, I asked JJ, "Why would the Governor himself assign a prosecutor to my case?" JJ shook his head. "Best I can reckon," he said. "it is because this case touches on some sensitive issues. There is little pride of the guerrillas who flourished in this valley during the War. Now that reconstruction has begun, their actions could come back to haunt the State. And you are alleging that Jacob Hayes and Manson Bowley were members of The Golden Knights, a well-known guerrilla group."

"But that will come out in the Hearing no matter who the Prosecutor is."

"True enough, but I suspect Mr. Botelier will try to keep a rapid pace and settle this issue as quicky and quietly as possible." JJ winked at me. "Might be good for us, give us a little leverage."

Testimony in the Hearing began behind closed doors—at the request of JJ—on June 24. Eugenie and I were not allowed to attend. When it was finished for the day, JJ returned and sat down in the jail to tell us about the Hearing. "There was only one witness called today and that was Doc Heinemann," he said. "Doc repeated what was in his earlier verdict, that Jacob Hayes was killed by a blow to the head. He would not speculate on whether it was homicide or self-defense, which irritated mightily Mr. Botelier." JJ put his feet up on the desk. "But I accomplished what we needed. I told the Justice that we would be presenting all our witnesses at the hearing." JJ smiled. "Mr. Botelier about went apoplectic, objecting to everything and going on and on about normal procedures being followed. But the Justice knew we were within our rights and overruled him."

Eugenie and I just looked at each other. Only one day of the Hearing under our belts and we were already lost in a legal morass. "Please explain, Uncle," asked Eugenie.

"Most times, Preliminary Hearings are rather perfunctory affairs," he said, "because defendants concede the inevitability of a full trial. With that in mind, they do not want to expose their defense strategy to the prosecution too early in the game. Likewise, the prosecutors present only enough testimony to meet the legal standard."

"But you are saying that a trial need not happen?" I asked.

"Just so," said JJ. "I know Justice of the Peace Forsberg and believe him a fair man. I think him a better hope for your freedom than a jury of twelve men selected from this County."

The second day of the Hearing was in the County Courthouse and open to the public. Every available chair was filled with spectators. I sat on a chair at a table next to JJ while Eugenie sat behind me on a row of pew-like chairs. To my right, the prosecutor sat at an identical table with a young man I assumed to be his assistant. We all stood when Augustus Forsberg, the Justice of the Peace, entered the courtroom. He nodded at JJ and Alexander Botelier and told us all to be seated. "Are you ready to begin, Mr. Botelier?"

Botelier rose to his feet and said, "We are, your honor."

"JJ?" asked the Judge.

"We are, your honor."

"Very well," the Justice said, "you may call your first witness, Mr. Botelier."

Botelier paused dramatically and then said, "The prosecution calls Manson Bowley."

JJ leapt instantly to his feet. "Your honor," he said, "Mr. Botelier knows very well that Manson Bowley is deceased!"

"That is true, your honor, but before Mr. Bowley's untimely death, he left behind a sworn Statement of Charges. I ask that it be read into the record."

JJ was on his feet again. "I object! Mr. Botelier knows better, your honor! Under the Confrontation Clause of the Sixth Amendment, criminal defendants have the right to confront witnesses who testify against them. If a dead witness's out-of-court statement were admitted at trial, the defendant would have no chance to challenge it. The framers of the Constitution clearly recognized that without the chance to hear challenges to testimony, courts could be seriously misled. Defendants have a fundamental right to cross-examine, which is missing when the speaker himself is not in court."

"Now, your honor," said Botelier, standing up, "things are

rarely that unequivocal. There is precedent for the admission of sworn statements by deceased witnesses. For example, a court may decide to admit an out-of-court statement from an unavailable witness, offered by the prosecution against the defendant, if it is convinced that the statement is sufficiently reliable..."

"That is a gross misstatement of the law!" interrupted JJ. "The right of criminal defendants to confront witnesses who testify against them is fundamental to our system of justice..."

"Now, Boys," said Justice Forsberg, "I invite the both of you to debate Constitutional law over a beer when the Hearing is over. But as I am approaching 80 years of age, let us keep this Hearing short enough that I might survive to its conclusion." The Justice made a note on a pad of paper in front of him and said, "As there is no jury, I would like to hear the late Manson Bowley's sworn statement. I will give you both ample opportunities to question—or support—Mr. Bowley's trustworthiness."

Both JJ and Botelier sat down. JJ gave me a sideways glance that made clear his displeasure with the Justice's ruling. The Justice handed a piece of paper to the clerk and asked him to read it out loud. The clerk was a short man, but his stature was more than made up for by his booming voice. The words of the late Manson Bowley echoed in every corner of the courtroom:

"I, Manson Bowley, hereby swear in the presence of Peter Banks, constable of New Market, Virginia, that the statements I am about to make are true and accurate to the best of my recollection:

(1) On June 2, 1864, Theodore Miller, aged 16 or thereabouts, blonde hair, 6' tall, asked Jacob Hayes and me to meet with him to discuss some work he wanted done. Me and Jacob, we assumed it was farm work;

(2) During our meeting, Miller let on he was working for the Union government. He even bragged that he had saved his father from hanging by spying on Southern troop movements in the Valley;

(3) Me and Jacob, we are no turncoats and the discussion got pretty hot. Miller insisted the South was going to lose the War anyways so we might as well make some money by helping him spy on our troops;

(4) When I got up to leave, Miller pulled out a Colt pistol and placed it on the table. "Do not be saying anything about this," he warned me. I skedaddled as fast as I could;

(5) When I left, Jacob was still there with Miller and still alive;

(6) When Jacob's body was found the next day, I knew Miller had killed him;

(7) There is no doubt in my mind that Miller killed Jacob to keep him from telling anyone about his traitorous activities;

(8) I am in fear for my own life and plan on filing first-degree murder charges against Miller for my own protection.

Signed and dated, Manson Bowley and Peter Banks, Constable

I sat there in stunned silence. Not a word Manson had said was truthful and I could feel the Justice's eyes boring into me. But it was about to get worse.

"Do you wish to comment on Mr. Bowley's Statement, JJ?" asked the Justice.

"Not at this time, your honor, but I reserve the right to revisit this Statement at a later time."

"Very well. Mr. Botelier, you may call your next witness."

Botelier stood up and said, "I call Peter Banks, Constable of New Market."

After he was sworn in, Peter Banks sat down in the witness chair at the front of the court. The Justice had to remind him to take off his bowler hat. "Sorry, yer honor," he said.

"I have just a few questions for you, Constable," said Botelier. "First, do you believe Manson Bowley was of good character?"

"I have no reason to think otherwise."

Botelier nodded. "And Mr. Miller. Do you think him of good character as well?"

"No, I do not."

Botelier paused and let Bank's statement hang in the air. "Can you elaborate?" he asked. When the Constable looked confused, Botelier said, "Can you tell us why you feel that way?"

The Constable nodded and looked directly at me. "'Cause he killed two other men that I know of and grievously wounded a third. Murder seems to be a habit with that boy."

JJ jumped to his feet and said, "I object! Speculation!"

Before the Justice could weigh in, Botelier said, "Let us stick to what we know, Constable. Can you list the names of the dead and wounded men?"

"Yessir. Simon Helburg, shot and killed, Martin Malachai, run over and killed by a horse and Andrew Beaudine, shot and wounded, all here in New Market."

When Botelier said he was finished with his witness, Justice Forsberg said that JJ could cross-examine the Constable in the morning and ended the Hearing for the day.

CHAPTER 32

Cross-Examination

They speak to each other through the magistrate, like warring children communicating through a parent, their words are extravagantly emotive illustrated with flamboyant gestures that are wasted on the empty court room. — Clare Mackintosh

For the first time, I was glad to return to the little jail. I was emotionally exhausted and more than a little frightened. The reality of the Hearing, and its potential consequences, had hit me hard. I squeezed Eugenie's hand so tightly I was afraid I might hurt her.

We all sat down around the desk. JJ looked exhausted and I suddenly realized the physical toll the Hearing must be taking on him. He was of the same generation as Justice Forsberg and must be nearing eighty-years himself. Eugenie was the first to speak: "It was all lies, Uncle, every bit of it!"

JJ smiled at Eugenie. "The first day always belongs to the prosecution," he said. "Tomorrow, we will cross-examine Constable Banks. Then we will begin to chip away at the reputation of our local saint, Manson Bowley."

The next morning, JJ approached Constable Banks who was sitting in the witness chair with a sour look on his face. It was obvious to everyone that he would rather be anywhere else. JJ wished him a good morning and thanked him for his time. Then he asked, "Are you familiar with the Golden Knights, Constable?"

"Never heard of them," he said.

"Then, were you aware of the guerrillas that operated in the Valley during the War?"

Botelier stood up and said, "I object, your honor, relevance."

"I ask your patience, your honor, as this will go towards the character of the witnesses."

Justice Forsberg said he would allow it and JJ repeated, "Well, Constable, were you aware of the guerrillas that operated in the Valley during the War?"

Constable Banks said, "Never saw it myself."

"This is a simple 'yes' or 'no' question, Constable. Were you aware that guerrillas were operating in the Valley?"

"Yessir," the Constable admitted, "but I never heard of no Knights, Golden nor otherwise."

"Do you personally know the identities of any of the guerrillas?"

"No, sir."

"Did you know that Manson Bowley was a guerrilla?"

Botelier leapt up from his seat. "Objection, your honor, there is no evidence of Mr. Bowley being a guerrilla! And since he is dead at the hands of the Union army, he cannot defend himself from this defamation!"

JJ held up his hand. "I am sorry, your honor, I have gotten ahead of myself. I would hope, however, that the irony of Mr. Botelier's argument is not lost on the court; it would seem that the Prosecution supports the Confrontation Clause only when it benefits them."

JJ glanced at his notes and asked the Constable, "Were you present at the deaths of Messrs. Helburg and Malachai?"

"No, sir."

"How about the wounding of Mr. Beaudine?"

"No, sir."

"Then how did you come to know about them?"

"I was told about them."

JJ paused and then asked, "By whom?"

"By Manson Bowley."

JJ turned his back on the Constable and began to pace. Almost to himself, he said, "Manson Bowley again. He does seem to be at the heart of all this." He turned back to the Constable and said, "Perhaps we need to talk to someone else who was there. Do you know the whereabouts of Andrew Beaudine, the man you allege was wounded by Mr. Miller?"

The Constable looked visibly uncomfortable. "He is in a prison in Washington City."

"Prison? But why?"

"He was arrested by the Union army."

JJ feigned being shocked as I had already told him about Beaudine and his fate. He looked directly at Justice Forsberg as he asked Banks, "Why was he arrested, Constable?"

The Constable glanced at Botelier, as if looking to be rescued. "The Yankees plan to hang him. He is accused of being a guerrilla." There was a murmur from those watching the Hearing and the Justice had to bang his gavel to restore order.

The rest of the day was taken up by a parade of witnesses brought in to pay tribute to the late Manson Bowley. They were unanimous in their praise of him, though I did not recognize Manson from their descriptions. JJ pressed them to the best of his ability, but they stuck to their stories. "Manson, he were a good man," they said, "brutalized as a child by the Yankees, he was" and "would hurt nary a fly."

With that, the Prosecution rested its case.

Once again, Eugenie, JJ and I gathered around the desk in the jail. Eugenie and I felt it had been a good day for us. We both believed that Manson Bowley's credibility, if not fatally wounded, had at least been tarnished a bit. But JJ was dour. "We have yet to present our own witnesses, "he said, "but I do not know if they will remove all doubt about Mr. Bowley's bad character. That is the bar that has been set for us. Unless Justice Forsberg is fully convinced that Mr. Bowley's statement is unreliable, he will remand Teddy for trial." JJ reached for Eugenie's hand. "I am sorry, my dear, but I do not want to fill you with false hope."

"But, Uncle, I thought today went well for us."

JJ sighed deeply. "We have no witnesses willing to speak truthfully to Mr. Bowley's character. Perhaps they are afraid of Mr. Bowley's friends, I do not know. But without that, I do not know that we can erase all doubt from the Justice's mind."

Eugenie looked so sad that it was like a knife to my heart. "Can we postpone the rest of the Hearing for a few days?" I asked.

JJ said, "We can ask for a postponement, but I do not know that the Justice will grant it. May I ask why?"

I touched Eugenie's face and smiled. "I do not care to be the source of false hope either. But if you can get a postponement, there is one person I know that may be able to help us."

"In that case," JJ said, "I do feel a cold coming on. Mr. Botelier will not like it, but I think Justice Forsberg will grant us a few days. Will that be enough?"

"It will have to be," I answered.

CHAPTER 33

The Defense

Der Lebensschutz des potentiellen Opfers soll mehr wiegen als die Menschenwürde des potenziellen Täters. (The protection of the potential victim's life should weigh more than the human dignity of the potential perpetrator.) — Heribert Prantl,

A s JJ had predicted, Botelier did not like the idea of a postponement. He argued loudly that his time was valuable, and he needed to get back to his law practice in Winchester. When that did not work, he accused JJ of stalling for reasons unknown and probably nefarious. But JJ just sniffed and coughed and sneezed until Justice Forsberg told him to go home and go to bed. The Hearing was rescheduled to begin again three days plus a Sunday later.

When the Hearing resumed, it was the defense's turn, and the courtroom was packed with spectators. JJ rose from his seat and told Justice Forsberg, "We will only be calling one witness, your honor." The Justice looked surprised. JJ continued, "As Shakespeare put it, *...since brevity is the soul of wit, and tediousness the limbs and outward flourishes, I will be brief...*"

The Justice smiled. "Brevity is always appreciated, JJ. You may call your witness."

JJ turned to the courtroom door and announced in a loud voice, "The Defense calls Mrs. Kate Warne." At that, the door swung open and in walked Kate Warne. It was a theatrical entrance, I thought, worthy of the late Captain Quinn MacBrùn as she swept down the aisle towards the witness stand. She was wearing a dark blue silk dress with a high neck and black trim. She had on sheer black, beaded gloves but no hat and her dark hair hung down in soft ringlets. Every man in the courtroom followed her every movement. As she passed me, she turned and smiled, and I could smell the sweet scent of Jasmine that she always wore.

When Kate reached the witness stand, three men rushed to help her with her chair. Even Justice Forsberg looked about ready to jump down from his dais to help. When she was settled, JJ asked, "Will you tell the court your name and occupation please?"

Kate gave JJ a dazzling smile and answered, "I am Mrs. Kate Warne, and I am a Pinkerton Detective."

"And what is your relationship to Mr. Miller?"

"Mr. Miller—Teddy if I may—helped me catch the murderers of a Union officer."

"And was he paid for this service?"

Kate shook her head. "No, he did it to earn mercy for his father."

JJ paused, then said, "So Mr. Miller committed treason to curry favor with the Pinkertons?"

"Treason is a strong word, Mr. Johnson. I do not look at it as a betrayal. Teddy never revealed any troop movements or that kind of thing." Kate looked directly at Botelier. "Or do you equate murderous guerrillas with your gallant troops?" Botelier looked down at the desk in front of him.

"Now Mrs. Warne, are you familiar with the circumstance surrounding the death of Jacob Hayes?"

"I am. Under my orders, Teddy met with Mr. Hayes and

Manson Bowley in an attempt to infiltrate their guerrilla group. Manson Bowley caught Teddy in a lie and terminated the meeting. As Manson Bowley was leaving, he gave orders for Mr. Hayes to kill Teddy. Teddy and Mr. Hayes struggled, and Mr. Hayes was killed."

"But you did not observe this yourself?"

"No. But Teddy was completely distraught when he returned to our camp. He told me his story and I have no reason not to believe him."

JJ studied his notes and asked, "And are you familiar with the deaths of Simon Helburg and Martin Malachai?"

"I am," answered Kate. "I killed them."

There was an instant uproar in the court. Justice Forsberg pounded his gavel and demanded order. When things had calmed down, JJ continued: "Can you explain why you killed them?"

Kate smoothed her dress over her lap. "Certainly. Teddy and I had come here to New Market in search of Union troops. We happened to come across Manson Bowley and members of his gang trying to kill an innkeeper who had somehow insulted them. Teddy and I scattered the men, and the innkeeper was able to escape. Manson Bowley objected to our interference and formed a mob to find and kill us. Messrs. Helburg and Malachai were in that mob and were killed while trying to stop us from escaping. One was shot, the other I trampled with my horse."

Again, Justice Forsberg had to quiet the court. JJ said, "One last question, Mrs. Warne. The wounding of Andrew Beaudine..."

Kate nodded. "When we came across Manson Bowley, he and his men were about to scalp the innkeeper. Teddy and I opened fire to scatter the men and I would guess that is when Mr. Beaudine was shot. I do not know for a fact if it was Teddy or I who hit him." Kate turned to the Justice and smiled sweetly. "I sincerely hope it was I."

JJ turned to the Justice. "The defense rests, your honor."

Justice Forsberg glanced at the wall clock and said, "We will adjourn until after lunch. Then you may cross-examine Mrs. Warne, Mr. Botelier, and I will hear final arguments."

Eugenie, JJ and I ate a lunch that she had prepared earlier and brought to the jail. Our mood was light. We all felt that the direction of the Hearing had turned. "She is a force of nature, that Mrs. Warne," said JJ. "I do not envy Mr. Botelier the task of cross-examining her."

Eugenie nodded in agreement. "And she is very elegant," she said. "The dress she is wearing looks so expensive. I bet it is straight from Paris!" Then Eugenie frowned at me and said, "But I do not remember you telling me she was so beautiful, Teddy."

"Did I not?" I asked. "It must be because since I met you, all other women appear to me as grey cats in the dark, one no more memorable than another."

Eugenie laughed. "You are such a pretty liar sometimes!"

The Hearing began again at about 1:00 p.m. I noticed Kate sitting in the back of the courtroom in deep conversation with a man. He was well-dressed with a neatly trimmed dark beard and a slightly receding hairline. When he looked up, I recognized him from newspaper drawings and photographs. It was Alan Pinkerton himself.

Every head followed Kate as she made her way to the witness stand again. And again, at least three men rushed to help her with her chair. When she was settled, Botelier walked up to face her. "Good afternoon, Mrs. Warne."

"Good Afternoon, Mr. Botelier."

"May I ask how you came to be here today, Mrs. Warne?"

"Certainly. I received a telegram from Teddy two days ago asking me to come."

Botelier glanced over at me. "What is your relationship with

Mr. Miller?" he asked.

"Did I not explain that earlier? He was my partner in our quest to bring the murdering guerrillas to justice."

"Nothing more?"

Kate's face grew red. "What are you implying, Mr. Botelier?"

Botelier held up his hand. "I imply nothing, Mrs. Warne. I am just trying to understand your role in all of this."

"Then perhaps you should listen more carefully, Mr. Botelier, before you cast aspersions on a widow's good name."

Justice Forsberg admonished Botelier: "Mrs. Warne is here voluntarily, Mr. Botelier. I will have you treat her with respect in my courtroom." This time it was Botelier who blushed. "I apologize, Mrs. Warne," he said. "Would you care for a moment before we begin again?"

Kate shook her head as she dabbed at her eyes with a handkerchief, although I could see no tears. "No, no, Mr. Botelier, let us finish."

"Very well. During your testimony earlier, you called Jacob Hayes and Manson Bowley 'murderous thugs and guerrillas.' Yet I know of no evidence that either Mr. Hayes or Mr. Bowley were either of those things. As you freely admit your complicity in murdering these men, and others, perhaps you can understand my skepticism."

Kate smiled at Botelier. "You are doing better, Mr. Botelier. It is best to call a lady a liar as indirectly as possible." Kate turned to Justice Forsberg, "May I retrieve some documents, your honor?" When the Justice nodded, Alan Pinkerton got up from his seat in the back and carried a large brown envelope up to Kate. When Kate said, "Thank you, Mr. Pinkerton," there was a collective gasp in the courtroom.

Kate undid the envelope and pulled out some papers. "Let me see... ah, here is one. This is a sworn affidavit by Andrew Beaudine stating that he, Jacob Hayes, Manson Bowley, and others, were members of the Golden Knights, a known guerrilla group operating in the Valley. Further, he describes a number of crimes they committed, including the murder of a Union officer named Thomas Ferguson." Kate handed the paper to the court clerk who carried it to the Justice. "By the way, Mr. Beaudine is still available for cross-examination if you hurry as he is scheduled to hang next month."

Kate shuffled through the papers some more. "Here is one that regards Jacob Hayes specifically. Apparently, he attacked a Union wagon train with a group of guerrillas and one of the Union soldiers recognized Mr. Hayes from before the war." She looked the paper over until she found the signature. "The name of the Union soldier is William Tanner and I know he survived the War as I spoke to him just before I came here." Again, the clerk carried the paper to the Justice.

Justice Forsberg quickly reviewed the two sets of papers and had the clerk pass them to Mr. Botelier.

Kate was excused and Botelier made only desultory and brief closing arguments. JJ was even more brief: "Teddy Miller committed no crimes, your honor."

Justice Forsberg looked out over the courtroom and said, "Normally, I would retire to my chambers to consider my decision. But in this case, the State has so clearly failed to demonstrate any evidence sufficient to bind Mr. Miller over for trial, that I do not feel it appropriate or necessary to hold him in further suspense." Justice Forsberg looked at me and said, "You are free to go, Mr. Miller." At with a bang of his gavel, I was a free man.

When Eugenie and I walked out the front door, Kate and Mr. Pinkerton were waiting for us. Kate rushed up to me and gave me a big hug and I found myself enveloped by Jasmin and silk. "Teddy!" she said. "It is so good to see you!" Kate held on to my arm as she turned to face Eugenie. "And you must be the Botticelli girl!" Eugenie looked confused. "When Teddy first met you, he told me you were as pretty as a Botticelli painting," Kate explained. "He was wrong. You are far more beautiful!"

Eugenie blushed and I rushed to make the proper introductions. I did not want to give Kate time to reveal any more of my secrets. When I shook Alan Pinkerton's hand, he said, "Mrs. Warne has told me a great deal about you, Mr. Miller. She thinks you quite intrepid." Pinkerton reached into his pocket and pulled out a carte d' visite. On it, he had written contact instructions. "If you are ever of a mind, I can always use another good detective."

Eugenie had taken Kate's hand and was in deep conversation with her. When they noticed that Pinkerton and I had stopped talking, they turned to us. "I was just telling Mrs. Warne how grateful I am for what she did today."

I took Kate's other hand and said, "As am I, Kate." Kate pulled us both towards her and gave us one last hug. "I wish you both years of happiness," she said. "Which reminds me, Mr. Pinkerton, do you not have something for Teddy?"

"Ah, I almost forgot!" Pinkerton reached into his coat pocket and pulled out an envelope with my name on it. He handed it to me and said, "This is from Senator Ferguson."

"But what is it?" I asked.

"It is the deed to your farm which has been restored to you and your brother. Senator Ferguson quoted Deuteronomy as he handed it to me: *Fathers shall not be put to death because of their children, nor shall children be put to death because of their fathers. Each one shall be put to death for his own sin.*" Pinkerton laughed, "I personally do not find that verse particularly comforting, but the end result is that you have your farm back."

Kate kissed Eugenie and I on our cheeks and walked away, arm in arm with Alan Pinkerton. When they were gone, Eugenie asked me who Senator Ferguson is. "It was his son Thomas who had been killed by the guerrillas. And it was he who hired the Pinkertons to find his son's killers." Although I said nothing to Eugenie, I was surprised at the Senator's generosity, and I suspected Kate had had a hand in all of this.

CHAPTER 34

The Hearing's Aftermath

Time and Nemesis will do that which I would not, were it in my power remote or immediate. You will smile at this piece of prophecy - do so but recollect it: it is justified by all human experience. No one was ever even the involuntary cause of great evils to others, without a requital: I have paid and am paying for mine - so will you. — George Gordon Byron

A round 1,000 people lived in New Market and the general vicinity. Not surprisingly, there existed a wide diversity of political opinions and beliefs. There were those who had supported succession, others that had not. In both cases, feelings were strong, often colored by personal loss.

My acquittal was greeted by a similar ambiguity. To some, I was a traitor, an unforgivable crime in their eyes, especially as they mourned their deceased sons, husbands, and fathers. A few others—a distinct minority—accepted my actions as the explicable attempt of a young man to save his father's life. And they did not elevate or glamorize the role of the guerrillas I had betrayed; quite the contrary, they despised those who would strike only in darkness and anonymity. But it was dangerous for anyone to express sympathy for me as they themselves could find themselves painted by the same brush as I.

The reality of my situation became apparent to me as soon as I had been released from jail. The first three boarding houses in which I tried to find a room slammed their doors in my face. By the time I found one that would take me, I had lowered my standards to a level barely above a hovel.

Employment was another issue. It was fortunate that I still had some money left from my work at The Crossroads. Although the South's workforce had been decimated by the War, the demand for labor was still slight. There were few working farms, at least in the Valley, and what factories there had been lay in ruins. Add to that the stigma that had attached itself to me and I could find no work at all.

Each day, I visited Eugenie at her farm. I would not say her father began to warm to me, exactly, but I no longer feared he would shoot me when I stood at the front door. His comments to me grew from grunts and long pauses to grunts and shorter pauses. And it was clear to me that his love for Eugenie would always temper his harsher inclinations.

I saw no more of Simon. The sheriff had broken Simon's jaw and he had been humiliated by his 'friends' decision to leave him lying on the ground at the jail. Eugenie said he packed up immediately after he heard the Hearing verdict and left the Valley.

While there is little nice that can be said about Simon, he was apparently a good farm manager. With Mr. Martin being away from his farm more and more, it was difficult for him to manage his interests both in town and at the farm. It was clear he needed a new farm manager and Eugenie lobbied for me to fill the position.

Mr. Martin finally agreed saying, "Hell, he is here all the time anyways. I might as well get some good from it." Eugenie kissed him on the cheek and said, "Thank you, Daddy," which elicited a grunt from her father. He turned to me: "I will move Billy and Edward into the house. You bunk in the old sharecropper's cabin. Tomorrow, the boys will show you your duties."

I quickly found that I had a lot to learn as farm manager. Although I had grown up on a farm, mine was one where crops and methods changed little over generations. Eugenie's father, on the other hand, had invested heavily in the future of farming. Before the War, he had bought expensive mechanical implements for producing wheat—drills for sowing, reapers for harvesting, and threshers and fans for cleaning the grain. While this was a sizable financial investment, it turned out that the post-War shortages of labor and animals would affect him much less than others who had not been so prescient.

Mr. Martin practiced 'mixed agriculture,' in which he produced a broad array of field crops— including corn, hay, and the various cereal grains—and kept on hand a full complement of the usual types of livestock such as horses, cattle, sheep, swine, and barnyard fowl. But even with this diversity of crops and animal products, which characterized Valley farming, wheat still served as his principal cash crop.

It was not long before I began to 'think long term,' as Mr. Martin called it. I encouraged him to increase his commitment to the diversity of his agrarian enterprise. The exploitation of alternate market opportunities in grass farming (hay), dairying (butter), and orcharding (apples), for example, would enable him to sustain the farm regardless of the vagaries of constantly changing wheat prices.

During the weeks and months that followed, the gulf between Eugenie's father and I continued to close, if ever so imperceptibly. He appreciated my enthusiasm for new technology, and we would read agricultural research studies with the enthusiasm of a new novel. Mr. Martin and I would then discuss the new ideas and proposals while Eugenie sat next to me, her hand resting on my arm, a gentle smile on her face.

It was a good time for Eugenie and me. The days were filled with healthy labor and the evenings with good companionship. I ate my meals with the Martins and slept in the old sharecropper's cabin, which Eugenie had cleaned and made comfortable for me. Even my relationship with my brother appeared to be on the mend. Malcolm's farm was only a short horse ride away and Jed and I spent many Sunday afternoons discussing what to do with our newly returned farm. Eugenie would sometimes accompany me, and she quickly became a favorite of Mrs. Davies and the twin girls.

But, meantime, the Valley did not take well to reconstruction. Everyone seemed to have their own idea of how the South should behave after the War. There were those, sick of the death and suffering that had already occurred, who sought reconciliation with their neighbors and the North. Others wanted to preserve racial segregation and White political and cultural domination. And a third group sought full freedom, suffrage, and constitutional equality for the former slaves.

Feelings ran hot. And the situation was not helped by the arrival in the Valley of hundreds of 'carpetbaggers'—Northern businessmen, teachers, politicians and even missionaries.

I understood the frustration rampant in the Valley. The loss of the War and the Confederate loss of life (more than 260,000) left the Southerners feeling humiliated and helpless. But I could not condone the brutality by which this frustration was sometimes expressed. And, in those moments between wake and sleep, I often worried that violence would someday seek Eugenie and me. I remembered all too well the hisses, threats and insults as Eugenie and I had ridden to the jail in New Market.

CHAPTER 35

The Bloody Night

What can you say to a man who tells you he prefers obeying God rather than men, and that as a result he's certain he'll go to heaven if he cuts your throat? — Voltaire

I t was one of those hot August nights where the air was heavy with moisture. I had half-closed my window before turning in, convinced that it would storm before the night was over. I had tossed and turned before falling asleep. My mind was full of new ideas for the farm and Eugenie and I had begun to speak of marriage. I felt overwhelmed, in the best of ways, by it all. Quieting my mind had seemed to take half the night.

When the first gunshot came, I thought it thunder, and congratulated myself on my foresight. But by the second one, I realized the truth and jumped out of bed. Without shirt or shoes, I ran towards the farmhouse, a quarter-mile away. My heart sank as I noticed a glow on the horizon. There was a sudden increase in the intensity of gunfire and then everything went quiet.

I burst into the front yard and saw the front porch on

fire. Lying on the ground was a man I did not recognize, and Edward was running from the well with a bucket of water. He threw the water on the fire and then ran back for more. "Eugenie!" I screamed. I started to enter the house through the flames when Eugenie appeared from the back. She was covered in blood.

She fell in my arms, sobbing. "Are you hit?" I cried. "Are you hurt?"

Eugenie shook her head. "No, no. It is Billy. They have killed him."

I held her tightly, pressing her head against my chest. I had no words and we just stood there in the middle of the yard, gently rocking and crying.

When Eugenie had calmed, I joined Edward. Working together, we soon put out the fire which had not spread from the front porch.

Edward and I sat down in the yard, exhausted. Tears streamed down Edward's face. "Billy did not deserve this," he said. "He was not armed. They shot him down, casual-like, without a word."

"Did you recognize any of them?"

Edward hesitated for a moment and then said, "Jest one."

I sent Edward on horseback to fetch the Sheriff. When the Sheriff arrived at the farm, we all gathered in the kitchen around the table with a pot of hot coffee. Dawn was already beginning to lighten the sky and we had all been up most of the night. Billy lay in the other room, while the man outside lay in the dirt where he had died.

"Tell me what happened, Uncle," asked the Sheriff.

"Some time after midnight," said Mr. Martin, "I ain't sure of the exact time, I was woke up by a commotion in the front yard. Three, mebbe four men on horseback. I could not tell for sure in the dark. But I did see that one carried a torch, another kerosene. I watched the man with the kerosene dismount and approach the porch when Billy come runnin' around the corner of the house, probably woke by the noise as well." Mr. Martin reached over and placed his hand on Edward's arm. "One of the riders pulled out his pistol and killed Billy where he stood. The man never said a word. I ain't never seen anything so cold. So, I grabbed my shotgun and used both barrels on the nearest rider. Shot him right through the window." Mr. Martin nodded towards the front yard, "That is him lying out there. Anyways, that seemed to take the steam out of them. They took a couple of potshots at the house, threw the kerosene and torch on the front porch and skedaddled."

"Did you recognize any of them?" asked the Sheriff.

"Nah, Dougie, my eyes ain't what they was."

Edward spoke up, "I did." All eyes turned to him as he said, "I got there just as Billy was shot. I hid in the bushes until they was gone, but I seen them clearly enough. All was strangers to me 'cept one: Simon Pitchford."

The Sheriff sat back in his chair. "I thought that sumbitch had left the Valley for good." When he realized what he had said, the Sheriff blushed and glanced at Eugenie. "Sorry, 'Genie," he said.

Eugenie reached over and patted the Sheriff's cheek affectionately. "That is alright, Dougie, he is a 'sumbitch.'" Eugenie offered to make a fresh pot of coffee, but the Sheriff declined. He asked me to go outside with him and help load the dead man into Mr. Martin's wagon. "I will have it returned tomorrow, Uncle," he said.

The night air stank of kerosene and wood smoke. We lifted the body into the wagon and as the Sheriff made ready to leave, I said, "I reckon you are going after Simon, Sheriff. I would like to go with you."

The Sheriff studied me for a moment. "I will not be part of any vendetta. I will take him alive if I can." When I nodded, he said, "Then be at the jail tomorrow morning 'round 8. I will supply the weapons."

I returned inside and sat with Eugenie at the table. Both Mr. Martin and Edward had apparently retired. I told her of my plan to go looking for Simon with the Sheriff. Eugenie laid her head on my shoulder and said, "Must you, Teddy? I would feel safer with you here."

"I do not believe we will ever be safe while Simon is still out there."

Eugenie squeezed my hand. "I know I do not need to say it but be careful."

I squeezed back and smiled. "I love you, too."

CHAPTER 36

The Posse

Deep in the guts of most men is buried the involuntary response to the hunter's horn, a prickle of the nape hairs, an acceleration of the pulse, an atavistic memory of his fathers, who killed first with stone, and then with club, and then with spear, and then with bow, and then with gun... — *Robert Ruark*

When I arrived at the Sheriff's office the next morning, two other men were already waiting. One was tall, thin, dark-haired, and maybe 10 years older than me. The second was tall as well, but stockier, his hair and beard streaked with grey. He was wearing leather clothes and had a large knife on his belt. When introductions were made, I learned that the younger man was named David Eicher, the older man was Marcus Wright. They had both been Confederate soldiers and had been mustered out with Lee at Appomattox Court House.

"I heard about you," Marcus said to me. "You are the kid that sold out the guerrillas to the Yanks." When I started to protest, Marcus just waved me off. "Do not matter none," he said. "Whatever you got for them, it was more than they was worth."

I heard the door shut at the Sheriff's house and looked over as he walked to the jail. He was carrying 4 muskets, as well as 4 leather ammunition pouches with a big 'US' stamped on them. "Glad to see you boys," he said, as he walked over to the jail where he stood the guns against the wall.

"Any others coming?" David asked.

The Sheriff shook his head. "No, I reckon this little army will get the job done well-enough." He walked over to us and asked, "You boys get a chance to know each other?" When Marcus shrugged, the Sheriff said, "Well, let me tell you what we got here. Now David, he was a sharpshooter in the Army. He always was a good shot. Before the War, I never saw him lose a turkey shoot." The Sheriff turned to Marcus. "Marcus, he is a trapper. In the Army, he was a scout. I hear tell that he can track an ant over a mile of bedrock." Then the Sheriff turned to me. "Teddy, here, was a blockade runner. He had his ship shot out from underneath him at Wilmington. Teddy is the only one who lived to tell the tale."

"The Sheriff will not speak of himself " David whispered to me. "But during the War, he was a Lieutenant in the First Corps under Gen'ral Longstreet hisself. Survived Pickett's Charge at Gettysburg, he did, though he lost nearly his whole regiment."

We started our search for Simon in the Martin's front yard. When Eugenie heard the horses, she ran out onto the porch, her shotgun raised. "Whoa, 'Genie, do not shoot," said the Sheriff.

Eugenie lowered the shotgun and scolded the Sheriff, "This is not the best time to come charging into the front yard unannounced."

"You are right, 'Genie, I am sorry. How is Uncle?"

"He is as well as one can expect. You know that Billy was

like a son to him." Eugenie leaned the shotgun against a wall. "Good morning, Mr. Wright, David," she said. I cannot say I was surprised that she knew them; it seemed everyone in this part of the Valley knew, or was related to, everyone else.

"Good morning, Miz Eugenie!" They answered with such formality and obvious affection that I believe they would have bowed if they had been standing. Eugenie rewarded them with a bright smile.

"'Genie," asked the Sheriff, "do you know any of Simons friends? Anyone he spends time with?"

Eugenie paused for a moment. "I have never known him to bring anyone here. But I have heard that he has been seen around town with a man named James Washington, the manager at Sam Lowry's farm up around Edinburg."

I noticed that while the Sheriff and Eugenie were talking, Marcus was walking his horse slowly around the perimeter of the yard, staring at the ground. When he finished the circuit, he returned to the group of us. The Sheriff tipped his hat to Eugenie. "Thank you, 'Genie. Please give my regards to Uncle."

With that, the men turned and galloped out of the yard. I jumped off my horse, ran over and kissed Eugenie, then remounted and raced to catch up.

I caught up with the men at the Valley Pike. Marcus was on his knees looking at hoof prints in the dust. He stood up and said, "They turned north." Then he motioned for the Sheriff to join him. When the Sheriff had dismounted, Marcus pointed at one hoofprint. "See this?" he asked. "There is a nick in the horse's shoe. Distinctive enough I will know it if I see it again."

The Sheriff nodded. "The Lowry farm is north of here, rounds 'bout 15 miles up the Pike. I reckon we should check it out."

But we did not proceed directly to the Lowry farm. We stopped at various farms along the way as well as a tavern or two in Mt. Jackson. While everyone we talked to knew who Simon was, they all claimed not to have seen him in weeks if not months. There appeared to be great resentment of Sheriff

Martin who was so clearly out of his jurisdiction. Marcus, however, had slightly better luck getting information. With his large stature and large knife, he was difficult to ignore.

We had stopped at a rundown tavern on the outskirts of New Market which was to be our last stop of the day. Inside, there were only a few customers and a bartender who was surly and uncommunicative. His answers to the Sheriff were monosyllabic and unhelpful. Marcus watched this, clearly losing patience. He finally took the bartender firmly by the arm and walked him away from our group. I could not hear what Marcus said to the man, but I could see the bartender's eyes grow wide and then he began to nod his head as Marcus spoke. After a few minutes, Marcus slapped the bartender on his back, as if they were great friends, and returned to us.

When we were outside, Marcus said, "Simon was just here this morning. He has two men with him, 'ruffians' the bartender calls them. They was drinkin' whiskey not yet 10 in the morning and braggin' about a lesson they taught some farmer down around New Market."

"Did the bartender know any of their names?" the Sheriff asked.

Marcus shook his head. "Only Simon and James Washington, the Lowry farm manager. But he described the third man. Says he had pure white hair and beard, 'though he could not be more than 30-years old. The other men called him Whitey."

The Sheriff grew pale. Marcus asked, "You know him?"

"I served with him." The Sheriff shook his head at the memory. "A natural born killer. I suspected him of killing some Yank prisoners, 'though I could never prove it."

"One other thing," said Marcus. "Bartender says they were armed better than Stuart's cavalry."

Because we were all no more than 10 miles from home, we elected to sleep in our own beds that night and meet again in the morning at the jail. We trotted out of Mt. Jackson and each of us made our own way home.

When I finally fell asleep that night, I dreamt about Billy lying dead in the dust, a white-haired man standing over him, laughing.

CHAPTER 37

The Raid

In every battle there comes a time when both sides consider themselves beaten, then he who continues the attack wins. —Ulysses S. Grant

In retrospect, it would have been better if we had gone straight to Lowry's farm the day before. But we had no reason to believe that Simon, if he were even there, had received any warning that we were looking for him. So, we took no special precautions other than to ride single file, a horse-length between us, up the long driveway to the farmhouse.

The driveway was flanked by fields of green spring wheat and there was a deep, dry drainage ditch on one side. The wheat undulated in a slight breeze and the sky was a perfect blue. I thought about how nice it would be to dismount, to sit beside the wheat and turn my face up to the sun. I was deep in my fantasy when a shot rang out and the horse in front of me screamed and fell to the ground. Marcus, who had been riding her, jumped off as she fell and dove into the drainage ditch.

There was a second shot and a puff of dust appeared in front of my horse. "They are trying for the horses!" yelled the Sheriff.

"Scatter them!" We jumped off our horses with our weapons and swatted them as hard as we could. "Hah!" we yelled, "Git!" The horses took off across the fields just as another shot landed among them but missed.

The four of us sat in the drainage ditch, shoulder to shoulder, our backs against the wall. There was an occasional shot that buzzed over our heads, but they seemed unaimed and almost desultory. "They are going to flank us, Sheriff," said Marcus.

The Sheriff nodded. "I reckon." He peered cautiously above the rim of the ditch and dirt erupted just inches from his face. He ducked back down. "I cannot see anyone, but I think that shot came from the woods on the other side of the field."

Marcus said, "Then there are at least two men. The shot that killed my horse came from up the driveway near where I figure the farmhouse is."

The Sheriff shook his head. "They get someone on the other side of us and we will have no cover." He motioned to David and me to move up the ditch in the direction of the farmhouse. "Keep your heads down, boys."

For several minutes, the Sheriff and Marcus sat heads together, deep in conversation. Then the sheriff nodded at Marcus and crawled up the ditch towards David and me. "Here is the plan, boys, such as it is," he said. "When I signal you, you start shooting, fast as you can, up the driveway. The farmhouse is just around that corner. I will shoot across the field towards where the other man is. Meantime, Marcus will make his way down the ditch, try and cross the field, and reach the shooter." David and I nodded and watched the Sheriff make his way back to Marcus. When he got there, he yelled, "Now!"

David and I began firing. I aimed at some woods near the driveway where I figured someone might hide. I was not very adept at reloading the musket while David was firing and reloading at least 3 times a minute. It was easy to see who the soldier had been. Nonetheless, between the two of us, we made a lot of noise and hopefully kept the other guys under cover.

After a couple of minutes, I felt the Sheriff tap me on the shoulder. "He is across," he said. David and I stopped firing and we settled down in the ditch with the Sheriff. After about 10 minutes, the sheriff lifted his hat above the rim of the ditch with a short stick. Immediately, there was a gunshot which tore through the hat and shattered the stick. The sheriff looked at his hand as if counting his fingers and then said, "Not yet." Ten minutes later, he tried again. This time there was no gunshot. David and the Sheriff looked at each other and smiled.

The Sheriff told David and me to again fire up the driveway. "Let us get Marcus back safely," he said. My ears were ringing, and I was covered in burnt gunpowder by the time the Sheriff again tapped me on the shoulder. I looked back and saw Marcus crouching behind the Sheriff.

When we moved this time, it was like a military operation. We formed a line in the ditch. The last man in line would stand up and shoot up the driveway, then run to the front of the line. He would then duck down and reload while the next man, and then the next, repeated the same process. When we finally left the cover of the ditch, we were no more than 100 yards from the farmhouse.

I do not know if we had been fired upon as we moved up towards the farmhouse because of the noise we were making, but we saw no one when we got there. But the farmhouse had been directly in line behind the little grove of trees at which David and I had fired. Nearly every window had been shot out and there were multiple bullet holes in the siding and front door.

It was several minutes before we felt it was safe to enter the farmhouse. I had gone around back while the Sheriff, David and Marcus approached it from the front. I had been afraid that some innocent person may have been in the farmhouse during the fire fight, but we found no one.

As I walked back around the house, I saw the 3 men staring at the ground. "There, do you see it?" Marcus asked. The Sheriff nodded. "I see the notch in the hoof print. So, you think it is Simon?"

"Or one of his men," answered Marcus. Marcus made a slow circle around the yard. "There were 3 horses so 3 men, including Simon." Marcus had killed the man in the woods, so I asked, "Where is the third horse?"

The Sheriff and Marcus looked at each other. "Check the outbuildings, David."

When David came back, he was leading a brown mare. "One horse all saddled and ready to go," he said. "From the droppings, it looks like there had been a couple more not long ago." Marcus checked each horseshoe of the mare. "No notch," he said.

The Sheriff sent David and me out to retrieve our horses. When we were all remounted, we stopped in the woods where the third gunman was. His throat had been cut and his eyes were open, a surprised look frozen on his face. "Anybody know this man?" asked the Sheriff.

"Gotta be James Washington," said Marcus. "One down, two to go."

CHAPTER 38

The Hunt Continues

There is no hunting like the hunting of man, and those who have hunted armed men long enough and liked it, never care for anything else thereafter. –Ernest Hemingway

Marcus circled the area behind the farmhouse, his eyes locked on the ground, looking for all the world like a hound seeking a scent. "That way," he said, pointing to the east. "Two horses, one with a notch in the horseshoe."

We followed Marcus, our senses heightened. We had no intention of falling into another trap laid by Simon. Although I saw nothing to indicate anyone had gone this way, it seemed as obvious to Marcus as if he were following a street sign. We passed again through New Market and turned east towards Luray. But before we reached Luray, Simon's trail turned and led up into the Blue Ridge Mountains.

The trail Simon had chosen deteriorated quickly from a road to a path and finally... nothing. It seemed he intended to lose any who pursued him in the ridges and valleys of the Mountains. But Marcus was a bulldog, unwilling to let go of his prey. Somehow, he followed Simon across meadows and rock ledges alike.

On our first night in the Mountains, we lit no fire and ate a cold dinner of hard tack and salt pork. We spoke in low voices, unwilling to alert Simon as to how close we were behind him. Even though it was summer, the nighttime temperature fell to near freezing in the Mountains. We all slept wrapped in our blankets, our muskets within easy reach.

I awoke the next morning to the Sheriff and Marcus packing their horses. I was stiff from a night on the cold ground and I would have given anything for a cup of coffee. Instead, it was another cold meal of hardtack and salt pork, and we were on our way again.

Marcus followed their trail as it led higher into the mountains. We had just come to a small clearing when Marcus dropped to his knee and signaled us to stop. We could see two horses picketed between two trees and their saddles and other tack piled under a nearby bush.

Marcus whispered for us to sit where we were while he circled the clearing. He came back a few minutes later and said in a normal voice, "They are gone, headed for higher ground where the horses cannot go."

The Sheriff nodded. "I reckon they seek an advantage to stand against us."

We walked up to the picket line to which the horses had been tied. Marcus untied them and they wandered away aimlessly, seeking fresher grass. "Simon and Whitey will not need them," he said. "They will not be riding back down this mountain."

We picketed our own horses, making no attempt to hide them or our tack. Then Marcus led us to the killers' trail where it left the clearing. We walked around several large, white boulders and began to climb.

The position of the sun indicated it was some time around noon when Marcus stopped again. We had been walking along a ridge line with another ridge above us. We had few trees for cover. I was not a tracker like Marcus, but even I could sense that Simon and Whitey were close.

"They have stopped making any effort to hide their trail," said Marcus softly. "I believe they àre planning a surprise for us." He pointed ahead to a gap in the ridge above us. "They climbed the ridge there. How high they have gone, I do not know. But if I were to plan an ambush, it would be there."

The Sheriff looked at David and me and said, "You boys wait fifteen minutes and then make your way carefully to that gap. Keep your heads down but make lots of noise. Make sure they know you are coming." We are decoys, I thought, while a chill moved down my back. The Sheriff continued, "Marcus and I are going to backtrack a bit and see if we can come up behind them. Understand?"

David and I nodded. David pulled out an old pocket watch and said, "Fifteen minutes."

The Sheriff and Marcus turned back and presumably went to look for another way up the ridge.

David and I checked our muskets, then rechecked them. When the fifteen minutes was up, David closed the watch with a snap and said, "Let us go now."

We approached the gap with great caution, keeping our heads below the ridge line as much as possible. Along the way, we kicked rubble over the edge of the ridge we were on, making enough noise for four people.

My heart was pounding against my chest. I imagined gun sights on me with every step I took. David was just starting to peek around a large boulder when a gunshot rang out from above us. David cried out in surprise and pain and fell to the ground. The minié ball had struck the boulder just inches above his head and sprayed rock chips and lead fragments. Blood ran down his face, but I was relieved when it did not appear he had been struck directly. "Stay still," I said. I took his musket and fired a quick shot over the boulder and then ducked down again. Two shots quickly followed from above, slamming into the boulder. What concerned me was that the shots seemed to have come more from the side than above. I feared I was being flanked. Where were the Sheriff and Marcus? I wondered. I could not withdraw and leave David where he lay.

Two shots rang out from above and there was a cry of pain. Only one shot answered the two. Then Simon came charging down the gap, his eyes wide, screaming as he ran. He caught me completely by surprise and he collided with me with such force that I nearly rolled off the ridge. By the time I retrieved my musket, he was gone.

The Sheriff and Marcus climbed down the gap and walked up to me. Marcus was holding his left arm and blood flowed between his fingers. "How is David?" the Sheriff asked. I lowered my voice. "I fear he may be blinded in one eye."

The Sheriff and I tended to Marcus' and David's wounds as best we could. We used water from our canteens to clean the wounds and then bound them with strips from one of our blankets. We were able to stop the bleeding in both cases, but it was obvious that neither Marcus nor David would be able to continue with the posse. "You boys need to get back to town and get some medical help," the Sheriff said to Marcus and David. When Marcus started to argue, the Sheriff said, "We got Whitey and James Washington, thanks to you. You boys done your duty and the County is grateful. Teddy and I can deal with Simon." The Sheriff turned to me, "That is, if Teddy, wants to see this through."

"Yes, sir," I said. In my mind, I could still feel the dog collar that Simon had put around my neck. I had promised an accounting.

Marcus gave us one last piece of help. He walked us over to the point at which Simon had scrambled off the ridge. He pointed and said, "There." It took me a moment to see it: two small droplets of blood.

"We must have hit him," said the Sheriff. "Else he cut himself jumping around the boulders."

"Either way," said Marcus, "he left a trail for you."

As Marcus and David made their way back down the mountain, the Sheriff and I walked in the direction Simon had fled. There were many hiding places in the ridges and gulleys, and I felt vulnerable without Marcus. I could not shake the feeling that we were being watched and I expected Simon to jump out around every corner.

As the day wore on, the temperature kept rising and there was no breeze and no water to cool us. My musket was slippery in my hands, and I kept wiping sweat out of my eyes with my shirtsleeves. I stumbled over loose stones and cursed Simon with every misstep I took.

Many times, we thought we had lost Simon's trail, but luck was with us; every time it seemed we had lost his scent, we would find one or two little droplets of blood that showed us his direction.

CHAPTER 39

Mano a mano

There is only one purpose in hand-to-hand combat, and that is to kill. Never face an enemy with the idea of knocking him out. The chances are extremely good that he will kill you. --William Powell

With David and Marcus on their way back to town, the Sheriff and I continued our search for Simon. Without Marcus to track Simon, we could only follow in his general direction. My greatest fear was that he would double back and sit in ambush.

The sun was beginning to set on our second day in the mountains. We were approaching another of the ubiquitous white stone ridges in the Blue Ridge when the hairs rose on the back of my neck. I motioned for the Sheriff to stop and dropped to one knee. "He is near," I said.

"How do you know?"

"I just know," I answered. Perhaps I had heard something, or maybe it was just a sense I had. I could not have explained it at the time, but I knew it was true. The Sheriff looked at me skeptically, but I noticed he kept his head down as we inched forward. I took the lead as we approached a blind corner, the

Sheriff close behind me.

I had just begun to peek around the corner when Simon rushed around the boulders, screaming like a madman. Whether it was intentional or simply primal, I could not say, but the screaming paralyzed us if just for a moment; but it was long enough for Simon to fire at me, his musket held hip high, from no more than 20 feet away.

The minié ball tore through my shirt, scoring my side as it passed by. I had been lucky, but I heard the Sheriff grunt and fall to the ground behind me. Simon's shot had hit us both.

I raised my musket to shoot, but Simon was already on top of me. He ripped my musket away from me and threw it over a ledge. He seemed to have the strength of a madman. His eyes were wide and his hair unkempt, his clothing dirty and covered with burrs.

When I was disarmed, he stepped back and stood looking at the Sheriff and me for several seconds. Then, at the same moment, we both seemed to notice the Sheriff's musket lying a few feet away.

I was slightly faster than Simon and I managed to reach the musket first. But Simon threw himself on my back, reached over me and grabbed the musket with two hands. Slowly, he began to pull it back against my neck. He had the leverage, and I could barely hold the musket back. He was trying to garrote me.

I summoned all the strength I had and pulled Simon over my head. He landed hard on his back, and I heard the breath explode from his lungs, but he would not release his grip on the musket. We both knew that the first person to let go of it would die.

Simon used the musket to pull himself up off the ground, then head-butted me so hard that I nearly lost consciousness. Somehow, I still did not let go. Simon growled and cursed me as we danced around the Sheriff's body. I kicked at Simon several times, but I did not connect, or did little damage if I did.

The Sheriff's body lay near the edge of a steep precipice.

Several times, we both stepped around him as we tried to push/ pull the other over the edge. First I, then Simon, danced on the very edge of the cliff, neither able to get an advantage over the other.

My strength was fading fast. Even though I finally had him at the edge, I could not seem to manage the final push. Then, the Sheriff's hand reached up and grabbed Simon's ankle. Simon gave a cry of surprise and, for just an instant, stopped fighting for the musket. I sensed the moment and pushed him backwards until only his grip on the musket kept him from going over the cliff. I let go.

Simon flailed for a moment but then raised and cocked the musket even as he began to fall. He shot me from no more than a few feet away and I fell next to the Sheriff. If Simon screamed as he fell, I did not hear it. For me, the world had gone black and silent.

When I awoke again, it was fully dark. I tried to get up off the ground but could not summon the strength. All I could manage was to reach about with my hands and arms. I felt the Sheriff's body next to mine and I was surprised to find it warm. "Sheriff," I asked, "are you alive?"

"I am. I was not sure about you."

"Can you move?"

I felt the Sheriff stir, "Mebbe," he said. "I have been shot through the side. I vary between wake and sleep. Hurts like a sumbitch. You?"

"I can move a little," I said. "I feel no pain. I do not even know where I was shot."

I began to shiver. "We need a fire," said the Sheriff, "but I do not possess the strength to gather wood and light one." Once again, I tried to move, but I could barely raise my head and only for a moment. "I cannot help. I am sorry, Sheriff."

I felt the Sheriff move his body next to mine, groaning with the effort. I fought my way onto my side and the Sheriff nestled close against my back. I could feel his breath warm against the back of my neck. I drifted in and out of consciousness, waking up cold and confused, then falling back into a troubled sleep.

I lay in my bed, covered with blankets, and yet I could not get warm. I shivered from somewhere deep down inside me where the heat could not reach. I felt my mother's cool fingers on my brow and heard footsteps in the hallway. My father looked in the doorway and asked, "How is he?"

"Burning up," answered my mother.

My father entered my room and sat on my bed opposite my mother. I could see the deep concern in his eyes. "Perhaps I can read you something, Teddy. Would you like that?"

I nodded, too weak to say anything.

My father opened his Bible to a page marked with a piece of blue ribbon: "Jeremiah 29:11," he read. "'For I know the plans I have for you,' declares the Lord, 'plans to prosper you and not to harm you, plans to give you hope and a future.'"

We were on the west side of the mountain and the sun did not reach us until afternoon. The sun helped to warm us, although I could not stop shivering. The Sheriff and I lay where we had fallen, neither capable of moving or of helping the other beyond sharing our body heat. "You must hang in there, Teddy," he said to me, "for I have promised 'Genie to keep you well."

At Eugenie's name, my thoughts came more clearly into the present. Visions of her filled my mind and I vowed to live to return to her. I tried to have a conversation with the Sheriff because I had begun to fear sleep; sleep was a seductress from whom I might never escape. "Will they come looking for us?"

I could feel the Sheriff nod his head. "Marcus and David will have expected us to return by now. That we have not will surely alarm them."

"Then soon..." I started to say. But shivers so severe racked my body that I could speak no more. I felt the Sheriff cover me with his arm. "Teddy!" he said. "Teddy!" But I could hear no more as I began to slide down the sides of a deep hole. It became darker and darker the deeper I slid. And quiet. And warm.

CHAPTER 40

5 Years Later...

A child's tale, perhaps, to hope for more than what you see, And what could be better, anyway, than to sail upon the sea? --from The Sailors Song by J.W. Bebout

The sloop Jerimiah seemed to fly over the water. I pulled the sail in tighter and tighter until we heeled well over to starboard. Sea water sprayed over the gunnel, refreshing us all in the afternoon heat. I glanced over at my 4-year-old son Eli who was squealing with pleasure. Eugenie, dressed in my old sailor pants, her hair wrapped in a colored scarf, scolded me: "Now, Teddy, you will scare the children!" But Eli just yelled, "Faster, Daddy, faster!" Even Anna, not yet two, smiled with delight as she snuggled in her mother's arms.

"They will be sailors someday," I said. I smiled at Eugenie, "Even you."

"Not if you drown us all," she teased. But I knew that she had come to love the sea almost as much as I. I let the sails out and slowed as we made our way around Big Pine Key and then tacked alongside the dock on No Name Key.

Amos Semissee, who had been sitting in the shade mending a net, got up and caught my lines. When the boat was secure, he helped Eugenie and Anna off the boat. I lifted Eli over the gunnel, and he ran to catch up with his mother and sister as they walked down the dock. Eugenie shouted back at me over her shoulder, "We will see you back at the house. Do not forget dinner!"

Amos gestured for me to follow him. "I have beer," he said, as he led me back to his nets. I sat on the ground next to him, grateful for the drink. "Is this not the same net you were mending when we left this morning?" I asked.

Amos grinned at me. "I sit down here in the shade, and I look busy. One stitch, one sip of beer, perhaps a brief nap, then another stitch... That way, Amesta will not find other less pleasant ways to keep me occupied." I grinned back at Amos, although I suspected that Amesta was not fooled at all.

"How were things up at the plantation?" asked Amos. He watched me with a twinkle in his eye as I reacted to the word 'plantation' and its connotations.

"Things at the *farm* are good," I answered. He knew I had formed a partnership with 3 Bahamian families to farm around 600 acres on Upper Matecumbe Key. We raised pineapples, tomatoes, various root vegetables and several different tropical fruits. I provided crop transportation, they the labor, and we split the profits evenly. Farming—new to the keys after the War—was proving lucrative. Our average crop of pineapples alone returned more than $100,000 per year.

"I do not understand, Amos, why you will not join me in this business."

Amos smiled. "Then who will mend these nets?"

I bought a fresh tuna from a local fisherman on my way home. I waved at friends and passers-by as I crossed town towards our little cottage. I filled my lungs with the fragrant air and enjoyed the feeling of the sun on my back.

I stopped on the street to watch my children playing on the

front porch. They were both tanned nutmeg dark from the sun and had sun-bleached highlights in their dark hair. Eli was looking more and more like my father, for whom he had been named, all the time. Anna, named for Eugenie's mother, was already a beauty like her mother.

When they saw me standing in the street, Eli and Anna ran into my arms. I asked Eli to take the fish to his mother and I carried Anna into the house. Eugenie met me at the door with a kiss and handed me a glass of lemonade. "What a remarkable place this island is," she said, not for the first time. "That lemonade was a lemon on a tree in our yard not 30 minutes ago." She shook her head in apparent wonder. "When you told me it was paradise here, Teddy, I thought you had to be exaggerating. Now, I think you understated it."

I put my arm around her waist. "Then you still like it here?" I asked.

"I would like anywhere so long as it is with you. But yes, I still like it."

Eli had been born not long after we first arrived. Over 4 years ago, I thought. How quickly the time had passed.

Eugenie turned to go into the kitchen while I sat down in a rocker on the front porch. I sipped the lemonade and thought about the Valley. I would be lying if I said I did not miss it sometimes. But my presence there had become hazardous to all who loved me. The death of Simon had done little to lessen the resentment of my acquittal for what most saw as treason.

Most of the hatred was expressed subtly, but not all; while I was recovering from my gunshot wounds at the Martin farm, I was awakened one night by a cross burning in the front yard. And there were death threats, even against Eugenie and my brother Jed. It seemed like everyone was looking for someone to blame for the perceived indignities being inflicted on the South by Reconstruction.

I shrugged my left shoulder and tried to uncramp it. The minié ball Simon shot me with had nicked my lung and then shattered my left shoulder socket. I had been lucky that my arm did not have to be amputated. My recovery took months. Eugenie nursed me through the fevers, then worked with me every day to rehabilitate my shoulder. I still could not lift my arm above shoulder level, but it was useful for most things.

Eugenie came out onto the porch with her own lemonade and sat next to me. I could hear the children playing in the house. "I was just thinking about Sheriff Martin," I said.

"Dougie? Why, have you heard something?"

I shook my head and smiled. "No, I am just feeling grateful for all I have. You know that the Sheriff kept me alive up on that mountain until help arrived. You know he used his own body to keep me warm." Eugenie nodded. "But there is more," I said, "more than I have told you."

Eugenie covered my hand with hers. "Tell me, Teddy."

"I kept falling asleep. Each time, it was deeper, more deathlike, than the time before. I felt as though I were sliding down the side of a bottomless hole. And each time it became more difficult for me to climb out again.

"The Sheriff somehow sensed this. Every time I seemed to have reached the point of no return, he would pull me back. He would yell my name and tell me you were waiting for me over and over again until I would stir. He did this all night and for half of the next day." I shook my head. "Where he found the strength, I do not know, as he was grievously wounded himself."

"Dougie is a good man," said Eugenie. "He will have my gratitude for the rest of my life."

The next morning, I again made my way to Upper Matecumbe Key. This time I made the journey alone. It was to be a quick business trip.

As always, my heart soared as I left the shallow waters of the keys, crossed the reef, and entered the Atlantic Ocean. Through some unexpected metamorphosis, I had become a sailor. Sea water had clearly entered my bloodstream like a benign infectivity, and I did not believe there would ever be a cure for it.

The water darkened into an indescribable shade of blue and long swells gently rolled under the boat. I closed my eyes for a moment, and I could imagine Captain MacBrùn standing in the bow with his telescope. I half expected to hear him say, 'Stop lollygagging and mind the rudder, helmsman!'

I opened my eyes and allowed myself to bask in the happiness my life had become. I did not know what the future held, but I looked forward to it in a way I had not thought possible. But however it would turn out, I approached it inexorably at 5 knots under fair skies and calm seas.

Epilogue

Theodore Miller
No Name Key, Florida

Jedidiah Miller
Davies Farm
New Market, Virginia

Dear Jed,

I am in rect. of your letter of the 18th and Eugenie and I are thrilled to learn of your betrothal to Sarah Davies. I shall have to stop referring to her as 'Sweet Davies,' as Eugenie tells me it is disrespectful of 'Sour' Davies, though it will be a hard habit to break.

For your wedding, Eugenie and I would like to gift you with our half of Daddy's farm. As you know, I borrowed money against it to settle here in the keys. That money has long been paid back and you will receive the deed, free of any encumbrances, under separate cover. I know Daddy would be thrilled to know you will cherish it as he did.

Please remember Eugenie and me to any of our friends whom you might encounter. Eugenie sends hugs and kisses to Sarah and her sister Jenny (see how much better I am doing with their names already?). And if you would, please tell Malcolm and Mrs. Davies that I am forever grateful for all they have done. They, like you, are always in my prayers.

Stay well.

Your loving brother,
Teddy